man without a star

═ man
without a star

═ by dee linford

── sears readers club · chicago

To Mike Tilden and Joseph T. Shaw

man without a star

part 1

1: Injun Boy

Jeff Jimson wasn't home the day his Uncle Ed turpentined the white stray mare up the river lane. But he heard the awful screaming, way over in the off-forty below Larkin's place where he was hoeing corn, and figured Uncle Ed must be killing Aunt Em at last. But when he'd listened for a while, he knew it was a horse and not a woman carrying on. And that evening when he'd knocked off work, he walked around past Larkin's cow corral to hear the low-down.

Nothing ever happened on the lane that old Eph Larkin didn't know the whole details and welcome the chance to make them known. And, sure enough, he called to Jeff just as Jeff came even with the milkstand.

"You, there, boy. You work right through the circus show this evening?"

Jeff stopped out in the road and brought the hoe to order arms. He slanted a glance on down to Buck Creek to check on Uncle

1

Ed, then stepped over to the milkstand that straddled the fence like a stile.

"I reckon so. What went on?"

"Well, now, your uncle Ed, he shot a syringe full of turpytine into that old white crowbait mare you and Roddy been a-riding on behind his back. Sent her up the lane here, dragging her tail-butt like a wormy dog. It being Ed, he never thunk to look up the road first, to see if it was clear."

Jeff shifted his weight to the other foot. "What was on the lane?"

Larkin cackled like a hen. "Nothing but Tom Peebles' young 'uns, driving all Tom's stock down to water. Them, and Sam Sea-bold with two freight teams, and Court Savage on his buggy, up ahead of Sam. . . . Well, sir, Peebles' cows heard the mare a-faunching. They took one look, and lifted their tails and tore out like flies was at 'em, taking the horse and kids along. Whole outfit piled into Seabold's teams, and they stampeded, too. Court Savage was headed up thisaway, but his bays whirled so short they snapped the reach and run off with the front wheels flying up and down behind 'em. Whole skittaree hit the bridge all at once and smashed the railings off. Seabold's wagons ended up down in the river, and Crust only knows where the others went to."

Overcome by laughter that could find no out, Eph bent over his milk bucket, thin shoulders shaking.

"If you ever seen three mad Dutchmen, it was Tom and Court and Seabold. Tom and Court was all for lynching Ed, but Sam said that wouldn't pay him for his loss, so they called it off. Sea-bold says he'll sue the beleaguered by-Crust out of Ed!"

Once again, laughter choked the speaker down, and such desolation poured in upon Jeff that he wished he could just dry up and blow away.

"What happened to the mare?"

"Her? Oh, I expect she's wore her hind end plumb off now, the way she was going! It was a comical thing to see."

"I guess," Jeff said, looking down the road and seeing nothing. "I wonder if you would lend me the loan of your old needle gun. I'd bring it back, sure, tonight."

2

"Which you aim to shoot?" Eph cackled again. "The mare or your uncle Ed?"

"The hell with Ed," Jeff said. "I aim to shoot the mare."

Eph fetched the gun, and Jeff thanked him and started down the road toward the river, the rifle in a soldier rest upon his shoulder. Knowing that Eph still watched him, he struck a reaching stride that said he wasn't fazed by Ed or the white mare either—that nothing could happen here in damn-Missouri that would be any hide off him. But he was tired and hungry, and he knew that he'd catch it worse than ever now for missing supper. Pretty quick his steps began to lag, but he kept on walking, pretending he had run away, back to Kansas.

It was coming on for midnight when he found the dying mare, stretched out on her side inside a gap she'd torn in Pete Wen's pasture fence. He was guided to where she lay by the muted, rhythmic pounding of her head upon the ground. Dark, glistening pools had formed at both ends of her, and with every falling blow there was a faint mewling sound such as he once had heard a mangled kitten make, when he'd kicked the dogs away.

The shot he fired into the hammering head drove one long shudder through the ruined body. Then he squatted down and watched until the twitching legs were still.

"I guess it was all my fault," he said to no one in particular. "I knowed how mean he was. I shouldn't ought of baited her into staying around."

The stars were still popping brightly when Jeff let himself through the dooryard gate and approached the house, calling softly to old Shep, so he wouldn't bark and rouse the sleepers within. He removed his shoes out on the porch and was fumbling his way up the dark stairs when Uncle Ed's voice came to him through the open bedroom door.

"I tell you, Em, that boy is just too damn much Injun for me to handle. If I could afford to hire a man around the place, I'd purely give him a shot of turpentine, too, and git shut of *him*. He's fetched us nothing but trouble, from the first."

"Why, the very idea, Ed Roundtree!" Emma's voice said in the special put-out way she had of speaking back to Uncle Ed. "You can't call him Injun. Rebel Jimson was wild, the goodness knows.

3

And whatever Teena saw in him, I never *did* know. But he was white as we are, and Teena was my own blood sister, even if she did go chasing off after a no-good roughneck like that Jimson!"

"Well," Ed said grudgingly, "this young 'un might not have the blood, but he's hell-sure got the Injun ways. For all we know, he's somewhere in the house right now, listening to every word we say. I half-expect to wake up every morning with my throat cut and the house on fire. If I was fixed to hire a man, I'd call the sheriff and have him committed for a spell. Maybe, and he's locked up a piece, he wouldn't try to be so muley headed. He's got no more respect for you and me than if we was Reb and Teena."

For many minutes, Jeff stood motionless in the dark, torn between indignation and a sense of guilt, assailed by the shadows of fear and loneliness that always closed in like nightmare whenever he eavesdropped on Ed and Emma. And later he lay wakeful on his bed, hating his aunt and uncle for the things they said and did—listening to Roddy's fretful breathing and hating him worse than he could hate the grown-ups. For even when he hated Ed and Em the worst, he knew that Roddy was his real enemy in the Roundtree household.

Roddy was only twelve, and puny, and hadn't wanted his orphaned cousin to come to Missouri in the first place. Roddy was shady and mean about his grudges, and too dogie small to pick on. When it came to Roddy, Jeff just didn't have any weapons to fight back with. He didn't understand how Roddy figured things.

"I'm going to tell Ma!" Roddy had threatened, that first day in Missouri when Uncle Ed was gone to court and Jeff had played Kansas rodeo with the Holstein heifer calves, scratching their tender flanks with the spur he'd fetched from home.

"Tell 'er and smell 'er and kick 'er down the cellar, and when she comes up she'll have a new feller!" Jeff had chanted scornfully, never dreaming that Roddy would be rotten mean enough to really tell. But Roddy did tell. Roddy told everything, including the smart-alecky thing Jeff had said. Then he stood by smirking while Aunt Em whaled Jeff proper, with an elm branch.

"You're just your reprobate old father, all over again!" Aunt Em said, crying as she always did whenever she took a switch to

4

Jeff. "He wouldn't take correction either, and you know how he died. You'll come to a hanging end yourself, and you don't mend your wayward ways. Just once, I'd like to make you break and holler, like normal, healthy boys!"

So Jeff gritted his teeth and wouldn't yammer. His eyes discovered in that moment that they could drive the faded, tear-bright eyes away. So they did it, even knowing that the switch would hide him all the harder. In that moment, too, he lost all confidence in grown-ups and set out to win Roddy to his side.

As a starter, he explained to Rod that Rebel Jimson had never been the kind of man who sold out his friends. He made it clear that Rebel let the Jayhawkers hang him before he'd lead them to the States' Righters' camp in the river bottoms—not for murder and all the crimes that Aunt Em mentioned. He told Roddy that his own ma always hided him worse for tattling than for anything else wrong that he could do. He worked on Roddy in every way he knew to put across the notion that they were in the same boat and had ought to stick together against the common enemy. Being the elder, he was quite willing to set the example.

"You'd ketch it good, if I told Uncle Ed," he warned the day he caught Roddy in the market melons they had been cautioned not to tamper with. "But I ain't going to. My ma told me that spies and informers go to hell—deeper than a anvil could drop in fifty years."

But Roddy was without concept of loyalty and secret alliance against mutual foes. That very evening when Jeff came up from the field, hot and tired from shocking corn, Ed met him by the stable with a harness strip in his hand.

"Didn't I tell you to keep out of them market melons?" he said, his voice all shaky and choked up till you'd have thought it was Jeff that had the strap. "You think I just talk to hear myself?"

Jeff looked at Roddy over by the stable, expecting him to step up and take his medicine. After all, Jeff had refrained from tattling on Roddy when he'd had the chance, and he couldn't see anybody being so low down as to sell out the one that had saved him. But Roddy just stood there, looking scared and smirky, and Jeff knew then that Roddy had done worse than just to tattle.

5

Roddy had lied against the one that saved him, to save himself again.

"I didn't do it," Jeff said, ashamed of the girlish tears that stung his eyes—ashamed that Ed could accomplish with words alone what Emma could not succeed in doing with a whip.

"If there's anything I hate worse than a sneak thief," Uncle Ed said loudly, "it's a lying sneak thief. You've had this coming for quite a while."

Jeff tried to get away, but Ed cornered him where the high pole fence met the stable, and laid the strap on harder than Emma could ever hit. At first, Jeff thought he couldn't stand it. But after a while he found he could.

That night, he caught Roddy in the outhouse and put a face on him. But Roddy's yells brought Ed and Emma out, and Jeff only caught more of what he'd had.

That was the first time Ed had whaled him with a tug, but it hadn't been the last. About a year ago, he'd tried to run away. Somehow, Ed got onto him in time, and for that once Jeff stood up to him. Their eyes were on a level, and the knowledge that he could now strike back was a sickness in Jeff's belly.

"Now, if you're bound to go, I expect you'll go," Ed had panted when it was all over and Jeff couldn't stand up to take any more. "But if you do go, why, just remember that the last time you got ideas around here you got 'em knocked out of you. And remember you'll ketch it a lot worse when the sheriff brings you back. . . ."

For what seemed an endless time, Jeff lay hot and rigid on his bed, staring into the chambered dark with bitter, stinging eyes—his unforgiving mind encompassing the years. He thought of the dead mare, and the secret place they'd had for her down in the brush in the creek pasture where Ed would never have discovered her without outside help. He thought of the many times he'd practically forced Rod to ride her, in the foolish hope that Rod would see the light at last.

"The hell with it," he muttered, sitting up and groping for his hat and spur. "I ain't got to stay."

Jeff had heard it said that Kansas City was only eighty miles from Buck Creek, straight toward the setting sun. But eighty

6

miles was quite a stretch, in early August, with the sun scorching down hot enough to cook the blood in him, and only his legs for locomotion.

Besides, he had to follow the brushy trails and be careful who got a look at him, in case Uncle Ed had gone to law to get him back. He had to forage nights, and sometimes in broad day, to appease the gnawing in his belly and keep the muscles in his legs. But a straight diet of uncooked fruit and vegetables left him loose and windy, without much get up and go. And he couldn't remember the time when he wasn't hungry. So, after a week of dodging people like a hunted fugitive, he gambled on Ed and the sheriff and took to knocking on the farmhouse doors at mealtime.

He wasn't often turned away. Women at most of the places he stopped in at had a funny way of looking at him, like maybe they had seen him someplace before and were trying to remember where. When the women were alone, they usually fed him and sent him on his way. The men would look at him in a different way, and usually mentioned helping with the harvest. At first, he shied from work, being in a hurry. But after a while he found that if he bargained in advance, he could get a little pay, in clothes and food to take along. So he slowed his pace considerably, and when he reached Kansas City it was coming on for fall.

Kay Cee was bigger than he'd imagined New York and London could be. He was confused and daunted by the jungles of crowded buildings, by the throngs of people that swarmed aimlessly, like ants. But once he was on the Kansas side of the river, where the stockyards were, he felt more secure. The fall beef shipments were coming in, and he found it no trick to get work around the pens.

"Yeah, I could use some help," a whiskered hustler told him, looking him up and down. "You ain't afraid of work, you can be the pilot."

"The pilot?" Jeff echoed.

The hustler smiled triumphantly. "That'll be your job—to haul it and pile it. Pile it here, pile it there."

It was hard work, being pilot, when the pens were full. Harder in some ways than working for Uncle Ed. But this job paid in coin of the realm, and he was working with cattle again, like back in Kansas. Then there were times when the piloting didn't fill all his hours, and he could ride the hustler's horse and work the cattle from corral to corral.

McCord, the hustler, acted pleased with him, and when the fall rush was over at the railroad pens he took Jeff with him to the packing-house corrals. In the spring, he offered to take Jeff booming, and they hoboed north to Omaha.

In Omaha, Jeff found a country that was more like Kansas than Kansas was, and there he made the acquaintance of a new kind of cow critter: one that was lean and big-chested and angular, with hoofs of flint and horns that must have made the devil jealous, down in hell.

"Them there are Texas caddle," McCord informed him. "They're half-tiger, half-mule, and half-Comanche Injun."

Jeff grinned. "You mean each one's a cow and a half?"

"And then some!" McCord said fervently. "For anything but eating, they're the best beef in the world."

Spring marketing was in full swing, and together they found work around the yards. Jeff, now seventeen and growing like a weed, commanded a man's pay.

"Dollar a day is wages, kid. All you got to do is lay it by, and in a million days you'll be a millionaire."

There was no arguing with McCord's arithmetic. But Jeff hadn't yet found the kind of work he felt a man should do. By early summer, he was ready to give up on his first million and start in on the second.

In Omaha, everything was moving west. And from the talk he'd heard among the brown-faced shippers, the second million would come easier farther out.

"Don't know as I blame you," McCord said wistfully, when Jeff spoke of his intention. "If I was seventeen, I'd pack my carpetbag and go with you. . . . Well, I've learned you how to ride the freights, and pay the brakies off if you git caught. And the U. P. will haul you as far west as you can go. But take my advice and don't never offer money to a shack with anybody watching. And don't ride the rods with any shaker you don't know. You might git in with some lousy Pink the brakie's spotted. And that could be tough."

"What's a Pink?" Jeff had to ask.

McCord spat in great distaste. "A Pink is a pimp detecative that hires out to them with money to make trouble for them without. Railroads git 'em to pose as bums and hoboes, to spy on shacks and conductors that take tips from poor folks to let 'em ride the freights. I've knowed shacks to spot a Pink down on the rods and let a coupling pin down on a chain from the front end of the car. Pin churns around and knocks the Pink off under the wheels. Then they's one less bastard around to devil folks."

Jeff didn't know that he'd spot a Pink if one came up and hit him in the face. But their way of doing put him in mind of Roddy, and he wasn't sure he blamed the train crews for making them hard to find.

Jeff was halfway across Nebraska when his finances gave out. The shack who accosted him at a place called North Platte was cross about it, but let him stay on the train if he would ride the rods and not let the conductor see him.

At the next long stop, called Julesburg, he was joined underneath the car by a man who was somewhat better dressed than most the fourth-class passengers. But the dude seemed as hard up as any of the rod riders. He was froze to know all about how much it cost to buy the brakie off, and Jeff told him what he could.

"Then take this here, and give it to him for both of us," the stranger said, handing him a dollar. "Tell him I'm going as far as Utah."

"Speak for yourself, John," Jeff declined tartly. "I done made my arrangements."

The hobo scowled. "You've already dealt with him. He knows you. Besides, like I say, it's for both of us. Be a good kid, now, and do as I say."

Jeff yielded, valuing the good will of all traveling companions. He then went off to approach the brakie in private. The shack took the dollar, and grabbed him by the arm.

"You said you was broke. Where'd you come by the buck?"

Jeff told about the man under the boxcar, and the brakie turned more friendly. "You ride in that empty coal car, yonder, kid. It's a mite dirty. But you can lay down and rest."

That afternoon, the train ground to a stop in a big yard where

9

the station sign said *Quadrille*. Jeff was climbing out of his car when a hobo he'd seen two stops back came loping down the tracks.

"Better ditch, kid," the bum said from one side of his mouth. "They're a-combing the train for hoboes."

Jeff's car was near the station house and a big crib of ties that joined it. He hit the cinders in a running crouch, and ducked behind the rick, where it made an el. He could hear talk and movement up the platform, but no one bothered him, and in a minute he began to feel secure. He was experimenting with a sack of makings he had bought in Ogallala when a child-like voice spoke at his back.

"Why are you hiding?"

Jeff's head pivoted, hot words of rebuff and denial forming on his lips. But when he saw the speaker, his voice stuck in his throat. He hadn't known many girls, and the pretty ones always made him embarrassed. The one who stood there looking at him was almost too pretty to be real. He reckoned her age to be somewhere near his own. In the face, she looked much younger. But in the places where girls grew up, she had.

"I ain't hiding!" Jeff exclaimed indignantly, when he could speak again. He started to stand up, then thought better of it and eased back down.

"I'm just tired," he added.

"I wondered," the girl said, plainly seeing through his weak subterfuge, "because I was just in the station, and they're all excited about finding a Pinkerton agent killed, somewhere back along the tracks. Somebody found his corpse and wired ahead to hold the train. They think he was pushed off one of the cars, and the sheriff is rounding up everybody who was on the train."

Jeff remembered the dude with the dollar, and the warning he'd had from old McCord. He remembered the way the brakie took him off the rods, and his heartbeat slowed.

"I don't know nothing about that," he said quickly—too quickly, he feared—and instead of trying to drive the intruder away he now started making conversation to keep her from leaving.

"You live in this burg?"

"My father's ranch is thirty miles out. The town would have

10

been at the ranch, but he didn't want to have it cluttering up the land."

The easy, absolute assurance in her manner smacked of arrogance. Jeff regarded it as a challenge.

"So you come in today to see the trains, huh?" he sneered.

But sarcasm was wasted on the girl. Her intense blue eyes widened with protest. She shook her head with disarming sincerity.

"I hate trains. They're noisy and dirty, and—and scare the livestock. That's another reason why my father had them put the town off here. He didn't want the trains running through his range."

Jeff had cut his eye teeth on the stories of how the railroads in Kansas and Missouri had taken the right-of-way wherever they wished to go, crowding the people off their land, smashing homes for fuel to fire their en-jines. He thought it unlikely that one rancher in a wild, unsettled land like this would be shoving the roads around, telling them where they could build and where they couldn't.

But before he'd thought of anything uppity to say by way of retort, he heard footsteps coming along the platform. They were hard, punching steps that telegraphed a warning. It might have been accidental, but as the steps approached, the girl moved closer to Jeff, as if to screen him with her skirt.

"Hello, Miss Abby," a hoarse voice said, when the steps had ceased. "You still waiting on that pap of yours?"

"Hello, Sheriff," the girl answered easily. "I always wait on that man."

"Well, there's no better man around to wait on," the other voice declared with fawning reverence. "You see any suspicious characters dodging around this woodpile? Any hoboes off that train?"

"I saw two men running up toward the caboose just now," the girl said. "I don't know if they were hoboes."

"Likely was," the other said. "Anyhow, I'll have a look. Remember me to your pa, if I should miss him."

Jeff sat hunched and motionless, listening to the steps recede.

Then he looked up at his benefactress. "Why did you tell him that?" he asked.

"Wasn't it what you wanted me to say?"

"Yes, but—well—thanks."

He was still fumbling for words and thoughts that eluded him when a grainy voice shouted "*Abby!*" He saw the girl turn obediently.

"I have to go now," she said with resignation. "Good-by."

"Yeah," Jeff answered. "So long."

As he spoke, he retrieved his tobacco sack and started another cigarette. But the girl paid no attention to his skill at rolling them. She didn't even appear impressed to know he smoked.

Watching her graceful, departing figure, Jeff himself forgot the tobacco, and sat thinking novel thoughts that made smoking seem a tame and unexciting pastime.

All too quickly she had passed from view, and fancy failed him, and his thoughts swung back to tobacco and his predicament. He had finished fashioning the cigarette and was lighting it when a new buckboard with red wheels and fancy black upholstery appeared around the corner of the grimy station house, drawn by a team of high-stepping bays. The high-breasted girl of his reverie was on the seat, and at her side was a hard-faced man in boughten clothes and big hat. He looked more like a witch than a man.

Behind the buckboard jolted seven high-bedded, springless Peter Schuttler wagons, all freshly painted and all drawn by well-matched four-up teams. Each animal was branded low on the shoulder with a strange design that resembled a man's head, in profile.

It suddenly occurred to Jeff that he might have hit the girl up for work on her father's ranch. Intending to remedy the oversight, he came to his feet, picked up his bundle, and started off to intercept the buggy. He'd taken maybe a dozen steps when a shout caught him in the back like a meathook.

"You, there! Hold on. Hold on, I say!"

He turned to see a mustached old man in cowboy clothes waddling toward him on high-heeled boots that seemed to hurt his feet. Except for his paunch that hung far down over his belt, he was thin and stringy, like Aunt Em. He had a straggling white mustache that rose toward his nose and fell again every time he breathed. His enormous belly hindered his walk. But he still made good time as he came boring down. A tarnished law badge was on his vest.

"You ride that there train in?"

Jeff stood stiffly silent, feeling trapped and helpless, like the time Uncle Ed had jumped him about the market melons.

"I—no."

"You're a damn poor liar!" the big-gutted man shouted, though he now was close to Jeff. "Cinders and soot all over you! Come on!"

"I ain't done nothing," Jeff said defiantly, stepping back.

"Well, somebody done something!" the lawman spouted, lifting a pistol from his holster. "And we aim to find out who. Lift your hands. Turn around."

"All right," Jeff growled, scared but trying hard to put up a front. "But you ain't got to bark at me. My mother wasn't no dog."

"A smart one, huh?" the sheriff sneered, getting rough about his searching. "Not so smart, I guess, that we can't learn you a few things. . . . Flat broke, too, just like all of 'em. Well, he wasn't robbed, so that don't cut no ice. Where you from?"

"Back east."

"Where you bound?"

"Out west."

"Just full of information, ain't you. Well, you'll talk. Come on."

Inside the station house, the train crew was lined up against one wall, presided over by a man with a rifle. There were four hoboes against the opposite wall, watched by another man, similarly armed. They all looked curiously at Jeff as the sheriff shoved him into the room—all but the shack who'd taken the dude's dollar. The shack glanced at him and quickly looked away.

"Now. You ever see any these men before?"

"Hell, yes. They run that train out there."

"You see a short-complected monkey with a mustache, bum-riding on that train?"

Jeff hesitated, wondering which way to go. Finally, he nodded. "Yeah. I seen him."

"Where?"

"Place called Julesburg."

"You see him talk with any these here boys, in Julesburg?"

Jeff had learned the finer points of honest lying back at Em and Ed's. He looked carefully at every man before he answered. The shack met his look now, and the heavy-lidded eyes hurled a warning and a threat. The look brought Jeff's blood pressure up. The brakie didn't need to think he was any Roddy.

"Can't say I did," he said.

"You lied once," the sheriff snarled. "You would again."

Jeff looked at him and said nothing.

"We got ways to make you talk," the sheriff warned.

At that point, another rifleman came in, herding before him the hobo who'd warned Jeff off the train. The bum looked scared and crawly.

"Ketched another one, Gut. That train was purely lousy."

The sheriff gave his attention to the newcomer. He put him through the same line of questioning to which he'd subjected Jeff. When asked if he'd seen the short-complected man engage in talk with any in the crew, the hobo pointed at the shack.

"See him chin with anybody else?"

"Yeah." The accusing finger jabbed at Jeff. "Chinned with him—first."

Jeff said a short word, and the sheriff cuffed him hard.

"What'd he say, when he talked with you?"

"Asked me where I was bound to, like you done. I told him it was none of his dirty business."

The informer pointed at Jeff again. "He talked to the brakie first. Then the shack went and talked to the short fella. Short fella was on the rods, underneath a box."

The sheriff nodded. "Now we're gitting some place."

He swung on Jeff again. "What did you tell the brakie, about the fella on the rods?"

Jeff could sense a thinning of the ice beneath his feet. He knew he'd rubbed the sheriff so hard that the old man was more inter-

14

ested in him than in the shack. He returned the sheriff's look,
with interest.

"I didn't tell him nothing about nobody. I asked him could I
ride a coal car on from Julesburg, so I could sleep. He told me
yes."

The sheriff spun on the informer. "Where'd this bellery calf
ride, from Julesburg?"

"In a empty coal car."

The sheriff looked crestfallen. He glared at the sagging shack.
"I'm holding you, suspicion of murder." Then his eyes swung
back to the informer.

"I got to hold you, too. But I expect it'll be worth your time.
There's a five-hundred-dollar reward been offered. I'll see you git
your share."

After that, he turned and stared at Jeff again, his eyes and
mouth screwed up. "I don't see no reason for the county to board
and bed every stray dog that comes skulking through. So I ain't
going to run you in. But don't try to leave town until I say. You
understand?"

"I'm commencing to," Jeff admitted.

Jeff liked the way the railroaders all looked at him as he turned
to leave the station house. But now that the excitement was over,
he felt a faintness that reminded him he hadn't eaten since the
day before. The thought of being hungry, of eating again sometime, set him to thinking of the five hundred dollars he could
have shared in, if he'd been another Roddy. The suspicion even
rose in him that maybe the Roddys and Pinks and Jayhawkers
were way ahead of him.

Behind him, the wheezing locomotive let off a warning shriek as
the liberated train crew hustled to make up lost time. As Jeff
stopped to look around, a clanging jolt ran backward through the
cars. The big-gutted sheriff was not in sight, and his coal car was
there within easy running distance if he chose to skin out. But,
just as he'd about resolved to chance it, memory brought up a
picture of a pretty face and a red-wheeled buckboard, and he stood
motionless, watching the train depart without him.

The whistle hooted again, as if bidding for his attention. He
glanced toward the locomotive and saw the engineer lift a gloved

15

hand in a farewell salute. Instantly, all misgiving evaporated, and —hand uplifted in answering salute—he turned and started up toward the board-front town, walking in time with the train's labored, rhythmic chuffing.

Almost without knowing, he started humming a catchy tune that had been born out of that same snort and chuckle to which he stepped:

> Jay Gould's daughter said before she died,
> "Papa, fix the blinds so the bums can't ride.
> If ride they must, let 'em ride the rods,
> And put their troubles in the hands of God. . . ."

2: Man From Texas River

The beaten sign nailed to the telegraph pole said *Welcome to Quadrille*, and Jeff tried to take it at its word. A long row of buildings, mostly false-fronted, faced the tracks, and the town that spread out beyond was the biggest he had seen since leaving North Platte. Farther on, tawny grasslands rolled away in all directions, as far as eye could see.

Jeff walked up past a blacksmith shop and a harness and saddle store, to a taller building signed *The Drovers House Hotel*. From this point west, the street was two-sided, canyoned by facing rows of trade houses that shouldered one against the other, like people pushing for room at a racetrack. The street between was a ribbon bog, but plank sidewalks made walking possible, and—having nothing to do but walk—Jeff turned west past the Hat Saloon, whose sign was in the shape of a derby hat, well-ventilated with holes the size of bullets.

There was a Cheyenne-Black Hills Stage Line office, a gun and hardware store with rooms above. There was a large building faced with tin stamped to look like brick. Its sign said *Warbonnet Café and Rooms*, and the smell of cooking that wafted from its open door played cat's cradle with Jeff's intestines.

"What I couldn't do with five hundred dollars!" he groaned.

16

He moved fast away from the smell, and kept walking until he'd reached the end of the sidewalk and the end of town. There he stood awhile, looking off across the rolling earth to blue mountains in the distance, where the sun was setting, pulling the whole sky down with it, into a sea of fire.

The vastness, the hypnotic emptiness of distance, filled him with a vague unease, compounded of loneliness and awe and apprehension. It was as if he stood on the brink of a bottomless abyss, where if he lost his balance he would fall forever.

In that instant, he had a glimmering of insight into the reason why people huddled so close together in a land that offered such a wealth of space. He found himself edging back into the protective limits of the town, as though a stockade surrounded it and security lay within.

A hundred yards or so from where he stood, a tree-hedged creek coiled snakewise between low banks, describing a wide bend to avoid the town, as though it too respected the flimsy man-made barricade against encroaching space. A trestled wooden bridge carried the railroad tracks across the stream, but no bridge was visible along the wagon road that stretched off toward the mountains, straight as an arrow, until it dwindled to a hair.

Midway between him and the creek, bordering the wagon road, stood a high log livery stable and several adjunct pole corrals. Trying not to think of hunger, he hefted his bundle and stepped off into the mud, meaning to investigate the sleeping accommodations of the stable loft.

The first corral he encountered enclosed an open shed where a dozen or so horses were still shaded up, switching and stamping at the flies. The animals differed radically from the long-lined Kansas and Missouri horses, and Jeff paused to inspect them closer. All were short-coupled and big-chested, with small hoofs and long tails and sharp, well-set ears. He was puzzling what the breed might be when he became aware that he was being similarly inspected by a man lounging in the door of the big log barn.

The watcher was built like a flagpole, and his long whiskery face had only one eye. The sign above his head said Star Livery Stable, A. B. Hitchett, Prop.

17

"You use a horse today, skipper?" a nasal voice intoned when their eyes had met and words were called for.

"You use a stablehand?" Jeff countered instantly.

The single eye went over him appraisingly. "Could be. You thinking of men's work, or boys'?"

"Make it easy on yourself," Jeff invited. "If it's men's work, I reckon I'll grow into it."

The stableman was silent.

"I can shoe, and curry, and almost anything," Jeff mentioned hopefully.

The tall man spat. "Can you shovel out after thirty, forty head?"

Jeff spat likewise. "Hell. I been the pilot where they was something to pile."

The pale eye gleamed, and Jeff spoke hastily. "I don't aim to make no career out of it. What I really figured, when I got strung out, was to punch cows."

"They all figure that," the other sneered. "Trouble is, when them cow fitouts hire a man, what they mean is a man-and-horse."

The speaker paused sufficiently long for the item of information to sink in. Then he pointed a bony finger. "Now there's a good mare, over yonder, I could likely spare. A mite old, maybe. But she's transportation, and tough as bullneck rawhide. Now I'll tell you what. You help me here a month, for bed and board, and that mare is yourn."

Jeff climbed the fence to inspect the nag. Unlike the other animals in the enclosure, she was long and lean, so poor her ribs stood out like the bars of a cooking grill. She was one-eyed like her owner, bottlenecked like an old ewe sheep.

"She must be tough, to be alive," he conceded.

But the offer of bed and board appealed to him. Besides, he reasoned that the red-wheeled buckboard was bound to put in at the stable whenever it came to town.

"Well," he said, "part of a horse is better'n none. I guess you've hired a hand."

The week that followed was not an auspicious one. The promised bed was just a quilt whose smell indicated that its previous

18

occupant had been a horse. Loft privileges were extended, but in wintertime, the wind would blow cold as a stepmother's breath, and the board was so bad he almost was homesick for Aunt Em. More disappointing yet, the red-wheeled buckboard did not return, and he found himself working for work alone.

But old Hitch's one good eye seemingly saw all that was to be seen around, and Jeff's labors did pay off in information about the country and its people.

"Old Scissorbill with a face like a knife, and silver dollars for his eyes?" Hitch said, when Jeff mentioned the red-wheeled buckboard and its driver. "Why, that's Christ-God's secont cousin, Wateman Garrett. Owns the whole damn country hereabouts. You stay around, he'll own you, too."

"You mean that old witch is Abby's pa?" Jeff blurted.

Hitch grinned crookedly. "That's what everybody says, when they first see the pair of 'em together. Abby, now, she looks and acts more like her ma. Ma was a stage girl, from back East. Purtiest thing you ever seen. But this country withered her, seemed like. Died directly, when the babe was borned."

"Where do they live?"

"Home ranch is out at Rifle Mountain. Thirty miles northwest. But you ride across Man Head range all the way to git there."

"How old's the girl?" Jeff asked, determined to keep the talk on things that mattered.

"What's the difference?" the stableman leered. "When they're big enough, they're old enough."

Jeff resented the lewd remark. But he was too fascinated by their topic to break off the talk. "She live out here all her life?"

Hitch grunted a negative. "Lived mostly with high sassity relatives, back East, except for summers. You'd figure, from that, that she'd be more stuck-up than Wate. But it ain't so. She's nice as she is purty. Big-hearted, too. Ol' Wate, he's so hidebound he squeaks when he walks. They say that when he left his home in Boston, heading west, his pa handed him a lunch and a check for ten thousand dollars. They do say he's still got that check, and most the lunch, locked up in his strongbox, in the bank right here in town."

"Well," Jeff stated thoughtfully, "I git me a horse, and I'm going to hit him for a job."

"Not a chance," Hitch sniffed. "His foreman is a Texian, and don't hire none but longhorns. On top of that, Man Head hands don't never quit. They git too old to work, Wate pensions 'em off to do chore work. He don't even hire new people to swamp and fence. Raises his own, sort of."

"Sounds to me like a good place to work," Jeff maintained.

"Best work in the country, if you can git it," Hitch confirmed.

Jeff had been shoveling stables for about a week when he met the sheriff on the street, and the lawman stopped him with a stare. "We got this murder case all wrapped now, Cocky," he remarked. "You can hit the grit now, for wherever you was bound."

"I wasn't going nowhere," Jeff disclaimed. "I kind of like it here."

"Well, the place don't like you," the lawman said. "We keep your kind on the move—right on through. We got no crime here. We don't intend to have none."

It was the first time Jeff had been called a criminal. But he wasn't entirely unfamiliar with the point of view. Uncle Ed had mentioned having him locked up, and Aunt Em had foretold a hanging end for him. Besides, he'd been floated out of other towns, back in Nebraska, when it had been determined that he'd had no money to leave with the shopkeepers. The crime, it seemed, was being broke.

"Now see here, Sheriff," he protested. "You can't run me out. I got a job here. I'm working in this town."

"Where you working?"

"Down at Hitch's livery. Been working for a week."

"Well—that can be checked on. Even if you are, I don't expect you're gittin' rich."

"Well, hell, Sheriff. A man got to be rich to live in your town?"

The lawman glowered. "Still the smart one, ain't you? Well, I can't make you leave. But you git in trouble here again, and I can hell-sure make you wish you'd went."

The words killed what good feeling Jeff had managed to generate toward the world, and he went quickly about his errand before his tongue got him in bad again. At the blacksmith shop, he picked up the horseshoes Hitch had sent him for. In the Hat Saloon, he spent part of a quarter tip a drummer had given him for a sack of makings. He fingered his change and considered ordering a nickel beer, but decided not to risk the bartender's scorn and departed, resigned to more moderate measures of retaliation against an unfair world.

After, he was sorry, because the minute he stepped out on the sidewalk, he met the sheriff again, walking with the hobo who'd put the finger on the brakie. The informer must already have collected his reward, for he was dressed up like a drummer and smoking a big cigar. They both acted plenty brotherly, and neither had any time for Jeff. Gut Desmond looked at Jeff and looked away. The hobo stared straight through him, and didn't return his nod of greeting.

"Well, some people have come up in the world!" Jeff said punitively as they passed. And, for days, a rancor burned in him, making him short-tempered with Hitch and the horses, giving him a savage energy for his work.

"What's eatin' at you, boy?" Hitch begged to know, seeing him break a pitchfork handle in a senseless burst of exertion, when a tine hooked under a rotten board. "You been fightin' something for a week. What you got under your tail, anyhow?"

Half in anger, half in shame, Jeff related the whole story of the brakie and the Pink—of his own behavior with the law and of the informer who collected the reward. He told of the sheriff trying to run him out of town, while currying the informer like he was high-proof stuff.

But when he tried to put the story into words, it did not hang together and make a point, the way it did in thought. He wasn't much let down when Hitch looked unimpressed.

"So what rasped you? You had your chance at the blood money, and didn't want it. What you care what somebody else does?"

"But I did want it. Anybody wants five hundred dollars!"

"Then why didn't you go after it?"

"Oh—forgit it!" Jeff snapped. "Forgit the whole damn thing!"

"I ain't about to forgit about that fork handle," Hitch retored.

21

But there were better days at the stable. Days when Jeff liked Hitch and liked the work, liked the things he was learning. Hitch had explained early in their association that the small shaggy ponies were Texas horses, descended from the high-toned stock the Spanish had fetched to Mexico a good long while before.

"They're spidery and tough as them Texas caddle."

"How come all this noise about Texas, way up here?" Jeff inquired. "I thought Texas was down way south."

"Texas is where Texians are," Hitch maintained. "And ever since the war, they been moving it up here to Wyoming. Occupying the North, they say, leaving their own country to the carpetbaggers. Scratch nine out of ten Wyomians, and you'll find a longhorn. Other one will be a Eastern capitalist, or a English hawhaw. You can spot them, 'cause they bleed blue."

"You from Texas?" Jeff asked artlessly.

Hitch snorted disdainfully. "Every man out here's from Texas— till he's got to be a bullionaire. Then he buys hisself a seat in Parleyment, and jines the Cactus Club in Cheyenne. After that, he can be from any damn where he wants."

It didn't make a hatful of sense to Jeff. But it made a big impression. He'd been hearing of Texas in one way or another ever since he'd heard of anything. Back in Kansas and Missouri, when any man dropped from sight and never was seen or heard from again, it was whispered about that he was "G. T. T." And even before he'd learned the other facts of life, Jeff knew that the letters meant "Gone to Texas" instead of "Gone to Torture," as he first had believed. Just where or what it was he never had been wholly certain, except that it was a kind of mythical far-off place where missing things turned up and all heroes gathered after death. A place of giants and raw force, out of time and space, having location in thought and talk but none in geography, like heaven and hell and Washington, D. C.

But out here in Wyoming, the normal processes seemed to be reversed, and all things came from Texas. The men and the horses, and the flint-hoofed, devil-horned cattle. The highest moment of his life was when he saw his first trail herd winding up from south.

At first, it was nothing but a billowing dust cloud on the skyline: a tall, feathering cloud that seemed stationary, but moved closer if you didn't watch it for a while. Then, after an hour or so, the herd itself was visible, coiling like a sluggish river, giving off a yellow mist. A pushing river that has no channel and must follow the warp of the land.

"I expect I'll just ride out and hit the boss for work," he said to Hitch, a little breathless at the reckless nature of the impulse.

"Well," Hitch said, without visible enthusiasm, "they can't shoot a man for trying. But be sure and tell 'em you're from Texas. These Texians, they don't figure ary but a longhorn knows which end the horse goes to the manger. They're stuck up as Boston Brammers. . . . And don't leave here on that mare till I fix you up a bill of sale. People here don't care how many folks you salt away. But they're hell-fired touchy who owns which horse."

While Hitch wrote out the title, Jeff fetched an old cavalry saddle someone had left to satisfy an unpaid bill, and which Hitch had given him as a bonus for his work, together with a horsehair bridle with maguey reins. Then, buoyed by the stableman's good wishes, he left the scene of his labors of a month and rode out to face the world, proudly regarding the shadow that moved beside him on the ground.

As Jeff approached the herd, it changed from a winding river with a rising mist above to a multicolored aggregation of gaunt, long-legged cattle: roans and reds and blacks and blues; brindles and brockos and spots; all high-headed and wide-horned, all marching along like soldiers. Jeff could smell the dust and sweat and rank cow smell. Above the bawling and the grind of hoofs, he could hear the muted clash of rocking horns.

Each animal was marked on the hip with a scar that looked like a high-tailed snake. But the months had made Jeff sophisticated when it came to brands. He pegged it as a flying V.

The rider up on lead was tall and lean as Hitch, with yellow hair, white eyes, and the thin, transparent skin that burns and reburns, never tanning. He was riding a short-coupled pony that made Jeff's mare look worse than she really was. He was higher-crotched and rode deeper in his saddle than any man Jeff had ever seen.

"Whose herd is this?" Jeff asked, when the rider did not deign to return his nod.

The rider looked him up and down, and didn't speak. Undaunted, Jeff turned his mare and fell in beside him. After a time, the supercilious one spread his lips and spat brown upon a thistle.

"Till we tally out, it belongs to Matador. Can't you see the brand?"

"Is he around?" Jeff asked politely.

"Who?"

"Mr. Matador."

The rider's white eyes flicked toward him and away again without really touching him. The lean, hoglike jaw chewed gently.

"Yeah. He's around. He's next man back, on flank."

Jeff thanked him for the information, and wheeled his horse toward a second rider, just visible through the dust. He decided, coming nearer, that his informant must have erred, because this one looked like a boy much younger than Jeff himself. But by the time he'd got within speaking distance, he could see the boy's face was wrinkled and thatched with white.

"Mr. Who?" the old-faced youngster said, when Jeff had put his question.

"Matador," Jeff repeated. Then suspicion struck him. "Don't he own this herd?"

"Why sure he owns it," he was told. "Who the hell you think?"

In other circumstances, Jeff would have resented such pointed lack of sociability. But these were supermen, and he accepted their scorn of him as natural and just. They were Texians, afterall.

"Could you tell me where I'd find him?"

The wide-brimmed hat jerked backward. "I think he's riding next behind."

The next man, red-eyed and apparently without a tongue, didn't utter any word. He just turned in his saddle and pointed at another rider on behind, with his chin, like an Indian.

The herd was strung out for more than a mile, and Jeff kept working back, each rider passing him on back to the one behind. By the time he'd arrived at the herd's rear, he'd started to suspicion that it all might be a game—though just what the point of

24

it might be he couldn't comprehend. Anyhow, he reasoned that someone in authority must be along, so he stopped one of the two riders on the drag, and put his question again.

"Mr. Matador?" this man repeated. "*Mister* Matador?"

The cowboy's eyes and voice were filled with wonder. He didn't seem to know which of the two words to give emphasis, and ended by emphasizing both.

"The man that owns this herd," Jeff said quickly.

The cowboy stopped his horse, and looked at him again. Dust was so thick all over him that it was hard to tell much about his clothes. His mud-rimmed eyes were tawny, luminous as a cat's. He was high-crotched like the man on lead, and didn't seem very tall until you noticed how far his legs hung down.

The eyes took detailed inventory of Jeff's person and outfit, and Jeff had the feeling he was being smiled at. But he couldn't be certain, because all the face below the eyes was hidden by a kerchief the man wore bandit-fashion over his nose and mouth.

After a while, the man reached up and pulled the kerchief down. The smile was there.

"Kid, the boys been hoorawing you. Matador does own this herd. But Matador ain't here, on account of he never learned to ride. He ain't no cowboy, nohow. He's a whole damned Scotch syndicate."

Jeff's face felt hot and red. The cowboy let his grin come out, and laughed. Unlike most laughter, it was a pleasant sound.

"Don't let it rasp you, kid. The boys just played a ranicaboo. Ain't many laughs on a jant like this, without you make your own."

Hoorawing . . . ranicaboo. . . .

They were new words to Jeff, but he got the drift of them, and marked them for remembering.

"Was that the wagonboss, up on point?" he asked, parading his knowledge of the lingo, picked up at Hitch's place and around the yards. "White-eyed longhorn on a buck?"

The cowboy's manner turned scornful. "Naw. That's just Sundance. Spy for the company sent along to see we don't sell off none of these walking cowhides and report they died. . . . He might think he's boss. But he ain't, nor won't be, long as Hasty is

25

alive and kicking. Hasty's off yonder with the wagons, scouting for a place to camp."

Jeff followed the incline of the high-hatted head, and saw two wagons, canvas-covered, pulled by four-horse teams, working down toward Trail Creek.

"You say his name is Hasty?"

"Hasten. Jesse Hasten. We call him Hasty, and sometimes harder names. He's one the old-time rawhiders. Cranky old fart, and set in his ways. But he knows what a cow is going to think before she knows herself. He's first rate to trail with."

"I was thinking I would maybe hit him for a job," Jeff confided, trying to sound casual.

The cowboy sized him up again, and kind of shook his head. "We're full handed, and ain't got far to go."

"Well," Jeff said doggedly, trying to cover his disappointment, "they can't shoot a man for trying, can they?"

The cowboy's shrug was a thing of poetry. "Depends on what he tries," he said.

The outfit went into camp about five miles from town, out where there was grass and the herd was safe from dogs and the frightening sounds of town. Jeff had felt himself drawn to the tawny-eyed man from the first, and stuck with him while the cattle were watered and scattered out to graze. The cowboy appeared to return his friendly feeling, and by the time the herd was settled, Jeff had learned that his name was Dempsey Rae, that he was a Texian by adoption rather than by birth; that he had made other trips to Wyoming with trail cattle; that he had spent a year in the territory riding for one of the big outfits; that he had a brother in the crew, named Harley.

"Me and Harley, we are brothers, but we ain't much relation, twice removed," he explained carefully. "He's quiet and touchy, and stands by Texas. For all I care, they can give it back to the Texians. I'm from Arkansas, myself. Harley, he's a pistol."

"I see." Jeff nodded wisely.

Camp was made in a cottonwood grove beside the creek. Ropes stretched from tree to tree formed a flimsy kind of corral that held thirty or forty loose horses. A low wood fire was burning between the wagons, and a sour-faced man in shapeless hat and flour-sack apron was morosely superintending a half-dozen Dutch ovens on the coals around the fire's edges. Nine or ten men were sitting on the grass around, their attention given wholly to the plates upon their laps. Their faces were lean and reckless-eyed, almost black from exposure to sun and wind. The state of their clothing made Jeff rejoice that his own apparel was old and faded and falling apart. The bodies that showed here and there through rents in shirts and pants were thin and wiry as the Texas cattle, similarly hipless and taut-strung. They all were shaggy as the Texas ponies, running the same to chest and shoulder, with small, dainty feet.

The white-eyed man Jeff had seen up on point was in the group, and Jeff expected to be hoorawed some more, as Dempsey expressed it. But no one seemed to notice him any whatsoever, and he concluded that Texas humor was short as the Texas memory.

Dempsey Rae watered his horse, unsaddled it, and turned it into the rope corral. He walked to the creek and washed, drying on a dirty canvas towel spread on a bush by the stream. At a sign from the cowboy, Jeff tied his mare back out of the way, walked with Rae to the cupboard at the wagon's rear, got tin plate and cup and tools, and helped himself liberally to the contents of the Dutch ovens and the barrel-sized coffeepot.

The fare was beans and roasted meat, tough and stringy, with fried bread smeared with blackstrap molasses. Jeff hadn't known that food could taste so good.

They ate in silence like the others, and when they'd finished, they deposited their utensils in a pan by the endgate. Rae stood rolling his cigarette, and when Jeff caught his eye the cowboy pointed with his lips at a wizened, bald man who sat with his back against a wagon wheel, still eating. Jeff took a breath and stepped up to him, and put his question straight.

"My name is Jimson, mister. I'm looking for a job."

The old man finished chewing, swallowed carefully, and looked him up and down with a swift flick of sardonic eyes. He wiped his mouth on the back of his hand.

"Where you hail from, boy?"

"Texas," Jeff said grimly, half-expecting to be struck dead for such a blasphemy.

The faded eyes touched his stogie shoes and highwater pants, rested on the big farmer hands that hung too far out of ragged sleeves, then drifted over to the crowbait mare with her cavalry saddle and collar marks and spavined feet.

"Any special part of Texas, boy?"

The question caught Jeff off-balance, and he floundered for an instant, trying to recall a Texas place name he had heard.

"Our place is down on Texas River," he said finally.

Laughter exploded all around him. As with the business about Mr. Matador, he didn't clearly see the joke, but the merriment was so spontaneous and genuine that he felt obliged to join in it, for politeness' sake. Instantly, it ceased, and he found himself laughing alone. And he sensed, without knowing just how, that he had committed a prodigious social blunder. He guessed there must not be any such river, so-called, down where the cattle came from. He saw that even Rae was mortified with him, and wished he could somehow just evaporate and disappear.

The wagonboss wiped his plate clean with a chunk of bread, and ate the bread. Then he stood up.

"Sorry, boy," the godlike arbiter of destiny said. "You better try the places over yonder there in town. You Texas River roarers run us common ordinary Texians off the range."

Turning, the old man dropped his plate and cup into the wreck pan, and—leaving Jeff desolated—walked to the rope corral to catch himself a horse. The minute the boss's back was turned, the others came to life, and the hoorawing began, proving to Jeff that he was remembered after all.

"How about it, Hack? You ever see one like that, in Texas?"

"Not on Texas River. You ketch 'em big, sometimes. But, that size, they commonly got whiskers."

"Maybe Mr. Matador could tell us. The one that owns them caddle."

"Yeah, but ol' Mat, he's tough to find. 'Specially when they's work to do."

"You think that's tough, just try looking for Mrs. Mat and Little Mattie. Them there Scotchmen have got 'em run plumb ragged."

They all spoke in a soft, slurred drawl that Jeff could have listened to forever—and strictly to themselves, as if Jeff did not exist. They made Texas sound like "Takes us," and cow like "cay-ow." They looked wild as warpath Indians. Jeff would have given his right arm to have been one of them.

The wagonboss saddled a tight-knit little black geld and looked at Jeff again. "You still want a job, you can be my guide—to town."

Jeff took the hint, and walked to his old mare, his eyes carefully avoiding the eyes of Dempsey Rae. He was settling in the saddle when he heard a step behind him. Before he could turn, the mare let out a bellow of pain and leaped high into the air, swallowed her tail, and came down standing on her head. With no cantle to give him purchase, Jeff lost his iron-ring stirrups and sailed through space. He came to earth on all fours, his head thrust between the spokes of a wagon wheel, like a cow in a stanchion.

He didn't feel much at time of impact, except thankfulness that his head had missed the hickory spokes that stopped his shoulders. But then he began to hear the wild hilarity, the jokes about milking him and all, and he started feeling pain acutely. When he got back up to his feet, he discovered his head had gone through his hat and he was wearing it like a horse collar.

Dempsey Rae had caught his mare and was earing her down, just outside the camp, while another of the cowboys removed a hot Dutch oven lid from underneath her tail. There was a smell of burned hair and flesh around, and Jeff stood remembering one other mare that had been tortured to death, to make a joke. Suddenly, he hated all Texians.

"That the way they top their broncs off, down on Texas River?" a voice said near at hand. He turned and saw the white-eyed man who'd started the game about Mr. Matador. White Eyes was wearing gloves and they were smeared with soot and ashes. He was grinning, and his grin was oddly like Uncle Ed's. Jeff had either to fight or cry.

"That's one way," he choked. "Here's another."

As he spoke, he let his fist fly. In his mind, it was Uncle Ed that he was striking, and years of held-in wanting to hit back powered the swing. His knuckles smashed into the face with such force that Sundance's hat fell off frontward, and he was thrown backward, floundering to keep from going down. A bedroll tripped him and he fell heavily.

Jeff's arm was numbed to the elbow, and he knew if Sundance got back up he would take a beating. But Sundance didn't seem inclined to get up. Not all the way. He rolled over and came only to his knees. He was bleeding from the nose and mouth, but he wasn't too bad hurt to cuss. He was calling Jeff every foul name in the language, and he was tearing at the bedroll like a crazy man.

For a minute, Jeff didn't understand. Even when Sundance came up with a holstered pistol, Jeff didn't really think he meant to use it. It wasn't until the other men all scattered back away from him that he began to get the drift. By then it was too late to help himself. The kneeling man had the gun out of its leather and was pointing it, still cursing like a maniac, when Dempsey Rae stepped calmly up behind him and kicked him in the neck.

Sundance collapsed and lay twitching like a sledge-hammered hog. Jeff stood still rooted to the ground, watching him in fascination. Then he stirred again, and looked around in wonderment. The cowboys who had scattered like quail a moment before now came drifting back to the fire, no more concerned than if the near-killing had been just a friendly scuffle. Except for Hasten, they scarcely glanced at Sundance.

"Well, goddammit, you-all didn't need to break his neck!" the old man groused. "Looks like you've fixed his clock."

Rae picked up the dropped pistol and hurled it into the creek. "There's plenty sonsabitches in the world," he said cheerfully. "One less won't be missed."

Hasten turned the hurt man over on his back, and felt his neck. "Feels busted." Then, belatedly, Rae's words seemed to register. "He'll be missed in this here outfit. Leaves me short a man."

"You got a man right here, asking to take his place," Demps reminded, sliding Jeff a wink. "From Texas, too, I'd say—the way he handles his fists."

"That's the drawback," Hasten growled, standing up. "To my thinking, he's too damn much from Texas—like some others I could mention. It's plenty, having you and Harley in my hair. I don't need no other like you."

"You could take Beans off day wrangling, and put him on the

bed wagon," Rae persisted. "Texas River there could handle the horse herd days, while we break him in."

"You telling me how to run this outfit?"

"Hell, no. Just how you'd *ought* to run it."

At Hasten's instruction, they hitched a team to the bed wagon and lifted the hurt man up into the box. When all was in readiness, the old man gave a few last instructions to the men assigned to camp, then climbed up to the seat and took the lines himself.

"Well," he snapped at Jeff, looking at him for the first time since the fight, "you figure you could drive sixty trail-broke horses from here to Rustler's River, in broad daylight, at a walk behind the herd, and not lose fifty-nine of them behind the first willow bush? Think you could learn to keep them hands to yourself, and not git somebody killt whenever they's a laugh on you?"

Jeff nodded, too overcome to speak.

"All right, then. We'll give you a try. Pay is thirty dollars a month, and found, and you'll find pretty good at Cranky's wagon. But you lose a horse or start another fuss in camp I'll fire you like a gun."

Minutes later, Jeff found himself alone in camp with Rae. He started, awkwardly, to speak his thanks. But the cowboy turned on him, cross as Hasty.

"You're the damnedest fool I ever seen! Hit a man with your fists, then stand around like you was being milked, and let him git a gun! How'd you ever live so long?"

"I didn't have no gun," Jeff said defensively. "I didn't think he'd go for one."

Rae wagged his head, as if the case were hopeless. "Listen, Tex, and listen good. I don't know how it was back where you come from. But here, there ain't none that schoolyard fist-throwing, see? People here don't fight for fun. They fight for keeps, and a gun does the cleanest job—and next to that, a knife. You figure to stay alive, you git you a hoglaig, and keep it where you can git at it. Gun, knife, or fists—you fight, you keep fighting till the other fella is out of commission, else just write yourself off. You savvy that?"

Jeff nodded, chastened. He started to remark that he owned no gun, then changed his mind, deeming such a statement unseemly.

But his surprising friend appeared to anticipate his every thought. Dempsey Rae walked to the great heap of bedrolls and warbags upon the ground where the wagon had stood, dug into a sack, and came up with an old single-action Colt .38 in a worn leather holster with a looped belt wound tightly around it.

"Here's an old equalizer I growed out of, when I went to a forty-four. Take it, and pay me what it's worth to you, when you can afford it. I don't know how long I put Sundance down for, so I wouldn't lose no time learning how to use it. Bible says the race ain't to the swift nor the battle to the strong, but time and chance happeneth to us all. Me, I notice time and chance usually happeneth to the man that's caught short, like you was just now. So put your faith in that, and keep your powder dry."

Jeff was buckling on the gun, expressing his gratitude, when a voice spoke balefully from the fire. "All right. If Bible school is out, I could use some help here."

Jeff turned, and found the cook's unfriendly eyes on him. There appeared to be no doubt that he was the one addressed.

"Hasty neglected to tell you," the hostile voice went on, "but the day wrangler is the chief wood rustler and wreck washer. So grab them empty ovens and git water started to heat, without you intend to bathe the dishes cold. After that, you can round up some wood for morning, and dig me a pit to bury a oven in to-night. Axe needs filing, and my knives is all so dull they won't cut hot butter. Ain't no coffee ground for breakfast, and they's a hundred pounds of beans to sort the rocks out of, to save the wear on teeth. You run out of work, I'll let you patch the fly we'll need next rainstorm, and fix the harness I been using broke a month. Wagon hubs need doping, too, if Hasty don't forgit the grease. And that big bay in there threw a shoe this morning, so I kept him up today. I think I got another that'll fit him, in the jockey box."

Having spoken thus, the chancellor of pots and pans turned his back and thrust his dough-covered hands back into the bread pan on his cupboard. Jeff caught a nod from Dempsey Rae, and went to work.

3: The Bulls of Jajaral

Jeff slept that night in a ripe-smelling bedroll inherited from the vanquished Sundance. He thought he'd only closed his eyes when the cook was shaking him awake. "Come on. Rise and be made whole. Hit'll be daylight in another hour. You going to lay right there and sleep your life away?"

Jeff kindled the fires and carried water and kept busy choring for an hour. As quick as it was fully light, the nighthawk, Beans, brought the horse herd in. Jeff helped him corral the bunch, between the ropes. By then, the other hands had eaten, and he and Beans sat down together. When they'd slicked their plates, they both turned to and washed the wrecks. After which, they dismantled the field kitchen and stowed it on the wagon, and hitched up the cook's team.

This accomplished, they hooked the other four-up team to the bed wagon, which Beans was to drive by day.

"When are you going to sleep?" Jeff asked him.

"When I've made money enough on this job to retire, I guess," the heavy-eyed youngster said.

Already, the restless herd was up and moving, resuming its strange migration to the north. The cowboys were whooping as they got the bunch strung out and trimmed to trail formation. Before riding out, Hasty told Jeff to get the horses on the move as quick as the hands had all caught up fresh mounts for the day.

"Just nudge 'em along, behind the ca-ows—off to one side, out the dust and on the grass. They'll mostly trail theirselves, if you don't git in the way. You ain't got to crowd 'em to keep up with the caddle, so when you hit a stand of grass, stop and let them pick. I see you got a gun. If you git in any trouble, shoot it in the air three times. Out of all us, somebody's bound to hear."

Jeff was fixing to saddle his mare when Dempsey Rae rode over, a dead cigarette between his lips.

"Tex," he said, "you wrangle any time for Hasty you're going to need a horse. Give that old carrion back to the coyotes, and rope one out the bunch. That little bangtail dun don't claim no

33

man in this outfit. Rope him out and top him off. Let 'im know he's yourn."

Jeff took the rope offered him, but when he tried to swing it, he didn't catch much except himself.

"Here," Demps said, swinging down. "Make your loop a mite smaller 'n all outdoors. Git it to swinging round, like so. Then look where you're throwing, and throw where you're looking. Savvy?"

Demps made it look so easy that Jeff wanted to take the loop off and try his own skill again. But this Demps wouldn't have.

"Not on outfit time. There's a rope in the bed wagon you can have to practice with, while you're sheepherdin' them switchers along. Extree saddle in there, too, that Sundance rode. Fetch it, and give that old postage stamp back to the boys in blue."

The saddle was a big-skirted, double-rigged affair such as all the Texians rode. Thrilled to his haunches, Jeff adjusted the stirrups to his reach, and screwed the cinches tight. Demps stepped up and showed him how to blindfold the digger with his scarf and hold its near front foot off the ground with his ketch rope, until he was safely mounted.

But Demps couldn't show him how to stay up where he was, once rope and blind were off. Jeff only lasted for three short jumps.

"Lend me the loan of your spurs," he begged, spitting out a chunk of prairie. "He might shuck me again, but he'll loose some hair a-doing it."

"There's spurs in the wagon, too," Demps told him. "But spurs ain't for making horses buck. Bucking is foolishment, for horse and rider both. Thing you got to do is sell the horse."

Jeff got the spurs, and next time up, Demps was on his sorrel, a riding quirt in his hand. When the dun began his pitch, Demps laid the whip across his rump, and the buck ended in a wild run that carried Jeff halfway to Quadrille.

Demps stuck alongside, on the sorrel, and each time the dun tried to buck, the quirt straightened him to a run. Once Jeff grabbed the horn, and Demp's quirt descended on his hand. Jeff made a one-point landing in some prickly pear, and bounced up, swearing like an expert.

"Now there's a proposition," Demps said gravely, riding up with the sweating dun in tow. "You hear a bunch of talk about how come the fine art of rough-riding has been developed to such a high degree, here in this north country. But, put credit where credit belongs, and honor the lowly prickly pear. No man that lights in it once will ever git shook loose again."

"You go to grass!" Jeff fumed, prying another pin cushion from his flesh. "I wouldn't of got shook loose that time, if you'd kept that damn dog whip to yourself. Git down here, and I'll honor you!"

But Demps let his eye-shutting grin come out, and Jeff learned right then that he couldn't stay peeved at Demps when Demps was grinning.

"I done it for your own good, Tex. You won't learn to ride, choking the apple. You ride with your laigs and haunches, not your hands. Better try and remember that."

Jeff didn't argue the point. But, next time up, he held the quirt himself. Inside of another ten minutes, the saddle had spanked him raw and his interior department felt scrambled until nothing was left in place. But he hadn't touched the horn again, and there wasn't any more jump left in old Clay.

"Handle him right now, and he'll make a horse," Demps told him. "He's rough-gaited and got a belly full of bedsprings, so none the boys been using him. He'll be broncky and full o' snorts for a while yet, but you've topped him off. He'll settle down, as quick as you do."

"Who's he belong to?" Jeff inquired.

Demps shrugged. "You, I expect. You twisted him out. He joined our band, clean down on the Canadian. That star there on his shoulder could be a wire scar."

"What'll I do about a bill o' sale?" Jeff asked, remembering Hitch's warning.

Demps looked at him, and his tawny eyes glowed. "You got a thirty-eight caliber bill o' sale, right there on your hip—if you'll learn yourself to use it."

"Hey, you *fairgrounders!*" the nighthawk yelled. "If you've finished your ro-day-o, how about gittin' the cavvy on the move, so I can have my ropes and git this wagon rolling. Cranky'll be so

35

far ahead o' me I can't hand him his lines in case he drops them. Then they'll be hell to pay!"

Demps helped dismantle the corral and stow the ropes. Then he dug into his bag of tricks again, and came up this time with a pair of old runover cowboy boots.

"Here," he said. "Try these here for fit. Man needs footgear that fits a stirrup, with a heel to keep it from pushin' through the bucket and gittin' him drug to death. And shorten them stirrup straps some, and put your weight in them instead of on your horse's spine. Man that rides like a sack of salt had better git a pack horse."

They got the nighthawk rolling, then Demps swung up to his saddle. "Well, Tex, I can't do no more for you. If I don't git on them drags, Hasty'll git on me. You're on your own, now."

You're on your own. . . .

Jeff found the words both daunting and assuring. And there he was, still seventeen and scarcely a year away from home, all set up as a practicing cowboy, horse herding with a Texas trail outfit, bound for the deep range country of Wyoming. Thanks to the puzzling interest and benevolence of a tawny-eyed man with an eye-shutting grin, he was fully equipped as a cowboy ought to be, living a dream whose beginning he could not recall.

He wasn't even Jeff Jimson any more. He was Texas River, and just plain Tex. Texas was where you found it, wherever Texians were. Jeff was G. T. T., and wished the world could know it.

From time to time, he pinched himself to see if he were dreaming.

They stalled along, on Hasty's orders, feeding off the grass, putting meat on knocking bones. "New grass makes new cay-ows, and we'll turn this bunch over in good shape—even if we don't have no company spy along to see we do things right," the wagonboss announced.

Cranky Crowe, tyrant of the chuckwagon, was an exacting taskmaster, and Jeff found himself working hard around the camp, night and mornings. But when it came to his day work, the horses were completely broken to the trail, and minding them was not work at all. He soon made the acquaintance of the other riders,

36

including Harley Rae. He found that a man was accepted in the crew so long as he did his job, regardless of past jokes and persecutions.

After the first few days, old Hasty himself unbent and hinted that he wasn't shedding any tears for Sundance.

"Wasn't no Texian at all," the trail boss derogated, as if that fact itself were sufficient to make a man suspect. "Ornery-eyed Montanan, is what he was. Good hand with the ca-ows, but always sucking up to a boss. Always figuring the way to git ahead is to knock the other fella. I don't hold with that."

"You figure he might git over that stomping Demps handed him?" Jeff inquired uneasily.

"The medic said he might." Hasty nodded sourly. "I've saw coyotes git up and run off with a broken back. He might take the affair up with you, and he might not. I don't expect he'll tamper none with Demps. Ain't many men that know him will ask a fight with Demps. He's a he-horse, with the hair side out."

Thereafter, lazing along with his horse herd, Jeff managed to keep the rest of the outfit always in view. And he gave less time and attention to his rope practice, more to the .38. Most of the riders used pistols of like caliber, so ammunition wasn't a problem. It wasn't long until the dun would let him shoot off its back without boogering, and he could hit a tin can up in the air two times out of five.

"What you practicing up to be—another Wyatt Earp?" Beans asked one day.

The name was strange to Jeff, but as with some of Demps's talk, he got the drift.

"Just practicing up to practice up," he stated modestly.

It was on the third day out of the Trail Creek camp when Jeff learned that the Rustler River whence they were bound was only fifty miles away. His hard-won job was going to be over with almost before it had begun, and the knowledge left him desolate. But then he found the cattle were consigned to Man Head, and his hopes and interest quickened.

"Man Head, eh?" he said. "Ain't that Wate Garrett's brand?"

"That's Garrett's," Dempsey nodded. "Most owners only burn

37

their monogram, as the Haw-Haw said. But Old Wate, he puts his whole damned picture on his. I guess he's smart. Keeps the bears and wolves off—like a scarecrow. Put a pair of crossbones down below it, and it would tell the whole damn story."

"I thought his ranch was off to west," Jeff mentioned. "Over by Rifle Mountain."

"Wate's ranch is every damn direction," Demps said ruefully. "We been on Man Head ground ever since we left Quadrille. Home ranch is at Rifle Mountain, but he's got others all over this end the territory. Upwards of half a million acres, all together."

Jeff whistled, thinking of Uncle Ed's quarter-section, which had seemed like plenty acres in Missouri.

"He own the whole damn territory?"

"Owns damn little of it," Demps refuted. "Just a homestead here and there, that he hired some his hands to take up for him. But he's got it all sewed up. Only difference is, he don't have to pay no taxes."

"He have it leased?"

"Naw. It's government grass. No way a man can lease the public land. But the big bullionaires, like Garrett, they take a kind of shotgun lease. All it costs is wages paid to toughs that stand the people off."

"What about the Homestead Law?" Jeff asked, recalling talk he'd heard from hoboes and around. "If it's public land, can't anybody go in and fence a hundred-sixty, long as he files on it?"

"Anybody could try," Demps admitted. "And some do. But Garrett's shotgun men make homesteading plenty tough. . . . Oh, the plowmen are gradually moving in. Maybe in a hundred years or so, the big operators like Garrett will have to own their ground—or at least rig things with the government so they can lease it for a little of nothing. Way things stand, there's damn few filers stay long enough to prove up. Takes five years to git a patent, you know. A lot can happen, in five years."

"What about the law?" Jeff insisted. "Ain't the law enforced?"

"In this country, Tex, the bullionaires are the law. They run the legislatures that make it, and they name the sheriffs that enforce it. The Governor's one of the crowd. So's the delegate to Congress. Governor runs the territory, and the delegate appoints

38

the U. S. marshals that are supposed to see the Federal laws git heeded. They got it all sewed up in a sack. Ain't no way to crack it."

Jeff was silent a time, trying loyally to generate indignation, but finding his real concern with more immediate things.

"You think I might git on with Man Head?" he asked, queerly short of breath.

"Why not?" Demps shrugged. "You're from Texas, ain't you?"

It was on the seventh day of Jeff's employment when they came in sight of a long plateau that ended in sheer bluffs at the edge of a considerable creek valley.

"That there is Rustler River," Demps announced, pointing at a narrow hedge of trees that marked the course of the valley stream. "Owned by the biggest rustler of them all."

"You mean we're already there?" Jeff asked unhappily.

"Them buildings you see on the crick, under the big bluff, that's Garrett's Rustler ranch. We'll sleep under a roof tonight."

True to the prediction, they took supper that night in the Garrett cookshack, and bedded down after in the bunkhouse. Directly after breakfast in the morning, Wate Garrett put in appearance, accompanied by a retinue of cowboys. He looked sharper of face than when Jeff had seen him in Quadrille, and once again Jeff wondered how a thistle seed could grow into a flower like Abby.

The ranchman greeted Hasty warmly, but had no eye for the rest of the ragged crew. He commanded that the grazing herd be strung out and dribbled past him through a narrow bottleneck where the bluffs closed in to canyon the stream. Hasty issued appropriate orders, then joined the receiver to make the tally. Jeff rode out with Demps.

"Couple years ago, I was with a layout that delivered a herd to one the Haw-Haws, up on Powder River," Demps related. "He took the tally at the bottom of a hill that set out in the middle of the valley. We drove the herd around that hill three times, and Sir Mortimer paid according to his tally. We sent the company theirn, and divvied the profits amongst us. But you wouldn't put nothing like that over on Garrett. Old Wate, he's sharp as they come. Tighter'n a young bull's butt, going uphill."

39

"Ain't much of a layout he's got here," Jeff mentioned, eyeing the shabby buildings. "I figured he would do things up in style."

"He does," Demps averred. "Home ranch, out at Rifle, is a regular show place. This here, it's just a way station. He only gits up here once a year or so."

"How far to Rifle Mountain?" Jeff asked, looking off to west.

"Oh, twenty, thirty miles."

Jeff laughed shortly. "Funny thing, I can travel round and round this country, and never git no closer to Rifle than twenty, thirty miles."

"Why you want close to Rifle?" Demps demanded. "What you lose up there?"

"Ain't lost nothing—yet," Jeff said, blushing just a little.

That afternoon, when the tallying was done, Jeff made the acquaintance of the Man Head crew. Strap Bowman, Garrett's foreman, was a lean wolfhound of a man, maybe in his thirties, with luminous green eyes and a hardness about him that made Jeff uneasy from the first. He was good-looking, in a predatory sort of way, and didn't use two words where one would do the job. He told the trail crew he was short-handed, it being roundup time. He promised to pay better than going wages if the Texians would stay and help process the cattle they had fetched. He said there would be winter work, for two or three, there on the Rustler range.

"Well," Hasty said, "it's up to the boys. I ain't got to be back to the Pecos until time to gether another bunch for spring. I and the wagons ain't in no sweat."

"How's about it, Harley?" Demps asked his brother. "Do we want one them winter jobs?"

Harley was red and ruddy where Demps was brown and tawny, quiet and drawn-in where Demps was wordy and aggressive. Harley shook his red-thatched head.

"Not this Texian. If I owned hell and Wyoming, I'd deed Wyoming to the devil, and live in hell."

Demps sighed and shook his head. "Then I and Tex will have to go it all alone. You got two takers, Strap. Eh, Tex?"

Jeff nodded fervently. But Bowman didn't favor him with a glance. Bowman was noticing Demps, apparently for the first time, staring hard. Demps was handing back his look, a kind of challenging smile upon his mouth. For a minute, neither of them said any more. They just locked eyes and pushed at one another, like a pair of range bulls. There was something in the air, and it wasn't just autumn leaves.

"So, you're back," Bowman said at last.

Demps nodded, still grinning on one side. "I finally made it, Strap. Ain't that purely hell?"

The foreman sneered. "Well, if you stay around, you got a job. That way, I can watch you."

Demps placed a hand on Jeff's shoulder. "This here is Texas River. He's my pardner. You hire one, you hire us both."

The foreman shrugged. "I didn't think I'd ever be this short-handed. Good thing there's only two of you. I only got two eyes."

Jeff was elated to be hired, but it seemed a doubtful beginning. After supper, he caught Demps alone out by the corrals and tried to learn something about the quarrel he feared he was inheriting.

"You know Bowman somewheres before?"

Demps nodded. "I knew the bastard, when. We went to different schools together. I learned the most. But Strap, he got the honors. I even worked for him here, once. But I quit."

"Why?"

The tawny eyes glowed. "There was too much to take from the bastard!"

"Well, is he from Texas, too?"

"In a kind of unmentionable way," Demps answered, savoring his words. "He was borned twin to a stinking snake, and he died, whereas the snake lived. But nobody never noticed, them being identical."

Jeff stared at his friend, fascinated by his eloquence. He hoped to hear more details of their feud. But when Demps spoke again, it was only to heap more vilification upon his enemy.

"Yeah. That Strap is a little house, out behind a big one. But I hear he's about to hitch up with the big house's daughter, and move inside."

Jeff's heart missed a beat.

"What do you mean by that? Bowman surely ain't going to marry Garrett's daughter?"

Demps shrugged. "Why not? Wate's got no son, only one little blue-blooded filly, in all that big white stable he keeps up at Rifle Mountain. Naturally, he'll pick a stud horse in his own image, to perpetrate his line. And he's got one in that Strap. Choice seems to be all right with the filly, too. I ain't seen her in two years. But the way she was horsing around Strap then, I wouldn't be surprised if . . ."

Jeff was shocked to see a hand flash out and slap his friend across the mouth. He was more shocked yet to know the hand was his own.

The open-handed blow was hard enough to knock the speaker off balance. By the time he'd struck a compromise with gravity again, his pistol had cleared leather. The tawny eyes were hot and bright.

Jeff stood rigidly motionless, hands at his sides, returning the heated stare. He was appalled at what he'd done, but he was angered, too, ready to take his medicine.

"You don't learn worth a damn, do you?" Demps said in a voice that was too quiet to match his cheeks and eyes. "What'd I tell you about laying your stubby hands to people, when you got no gun? And what the hell's this all about? What you slapping me for?"

Jeff was getting scared, but he still had anger to sustain him. "I won't have you laying your vulgar tongue to Abby Garrett," he stated, trying without success to keep his voice steady. "Maybe I shouldn't of slapped you. But I won't stand by and hear you run that girl down."

Demps's tautness left him. Stupefaction replaced the fury on his face. "I didn't know you knew the lady," he said.

"I know her well enough I ain't about to stand by and hear her slandered. Ain't a nicer girl than her in all creation."

Demps stared at him in uncomprehending amazement. "Well, godamighty," he complained. "I'll take your word for it. I didn't mean nothing. Why, I don't scarcely even know the gal, to speak to. I was just running off at the mouth. I baig your pardon, all to hell."

"I expect I should baig yours," Jeff said awkwardly, starting to feel foolish about the whole thing. "I just kind of lost my head."

42

"Well, maybe I asked for it," Demps conceded aggrievedly, blotting a drop of blood from his mouth with his hand, then staring at the hand.

"But, dammit, kid, you're going to die of sudden death someday, if you don't learn to curb them hands. And one other thing. Ever you have to hit me again, you use your goddam fist, see? I won't take a slap from God's own hand!"

It was heavy work, branding and marking the two- and three-year-old steers that weighed all the way from five hundred to eight hundred pounds. Jeff's participation was limited largely to tending fire and handling irons. But he learned a lot, just watching the others function. And it was a thing to see as they went about the roping, catching the breachy animals by the feet, spilling them to the ground for the flankers who held them by horns and nostrils while the brands were burned. The ropers worked with incredibly small loops, always with the rope's other end tied fast to the saddle horn. And as the ten-ring circus progressed, Jeff began to understand the purpose of that second cinch one saw on all the Texas saddles. Many of the cattle were as large and heavy as the horses. The instant a catch was made, the ponies wheeled to face the caught critters, braced their forefeet, half-squatted on their haunches, and started backing off. Often, when a big steer busted itself at the rope's end, the impact would lift the pony's hind feet off the ground and come near to standing it on its head. If secured with one cinch only, the saddles would have been torn loose and snaked halfway back to Texas.

Superior equipment and the skill of men and horses notwithstanding, the work did not go off without its slips and smashups, its casualties and near-casualties. Sometimes a pony would not be braced when a proddy old steer hit the rope, and the pony would be jerked from its feet, the rider sent hurtling through the air as if thrown by a catapult. In some cases, ponies were dragged over the rough ground, kicking and bellowing, until ropes parted or other men came in to make good the catch. Once in a while, a leg would be broken, and a game little horse would have to be destroyed. More frequently, a falling steer would snap off a horn,

43

and when freed would leap to its feet with mayhem in its heart and scatter the flankers and iron men like a whirlwind.

Men were trampled. Men were spilled from horses and kicked and cut by knife-sharp hoofs. Men were burned by hot irons and bruised in jarring falls. But none were put out of action, and the work went forward. The thought was planted in Jeff's mind as he watched that the men were tougher than the cattle or horses either —that maybe it did take Texas men to handle the Texas cows and horses.

"'Para los toros del Jajaral, los caballos del Jajaral,'" Demps quoted with a shrug, when Jeff mentioned the notion to him.

Jeff waited, not understanding, and Demps read the question in his eyes. "That's a saying they got, down in Jajaral in Old Mex, where they raise them fighting ring bulls. Means, 'For the bulls of Jajaral, the horses of Jajaral.'"

"And, for them both, the men of Jajaral, eh?"

Demps shrugged again. "I wouldn't know. The saying didn't say."

One afternoon when the rebranding operation was nearing completion, Bowman sent Jeff off to Rustler Station, some five miles from the Man Head ranch, to buy horseshoes. He was on his way back, the horse iron in a gunny-sack tied to his saddle, when he saw a well-shaped brown pony coming toward him across the low valley, bearing a well-shaped rider in matching brown riding habit, sitting sidesaddle. He knew somehow that it was Abby, long before he could distinguish her features. And when they'd drawn close enough together that he could see her clearly, he was exulted to see her face light with recognition.

"Why, hello!" she called, her voice as rich and musical as he had remembered it. "I didn't expect to see you up here."

"I didn't expect to see you!" Jeff responded heartily. Then his bolt was shot, and he could say no more.

Their horses came together, and both pulled rein. Jeff knew that he was staring, and it was wrong to stare. But he wasn't able to do anything about it.

Up close, Abby was even prettier than at a distance. Prettier than the picture he'd carried in his mind ever since that memorable day when he'd first seen her, back in Quadrille. She had blue eyes and copper-red curls, just as he remembered. Her well-kept skin was like the rose-tinted china his aunt Em had always used for company. Her chin was some like old Garrett's, but an awful lot nicer.

"I didn't know you were a cowboy."

Jeff saw the blue eyes inspecting his clothes, and suddenly the pleasure went out of the encounter. Around the ragged, unkempt ruffians who had been his companions of late, his shabby getup had been in style and helped to make him one of them. But Abby looked as if she had just stepped out of a mail-order catalogue, and —remembering Strap Bowman's good clothes—Jeff was painfully aware of the bare knee that winked through the hole in his pants. Of the places in his sleeves where his arms were out.

Remembering his hat, he reached up furtively to remove it. His fingers encountered the overlong hair sticking up through the hole his head had punched, and his mortification grew.

"I wasn't a cowboy when I saw you in town," he owned, seeing that she waited for an answer. He tried to make his voice and manner commonplace, to impart the idea he had changed his plans on the merest whim.

"I just decided to come up and try my hand at it, as long as I was in the country."

"Do you ride for one of the ranches here?"

"I ride for Man Head," he informed her, his pride returning. A bit of his earlier pleasure came back, too, when he saw she looked happily surprised.

"For my father?"

Jeff nodded. "I figured to ask him for work, that day in Quadrille. But you got out of town before I had the chance. So I tied on with the Texians that delivered the cattle here last week. I hit Strap Bowman for a job, and he put me on."

Comprehension lighted the girl's face as he talked. "So you came up with the Texans!" she exclaimed when he'd finished. "Now, I'm beginning to understand. You must be the famous Jeff Jimson!"

"The fam—" Jeff's mind and voice failed him, and he sat staring

45

at her in silence. After a time, he felt the wind blowing into his mouth, and closed it.

"The man who saved my name from being slandered," she went on. Then she observed his thunder-struck expression, and her bright laugh tinkled.

"My father was standing in the stable door one day, just after the herd came up, and heard one of the drovers say something bad about me. He said he started out, planning to have the man horse-whipped. But one of the other drovers was quicker, and slapped the slanderer's face. Dad heard my champion say he knew me, and I was the nicest girl in the country. He asked Mr. Hasten who you were, and Jesse told him your name was Jeff Jimson."

There was such warmth and approbation in the eyes and in the voice that Jeff's spirits more than just recovered. So the old man had overheard that conversation! He'd been pleased enough to find out what Jeff's name was! There seemed to be a kind of pattern in it.

Jeff knew he was blushing, and the blood was pounding at his ears until he almost missed the rest of what the girl was saying. Afterward, he was sorry he hadn't missed it.

"Father and I had a terrible scene, over that. He wanted to know when I had been consorting with Texas trail drivers, and all. He didn't believe me when I said I didn't know any Jeff Jimson. Now I can explain."

Consorting with Texas trail drivers. . . .

Long after Abby had stopped speaking, that phrase kept going through Jeff's mind, weighting him down like a load of stone. He was only vaguely aware of caste and class barrier, and didn't even know the terms that were used to describe it. But he remembered old Garrett's cold and proud behavior around the Texians at the ranch, and he sensed the thing it meant, even if the abstractions of it did elude him. He sensed that he might be reaching for the moon, getting ideas about the old man's daughter.

"Maybe you better not tell him," he said soberly, feeling the need to say something. "I mean about me not being from Texas. He might fire me."

"What's being from Texas got to do with being fired?"

46

Jeff shrugged and assumed a worldly mien. "For the bulls of Jajaral, the horses of Jajaral," he said darkly.

The blue eyes regarded him blankly. "What on earth are you talking about?"

"That's a saying they got, down in Jajaral, in Old Mex," he said casually, as if speaking of a place he knew well. "Means it takes one, sort of, to handle the other. I hear tell people in this country think it takes Texas men to handle Texas cows and horses."

"That's silly!" The blue eyes were scornful. "My father isn't from Texas."

"Strap Bowman is—or thinks he is," Jeff gloomed.

He fancied the girl brightened at the name. He remembered Demps's insinuations, and his unhappiness thickened into sickness.

"Strap thinks a lot of things that are not so," Abby said lightly. "I wouldn't worry about him."

Jeff brightened some, but could think of nothing else fitting to say. He sat looking at imaginary objects of interest in the distance. He felt the blue eyes studying him. He sensed that Abby felt his unhappiness, and was holding herself to blame. It gave him a feeling of advantage, but he didn't know how to exploit it properly.

"Well," Abby said in a moment, "I might not tell, if you'll race me to the ranch. Mouse hasn't had his run, and wants to go."

"You'll git beat!" Jeff warned, wanting bad for some reason to win a race from her.

But the girl already had gathered her reins, and now she lifted the wonderfully trained pony to a gallop from the very first step, and sped away from him. He had previously identified the brown as a Morgan geld, and knew that it was bound to be a race. But distance to the ranch was a long two miles, and he expected the tough little dun to shine in endurance, even if it couldn't match the stockinged brown at the getaway.

But even though he pushed the dun hard, using spurs the last half-mile, its choppy run could not begin to compete with the blooded racer. All the way, the Morgan kicked dirt and rocks in the dun's face, and the graceful, flashing feet were a taunt the dun could not rise to. When Jeff finally rode into the yard, Abby was already out of the saddle, waiting for him.

"You're slow," she said, laughing a laugh that stabbed him like

47

a blade of light. "You'll have to get a horse, if you expect to catch me!"

"I got a horse," Jeff said loyally, trying to match her smile. "We're just out of practice. I'll catch you yet—before I'm through."

At one moment, their mood was careless as their laughter. Then their eyes caught and held, and suddenly they were not laughing. It was as if both had suddenly become aware of a deeper meaning in their words, and their mood was not careless any longer.

Jeff kept the smile on his face, but it felt stiff and carved and out of place. Abby was blushing, and as tongue-tied as Jeff. After what seemed a long time and no time at all, the girl put out one hand in an aimless gesture of escape. She freed her eyes and started fussing with the Morgan.

"Well," she said in a commonplace voice, "I have to find my father. A telegram came for him, at the station hotel where I'm staying. I promise I won't tell him you're not from Texas, or Jajaral, or wherever you told him."

Then she was gone, leading her dainty pony away, and Jeff sat looking after her, sensing the lifting of a latch, the opening of a door which should have been locked and barred and guarded by the palace guards. When he finally recalled his errand and turned toward the branding corrals to deliver the horseshoes, the skyline in front of him had widened to horizons so broad and distant as to numb the mind.

"When I send you somewheres, after something, I don't look for you to go galivanting all over the country with the boss's daughter," Strap Bowman told him pointedly, as he took the proffered sack. "And that there is the lesson to write down and memorize for today. Wate Garrett don't put up with the hired help cutting shines around that girl. Nor I don't look for to have tell you so again!"

Ordinarily such a speech from the boss would have set Jeff back a notch, and maybe would have brought a sharp retort, before he could put a bridle on his tongue. But Bowman had a way of turning on his heel and walking away as he talked, so his words didn't hit as hard as they might have done. Besides, Jeff was remembering Abby's words, "Strap thinks a lot of things that aren't so."

48

Jeff was too high in the clouds to be reached by a jealous straw boss, however loud his bleat.

"We're a-going to make good here, Clay," he told the sweating pony as he tied him to the fence. "We're a-going to make so damned good we won't even know ourselves. Be some others around won't know us, too, by golly!"

The dun chomped its bit and stamped restlessly, as if it too were troubled by a maggot of hungering ambition. . . .

4: The Maverickers

Jeff didn't see Abby again before leaving the ranch. The branding was completed on the evening of his encounter with the girl, and after supper Strap Bowman came looking for Demps and Jeff.

"If you two lightweights still want a winter's work, why git your stuff together, and be ready to shove in the morning. I figure on you riding line, up on Paint Crick, between us and Muleshoe. Most of these new caddle go to that range. I'll give you four more riders to help shove the stuff over. Once you git it scattered, you'll ride the Paint Crick line. I'll send Hob Shaffer up with you, to git you located. He knows the country."

"We don't need no Shaffer," Demps spoke up. "I know that line."

"You'll each take four horses that I'll point out to you," the foreman went on, ignoring Demps. "You'll pack two, and ride two. Pack gear is in the harness shed, and you can draw what supplies you'll need, for trailing and to keep you awhile, up at the store in the house. Every month or so, a packer will come by and provision you. Any man caught butchering company beef to feed his face gits chopped."

"I'll only need two horses," Jeff interrupted to say. "I got a couple my own."

Bowman looked at him without friendship or favor. "If you got horses, you can sell 'em to Wate, if he wants them. Or you can find pasture for them, off the Man Head range. You won't use

49

them while you work for us. Now, it's rough country up there, and I want it understood . . ."

"Why not use my own horses?" Jeff broke in again, figuring there must be some misunderstanding. "It won't cost the company any more."

"You won't use your horses, because when you work for the company, you by-God use company horses," Strap explained carefully. "Now, like I was saying . . ."

"But I already got the horses," Jeff protested. "I want to use 'em."

Bowman pushed back his hat and oggled him. "You want this job, or not?"

"Why—sure."

"Then quit the hell talking when you should ought be listening! . . ."

"Don't worry about your switchers, Tex," Demps advised. "I know a place we can pasture 'em for nothing."

Bowman inhaled a big breath. He pursed his lips and said that if he could interrupt their private conversation for just a minute, he would like very much to finish giving them their instructions. He wrote them out an order on the store for groceries, and told them they could draw anything they needed in the way of bedding and winter clothing against their pay. He took them to the corral and pointed out the horses they would be using. He suggested that, if at all convenient to their plans, they transact all necessary business that night, because they would by-the-jumped-up-Jesus-Lord be up and on the trail by daylight in the morning. Then, still in a stomping huff, he went and left them standing.

"Tex," Demps said sadly, "that there man is plumb down on me. I'm afraid he's gittin' down on you, just because we're teamed."

"What's this about not being able to ride our own horses?" Jeff asked.

Demps shrugged. "Just a rule they got. It's the same with all the big layouts. Old Garrett didn't think it up. They got a system. They hire a man, he brings nothing to the job but himself and his saddle and bed. They fire him, he takes nothing away but what he brought. Most the outfits even furnish beds. Strap, he

50

don't, because he likes to fire a man just by telling him to pick up his bed and walk, which he couldn't do if it was company property. The notion sets right with Wate, too, 'cause like I say, Wate is tight as a Scotch virgin in a freeze."

Jeff scowled. "I don't git it. If Wate's tight as you say, I'd think he'd want us to furnish our own horses. Horses cost him money, don't they?"

"They cost him money—but the kind he can afford. The bullionaires are 'way ahead of you, Tex. They see around the corners. It's kind of hard to explain, without you know the system. Take Garrett, just for instance. He got control of this end the territory, because he was the first one here. There was others right behind him, moneyed, and hungry as Wate. But there was plenty ground, and instead of moving in on Wate, they went on up north and west. Instead of fighting amongst theirselves, they joined hands to stick together and keep others out. And they got things pretty sweet. They pay no taxes and they pay no rent. They stock and graze the whole damn plains."

"I don't see what that's got anything to do with me riding my horse."

Demps looked at him, and rubbed his neck. "That's because you ain't looking at it. Say you ride for Garrett, and keep your horses. First thing, you're going to have another horse, and maybe another. Pretty quick you want a place to keep them. So maybe you take a homestead. Then you got grass for still more horses, and maybe so a cow or two. Your cows calve out, and after a while you're short of pasture. You turn 'em out on public land. That cuts Garrett down, and Garrett ain't about to git cut down. Garrett likes things way they are."

"Well, it looks like a lot of fuss and rigmarole, just over a man using his own horses," Jeff said stubbornly. "And old Hitch sure put one over on me, in town."

"It ain't over a man riding his own horses," Demps said patiently. "I been trying to tell you. It's over the bullionaires keeping other people off the public ground. And there's another angle. A man that's got his own transportation is liable to up and quit the job any time he feels like it. Maybe then he'll hang around the country and practice what the company has learnt him.

But if he's out to hell and gone in some big gut of a place and knows he's going to have to ride Shanks's ponies, lugging his outfit on his back, he's going to count his many blessings before he takes the jump."

"Well, I'll take your word for it," Jeff said, losing interest. "I don't figure on quitting. If Strap says to ride company switchers, I'll ride 'em backwards, if I got to. But it sure seems complicated."

"Any system's complicated, till you know what's back of it," Demps grunted. "Then it's simple as what makes milk."

"That always struck me as kind of complicated, too," Jeff confessed.

"Well, I'll explain that, likewise," Demps promised, "as quick as you git your growth."

Besides a bedroll and new clothes from his skin out, Jeff's credit purchases at the company store included new boots and hat, and a saddle—big, wide-skirted, double-rigged. The value of his purchases totaled ninety dollars, and Demps condemned his extravagance.

"You're mortgaged to the eyebrows, kid. You won't draw no pay for ninety days."

"Nor I won't git fired for ninety days," Jeff pointed out.

Demps clucked, and clapped him on the back. "You'll be a bullionaire someday, Tex. You see around the corners, too!"

Paint Creek was a small, brushy stream in a spread of endless prairies, rolling like pictures of the sea. Their joint task was to patrol a sixty-mile line from the Upper Rustler to the Big Blue Plains to west. Their base camp was a one-room cabin of cottonwood logs, located roughly halfway between the line's extremities. By dividing the distance equally, each could ride the thirty miles to the end of line in one day and return the next. Smaller, more primitive shacks were located at both terminals, and their itinerary demanded that they cover the lines each day—camping together in the central cabin one night, camping separately in the terminal shacks the next.

"In other words," Shaffer told them, "you'll take the place of sixty miles of fence. You'll cover the line every day, turning Man Head stock back south, Muleshoe and anything else you see up

north. You'll keep your eyes open for predatories, too—two-legged
and four. Any homesteaders show up, discourage them. You run
up against anything you can't handle, ride like hell for Rifle Mountain."

As he listened, Jeff began to have a little clearer appreciation of
how the unfenced ground was held against trespassers, within the
law and out. And he felt pleased and flattered with the responsibility invested in him. He liked the idea of being on his own, the
chance to show the company what he could do.

"It'll be a little lonesome, out in the farther camps," Demps
mentioned.

"That's all right with me," Jeff answered. "I'd a heap rather be
lonesome than stuck around the home ranch, with Strap Bowman
looking down my neck."

But even as he said it, he was thinking of Garrett's daughter and
having heartburn at the thought of not seeing her again till spring.
He was thinking of Demps's story of Strap and Abby, and wondering if his horseback ride with Abby at the Rustler ranch had
brought on his sudden exile.

Summer had almost run its course before Jeff left Quadrille.
Now the leaves were off the brush and trees; the grass was gray
by day, frosted white at night. The creek wore a morning fringe
of ice, the ponies a morning knot in their backs that had to be
ironed out before the day could start. What rain they had was
cold, predicting snow. But Jeff was dressed against the wet and
cold, and the thought of spending a Wyoming winter out there
fifty miles from nowhere didn't eat at him as it seemed to eat at
Demps.

"Well, we better git our horses down to Ekard, while them caddle are still back from the line," Demps said a couple of mornings
after Shaffer had left them to their own devices. "Won't hurt if
a little Muleshoe stuff comes over onto Garrett while we're gone.
Them outfits both got rich stealing from each other, anyhow."

"What and where is Ekard?" Jeff asked.

"Road ranch, about twenty miles east of here," Demps explained. "Run by a longhorn name of Drake that used to punch
cows before he graduated to herding women. Gits the name by

spelling his own handle backwards. Ain't much there to speak of. Just a kind of cap-and-ball, muzzle-loading honkytonk. But his whiskey's got authority, and a girl's a girl—a bare necessity for any man. He pastures horses free for nothing, for his friends. I figured we'd leave our switchers there."

"I don't drink," Jeff demurred, uneasy at the thought of neglecting his job. "Nor I don't need no bare necessity. You go on—I'll stay."

But Demps laughed him down. "You ain't a true misplaced Texian till you've been to Ekard, and yelled the rebel yell. It's the snorting post for longhorns, coming and going and staying around. Strap's cows'll keep till we git back."

So Jeff yielded to influence and went along. Each rode his own pony, leading a bed horse and a company mount for transportation back. They arrived in midafternoon, and Jeff saw an ugly scattering of squat, one-story log structures, flanked by shabby pole corrals. But the stable was a qualified establishment, and a buck fence enclosed several thousand acres of good grassland along Drake Creek.

In the small, smelly café-barroom in the main hotel, Demps was greeted cordially by a hard-faced man he introduced as Drake. Olive complexioned and onyx-eyed, the man gave Jeff a small hard claw of a hand, but did not look at him.

"Glad to see you're back," he said to Demps, in the soft, slurred drawl. "Country's going all to pot."

At that moment, a heavy girl with the biggest bust Jeff had ever seen came bouncing up to hug Demps like a bear. "You sure keep a woman waiting, damn your eyes!" she said to him. "Where the hell you been?"

Demps slapped her where Jeff would never have slapped a girl, and grinned at Jeff. "Tex," he said, "I'd like for you to meet Boxcar Alice, my bosom friend. Alice, this here is Texas River. He's my pardner now."

"Then angels help him!" Alice said, staring at Jeff with bold, inviting eyes. "You're keeping awful bad company, sonny. My God, you're cute!"

Jeff stared at her helplessly, blushing to his hair roots.

Demps's bosom friend soon was joined by two other sirupy-

54

voiced females of less formidable proportions. These were presented as Big Casino and Little Lil—"the long and the short of it, as they say." Whimsically, Little Lil was seven feet tall, while Big Casino was no larger than a minute.

"I like Tec-thuth River," he heard Casino lisp, and—despising himself for it—blushed hot again.

"He's for me," Alice spoke up, trying to catch Jeff's eye. "My God, he's got it! Demps, you hound dog. What you been hiding from me?"

"I'll show you in a while." Demps leered.

They ate a greasy meal, fixed and served up by the girls, and soon the crowd began to grow. Customers for the most part were hard-looking citizens, roughly dressed and long-unshaven, armed like pirates. Whiskey did not improve manners or dispositions, and Jeff moved and spoke discreetly. But most of those present knew Demps, or seemed to. Most were effusively friendly or politely distant in their demeanor, and the same delicacy of behavior was extended to Jeff, apparently by virtue of his claim to Demps's benevolence. Here, as in the trail crew, Jeff found his friend a tower of protective strength.

Jeff had never attempted, consciously, to analyze his feeling for or relationship with Demps. But tonight he was especially aware of his growing dependence upon his friend. And it was odd how he hardly ever thought of Rebel Jimson any more—how, when he did, the face he conjured up was square and jovial, with wide full mouth and tawny eyes that closed with smiling. Sometimes it seemed to Jeff that Rebel Jimson had returned from Texas, and was here beside him.

"Demps," Jeff said that night on impulse, "if you was with a gang—people that was wanted, but you figured was in the right— and if you got took, would you let 'em hang you before you'd give your friends away?"

Demps set down his glass and looked him over curiously. Then he drank again. "That's a hard question, Tex. Why you ask it?"

"Oh, I don't know," Jeff mumbled, suddenly self-conscious, suddenly wishing he hadn't spoken. "I—I guess I just wondered."

Demps watched a minute longer. Then he reached across the table and clapped Jeff on the back.

"You damn betcha I would hang!" he said. "Hang and rattle. Wouldn't you?"

Jeff nodded, and looked away. It was the answer he had wanted. But the thought of Demps getting hung the way his father had, leaving him alone again in a world of Uncle Eds and Strap Bowmans and Gut Desmonds was almost more than he could bear.

Demps smiled at him, gently and wisely, like a father. "You've had too much bug juice, kid. You better take it easy."

Earlier in the evening, Jeff had joined Demps and his bosom friend in a social bottle. But it was his first real experience with hard liquor, and he'd taken it easy, at Demps's suggestion. So Demps was wrong. It wasn't the liquor that bothered him. Furtively, he drank some more, and found his reticence and blues were soon routed. A kind of golden haze enveloped him, and the first thing he knew he was joining in the fun.

At one time, he remembered seeing Demps seated in a corner, talking earnestly with Drake, seemingly unaffected by the incredible quantities of drink he'd put away. At another time, Demps was standing on a table in the middle of the floor, a bottle in each hand, leading the company in a smutty and tuneless ditty about "The Big Hole Girls and the Bitter Root Boys, way up in Montan'." Dimly, he remembered stumbling around the dancing space with Big Casino, while a banjo twanged some place. More dimly yet, he recalled standing at the bar, holding tightly to it for balance, staring at a homely framed motto on the wall:

WHATEVER YOU ARE—BE A GOOD ONE

"I ain't figured out just yet what Dempsey is," he confided to Casino. "But whatever he is, *he's* a good one."

"He's pure gold, honey," she agreed. "All heart above the waist, all guts below. You're lucky you got him for a friend. You love me, kid?"

She leaned gently against him, and her lips sought his. Jeff suddenly was conscious of her softness—the terrible softness of woman —and felt the blood pulsing through his body, the vital impulsion, strange but familiar as hunger or sleep. He felt the animal drive in him, and gave it rein. Then his mind showed him a heart-shaped face with two clear eyes, and a sickness spread in him.

"No," he answered hoarsely. "I don't need no bosom friend!"

Their stay at Ekard lengthened almost to a week. When they finally shoved, Jeff felt sophisticated and grown up. He felt a little dirtied, and contaminated, too. But he reckoned that feeling just went with coming into manhood. He was eighteen, now. He knew the score.

"That ain't a bad spot," he said to Demps. "I think I could git to like it."

"You're from Texas now, Tex." Demps grinned at him, still half-crocked. "Another trip or two, you'll be longhorned as they come."

Nor did Jeff's education cease upon departure from the road ranch. About a week after their return to the line camp, he came back early from patrol and saw smoke issuing from a draw, off along the line that Dempsey rode. He went over and saw his campmate dismounted beside a small fire. A scrawny yearling heifer was stretched out on the ground, hog-tied, and the wind brought the smell of burning hair.

Demps acted a bit upset to see him. He even made a quick move toward his rifle before recognizing Jeff. Even when Demps could see who it was, he hesitated before motioning him up. Then he went on with what he was doing, and didn't look up or say anything when Jeff drew rein beside him. Instead, fished a heated harness ring out of the fire and—holding it with shoeing pincers—burned on the heifer's ribs a mark that looked like Drake's Flying D.

Only when the job was done, the calf freed and the tools stowed in his saddlebags, did Demps favor Jeff with another glance. Squatting on his heels, he brought out tobacco and papers and rolled a smoke.

"I been meaning to tell you, Tex," he remarked, defiance and apology oddly mingled in his manner. "Drake's offered me ten bucks apiece for all the mavericks I brand in his iron. If you want in, we both can work, and split the take. Five bucks a head is five bucks ahead. With both us working, we could make it pay."

Jeff sat silent, feeling confused and worried and low—somehow betrayed. He remembered seeing Demps and Drake with their heads together, that night at Ekard. He remembered a motto on the rancher's wall. He wished he had never seen the smoke coming out of the ravine there. He wished he hadn't found out anything about the deal.

"It ain't Drake's stuff to brand, is it?" he asked finally.

"It's anybody's stuff that finds it," Demps maintained. "Mavericks belong to the man that gits his mark on them."

"But this is Garrett's range," Jeff said. "Don't that have something to do with it?"

"Damn little," Demps answered. "Why, caddle drift sometimes clean from hell to Texas. Every roundup here, they git drifts from Montan' and the Big Horn. Branded critters are private property, sure. But when they ain't been marked—who the hell can say who they belong to? People call 'em Maverick's cows, and let it go at that. You ever hear of Maverick, Tex?"

Jeff admitted he had not, and Demps told a yarn about a cowman down in Texas who went away to war and didn't brand his stock. With the passing of the years, his unbranded stuff spread halfway over the whole state, causing such turmoil that the lax rancher's name became a byword, a term for all unmarked kine throughout the West. But when the story was over, Jeff still sat silent, feeling bad inside.

"Maybe you ain't been told," Demps went on. "But Garrett pays each us boys five dollars a head for mavericks we turn up and brand in the Man Head iron. That's bonus, above our dollar a day. Now if Wate really figured the stuff was his, would he be paying us twice for work we already been hired to do? He knows damn well the stuff ain't all his. So, if it's wrong to brand for Duckbill Drake, ain't it just as wrong to brand for Garrett? As long as a man is mavericking, ain't he a fool not to brand for the highest bidder?"

The argument seemed unanswerable. But it did suggest a different line of thought.

"Well," Jeff said, "if the stock don't belong to nobody, and it's inside the law to brand it, why not mark it for yourself? Why brand for Drake?"

58

"Drake's got a brand registered. I ain't."

"Well, why not register one?"

"Because I can't git past the bullionaires to do it, that's why. And even if I could, I'd just git blacklisted. You ever hear of the blacklist, kid?"

Again, Jeff had to own to his ignorance.

"It's a kind of honor roll, kept by the Stock Association, run by Garrett and his cronies. Man can git his name included for trying to register a brand without their say-so, for filing on a homestead, or just for by-God talking when he'd ought to be listening. And any time they list you, you had just as well fold up your tent like an Ay-rab and as silently steal away. Because you can't work for none the outfits, and your brand is no good to you because they confiscate your caddle when you try to ship. You can't join the roundups to look out for your stock, nor you can't git no justice in their kangaroo courts. That's the system I was telling you about. It's just too tight to buck."

"From what you say, Drake must buck it," Jeff pointed out. "How come they don't blacklist him?"

"They did," Demps answered, a queer satisfaction in his voice. "Hell, Drake's name is first, in lettered gold. But Drake is set up some different from you and me. He's got a business, and he's got friends. He is a nasty cat to clean after, too. The big thieves just don't dast to tamper with him, the way they would with you and me. He markets his caddle inside the territory, to butcher shops and railroad camps around, and don't go through the stockyards where the Association watchdogs hang out. Besides, Garrett and the other big ranchers need Drake, and they know it."

"Garrett needs Drake?"

"You're damn tootin', Garrett needs him. So do the others, the way they operate. They won't hire a married man, if they can help it. Why? Because if a man has got a wife and fambly, he's going to be building a cabin somewheres, and staking out a piece of ground. They want bachelor bucks only, that crave no more ground than a six-foot plot to rest in, when they lay their bodies down. . . . Well, it's forty-fifty miles to Quadrille and more than that to Douglas. How long you figure Garrett would be able to hold men out in these line camps, if it wasn't for Duckbill's girls?"

Jeff found the question intriguing, but he had no qualified opinion.

"Well, that's the setup," Demps said, rising. "Garrett don't own this ground no more than I do. So I don't see but where unmarked cattle I find on it belong as much to me as they do to him. I'm earning the dollar a day he pays me. I'm working for myself on the side."

Jeff mulled it over, but couldn't seem to get anywhere with it. Demps made it sound right side up. Demps almost made it sound like the right and decent thing to do—to turn secretly against the man they worked for, and buck him on the quiet, while accepting his wage money. But Jeff didn't feel patriotic, the way Demps seemed to. Jeff had got hold of a good thing, and he didn't want to spoil it. He didn't want to mix in a thing that might lead to trouble, and put him back to mucking stables.

"Well," he said, "it ain't my style of doing. But, if it's yourn, I guess it ain't no hide off me."

"You don't have to give me no sermon," Demps said edgily, stamping out the remains of his fire. "I don't look on what I'm doing as any kind of crime. Course, it would be as well if you didn't say nothing to Garrett or Strap Bowman. Like I say, a man can git blacklisted for wearing his hat the wrong way."

"You didn't have to say that!" Jeff said in sudden heat. "I ain't any flannel-mouth informer!"

For a week or so, relations between them were somewhat strained. Jeff sensed a personal threat to him in Demps's activities, whether he participated or not, and he could not conceal his resentment. For the first time, Demps showed that he too could be sullen and sulky and vindictive. But as weeks lengthened into months and neither saw any other human being except the packer twice a month, Time the Healer took a hand, and eventually they were civil again, even if the old camaraderie was wanting.

The winter was wide-open, all the way. The winds blew strong, but only moderately cold. Sometimes there was snow, but it mostly blew on through.

"Horizontal percipitation," Demps called it humorously. "Makes you wonder where and if it ever stops."

60

Never, since that first encounter in the ravine, had they ever mentioned mavericking. But as the winter wore on, there was more and more evidence that Demps was working hard at his enterprise. And Jeff found himself in a dilemma that haunted him night and day. Shaffer had said that they were to watch out for predators and report them if they couldn't be handled on the spot. But Jeff couldn't see himself informing on Demps. Conversely, he couldn't see himself countenancing Demps's actions indefinitely. Nor could he see himself breaking up their association, asking for another partner on another part of the range. That would be like leaving home again.

So he worried, and did nothing, and tried to pay no attention to the growing number of young cattle branded in the Drake Flying D that he turned north off Man Head range.

But Strap Bowman paid attention that spring, when Drake and a following of toughs showed up at the calf roundup and drove off upward of a hundred head of yearlings. Strap talked turkey with Duckbill Drake. Then he caught Jeff off alone and bored into him.

"Quite a cut that Drake took out our herd this morning," he remarked conversationally, to start. "I didn't know he was ranching on such a scale."

Jeff looked at things off in the distance. He allowed it was quite a cut, quite a scale.

"Funny thing," the foreman said. "Lot of that stock matched ourn, for coloration. Most of it fresh-branded, too. Funniest thing, to my notion, is we gethered most of it from the Paint Crick range."

Jeff nodded guardedly. "Yeah. I seen some of it up that way, last winter."

Bowman laughed nastily. "I'll bet you did." Then, abruptly, his tone and manner changed. "All right, kid. Who's doing it? You or Rae—or both of you?"

Jeff made his eyes stand to the probing green eyes. He forced his head to shake.

"I don't know nothing whatsoever about it."

"I'm asking you nice, Jimson," Bowman warned. "I ain't got to ask you nice. I been hearing all winter about you two sports wallering your dodgers down at Drake's hog ranch, spending money wide and free, and neither of you drawing no cash against your wages. Now, I can add up two and two. I got some pretty unhealthy notions about you, but you're young, and I'm giving you the benefit of the doubt. If you want to show me where you stand, I'm giving you your chance."

Jeff knew then what was coming, and the knowledge made him ill. He felt intensely loyal to the company. He wanted to go on working for it almost as bad as he wanted to keep on living. He wanted to show where he stood. But he felt loyal to Demps, too. He couldn't squeal on Demps, not even if they hung him. He couldn't be a Roddy, or a lousy Pink. He couldn't do the way that hobo did, in Quadrille.

"I don't know nothing," he said, in misery.

"Well, I know something," Strap said briskly. "Man Head ain't hiring men to steal its stock. You're through, Jimson, and I'm keeping your wages as part payment on the stuff you've stole. Leave your horse at the wagon, and roll up your bed, and make long tracks. And one more thing before you go. We don't like snowbirds of your stamp hanging around the country without no visible means of support. If you're smart, you'll light a shuck for far-away places, and save yourself some trouble."

"Ahhh," Jeff said in futile rancor, "you sound like Gut Desmond now."

"Sure," Strap said inimically, turning his horse. "It comes to things like you, I and Gut see eye to eye."

Jeff sat staring at the exposed, retreating back. His hand touched his pistol, and a tremor went through him, leaving an ache in every bone and muscle. He shut his eyes until the seizure had eased somewhat. Then he turned and rode toward the wagon.

Demps had arrived ahead of him. Demps had his bed rolled up, his warbag packed, his saddle and bridle and chaps laid out, ready to travel. He helped Jeff round up his stuff, begged some bread and cold meat from the cook, and borrowed a canteen he said no one would be like to miss. Then, there being nothing else for it, they strapped the saddles to each others' backs, picked up their roped bedrolls in one hand, their warbags in the other, and set out.

"Maybe you see now why the bullionaires like to furnish the

62

horses," Demps grunted, after they had covered a mile or so in silence.

"I'm starting to see a hell of a lot that got past me up till now!" Jeff snapped. His feet were swelling in his boots, and bitterness filled him until he didn't see how he could contain it. Yet now, as when he'd had the heartburn over the reward money in Quadrille, his resentment was not directed so much at Strap or even at Demps as it was trained upon himself. Here he was, walking away from everything he'd ever wanted from life, and doing it voluntarily, without even being able to give himself a decent reason. There was a blue-eyed face that kept telling him to crawl back to Strap and spill his guts before it was too late. But he knew he wouldn't do it.

Nor did it help when Demps started taking a light view of the whole affair, prating optimistically about how bright their future was.

"Why, we don't need the damned old skinflint's wage money, nohow. They's a heap more profit in straight mavericking. I don't doubt Garrett will blacklist us. But we can brand for Drake, and split the take. Duckbill and his longhorns will come in handy, too, in case Strap undertakes to close us out. Give us a little time, we'll be on easy street."

Jeff looked straight ahead and didn't trust himself to speak.

As quick as they were out of sight of the roundup camp, they cached their saddles and beds in a cottonwood stand, and went on burdened with nothing but their bags and guns. The going was easier then. But Ekard was still twenty miles away, and high-heeled boots were not meant for walking. When they staggered into Drake's place, about noon next day, their bodies and their friendship both were strained to the breaking point.

Jeff had to cut his new boots in order to get them off his swelling feet, and when he sat soaking his barking dogs in half a tub of water, he needed no urging to join Demps in punishing a bottle of Green River.

"Yeah," Demps said to the leering Drake, who seemed to think it all a joke, "old Strap got wise, and canned us both. But he ain't heard the last of us. Time we git to ranching good, he'll see it would of been cheaper to kept us on the payroll. Eh, Tex?"

Jeff mumbled an incoherent reply, annoyed because Demps never once had let on that there was any difference in their degrees of guilt. Demps refilled the glasses and chanted an obscene toast Jeff had laughed at once. Now it filled him with disgust and fury.

"Yes, sir," Demps said, his spirits rising with the drink. "First time Strap fired me, I had it coming. This time, he just up and purely took it on himself. The bastard, he's opened a account with Dempsey Rae!"

Jeff drank with a kind of savage abandon, trying desperately to blot out a face that kept rising before his eyes. His thoughts and other objects blurred, but not the specter face that haunted him. So the Green River did not benefit him as it seemed to Demps. His thoughts became blacker with the night.

"Poor honey chile," Boxcar cooed at him, her voice like sweet molasses. "Mamma knows what you need. Come right here to Mamma."

"You go to hell, you damned old bitch!" Jeff snarled at her, and instantly was ashamed.

"You're a nasty little snot!" Boxcar said indignantly. "I'd ought to wash your mouth with soap."

"Leave him be, Alice," Demps said sternly. "He's had a hard knock. But he'll come out of it. Hell, he's from Texas River!"

In the morning, they wrangled their own horses and set out for Man Head range to repossess their cached equipment. All the way, Jeff listened to Demps's optimistic planning, and tried to study what to do.

"It takes power to deal with power, kid. Drake ain't got a whole lot, yet. But he's going to git more, as the homesteaders keep coming in. Takes a man like that, one that knows what to do and got the guts to do it, to stand up to the bullionaires. He'll be a big man in the territory, someday. I figure he's a good one to tie to. Why, he's so foxy-smooth, there's times when he ain't right certain what he's up to, his own self."

"Well, I ain't decided," Jeff mumbled, when Demps pressed him for a commitment. "I just might take Strap's advice, and light a shuck for far places. I don't want no trouble or bad name."

"Well, it ain't for me to tell you what to do," Demps said

64

slowly. "But you already got the bad name, as far as Garrett and his cronies are concerned. And I feel like it's my fault. I'd like to help you, if you'd let me. But running away never helped nothing yet. This here's as much our country as it's Garrett's. He ain't about to run me out."

To Jeff, it wasn't so much a matter of being run as wanting to run. He didn't want to stay in that country with Abby Garrett and never be able to see her. He didn't want to hang around and hear of her marrying some bullionaire, and not be able to do anything about it. He didn't want to be a homesteader, or another Duckbill Drake. The way he looked at things, he had got off on a wrong foot, and all he wanted was to get right again. But from all Demps had told him, he'd never get any second chance, there on Rustler River. So it looked like time to light that shuck.

But if he left the country, he would be losing Abby, even more surely than if he tried to stay. He would be losing her, and everything else that mattered, everything she represented. So he couldn't really see himself leaving. Staying on, he couldn't see himself breaking with Dempsey Rae. No matter which way he looked, the trail was blocked.

"What could we do, to keep us eating, if I stayed?" he asked finally. "I mean something that would be inside the law?"

He saw Demps's face harden, and he spoke again, in haste. "What I mean is, something Garrett can't grab us for, and run us out for doing. I don't want to throw in with Drake. I don't want to maverick. Irregardless of whether it's right or wrong, it'll git us trouble, and you know it."

"You shy from a little trouble, Tex?"

Jeff nodded, feeling himself on the defensive again. He couldn't tell Demps of his ambitions and big plans involving Abby and her father's barony. He couldn't be laughed at, on top of all his other raspings. He had to put it on another footing.

"I've had nothing but trouble, ever since I remember, Demps," he said, saying the same thing in a different way. "I've about had enough. My pap was hung as an outlaw. He figured he was in the right of it, but he bucked a sure thing, and he got strung up. Drake'll git it in the neck, too, before he's done. You know that

65

as well as I do. You've said yourself they got this thing rigged till there ain't no cracking it. So why try?"

Demps was scornful. "You mean, just roll over and play dead, on account of Wate Garrett thinks the good Lord God made the world and Wyoming just for his personal use and benefit? Go back and kiss his foot, and say I didn't mean it, Wate, just give me another chance?"

Jeff shook his head. "I don't aim to kiss his foot—or his anything else. But it seems like, in a country big as this, they'd ought to be something a man could do and not git in Garrett's way. My ma used to say you don't hunt grizzly b'ars with a razor strap."

Demps rode a ways in silence, his face dark and sullen, and Jeff figured the partnership was on the rocks. But after a while, the Texan's mood lightened, and he looked at Jeff again.

"Well," he said, "I know some people down in Texas that live by gethering up old buffalo bones. They ship them to a St. Louis concern that uses them in making some kind of soap and fertilizer. I've noticed a mighty lot of bones around here—buffalo and cow and horse. Human, too. If you're bound to do things the hard way, I got enough back from my Drake money to buy a team and wagon. Winter times, we could trap."

Jeff looked at him in gratitude. It seemed to be an out. Garrett wouldn't object to anybody picking bones, surely. And there wasn't any telling what it might lead to.

"Strikes me as a pretty good idea," he said with something like enthusiasm. "But I wouldn't expect you to throw in with me. If you'd set me up to a team and wagon, I'd give you half of what I made, till I got you paid back."

"Balls," Demps said mildly. "You pick bones, I'll pick bones. We're pardners, ain't we?"

Jeff looked at his square-faced friend, and once again he felt a vast affection for him. He understood, without it being said, that this was Demps's way of making it up to him for keeping quiet about the mavericking, and going down the road with him. Once again, it seemed that his way of doing was vindicated; that it did pay to stand by your friends. But at the same time, he was uneasy about continuing the partnership. He had been blamed once

66

for Demps's sins, and he didn't expect Demps would leave off the mavericking.

"We're pardners, Demps," he said. "But that damned mavericking got us in Dutch once. Wouldn't be no point in picking bones, if we just got ourselves in bad again."

Demps whitened as if Jeff had slapped him. But he didn't say anything until he'd managed a grin.

"I guess I had that coming, Tex," he said. Then he lifted his right hand.

"I take the pledge," he said. "No more mavericking—until we're bullionaires."

5: Scavengers

True to his commitment, Demps provided a team and wagon with which to start their bone collection, together with a tent and cooking outfit with which they set up housekeeping out on the prairies. While the good weather lasted, they maintained no base of operation. Instead, they set up camp in whatever locality they happened to be working, and moved it with them when they went on to greener pastures. Grass was plenty for their horses, which they hobbled out at night. On extremely rare occasions, they saw a few antelope and deer. And when they succeeded in bagging one, the meat helped piece out the groceries Demps had staked the outfit to.

Buffalo skeletons were still plentiful around, and cattle bones filled many of the draws, where they had been piled by winter storms. So they didn't want for raw materials. They even found a great many antelope and deer skeletons around—which, according to Demps, had starved by the thousands when overstocked cattle had depleted the range, or else had been shot down and let lie by Man Head hunters.

"Man Head hunters?" Jeff echoed.

Demps nodded. "When I first rode for the outfit, we got furnished all the ammunition we could shoot, so long as we shot at wolves and game. Sometimes the antelope got so tame and poor

67

we'd round 'em up with the cows in spring, and club 'em to death in the corrals."

"But—why?"

"Why? On account of they eat grass, that's why. People that raise cows got no tolerance for anything *but* cows. People that raise sheep the same. Anything that kills cows and sheep, they kill. Anything that eats grass, they kill same way. It's their religion, and by God they're a holy congregation. So holy they burn you at the stake, if you eat grass, or cows, or sheep. Or if you fence a homestead off.

"Besides," he added punitively, "homesteaders eat deer and antelope, like the Injuns done. So the Garretts take a lesson from the Army boys. Kill the deer and antelope, and the homesteaders got to starve—or kill branded beef. They kill beef, they git the treatment the bullionaires give wolves. It's simple as A. B. C. You know what A. B. C. means, Tex? Means Allah's Blessed Cows!"

At times, Demps's bitterness seemed a sickness, an obsession that promised to destroy him. It drove him to Herculean feats of strength and endurance, and day after day he did the work of ten.

Distance to Quadrille was too great to justify hauling the gather in as collected. Instead, they built vast dumps at scattered depots near the sources of supply, with the plan of hauling later.

After the first day or two, Jeff was glad to trade his riding boots for a pair of flat-heeled farmer shoes Demps had thoughtfully fetched from Ekard. And it wasn't long until he had the art of bone picking down to a fine point. It was quite a comedown, for a man who'd trailed Texas cows and ridden line for Man Head. But he got so he didn't mind the work so much, though he did live in horror of Abby or her father happening by and finding him so ignominiously employed.

"So what—if they do?" Demps shrugged one day when Jeff made reference to his secret fear. "This is good, honest work. Ain't that what you wanted?"

His partner's voice was bland, but Jeff sensed the gravel in the question. "Sure it's what I wanted," he replied. "But I'd sooner be punching cows."

Demps looked as if he'd been slapped again, and Jeff quickly repented the remark. "The only thing I don't like about the job

68

is that old Wate's bones ain't here amongst these others," he said to make amends. "That would make the work a pleasure."

One day Strap Bowman rode up to investigate their activities, and when he'd satisfied his curiosity, he sneered. "It appears you two are bound to live off Man Head stock—alive or dead. Well, you're welcome to the bones, as long as the meat's all off."

They were into a drift pile at the time, in the bottom of an eroded coulee. Jeff worked on, hot of face, pretending not to notice the horsemen on the bank above. But Demps heaved a thigh bone onto the load, then stepped up near the front endgate where the rifle was.

"Thanks, Strap," he called back. "We know you're big-hearted. You and Wate, you'd give us common people everything the hen lays any day—except the aig. Well, give us time, and we'll take the hen."

"I wouldn't bank too far on our big-heartedness," Strap retorted. "You're trespassing on our ground, and them are Man Head skeletons, if everybody had their own."

"It sticks in my mind this is government ground," Demps argued. "I am a voting stockholder in the government, the same as you, and got as much right here as you. These bones don't show no Man Head brand. I wouldn't try to butt in here, if I was you."

"I'm only interested in the coyotes that bother my live cows," Strap flung back, turning his horse to ride.

Many times, thereafter, they saw Man Head riders around. Some were derisive, some abusive, others simply curious. But the partners adopted a policy of ignoring all hecklers, and soon the cowboys' interest waned. By the time the crickets started chirping, late in August, they had worked most of the Rustler River country, and Demps suggested they swing over and "harvest" the Rifle Mountain sector. Jeff objected strenuously.

"Still afraid them blue-blooded Garretts will be shocked to find out people do this kind of work to git by?" Demps taunted.

"I ain't ashamed of what I'm doing," Jeff answered him. "But I ain't so proud of it I parade it, neither. I expect there's as many bones east as west."

Demps grinned and rubbed his neck contemplatively. "Someday you're going to have to tell me about this romance you got with Abby Garrett, kid."

Jeff nodded and turned away. "Someday, by God, I will."

Along toward the middle of September, they left off gathering, and started hauling. For this operation, Demps borrowed another team and wagon from Drake, so they both could work to advantage. To expedite matters, they split cottonwood logs and built a high, slatted rack upon each box, greatly increasing capacity. Their trips into Quadrille required all the way from one to three days, depending on the location of the dump concerned. They worked together at the loading, traveled together on the trips, and camped together nights when necessary.

Managed so, the hauling went fast, and the great white mound down by the siding grew at such a rate that late in November they packed and shipped eight full carloads of bones. The commission house check came just before Christmas, and Jeff felt halfway rich for part of a day. But by the time they'd bought steel traps and some needed clothes and groceries, they had an even forty dollars to split.

"Wages ain't high, this kind of work," Demps grinned as he spent two of his twenty dollars for a bottle of Green River whiskey. "But think of the experience we git!"

For a winter's trapping headquarters, they took over an abandoned line camp on Cat Creek, a tributary of the Rustler, about midway between Rustler Station and Quadrille. Both cabin and stable were mere excavations in a high cutbank, timbered up at the front, doored but possessing no windows for light. But they spent little time indoors in daytime, and Jeff soon learned that a dugout was the warmest kind of habitation known to man. They kept only two horses at the place, Jeff's dun and Demps's sorrel, having quartered the others on Drake for the cold months. There was a rusted cookstove in the cabin, and two bunks they were able to fix up. There was brush along the creek for firewood and ample grass to fuel their ponies for the easy riding they must do.

By the time they were located there on Cat, cold weather had primed the furs, and they swung right into their new industry. Once again, as in all their past occupations, Demps furnished the know-how. But he was a willing teacher, Jeff an eager pupil. Within a week or so, Jeff could make a satisfactory set, and didn't stint on assuming his share of the work—riding the lines, making the sets, pelting and stretching the furs.

Their sets were mostly for coyote and weasel, though once in a while they took mink, bobcat, and skunk, even a few muskrat from the creek. Foxes were around, but hard to catch. Wolves were about, too, but Demps explained that Man Head hired full-time wolfers to work on these, and it wouldn't pay to run the professionals competition.

"County offers fifty dollars bounty on every scalp. But it's Garrett money mostly, and he'd see that none of it come to us. He'd sooner have wolves than pay us for ketching them."

"What I wonder," Jeff said, "is that somebody don't offer a bounty on him."

"Shooting Wate wouldn't solve nothing," Demps said mildly. "It's the system that's at fault. You ever try to shoot a system, Tex?"

The stretched pelts did not dry readily in the damp stable. To combat the threat of mold, they took to placing the stretching frames around the cookstove for the first several days, removing them to the stable only when the drying was well along. The weather usually required that they keep the cabin tightly closed, and after a week or so the fetor of the dugout's interior clung to them like musk, even after a long day out in the cleansing wind.

"It's a good thing we live alone, and don't see nobody," Jeff remarked one night. "Take us both together, we'd stink a dog off a gut wagon. How many years you reckon it'll take us to git aired out?"

"Stink like this has got to wear off," Demps informed him. "There ain't no washing it, at all.

"But," he added cheerfully, "I expect the money them pelts bring will smell some better."

As the months wore on, Demps began to chafe and fret at the isolation and dull routine. As in the line camp the year before, he became morose and irritable, unpredictable in his tempers. He had a little money left from his mavericking, and started riding off to Ekard week ends to let off steam. As the year before, he invited Jeff to go along. But Jeff had other ideas for what little money he had left, and politely declined.

At times, Demps would be gone for days at a stretch, but Jeff told himself that it was all right. He didn't mind the extra work it threw on him, and Demps had furnished their outfit in the first place. Besides, he figured it did them good to have a little time away from each other. They had started getting on each other's nerves again.

Jeff never did know just what activities Demps indulged in at Ekard, other than the pleasures available to all. But, visibly at least, Demps was on the straight and narrow. Around the cabin, he made the law—Garrett's law—a shibboleth whose sanctity was never violated, by word or thought or deed. He spoke holy as a preacher on all topics related to the law he had once condemned so vociferously. And when their game meat was gone, he sternly vetoed Jeff's proposal that they beef a Man Head cow.

"What the hell," Jeff argued, after two days' hunting had turned up no deer or antelope. "Wate won't miss one measly critter. We can butcher one in the dark, and bury the guts and hide."

Demps shook his head. "You damned me for branding mavericks, which wasn't no infracture of the law. Now you'd let in to do a thing that's counter to law everywhere. How'd you git that way?"

"Well," Jeff hedged, "we could maybe still find a maverick, so it wouldn't be stealing. I'm gittin' hungry for meat."

But Demps still shook his head. "You don't approve of that way of doing," he reminded. "No man's morals ought to be shaped by his appetite.

"Nope," he added by way of emphasis, "you didn't like my way of doing. Now we're trying yours. And we're going all the way. What the hell, kid. You can't have things both ways."

Jeff felt chastened. But he started to suspect that Demps's purpose in agreeing to the new schedule of living in the first place had been simply to teach him a lesson. And, hungry as he was, Jeff still preferred his way to Demps's. It was harder at the time,

72

but there seemed more future in it, and Jeff was still living for the future.

"Well, I ain't complaining," he said with such lightness as he could command, surveying their barren cupboard. "Hell, we got a thousand different things to eat—beans!"

More and more as winter drew on toward spring, Jeff was left to himself at the dugout. But he wasn't often lonely. He had Abby Garrett to think about. And though it wasn't so easy now to imagine himself marrying her and inheriting her father's barony, she remained the symbol of his ambition—the goal to which his life now was dedicated. The star to which his wagon was hitched, even if only by thread.

He had other ambitions involving her, also, but these he kept secret even from himself, except at unguarded moments when certain pictures would creep into the fantasies he built around her. Then he'd try to conceive of what marriage to her would really be like—sharing her silken bed, smelling her perfumed hair, pleasuring in her body, fathering her children—and an old familiar thrill would course through him with his blood. But, exciting as these pictures were, they never would come entirely clear, perhaps because he could not completely believe in them.

But the other pictures, of Jeff supplanting Strap Bowman someday as Garrett's foreman, of Jeff somehow succeeding to Garrett's position of wealth and influence in the land—these he could believe in. Lincoln had got to be President, and they said that Andrew Carnegie started life earning a dollar a week in a cotton factory. Jay Gould himself had started out as a surveyor; Vanderbilt rowing people around in a boat in New York Harbor.

Jeff's mother had told him these things a good many years ago, as evidence in support of her contention that he could be a big man, President even, if that's what he set out to be. His mother hadn't said anything about the systems he would buck up against, but Jeff figured the systems must have been there then, the same as now. And he would have bet that Carnegie and Lincoln and the others had got to the top by getting into the system, not fighting it the way Demps seemed bound to do. Rebel Jimson likely would have still been alive if he hadn't been bound to buck the system.

"Demps is a good guy," Jeff concluded sagely, having studied the whole situation carefully through the colored window of his youth. "But he ain't the kind that will go very far."

Jeff Jimson, he figured, was something else.

When the warming winds had turned the coats of wild things rough and valueless, Demps fetched their team and wagon from Ekard, and Jeff set off at daybreak one morning to haul their fur catch into Quadrille and bring back some things they needed. He arrived that afternoon in time to get into the post office in the front of Gentile's store, and—with the packs consigned to the custody of the U. S. mails—he begged some old unclaimed newspapers and magazines the postmaster had lying around, then stepped into the Hat Saloon for a smile.

"In early for the big shindig tonight?" Paddlefoot Renfro, the mountainous barkeep, inquired as he set up a bottle.

"Shindig?" Jeff repeated, unfamiliar with the word.

"Big benefit dance, to raise money for the new skulehouse—over in Bard's new store building, by the courthouse," Paddlefoot elaborated. "Free to all, with free feed for the horses throwed in. Ladies are fetching lunch boxes that will be raffled off to the highest bidders. Better be there, if you can. Whole country is kicking up its heels."

Jeff fingered the seventeen dollars he had left out of his summer's earnings after paying postage on the furs, and allowed as how he guessed he couldn't make it.

"That's too bad," Paddlefoot clucked. "If I was young and in my prime, I'd be there with bells on, scraping my wings around little Abby Garrett."

Jeff stiffened, and looked hard at his glass. "Is Ab—uh, are the Garretts going to be there?" he asked with studied deliberation.

"Everybody'll be there!" the barman assured him. "And, by gum, if I was a looker like you, I'd just set my cap for that filly. I'd marry 'er, by duff, and fall higher to Man Head."

Jeff smiled a little, pleased in spite of himself. "I don't expect I could fall that high," he said.

He didn't believe that the bartender knew what he was talking about, when it came to the Garretts. But he resisted the temptation to buy another drink, just on the chance that it might be so. And when he stepped outside again and saw the red-wheeled buckboard of his memories tied to the rail in front of the Drovers House, he started making feverish plans for his social debut in Quadrille.

A half-dollar bought him a haircut and shave at the barbershop, and another quarter admitted him to a tub full of hot water in the room at the back. Remembering the way people had stood wide of him in Gentile's store and the Hat Saloon, he spent still another quarter for bay rum to sweeten his bath. The ten-dollar bill covered the cost of an army shirt and a cheap pair of pants and boots at Gentile's. He would have liked some underwear and sox as well, but neither showed, anyhow, and he figured he might need the five dollars left him to buy Abby's supper box.

He was early at the dance, and found the unoccupied storeroom prettily decorated for the occasion with long strips of colored paper, with lanterns dolled up in paper frills. Accustomed now to the pleasant effluvium of bay rum and moth balls in which he'd moved all evening, he stood back near the door, watching the crowd come in. Watching in particular for a heart-shaped face and a fairy head that were his destiny. Hair slicked back and box wrinkles in his shirt and pants, he felt debonair and confident, ready for whatever the evening might bring.

As Paddlefoot had said, everyone in the country was in attendance. Whole families, from Grandma to babies in arms; men in whiskers and clean-shaven, in new clothes and old; young bucks like Jeff, all angles and optimism; young ladies in gingham and silks, their hair braided so tight they couldn't blink their eyes.

Jeff was standing bashfully with the other young stags at the back of the room when Abby came in, all silk and loveliness, so wonderfully beautiful that it took his breath to look at her. She was squired by her rock-faced father and lank Strap Bowman, and she trailed a delicate perfume that smelled exactly as she looked. Jeff's throat almost closed when she saw him and smiled warmly in greeting. But he got a memorizing look at the supper box she carried, and after that when he wasn't watching her, he was watch-

75

ing the box, placed carelessly with the others on the big table up by the fiddles.

The box was wrapped in blue paper, and tied with a big ribbon as red as blood. The bow was so beautifully wrought that Jeff felt a little sad, knowing he soon must destroy it.

The fiddles were scraping now, and the dancers were taking the floor. Women were so scarce that some of the young stags tied handkerchiefs on their arms to identify themselves as females, and danced with their buddies. But Jeff didn't dance, and didn't want to dance, so long as he could watch Abby.

Abby's dress was spangled like a rainbow in moonlight, perpetually changing colors in the lantern light—from red to blue and purple-pink. Whether the dance was a waltz or a strenuous square, she was cool and neat and fairy-graceful, a butterfly among moths and grasshoppers. To Jeff, it seemed that her arms and neck and face would bruise like a butterfly's wings if touched by hands. He remembered painfully the things he'd subjected her to in his thoughts at the dugout, and wondered that he hadn't been struck dead on the spot.

Lordly and aloof, yet proudly watchful of his only chick, old Garret idled up by the music stand, solitary and self-contained, blessing the affair with his presence, but having no part of the frivolity on the floor. His great mop of white hair was in startling contrast to his purple face and somber black attire. He talked with a few other men who were there in store clothes, and once or twice he unbent enough to joke with the bald-headed men who swamped in the Drovers House. But most of the time he sat in a chair back of the lunch table, smoking his pipe, beating time to the music with one foot, watching his graceful child give meaning to the music's haunting story, in the arms of gangling Strap Bowman.

Bowman, too, was somberly garbed in black. In contrast to Garrett, who wore broadcloth as if born in it, the foreman looked laughably incongruous in Sunday clothes. His coat and pants hung loosely, as on a willow frame. His celluloid collar fit big as a horse collar, and his red neck stuck up out of it like a turkey's. His high forehead was white above the slanting weather-line left by his hat. But, grotesque as he was, the foreman managed his long body with a catlike sparsity of effort that was grace. And he monopolized his employer's daughter from the first, giving no one else a look in.

Watching Strap claim her, dance after dance, standing everybody else off, Jeff couldn't help remembering punitively what Demps had said of him, back at the Rustler River ranch: *Strap's a little house, out behind the big one, but he figures to marry the big house's daughter, and move inside. . . .*

Jeff wasn't the only one in the stag line who resented Bowman's possessive attitude toward Abby, as the dancing went on.

"That damn Bowman, he sure builds a fence around that Garrett girl, don't he?" a man next to him remarked to his companion. "Who the hell he think he is?"

"He knows who he is," the other responded sourly. "He's the Prince Concert, like old Albert, hoping that someday he'll be the king."

Jeff sneered at the notion, recalling how Abby had spoken of him, that day near Rustler Station. But the words did instill a fear in him that maybe Strap would bid more than five dollars for the blue-wrapped box, although five dollars seemed an awful price, just for a lunch.

After an eternity of waiting, the fiddles stopped their caterwaulering, and the musicians left the stand. There was a lot more pointless delay while the people in charge visited and killed time, as if they hadn't had the whole night to gossip in. Then old Jim Gentile, the postmaster and merchant, stepped out in front of the table, and talked until Jeff figured he never would run out of wind.

". . . And I'll remind you gentlemen here that the money you spend with us tonight not only will buy you a lovely supper and the female company of a lovely girl to eat it with. That money will go for one of the worthiest causes ever espoused in our community: To build and equip and put in operation a first-class, modern school for our young folks—the country's most precious resource, our white hope for the future. . . ."

Gentile had the blue-wrapped, red-ribboned box in his hands from the minute he'd started to talk. And when he finally paused to get his breath, Jeff could restrain himself no longer.

"Two dollars for the box."

77

Originally, Jeff had planned to bid the whole five right off, to discourage competition and wind the thing up in a hurry. But the thought occurred that maybe he could get it cheaper, and money didn't grow on the bushes around. So at the last second he had changed his mind. He could still go to five, if he had to.

The way all eyes turned to look at him when he'd spoken made him believe that maybe two dollars would buy it. And he guessed it wasn't everybody in the country who had hard cash to spend. The store man's glance wasn't as friendly as could be expected from somebody you had just spent money with, for clothes. But Abby was smiling at him from the fiddler's stand, where she stood with her father and Strap, and Jeff's heart suddenly felt too big for his chest.

"Two dollars has been bid," Gentile's voice droned. "Do I hear a higher bid for this lovely box? Remember, the money will be spent as an investment in our country's future."

Only silence answered the raffler's appeal. Jeff was pushing his way through the crowd to claim his prize, congratulating himself that he hadn't bid higher, when an awful, insolent voice he knew too well spoke from the musician's stand.

"Fifty dollars."

Jeff stopped, stunned. His unbelieving eyes found Bowman's face across the void of distance that separated them. The foreman didn't so much as glance in his direction, but something covert and gloating in his expression proclaimed that he was aware of Jeff's stare.

The saving thought came to Jeff that Bowman was only joking, having fun with him. Fifty dollars would buy a good horse, a fair team, with a wagon like Demps's thrown in. Fifty dollars was half a hundred dollars. No man would spend that much, just for a lunch box. Not even for Abby's.

By the time he shifted his gaze to Abby, he was quite confident that the whole thing was a prearranged joke, of obscure point, like the affair of Mr. Matador and the Dutch oven lid under his old mare's tail—that Strap was only joshing him, because he'd opened the bidding so high. But Abby smiled at him, a little pityingly, he thought, and looked away. And then the truth eluded his defenses, and he saw the naked fact.

78

He was a tinhorn, a penny-ante player in a blue-chip game.

"Fifty dollars has been bid. Do I hear seventy-five?"

"Seventy-five dollahs!"

Jeff looked dully around, and saw a whiskered cowhand he wouldn't have figured for seventy-five cents waving a handful of greenbacks that would have papered the dugout up on Cat Creek.

"Hundred dollars for the box!" Bowman called, in the same bored tone.

Jeff waited to hear no more. Jeff wanted only to get outside in the dark, to lose himself from sight, forever. But the crowd was pressed tightly around him, blocking the way. Writhing in ignominy, he used knees and elbows to force passage, and affronted faces snarled warnings and imprecations for his benefit.

One particularly malignant face spat a challenge that could not be ignored, and he made a move to smash the offending face away. But before the blow could be delivered, his fist was caught in a cool, moist hand. Turning, he stared unbelievingly down into blue eyes that looked black by lantern light.

"I want to thank you for bidding for my lunch, Jeff," Abby was saying to him, incredibly. "If you'd like, I'll save the first dance, after intermission."

Tongue-tied, still half-convinced it was another trick of an unreliable imagination, Jeff could only stare at her, and nod. It wasn't until she had turned to leave that he was aware of Bowman —aware that Bowman had followed Abby into the crowd, and wasn't following her back.

Until that moment, Bowman had not given the faintest sign that he remembered Jeff as the man he'd fired for rustling just about a year before. But recognition was on the lean face now. Recognition was in the voice that spoke to Jeff, loud enough that all around could hear.

"Why don't you go outside, and wait there till we have et? You stink like a dead dog, you know."

The words fell on Jeff like a ton of crumbling stone, crushing him, paralyzing every sense. As in a dream, he saw the hated face leering at him through a haze, and for the second time in a year and a half, he forgot a hard-earned lesson. His fist came up and smashed the face in a blow that drove his own heels down hard against the floor; that drove his knuckle bones back upon his wrist.

Still as in a dream, he saw the foreman floundering backward, arms swinging in a fight for balance. As in a dream, he heard the warning groan that came from every side as Strap staggered toward the heavily-laden lunch table. Then the dream and groan both were lost in a terrible grating crash as the table collapsed, scattering the boxes as if a whirlwind had struck.

Through a prolonged beat of silence, Jeff stood motionless, petrified by the frightful damage he had wrought. Worst sight of all, to his appalled eyes, was that of the blue-wrapped box, its ribbon spilled across the floor like blood, its sides smashed in, its sandwiches and fried chicken legs and frosted cake strewn about like garbage.

Then a single feminine voice was raised in a scream that rose like a rocket and swelled to agonized crescendo as other voices took it up.

Until the moment that he died, Jeff would never hear a sound more terrible than the one which beat against his ears as the indignant and disconsolate women thronged up from all sides to retrieve their ruined suppers.

"Throw the lout outside!"

Glancing in the direction from whence the crackling voice had come, Jeff had a vivid impression of Wate Garrett's purple face, behind a jabbing finger. Then the crowd closed in, and a hundred hands were tearing at his clothes and flesh.

Muscles crawling in a clamor for violence, welcoming any diversion from the untenable scene across the room, Jeff spun on his attackers and fought them savagely with fists and knees and feet.

For a moment, it was glorious. For a moment, he reveled in the wealth of targets upon which to spend his fury. Faces swam at him out of an encircling red haze, and he struck them down in ecstasy. At one moment, the pack was on him, like hounds upon a panther, baying for his blood. At the next, he was standing upright and alone, the pack drawn back to lick its wounds.

But the next rush carried him to the floor, where a booming yellow flood enveloped him like a raging river. For what seemed forever, he struggled against the buffeting current, trying to swim to shore, trying to break through to the surface, where he could breathe again. But, in the end, he was swept over a precipice, down into a whirlpool that had no bottom.

A long time later, swimming painfully back toward the light, he found himself stretched out on the counter in the Hat Saloon, raw-meat poultices upon his face, the raw burn of whiskey in his mouth.

"That's all right, boy," a soothing voice was saying somewhere. "We're all your friends. Ol' Hitch has got you, now. Just simmer down, and take it easy. Everybody tries to lick the whole damn world single-handed at one time or another. And everybody gits their tar tamped, just the same. Just don't let it git you down...."

When Jeff drove up to the Cat Creek dugout, late the next afternoon, Demps was down to the stable to greet him, hungry for news and companionship. He was plainly fascinated by the condition of Jeff's face and fists and clothes, by the scuffed new boots he wore on his feet. But when his eyes collided with Jeff's, he pulled his grin in where it didn't show.

"Anything special happen, down in town?" he asked obliquely.

"The news is all in these," Jeff snapped, tossing him the roll of reading matter the postmaster had contributed. "You can read it, at your leisure."

But that night, at supper, he opened up a bit. He told about the benefit dance and the lunches, and the fight with Strap, after his two-dollar bid. But there, at first, he was not explicit when it came to explaining why he had hit Bowman. It took a while to work up to the point where he could talk about that.

"Anybody that knocks Strap Bowman on his hinder is my candidate for Governor, and Injun chief!" Demps commented in warm if puzzled approbation. "But why rowel yourself over only having two dollars to bid for a box of put-up lunch? There's no shame that I can see in not being so damn-fool rich that you can't spend a hundred dollars for a perfumed sandwich. Two dollars is all any lunch is worth."

Jeff looked at his puffed, raw fists, and wished that there were words with which to tell things as they really happened—what it had done to him, seeing a broken-down old saddlebum bid more money for a box of chicken than he'd seen in all his life, then being talked to as Strap had talked to him, on top of everything else. But it was like trying to explain to Hitch about his run in with Gut Desmond, over his leaving town. There just weren't enough words in the language to tell some things.

"Bowman told me I stunk!" he blurted finally, rage and shame washing over him again. "Said I stunk so bad I better leave the place, while the rest of them et their supper!"

Demps hid another smile, and fed his face. "Well," he said in a minute, "it really ain't nothing to lay yourself out over. You just had your pride scorched, for the first time. Pride's a luxury, especially in this here country. I didn't know you could afford it."

"First time, hell!" Jeff flared. "I was fired for a rustler, wasn't I? And made to trap—and pick bones, like a vulture, to keep from starving!"

If Demps caught the dig about how Jeff was fired, he didn't let on. He just kind of grinned again. "You'd ought to try to git it through your head, Tex, that there's as much honor and all that old stuff in this kind of work as any we'd be doing for Garrett. The whole thing's just a pigment of your imagination."

"Don't you preach at me!" Jeff snarled. "You didn't git told you stunk, in front of the only girl that means anything to you, and a whole hallful of other people. You don't even see what I'm talking about."

Demps shook his head. "You're the one that don't see, Tex. If you did, you wouldn't be spreading your tail feathers around that Garrett chick in the first place, laying yourself open to hurt. Time you're as old as I am, you'll have your pride blistered enough times that you'll learn to keep it in where people like them Garretts and Strap Bowmans can't git at it. If it's marriage you got in your head, my advice would be to settle down somewheres with a good brood woman and start your baseball nine. Leave that Garrett girl to the Boston Bean Boys and the bullionaires like her pappy, or you stand to git hurt a lot worse than you already been."

"That's your notion," Jeff said sullenly. "I'm going to marry that Garrett girl, as you call her. Before I do that, I'm going to put a ring through Strap Bowman's nose, and snub him to my red-wheeled buggy. If I have to whittle old Wate down to size first, I'll do that, too."

"That's pretty big talk, for a boy," Demps said, looking bored.

"I'm a pretty big boy for the talk!" Jeff shouted.

"Big boy—big hurt," Demps sighed, reaching for something to read.

They were out on the prairie in the wagon next day, resuming their bone collecting, when the pressures building up in Jeff reached the danger line. His face was less swollen than the night before, and he was getting back the use of his hands. But the poisonous fester inside him continued to rankle—pouring venom into his blood, bile into his knotted stomach.

Demps was handling the team, and it seemed to matter none at all to him that the skeleton of the red cow in the meadow below the dugout hadn't been picked clean. Winter-killed, the animal had long been eaten out inside, but the hide was still intact —the hair scoured off, the leather dry and brittle like that of an old boot left to weather in sun and rain and wind.

Demps pulled up beside the uncleaned bones and leaped to the ground. With obscene relish, it seemed to Jeff, he grabbed the dry horns and started tearing the carrion apart, while Jeff stood back, his face twisted and screwed with distaste.

One mighty tug, and the head was loose in the big, hairy hands. Gray, fat bugs fell from the skull cavities as Demps hammered it against the ground. Hide still adhered to the nose and jaws, but the freebooter tossed his prize into the wagon, and grabbed a front leg with all the zest of a ravening scavenger.

His strength snapped the brittle tendons, cracked the dry hide like dead tree bark. Another twist, and the leg was free of the body it once had supported. Again, the obese bugs scurried.

"Come on, Diamond Jim," he said to Jeff. "This here's money on the hoof. If we got all our bones green, like these, they'd weigh up to where this work would pay."

Jeff closed his teeth against words that were better not spoken, closed his mind against thoughts which were better not thought. Stepping up to the carcass, he took hold of a leg, and tore it out of the hip socket. Before he would get it into the wagon, the dead stink assailed him sickeningly. He imagined he could smell bay rum and moth balls in it.

"The hell with it," he said, hurling the foul object from him. "There must be easier ways than this!"

Demps heaved a length of neck bone into the rack, and looked him over carefully. Before he could say anything, a group of Man Head cowboys broke from the brush down the creek and rode past them at a trot. They all wore town clothes, and Jeff recognized a face or two from the dance.

"Two dollars for the box!" one of them whooped. "Hey, sport! Could you make it two-fifty?"

"Must of been mixed up on where you was, Romeo, bidding that upstairs money. Think you was out to Ekard?"

"My God, boys. What stinks around here? You reckon all nesters smell thataway?"

"Damn near as bad out here as it was at that dance!"

A sob tore Jeff's throat, and he made a lunge for the head of the wagon, where the rifle was. Demps was on guard and intercepted him, thrusting him back. For an instant, Jeff fought to get past him. But it was like fighting a wall.

"Now you better take a tail-holt on yourself, and simmer down," Demps's voice strained at his ear. "It's all right to be a damn fool in a small way. But you ain't got to git both of us killt."

Jeff yielded and stepped away. He looked around, and saw the horse troop disappearing over a rise to the west. He watched the riders out of sight. When he turned back, he found Demps waiting, the quizzical, watchful look in his eyes.

"You look peaked, kid. You want to go up to the cabin and lay down?"

Jeff shook his head. "No. I don't want to go up to the cabin and lay down."

"Well, git that wild look out of your eye. And here. You're about to lose your makings. Must of tore your pocket in our scuffle."

As he spoke, Demps reached a gloved hand toward him. The stink that had become a darkness on Jeff's mind was there on the glove, and Jeff knocked it away.

"I say the hell with it!" he repeated with hot finality. "The hell with all of it. I rate myself above a buzzard, even if you don't!"

Demps gave him the careful look again. He shook his head a little. "One trip into town sure spoiled you for anything. If you think I got any love for this kind of work . . ."

"Bowman told me I stunk!" Jeff broke in. "And you heard what them other boys said. Well, God knows I do stink! How could anybody help stinking, living in a vulture nest like that dugout?"

Now that he'd started talking about it, Jeff could find no place at which he could stop talking. The memory of his humiliation in front of Abby Garrett was on him again. And once again it seemed that the tawny-eyed man had brought the whole degrading experience upon him. In that instant, his whole loathing for the stinking bones was transferred unreasonably to the man who dealt so cheerfully in stinks and carrion. In that instant, he hated Dempsey Rae as he'd never hated any man.

"Maybe it's your style to live like a carrion bird—and smell like one!" he shouted, fearing to stop shouting. "Well, it ain't mine. Only reason you can stand me within a half a mile of you is on account of you'd stink a skunk out of a backhouse your own self. Well, I'm belly-sick of it. I stay any longer, I might git like you—so used to my own stink that I wouldn't mind it any more—"

He stopped shouting then, because a fist as big as a maul had slammed against his mouth, and the ground had come up behind him and struck him again from the back. All his front teeth felt loosened, his eyes jarred out of their sockets. When his vision cleared somewhat, he saw Demps standing over him, the most dangerously angry person Jeff had ever looked at.

It occurred to Jeff quite lucidly that Demps had forgotten his own lesson, to use his hands on another man, in anger, instead of getting hold of a killing weapon. But he soon had more immediate things to think about.

"It seems to me you have developed one of these here obstacle illusions," Demps was saying to him, biting his words off close to his tongue. "I only went into this bone picking and trapping to make you happy. I don't like the stinks no better than you do. I've liked to stood on my head this last year to please you. But it looks like there ain't no such thing as pleasing you. So you know what you can do."

85

"That's right," Jeff rumbled, getting to his feet. "I ain't very smart. But I can sure as hell figure that one out. I'll do what I should of done a year ago!"

It was only a half an hour's walk to where his dun was hobbled out to graze, and Jeff didn't let any grass grow under his feet. Within an hour's time, he had the dun saddled and his bedroll tied behind the cantle. His warbag he carried on the pommel in front of him, and he rode at a long walking trot.

The trail toward Ekard took him within hailing distance of Demps, who was now on the wagon, driving slowly up to the dugout.

"Let me know your address," Demps shouted to him. "I'll send you your half the fur check."

Ashamed of his behavior, ashamed of shame, Jeff told him to keep the check, and where to shove it. "You'll be needing it a heap worse than I do!" he predicted.

"Like to bet?" Demps challenged.

6: Outcast

Throughout the ride to Ekard, Jeff toyed with the idea of heading straight to Rifle Mountain, of humbling himself before Garrett and Bowman, and begging to be reinstated on the payroll. But even as he tried to pretend otherwise, he knew in his guts that this would be no dice. He wasn't any more ready to peach on Demps and Drake now than he'd been the year before, and anyhow it was coming on for the slack season around the ranches, as soon as the calf roundup was over. Besides, if there'd ever been a chance that Garrett and Bowman would take him back, he knew he'd killed the chance forever, that night at the benefit dance.

"Jimson," he said in bitter self-denunciation, "you sure do make things hard for yourself."

At Ekard, Jeff roped his mare, and appropriated an old cross-buck pack saddle with open-mouthed panniers that belonged to

Demps, figuring that his share of the fur check would more than buy Demps a replacement. He spent his last five-dollar greenback with Drake, to buy a little flour and canned stuff, successfully parrying the roadrancher's curious inquiries into what was up. There was an old frying pan, a black Dutch oven and coffeepot already in one of the panniers, so he felt set up.

"You pulling out on Demps?" Drake asked bluntly, bringing his curiosity into the open.

"Hell, no!" he answered easily. "I'm just pulling out."

It was still early April, the weather cold and windy, washed by chilling rain. But daily the grass grew greener, and feed for his horses was plenty. About his only needs, for the first several days, were wood for his cooking fires and a dry place at night to put his bed.

He didn't doubt that he'd been blacklisted, so he was determined to ride well out of Garrett-land before trying seriously to find a job. As on one other occasion, he inspected his shadow on the ground as he rode, and was uplifted by the romantic form of it, comforted by the knowledge that he hadn't fared too badly in the last eighteen months, no matter what lay ahead. True, the second million wasn't coming any faster than the first had done. But he did have two horses and a good outfit, and the world was all in front of him. Sometimes people he passed on the road looked at him as if they envied him—riding a good pony like old Clay, leading his bed horse behind him, free as a bird in the air. And, as long as his groceries lasted, he took a melancholy pride in the knowledge that he was now proscribed, almost an outlaw. Practically a Rebel Jimson, and only nineteen this month!

There was no pleasure in the knowledge that he might never see Abby again, if things continued to go against him. But there was a kind of glory in the picture of her wondering about him, grieving for him, as she might. In the thought of her hearing of him again someday, a big man on another part of the range—maybe a hero in a big range war in which the bullionaires all got what was coming to them, and the people inherited the earth.

Then his reverie took a different turn, and he saw himself dying romantically, a broken old saddlebum in a dive like Duckbill

87

Drake's, just as Abby finally found him after much searching, having learned somehow of his innocence, of what he'd suffered because of his loyalty to his friends. The pathos of it touched him deeply, and as he rode he gave voice to the sadness that filled his throat and chest:

"I am an old cowpuncher, and now I'm dressed rags,
I used to be a tough one, and take on great big jags.
Now when I left my home boys, my sweetheart for me cried,
She begged me not to leave, boys. For me she would have
    died. . . ."

He had meant to ride further than Hat Creek Station on the Cheyenne-Black Hills Stage Line before seeking employment. But when he stepped inside the dirt-roofed log saloon to stretch his legs and kill some time, he saw by the bulletin board behind the bar that the Fiddleback outfit had work for a line rider, at forty a month and board.

He made the proper inquiries, and rode out to the ranch headquarters to investigate. He kept his fingers crossed, but the rancher, Tillitson by name, acted glad to have him, and let him ride his own horses. His camp was a dugout affair, much like the one he'd shared with Demps on Cat Creek. But it smelled some better, and he had it to himself, which circumstance right now was altogether to his liking.

He hadn't been on the job a week when he developed a strong suspicion that the riders on both sides of him were mavericking, for he kept seeing young steers and heifers branded in fresh irons that were not the Fiddleback. But the riders didn't bother him, and neither did his suspicions. He considered his neighbors' business to be their own. He was determined to make good this time, and aimed only to keep his own nose clean.

Then one day, about two weeks after he'd hired out, the foreman rode around to question him about the fresh brands. Jeff denied any knowledge of what was going on, and the foreman told him to roll up his bed.

"For what, and why?" Jeff protested. "I've did my job here. I haven't done nothing wrong."

"That's your story," the foreman said. "The evidence is otherwise. Besides, I been checking up on you. You didn't tell Tillitson that you'd made the Association blacklist, or he wouldn't have hired you in the first place. Fiddleback don't hire thieves."

This time, Jeff did not forget Demps's rule. He knocked the foreman down with his fist. But when the foreman rolled sideways to get at his pistol, Jeff's .38 was already in his hand.

"Go ahead, you mouth-Almighty bastard," Jeff invited. "Pull your gun—and I'll let some wind out of you another place."

"I'll make you wish you hadn't been born," the foreman warned, dabbing at his bleeding mouth, "if you don't make long tracks off Fiddleback range."

"This here's as much my ground as it is yours, or Tillitson's," Jeff retorted, recalling other lessons learned from Demps. "I'll take my goddam time."

The foreman climbed on his horse and departed meekly. Jeff smoked a cigarette, watching him out of sight, then went about his packing with a feeling of something like triumph. But after he'd stopped at the ranch office and picked up his bobtailed check, he began to know that he'd passed another milestone on the road to failure.

"I'm just hell-bent," he told the dun, midway between disgust and despair.

From Hat Creek, he angled east to Fort Laramie, and hung around awhile, dribbling out his money, trying to make some kind of contact. A fellow from the Mill Iron was hiring him, until he mentioned his name. Then the man looked in a notebook he carried, and shook his head.

"I don't know what you done to git yourself in bad with the Association," he said, half-kindly. "But I can't hire you, till you git clear with them. Be my own tail, if I did."

His next stop was at Lonetree, an eyesore burg that put him in mind of Ekard. A saloon signboard announced that the Jay Tee, a little English outfit to the east, was hiring men. But here too he was rebuffed.

"You'd ought to change your name, son—or else your line of work."

"It's the only name I got," Jeff answered hotly. "It's the only line of work I know. I ain't about to change either one, just to accommodate a hidebound old mossytail I never did no harm to."

His only answer was a shrug.

Through the rest of the summer, he rode grub line, asking for work—any kind of work—wherever he stopped. But there weren't any jobs in the towns he hit, not even swamping jobs for bed and board. And always, at the ranches, he encountered the invisible wall he'd run into first at Hat Creek station. The outfits that fed him and sometimes put him up at night pointedly hastened his departure, and he learned that life outside the pale was not entirely the romantic business he had fancied.

In the towns where he stopped, he was treated with suspicion. On a couple of occasions, he was thrown into jail and questioned tediously about fantastic crimes, then given a floater and warned to keep moving. At Julesburg, in Colorado, the town he'd first seen from the rods of a boxcar, his geld was taken from him, because he could produce no bill of sale. That night, he broke out of jail, stole the dun out of the stray pen, and made long tracks.

Finally, deep in the Nebraska sandhills, he did find winter's work—tending a windmill camp for the Spade outfit. The employment didn't pay anything besides his keep, and feed for his horses, and it was a comedown, even for a man who'd gathered bones. But he took it gratefully, and almost died of loneliness and despair before the cutting winds warmed up again. Early in the spring, he was fired again. This time he did not inquire into the reasons, and none was volunteered.

Beaten utterly at last, he swallowed his pride and rode the shortest route back to Rustler River.

He bypassed Cat Creek, thinking it unlikely that Demps would keep on scavenging after he had gone. Even so, he was two weeks on the trail—two weeks in which he avoided towns and the ranches he once had sought, living on sage chickens and rabbits that came within range of his gun; skulking like the fugitive he'd become. By the time he'd reached Drake Creek, he looked and felt like something the dogs had dragged around. But Duckbill greeted him casually.

"Dempsey allowed you'd be coming back," the barman said, setting up a bottle. "Said to have you fetch some things he's got to have. His homestead is off on Hurricane Crick, and he don't git in as often as he did."

"Homestead?" Jeff repeated. "You mean Demps has gone and filed a claim?"

"Gov'ment survey went through up there, right after you lit out," Drake nodded. "Demps got a couple of the crew likkered, and kidnaped them up to Hurricane, to git his corners located. He's got a nice little layout, now."

Jeff received the news with mixed emotions. It was nice to think of Demps having a place of his own, away from Drake's, where Jeff would be welcome to go. But he remembered Demps's own stories about the way homesteaders sometimes got treated. Hurricane Creek was Man Head range.

"Ain't Demps kind of courting trouble, staking out a claim on Garrett?" he asked.

"Demps courted trouble, and married the bitch, with a shotgun at his back," Drake said proudly, as if speaking of a favored son. "The bullionaires, they don't hamper Demps."

"Is Demps still mavericking?" Jeff asked, emboldened by the liquor to speak of a matter he had never discussed openly with the roadrancher.

Drake made a sound like a snapping dog. "Hell, no. The bullionaires built a fence around the mavericks last winter. Didn't you hear about their legislative act?"

"I was in a Nebraska windmill camp," Jeff answered. "I didn't hear nothing but that Sandhill wind."

"Well, Garrett and his crowd went down and rewrote the laws. Got one through saying all unbranded critters on the public land are the personal property of the Stock Association. They can be branded only at Stock Association roundups. Association sets the date and place for every roundup in the territory, and any man caught branding any cow anywhere outside them dates, without a Association stooge there tallying, gits five years in the pen."

"Can they make that stick?" Jeff asked.

"They're makin' it stick," Drake said. "Nor that ain't all. No man can register a brand or ride in a roundup without he joins the Association first. And you just by-God try to join!"

Jeff recalled his personal experiences of the past summer and winter, and felt a hot partisan sympathy for the Drakes and Dempsey Raes. He looked around him at the place again, and noted its deserted appearance. None of the displaced Texians who'd used to hang out with Drake the year around were in sight. The only horses he'd seen in the pastures and corrals were Drake's own stock. Boxcar Alice was the only one of the girls around, and she looked down at the mouth and heels.

"You mean you're letting that crowd bluff you out?" he said.

Drake's laugh was not a pleasant sound. "They ain't bluffing, boy. When you hold all the aces, you ain't got to bluff!"

It had been a week since Jeff had eaten what could be called a meal, and he was more interested in food than politics. Meat was cooking somewhere, and the smells put his stomach to digesting itself. When Boxcar Alice set a place for him and bade him to sit and eat, he found he loved her dearly.

"Boxcar," he said reverently, "you are my bosom friend."

"You're singing different from when I seen you last," she snapped, looking pleased in spite of herself. "I always said, a man ain't nothing but a stomick and a you know what!"

Jeff was off at dawn next morning, riding north and west, and it was after noon when he struck the little badlands stream he knew as Hurricane. It was nothing but a trickle of liquid mud, between two bars of shifting sand that looked as if it would swallow an empty sack. The country around was eroded and dry, unpromising as any Jeff had ever seen. But Drake had said that Demps's place was on the stream's headwaters, and he guessed that Demps would know good ground from bad. So he turned his unwilling horses north and rode toward the tablelands that rose bleak and massive in the distance.

The country became much rougher as he approached the mesas, and all afternoon he searched the broken landscape, looking for something that might be called a homestead, seeing nothing but the wild forlorn contours of the badlands. Late in the day, he found himself in breaks so jumbled and stood on end that he couldn't see fifty feet in any direction but straight up. But the trail he followed kept snaking around the chalk bluffs and buttes with an assuring appearance of purpose and direction, as if it knew where it was going. Suddenly he noticed that grass and shrubbery grew along the hitherto sterile banks. Water in the channel was clear enough that his horses no longer spurned it.

It was coming on for sundown when he heard a muffled pounding up ahead, and pretty quick he came in sight of some cottonwood bars across the trail—and Demps. Demps was off his horse, hammering at a post. His tethered sorrel threw up its head, and Demps made a grab for his rifle, much as he had done when Jeff had caught him branding mavericks in the draw on Paint Creek, except that his movements were more businesslike.

As before, Demps recognized Jeff in time, and didn't shoot. He stared long and hard, then set the gun down and resumed his labor. He didn't look around when Jeff pulled up against the bars and sat waiting to be greeted. He kept on hammering at the crosspiece he was nailing to the post, and Jeff watched him with a knocking at his heart, wondering if his partner hadn't forgiven him afterall.

In all his profitless drifting, in all the booting around he'd taken in the last year, in all the pride-swallowing he had been put to in deciding to come back, he had never for an instant doubted that Demps would welcome him. In all the bruising he had been treated to elsewhere, he had taken Demps's good will and friendship for granted—as he would have counted on the sympathy and benevolence of an indulgent parent, if he'd had one. Now the fear that Demps too would reject him descended on him like a smothering cloud. He waited, scarcely breathing, reminding himself of a stray dog that had approached him in the corrals at Ekard and had stood watching him similarly, wagging tentatively, poised to accept a pat on the head or dodge a kick at his guts.

He remembered with a pang how he had obliged with the kick to keep the cur from adopting him.

Demps finally finished driving his nail. He turned and pushed back his hat and looked at Jeff. The old mocking smile was there, and Jeff knew then that everything was going to be all right.

"Well, hi ya, Tex," Demps said, his voice as casual as if they'd parted the week before. "I was beginning to wonder if you'd make it. I hope Duckbill sent some things I been in need of."

"They're right there in the packs," Jeff said, blowing out his held breath. "He said you didn't git in so often any more."

"Tex," Demps said, "I used to hear it said there wasn't no Sunday west of Omaha. I never savvied what they meant, until I staked a homestead."

Demps let him through the bars, then walked to his sorrel and swung up to the saddle. There was something different about him, and Jeff couldn't say just what. He was thinner, and looked much older than when Jeff had seen him last. He didn't grin so easily or thoroughly. He seemed edgy and drawn in, more like his brother Harley than the Dempsey Jeff had known. More desolating yet, Jeff thought he detected embarrassment behind the outward cordiality. The conviction grew on him that he wasn't entirely welcome, and he wished bitterly he could go back a year and relive that day on Cat Creek when he'd behaved rottenly and said so many things he could not unsay.

They rode in silence, Demps thinking his private thoughts, Jeff groping vainly for words to express the apologies that were in his mind. Then, a hundred yards or so from the bars, the breaks opened suddenly onto a small meadow valley, a mile or so long and half a mile wide, all ringed by high chalk bluffs. The creek was clear as crystal glass, and brushed with cottonwoods and willow. The lush bottoms grass looked sweet and fat, and the sagebrush on the fringes grew to tree dimensions. Pine and juniper garnished the bluffs with green. Upward of a hundred horses grazed the meadow.

Jeff whistled admiringly. "Say, this is some layout. How'd you come to find it?"

"It's right cozy," Demps agreed. "Only two trails out, and I got bars across them both. Fencing ain't no problem here."

They were out onto the meadow now, and some of the horses came trotting up to snort at them. There were fine-looking saddle animals and heavy draft creatures with harness scars and work-bent knees. It was all branded stuff, but Jeff recognized none of the irons, and he had covered a considerable slice of the territory around. Almost no two brands were similar.

94

"All these switchers yours?" he asked.

"And the nice part of it is," Demps said, "it's back out the way. Ain't many even know it's here."

Jeff rode a ways in silence, anger and mortification burning in him. "Well, excuse me, all to hell," he said finally. "I only asked a civil question."

"Tex," Demps said, mild as milk, "the only civil question I ever heard was how-de-do."

Jeff's jaws clamped together, and he wished more than ever that he could just turn the calendar back a year and live one particular day again. Almost, he wished he hadn't come.

The cabin was set in some breaks above the creek on the far side of the valley. It was part dugout and part cottonwood log, with one unglazed window and a door of split cedar. It smelled something like a cellar inside, and wasn't very clean, having dirt for a floor and part of the walls. But it was a palace compared to the cave they'd lived in on Cat Creek. There was a tin campstove that looked familiar, and cupboards made of packing boxes. There was a hewn cedar table and benches to match. In the big windowless room off the kitchen there were bunks to sleep a dozen men.

Half a dozen questions crossed Jeff's mind as they stored the groceries he'd fetched from Drake's. But he saw to it they didn't cross his lips. Later, they took their horses up to a stable that was just a cave in a big mud butte, faced with log and doored with cedar, like the house.

Around the stable, in the breaks, were three natural corrals, separated by pole bars. There was harness hanging in the stable, but no riding gear. In one of the corrals there sat a funny-looking cart: cleated mowing machine wheels fitted onto a cedar axle, hand-hewn, with crude platform and seat built on.

"Ol' Clay looks some used up," Demps commented, when their horses were unsaddled and having their roll. "Well, a little of this Hurricane grass will put 'im on his feet. That damned old mare, she hangs on, don't she?"

"She's tougher 'n bullneck rawhide," Jeff confirmed.

Dusk was thickening to dark when they walked down to the cabin, and Jeff was interested to note that Demps lowered a wooden shutter to blind the window, before lighting the lantern that served as lamp. It struck him as especially odd, since the place was so far from everywhere, and Demps himself had said that not many even knew the place was there. But Jeff wasn't asking any questions.

Once the lamp was lighted, Demps kindled a fire with cedar choppings, and pushed a greasy fry pan up over the flame. Then he took the lantern into the bedroom and came out carrying a quarter of fat red beef that Jeff could have eaten raw. The meal he'd taken on at Ekard had worn off, and the smell of the steaks frying was almost more than he could stand.

Demps eyed him wryly. "You ready to put on the nosebag? Or do I got to show the hide the critter wore before you'll set?"

"I'm ready for the nosebag," Jeff said reverently.

The food dispatched, they sat awhile, smoking Demps's tobacco, a strained silence between them. Finally, Demps looked squarely at Jeff for the first time the entire evening.

"You must have had things kind of rough, by the looks of you," he said.

"It wasn't no picnic," Jeff confessed. "It's hell-sure easy to git a bad name in this country."

"I figured you'd find out," Demps said, not smiling. "Well, as you can see, I've gone to breaking horses. It don't pay much, but I eat, and I could use a hand. Blacklist don't hold here."

Jeff sighed in relief and happiness, and considered how good it was to be home again, even if Demps didn't act quite like himself. He felt a vast security, a vast affection for Dempsey Rae, a wonder that he ever could have hated him, even for a little while.

"You've hired yourself a man," he said.

7: Wild Bunch

After breakfast the next morning, Jeff roped a fresh horse out of the bunch on the meadow, and rode with Demps down to the lower bars to replace a post that had rotted off. They had to locate another cedar in the breaks, cut it and trim it to post-length, then snake it to the gate before they could set it and transfer the cleats and crosspieces from the discarded upright. It was nearing noon when they returned to the meadow, and saw a strange horse band stringing down into the valley from the table-lands above.

There appeared to be almost as many animals in the trail herd as grazed on the meadow, and altogether it was about the poorest aggregation of horseflesh that Jeff had ever seen. All were bony and rough-coated and so sore-footed they scarcely could walk. The seven drovers that Jeff counted looked as hard-used as the horses, and he figured it must be just some wild bunch, moving through. But Demps disabused his mind.

"More customers," Demps announced, "with more switchers to fatten and twist out. From the looks of them, we got our work cut out, this go."

They rode up to meet the newcomers, and Jeff was disconcerted to see Sundance among the drovers. He mentioned his discovery to Demps, but Demps only shrugged.

"Yeah, I've interviewed him, already. He got over that fracas we had, and been working around at odd jobs ever since. Says Matador tied the can to him, for not being present when Hasty tallied out to Garrett that fall, and he's just been loose on the country. His business is horses, these days."

Jeff looked the outfit over as they worked up one flank toward the drovers at the rear, and as far as he could tell none of the brands matched any on the horses down on the meadow. But the men all greeted Demps warmly and complimented him on the looks of the other bunch, so Jeff reckoned they must be old customers.

Demps introduced Jeff all around. The names he heard didn't

sound much like real names: Dabs and Slim Pickens. Bad Water. Bitch Crick. Hard Pan and Mon Tan.

"I believe you two already run into each other once." Demps smiled faintly when Sundance came riding up. And Sundance slanted Jeff a gargoyley grin.

"Well, if it ain't Texas River!" he leered, putting out a hand. "You ever locate that there Mr. Matador?"

Jeff felt the white eyes brace him, and he knew then that Sundance hadn't forgiven him, that there would be more trouble between them.

"You go to hell," he invited, ignoring the hand.

"Come on, you two pit cocks," Demps scolded. "That was a long time ago."

"A hell of a long time," Sundance agreed. "So long that this Texas River is growing chest hair. Way he's going, he'll be a man before his mother."

"My advice to you, Sundance," Demps said pointedly, "would be to lay off him, now—before you step into something that won't scrape off."

The white eyes leered again, but Sundance let Demps's statement stand.

They dropped the faltering horses at the head of the meadow, and rode on to the stable where the drovers commenced unsaddling and unpacking the four animals that transported their outfit. The talk Jeff overheard was general, but from the frequent mention of the Yellowstone River and Hardin and the Rosebud Reservation, he began to get the idea the men were all the way from Montana. He was remembering the dozen bunks in the cabin and listening to a number of conversations at once, trying to piece things together, when Demps noticed him and looked bothered.

"Tex," he said, "these boys say they dropped a couple likely colts, a mile or so back, up on the mesa. And they're all about rode out. Why don't you back-trail 'em a ways, and have a look around?"

Jeff had heard no mention of any colts dropped. He felt like a button ordered from the room so he wouldn't hear the salty

98

grown-up talk. But it was Demps's homestead. He bit back the retort that came to his lips, and turned his pony to ride.

The horse trail led up the canyon washed by the creek, through another set of bars, then angled off through more rough breaks. After a mile or so, it came out upon a vast tableland that stretched flat as a floor to where it blended with the sky and you couldn't see it any more. A circle of scrub brush off to left of him showed where Hurricane Creek headed, and other brush outlines indicated other marsh springs, other creeks that flowed in other directions. Given free rein and unhampered by any barriers, the wind blew warm and strong. In winter, Jeff speculated, such a wind would be hard to face.

Jeff looked for no lost likely colts, and found none. But he'd heard of Hurricane Mesa off and on ever since coming to Wyoming, and he was interested in looking around a bit. It was a wild, forlorn place, exposed to all of nature's excesses. But it was well-watered and judging by the early growth would soon be exceptionally well-grassed. Somehow, it seemed to fit Demps's personality, his outlook and inner nature. As he rode around it, Jeff began to envy Demps. Not only for his fitting land location, but just for being Demps.

Several times in his exploring, Jeff raised cattle, in little bunches. All wore the Man Head brand, and the circumstance puzzled him a little. He had been told once that the tablelands in this sector formed the border line between Garrett and Muleshoe, that Shoe herds grazed the plateaus, Man Head herds the prairies. He decided that either the line riders were dogging off, or Garrett was spreading out.

Riding back along the trail, he came upon the remains of a freshly butchered calf—head, feet, and guts, but no hide. The blood was scarcely dry, and the flies were swarming around in clouds. Jeff could only figure that the horse drovers had committed the act, and he was annoyed that they hadn't made any effort to conceal the evidence of their crime. He looked carefully around to make certain he wasn't being watched. Then he climbed down, tossed the head and feet into some nearby brush, and dragged the guts to a shallow draw where they would be less conspicuous. After that, he kicked dust over the blood pools, and swore again at the laxity of the drovers.

"The'd ought to be shot in five places—making trouble for Demps that way," he said aloud.

Dusk was falling when he returned to the homestead. A big fire was burning down on the creek bank, and a calf was roasting on a spit. A hide was stretched out on the ground not far away, a square piece cut out of it where the brand might have been. Two stone jugs were circulating, and when Jeff joined the party, Sundance thrust one at him.

"Texas," he said thickly, "it's time I and you buried the tomahawk, and I don't mean in each others' headbones. You slugged me onct, when I didn't look for it. But that'sh all right. Time now we had a drink. Any son of a bitch that's a friend of Demps's is a friend of mine."

Jeff had learned that hard names were not considered insults in this country if they were offered with a smile. Feeling two tawny eyes on him, he glanced over and saw Demps shake his head about a quarter of a turn. The glance told Jeff that Demps was cold sober, and he was the only one in the gathering who wore a gun. Jeff's head made the same motion at Sundance.

"Thanks, Sundance," he said lightly. "But some us sonsabitches got to stay on our feet, in case there's work to do."

At Demps's suggestion, Jeff went to the cabin and fetched eating tools, and they went to work on the barbequed beef. Being so newly killed, the texture was stringy, but the flavor was the best. And when Jeff commented on its goodness, Sundance grinned at Demps.

"You ever figured why it is, Demps, that the other fella's beef always tastes so much better than your own?"

Demps's glance touched Jeff, and slid away.

"I hadn't never noticed, Sundance," he said thinly. "I'll just take your word on it."

The air around the fire went still and dead. The drovers all watched Demps uneasily, and one or two hitched themselves away from him. Then, all at once, Demps let his eye-shutting grin come out.

"Hell," he said, "I don't ever remember tasting none my own!"

100

"Now, hit's a fact that down in the hill country of Texas a man is figured to be plumb shiftless, if he eats his own beef," the man known as Hard Pan put in, when the laughter had subsided. "I mind the time a neighbor of ourn invited Pa to supper, and fed him some Pa's own meat. Pa was dog-sick, when they told him. Said it was like eating his own kinfolks."

"My old man was just the same, only worse, but he got cured," another contributed. "We homesteaded in again' the big I-C outfit, up in Montan', and Pa started branding a I-C-U, which saved work no end, us just having to add the U. But one day he found somebody had tampered with one of his brands. It said I-C-U-2. Next day, he harnessed our team, and we changed climates for a while.

"You git it?" the narrator asked, nudging Jeff. "I-see-you-too."

The yarning went on endlessly, and Jeff couldn't help noticing that any reference to cow stealing was always good for a laugh, though just what was so humorous about it he couldn't clearly understand.

"Well," Demps said finally, "I don't know how it is in other places. But here in Wyoming, a man can't very well eat his own beef without he's a bullionaire. On account of the way they got it rigged, you got to be a bullionaire to own a beef!"

Nobody laughed at that, and Demps stood up and stretched. "Well," he said, "I and Tex have got plenty work looking us in the face, and the rest you Injuns got quite a piece to ride, starting in the morning. We better ring this down."

So they all turned in, and the drovers got off early next morning, taking the fat, trained horses with them, leaving the eyesore skates behind. They left Sundance behind, also, and when Jeff hit Demps up about it, Demps just shrugged.

"Says he got into trouble with the military at Fort Fetterman, and got to lay low awhile. Offered to help twist out these broncs for just his keep. I didn't like to tell him no."

"You're too big-hearted for your own good," Jeff told him, forgetting where he personally would be, except for that same generosity. "I wish you'd booted him. I don't trust the bastard."

"Hell, he ain't my notion of good company, neither," Demps

answered. "But he's a top hand with horses, and we can use his help. He gives us any bother, we will by-God run him off."

The trouble was, the white-eyed drover was crowding trouble right from the first, and Demps seemed not to notice. Sundance walked and talked soft around Demps. But around Jeff he was always snooping and nosing him, prying at things Jeff knew nothing of. Always leering and hinting at things Jeff took no stock in. Always trying, it seemed to Jeff, to drive a wedge between him and Demps.

"We'll have to let that bunch rest up and put on a little flesh before we start working on them," Demps announced that morning after the other riders had pulled out. "But there's a dozen or so colts, I notice, that need altering. I reckon we can tend to that."

There were more stud colts than Demps had estimated, and the surgical alterations consumed the better part of three days. As a rule, Sundance did the roping and throwing, and Demps the knife work. Jeff helped with the tying and kept the fire and handled the cauterizing iron—watching the other procedures to learn what he could.

Then, when each colt's destiny in life had been changed for all time, it also was Jeff's function to bang the tail off square, just below the tip of bone, to show its wearer was a geld.

When the doctoring was done, there followed several days of idleness, in which Jeff did considerable riding up on the mesa, considerable target shooting with his pistol, expending some .38 ammunition the long-trail drovers had left behind.

"Studying up to be a gunslinger just like Dempsey, eh, Tex?" Sundance said to him, once when Demps was down on the meadow, out of earshot.

"What's wrong with gitting to be like Demps?" Jeff challenged.

"Nothing wrong," Sundance said with an exaggerated shrug. "Demps is all wool and a yard wide. But dogs like me and Demps, we come to sorry ends. You'll come to a sorry end, too, kid, if you don't skin out of this."

"Skin out of what?" Jeff countered, angered but feeling a hairy spider crawling up his spine.

"Out of this whole damn country," the white-eyed man told him. "You're gitting yourself a bad name. Rustling calves from Man Head, and from Fiddleback over east. Stealing horses in Nebraska, gitting throwed in every jail around. What you think it's going to git you?"

Jeff stared at him. "How come you know so much about me and what I do?"

Sundance grinned his gargoyle grin. "I keep tab on all my friends," he said. Then, before Jeff could say more, Demps came riding up, and he had no chance.

At another time, Jeff was riding alone up on the mesa when he flushed a poddy Man Head calf out of some brush. He was getting rusty on his roping, and just to be doing, he shook out a loop and gave chase. He caught the dogie with one cast, dallied the rope and slid his dun to a stop, letting it bust itself at the riata's end. The bellow it let go brought a cow up out of a ravine close by, slobbering and shaking her horns at Jeff. He was just beginning to wonder how he was going to recover his rope when he saw Sundance come riding up out of the same draw the cow had emerged from.

For once in his life, Jeff was glad to see the white-eyed snoop, thinking that he might need help in getting back his rope. But when Sundance pulled up about ten feet away and just sat looking at him, Jeff began to feel the spider at his spine again. Sundance was carrying his rifle along in front of him, and Jeff had the nightmare feeling that the white-eyed man was there to kill him—gun him down and never say a word.

"Well," the twangy voice said finally, proving that Jeff's hunch was at least partly wrong, "don't just set there. Git off and tail him over. Where's your iron, and fire? Or are you using acid?"

"What iron?" Jeff burst out. "What acid? What are you raving about?"

His accoster laughed, but the sound served only to send Jeff's apprehensions up. "Hell, you and Demps don't trust nobody, do you? Well, you'd might as well trust me. I know what you're up to."

Jeff sat silent, not thinking of anything appropriate to say.

"I expect you're just up here roping Garrett calves for exercise," the sneering voice went on. "Well, it ain't no hide off me, long as you two hog everything yourselves, and won't cut nobody else in. But take an old hand's advice, and swing your rope in draws and gulches. Supposing I had been Garrett, or Strap Bowman, coming along right now? Where you think your address would be, the next ten, fifteen years?"

Raising one hand before his face, the speaker spread his fingers and leered between them, as if they were iron bars. Then, before Jeff could make reply, he turned his roan and loped away, leaving Jeff alone with his thoughts and the calf and proddy cow.

On the ride back to the homestead, Jeff resolved to go to Demps and tell him of their guest's behavior. But he recognized the difficulties involved, with Demps holding out on him about the horse deal, and pretending everything was on the up and up. Besides, when he got right down to it, he could see there wasn't much to say. Just that Sundance suspected they were rustling cattle, and wanted to be cut in. With Demps as touchy as he was about his private affairs, looking put out every time anybody made mention of stock stealing where Jeff could hear, he didn't know if he would dare.

As it worked out, Sundance stuck close to Demps all afternoon and evening, giving Jeff no chance to speak with him in private. And that night, in the cabin, Demps was all absorbed in an Eastern heart-and-hand bulletin he had got from somewhere. The pamphlet listed women by age and description and personal fortune, and according to Demps you could just order one, like something out of a mail-order catalogue, and she would come out and marry you.

"You thinking of gitting married, Demps?" Jeff asked, taken back.

"Why not?" Demps demanded. "Man needs a woman, and they don't grow on the bushes around here. This riding into Ekard twice a month gits old."

"But would you buy one, just like that?" Jeff pressed. "Sight unseen? Take what you git?"

"Why not?" Demps grinned. "We can't all marry Abby Garrett."

Jeff felt his face change colors, even though he could see that Demps was only hoorawing him.

"Don't seem like none of us can," Sundance put in from over in the corner. "Least, Strap Bowman's been a-trying for two, three years now, and ain't got the job done. Strap can't do it, I expect it can't be did."

Jeff looked at the outlaw, wondering again how he came to know so much about the country and all its residents. But the thought was off the top of his mind. He'd been trying to broach the subject of Abby and Strap ever since his return, but hadn't found a way to do it without laying himself open to a ribbing.

"Strap still ain't got her, huh?" he said, trying to keep his voice steady.

"Not the last I heerd," Sundance said. "But I don't doubt he'll wear her down. Strap gits what he goes after—I've heerd tell."

"I dunno," Demps disallowed. "That's one gal thinks her butt is a gold mine, and everybody's digging for it. I don't expect Strap will git to first base with her. Nor anyone else, this side of Bunker Hill."

Jeff felt the tawny eyes brace him as the lewd reference to Abby was made. He knew then that the remark had been deliberate, that Demps was openly baiting him. Oddly enough, he did not feel affronted, but he sensed a challenge that must be acknowledged. He reached the catalogue they used for starting fires, and ripped out a sheet.

"Here," he said easily. "If you've finished, you can wipe your mouth."

Demps scowled at him, and looked away. Demps had changed a lot.

8: The Killer Comes

Next morning, they started breaking out the rough bunch, and they were all kept so busy for a week or so that Sundance had no opportunity to nose around Jeff in private, Jeff no time to worry over the times he had.

With Jeff to help him, Demps took over the breaking of the animals they'd marked for harness, leaving those destined for the saddle to Sundance's brutal handling. Sundance employed the stomping tactics that were calculated to break a horse's spirit and instill in it so terrible a fear of man that it would never have the courage to buck again. And when the high-crotched rider wrapped his snaky legs around a bronco's belly, bucking was a waste of time.

Demps's method with the work and driving animals was gentleness itself. His way of getting them accustomed to handling was to snub them short, place a gunnysack over their heads, then tie one front foot and one hind foot up so they could neither kick nor strike without falling down. When they had ceased fighting the ropes, he would slap them around a bit and throw harness on their backs and jerk it off until they found it wasn't going to hurt. When they'd quieted down sufficiently, he would remove the sack and leg ropes and lead them around the corrals with tugs dragging and loose straps flapping, until they took it all in stride.

When a handled colt was ready for secondary education, it was hitched along with a gentled horse to the cart that had excited Jeff's curiosity. Demps had a rope device called a running-w which joined all the colt's feet in a kind of loose hobble that let it walk free, but was so contrived that one tug on the guide rope would jerk both front feet from under it and throw it to its knees.

When it came to driving, Jeff held the lines, Demps the trip rope. At the offset, the hitched colt would usually sulk and balk. But the gentled horse would crowd it with the tongue, and when it lunged in an effort to bolt, Demps would bring it to its knees.

In the beginning, this treatment, too, struck Jeff as severe. But Demps was patient, and the meadow ground was soft and spongy, easy on the knees. Pretty quick, the colt would discover it could keep its feet so long as it behaved. In the same way, it learned to stop when Demps called "Whoa."

"They sure do ketch on fast," Jeff commented, impressed at how well the system worked.

"Horses ain't cussed, like people," Demps opined. "Let a horse know what's expected of it, and give it a chance to come through, nine times out of ten it will. Let a man know what you want, and without you pack a club, nine times he will do the opposite.

And I expect that's where we git all the talk we got about horse sense. I sure don't remember hearing no talk about man sense."

With three of them working, the training progressed rapidly, and for a day or two Sundance behaved so well that Jeff almost got over feeling edgy and snorty in his presence. But as time went on, and as Jeff managed never to be thrown in with him alone again, the white-eyed drover began to dig and insinuate around Demps the way he had done earlier with Jeff. Not so openly, but plainly baiting and prying; seemingly unable to stop picking at a sore.

One day Demps snubbed up a little brown quarter-horse mare that Jeff had figured would make a fine riding animal, and Jeff asked an innocent question.

"Demps," he said, "why break an animal like that to harness? Why not twist her out to ride?"

"Mares ain't favored for riding in this country, kid," Demps answered. "Out here, on your cow roundups, you sometimes git five and six hundred horses all together, from twenty or thirty different outfits. All that many switchers is hard enough to hold in one band, without having mares around to keep the geldings all stirred up."

"I thought mares and gelds mixed all right," Jeff said. "I thought you took care the gelds' feelings and inclinations, when you cut 'em."

"You take care some of it," Demps conceded, grinning on one side. "But they're considerable like people. To git it all, you'd have to cut their throats."

"And there's another reason," Sundance put in. "Take a look at the Box brand on that mare's shoulder. Conspicuous as hell, ain't it?"

Jeff had to admit that the mark was easily read.

"Well, now, put a saddle on her back, and the brand stands out, just the same. But, under harness, it would be different. Draft work changes a horse's lines, and harness marks 'em up. Why, roach that little digger and work her in harness two months, and I could drive her right under the nose of the owner of that iron, and he'd never give her a second look."

Jeff tried not to look at Demps, but the silence lasted so long he had to look. He found Demps glowering.

"Sundance," Demps said finally, his tone flat and steady, "you talk too damn much. And that ain't the worst of your faults."

Sundance winked at Jeff, and leered. "Well, now, tell me, Demps. Tell me about the worst of my faults."

"I'll tell you," Demps said evenly. "You're too damn nosy, around other people's business. You asked to stay here to hole up awhile, and I let you do it out the bigness of my heart. But you figure to go on staying, you better put that nose in a sling, and git some shutters for your mouth. And that's the word with the bark on it."

"Why, now, what's the matter?" Sundance protested, spreading his hands as if to show they both were empty. "What'd I do to bring on all this, except to tell the button some things he's old enough to hear. Hell, it's time he knowed the facts of life."

"You're the one that will learn some facts of life, if you don't put a bridle on that tongue," Demps told him. "You don't believe me, you just keep talking, and put it to the test."

Sundance sow-bellied in the face of a direct threat, and for a day or so he sulked, saying no word to either of them. But his silence didn't last for long. The thought had come to Jeff already that Sundance could no more stop his prying insinuations than a crow could stop cawing. He seemed almost to be courting trouble, crowding a showdown with the man he had good reason to hate.

One night around the table, Demps was imparting his plans for future development of his homestead, and allowing as to how he figured to get started in the cattle business, on a small scale.

"How can you own cattle, if you can't brand?" Jeff asked him.

Demps looked thoughtful. "I been over all that. I been hearing some lately about a red bally-faced breed of cow the Haw-Haws up on the Powder been experimenting with. Brought it over from the old country. Called Hoford or Hearford, or some Hinglish name like that."

"Hereford," Jeff supplied.

"That's it." Demps nodded. "Well, that coloration would be

108

pretty damn conspicuous. Fella stocked Herefords, he wouldn't need no brand. At least not till Garrett stocked 'em."

"How will you market, if you can't ship?" Jeff countered.

"That's a horse of a different story," Demps admitted. "But I figure this way. There's a big demand amongst these freighters for steers for bull teams. Garrett and the other bullionaires won't sell to them, on account of they don't want to scatter their brands. Me, I wouldn't have no brand to scatter. I could train 'em right here, with my horse cart, and just let the bullwhackers come and git 'em."

"Where would you pasture 'em? Here on the meadow?"

Demps grinned faintly. "If I had my own colors, I could run 'em up on the mesa with Garrett's. That would make us pardners, in a way!"

Jeff was desolated by the way Demps kept saying "I" instead of "we." But he tried not to let his feelings show.

"How about the mesa?" he demanded. "I thought Muleshoe grazed up there."

Demps nodded. "They did. But Garrett brung in more Texas caddle last summer, and needed more range. He bought the mesa off from Shoe."

"I thought it was public ground."

"It is."

"Then how can Garrett buy it, from Shoe, if Shoe don't own it?"

"That's the question," Demps told him, tawny eyes glinting. "They hold it. They fence it. They buy it. They sell it. So, I expect they don't have to own it."

"Seems like a funny deal," Jeff said dubiously.

"It's funny, all right," Demps growled. "So funny I could bust a gut."

Until that moment, Sundance had not joined in the after-dinner talk. Now he hitched his chair around.

"Your idea strikes me as plumb good," he confided. "You could make money, and wouldn't need no special coloration. You could start tomorrow."

Demps looked at him inimically. "What would I buy my seed stock with? Gold dust out the stable?"

Sundance grinned. "Why buy stock, when it's all around you? Now, if I was you . . ."

"You ain't me, nor I ain't you—thank God."

"Well, just listen to me. All that stuff of Garrett's up on the mesa, and you in a place like this. Big barn out there, without no window, and calves don't bawl, if they're locked in where it's dark."

The suggestion appealed to Jeff. But Demps looked black again. "You're so damned smart, Sundance," he said venomously. "Why ain't you rich?"

"But I . . ."

"Shut up. I told you once, you talk too much."

"But—what the hell?"

"You heard me. You're not blind."

Next morning the three of them were riding up on the mesa, looking for a pair of breachy colts that had jumped through the bars in the night and made a getaway. They didn't find the colts, but they did raise a band of wild broomtails, over by the head of Cat Creek. The wild bunch was bossed by a tall red stallion that looked at a distance to be plenty horse. On its back was what appeared to be the remnant of a saddle.

"It *is* a saddle—or what's left of one," Demps said, when Jeff had mentioned it. "Belongs to Wate Garrett, I been told. That big stud belongs to Garrett, too. But he can't make his claim stand up."

Demps told a story then. "When I was first up here, three, four years ago, riding for Garrett, he went back to Indiana and paid fifteen hundred dollars for the stud, to breed up his riding string. Registered American saddle horse, with a pedigree longer 'n a harlot's dream. There was a big Fourth of July celebration in Quadrille, just a day or two after Wate got back. Governor was up to kiss fat babies and arses, and everybody put on his best bib and tucker. There was dignitaries around till you'd of thought somebody had dropped a dime, and the word had got down to Cheyenne.

"Well, they had a bunch of speeches, and a big pee-rade. Governor and Wate come first, side by each, not being able to figure out which one should ought to have the edge. Back of them come the lice and little shots, in order of their drag. Ol' Wate was riding that big red, and proud as Satan, hogging the whole show.

"Well, everything was going according to the book when old Pete Blue staggered out the Hat Saloon, carrying a load bigger 'n the Governor's horse. Let out a yelp, and started shooting in the air—a kind of six-gun salute, in honor of the honoraries. And that big red stud caught the spirit of things and put on a private show, just for him and Wate. Threw a wall-eyed fit, and piled old Garrett plumb through the window of the Hat Saloon. Broke a arm and collarbone, and purely crushed his pride. Busted up the whole affair, and was the hee-ro of the day!"

"What happened to Blue?" Jeff asked, seeing tragedy as well as comedy in the recitation.

"During the excitement, which went on for hours, Pete staggered to the livery corral, wrangled his horse, and lit a shuck. Never was heard tell of again. That big red Injun out there charged off, and was next seen up here on the benches, with Wate's silver-mounted celebration saddle still strapped to his snaky back. Been here ever since, squiring them spidery mares around. Siring blue-blooded colts with stud fees waived, and having himself a time. Garrett, he's imported racers from everywhere and spent a fortune trying to run him down. But he ain't got the job done yit."

"Why didn't he just spend that money on another horse?" Jeff asked naïvely.

"That's a good question," Demps glowered. "But you don't know Wate. He'd spend a thousand dollars to ketch and convict a ten-dollar thief any day. Same with that horse. He don't want nothing nor nobody gitting the best of him."

"Well," Jeff said practically, "he might as well spend his money that way as some other. He can't take it with him, when he goes."

"He don't have to take it with him," Demps said cynically. "Them that have it here will have it there."

Jeff was much impressed by Demps's story, and turned his dun off toward the bunch, hoping to get a closer look at the animal which had humbled the man who was, for practical purposes, the King. He was still half a mile away when the guardian stud snorted and started herding the band down toward the breaks, working back and forth behind the drags as skillfully as a well-trained dog.

The dun was hot and sweaty, but the instant the mustangs bolted, he got all bothered and wanted to give chase. Jeff had a moment's fight to bring him under control, and that incident made another deep impression on his mind.

"Now there's a deal I can't make out," he said to Demps, when he'd rejoined his two companions. "You'd think horses would hang together some, instead of always being out to do each other in. But I've yet to see a horse that wouldn't bust a gut to help run other horses down. How'd you explain that?"

"Why, it's easy," Demps said, only half-humorously. "All you got to do is look at it from the horse's angle. It got caught, so it hates to see other horses on the loose."

Jeff was dubious. But Demps talked on, developing his thesis. "Horses ain't so different from people, neither. I mean, most people have got riders, the same as horses. And them that do are always hot to help corral the ones that don't. . . . Why, take Strap Bowman and Gut Desmond, and most the others in this man's country. Ain't they just as quick as that blue pony to take after anybody that won't knuckle under and kiss Garrett's prat? Ain't they quicker than Garrett, even, to insist that everybody kiss him, just 'cause they do?"

Jeff thought back on past experience, and had to grant the point. But he made an important reservation.

"There's sure more truth than poetry in what you say. But all horses are that way. And all men ain't. You and me, we ain't that way."

Demps shrugged. "You and me, we ain't never really had a rider—yet. Maybe it's too soon to say."

As in all other conversations that had to do with anything but stealing stock, Sundance had remained stonily aloof, looking slightly bored, awaiting a chance to turn the talk to matters which he deemed important. The chance came when they were back at the homestead, unsaddling their horses up in the corral.

"I been thinking, Demps," he said, in his slanted, baleful way.

"There's some good stock horses running with them broomtails on the mesa. Lot of Man Head brood mares that damn stud has coaxed away. Why don't we run some these skates of ourn up there, as a decoy bunch, and pull them others in down here. I think it would be worth our time."

Jeff held his breath, remembering Demps's warning of several days before. But Demps just stood looking into distance, as if he hadn't heard.

"And another deal—" the white-eyed man went on. "I see Wate's got a bunch of brood mares, under wire, down on Cat Crick now. Long as we're operating, why don't we borrow some of them. Like you say, we couldn't market Man Head mares nowhere in the territory, because people won't tamper with the brand. But the colts don't carry no mark. We could slip down there some dark night, and push a bunch of mares and colts up into the breaks on Cat. We could file the mare's feet down, so they couldn't travel, and they'd stay put that way, till the colts was ready to wean. Then we drive the colts off, and the mares go back to Man Head, when their feet grow out. Looks air-tight to me."

"About as air-tight as you yourself," Demps said, turning. "Which ain't air-tight at all. Git something through your goddam head. My business is breaking horses. Yours is something else. So pack your bag and make long tracks."

Sundance looked at him, his long face sharpening. "You undertaking to run me off, Demps?"

"Undertaking—hell!" Demps said, an awful mildness in his voice. "I'm gut-sick of you and your everlasting yawp. Git your stuff together now, and drag it out of here, or you'll need some undertaking done."

Sundance didn't move, and Jeff smelled trouble. But just as he started backing off, Sundance started caving.

"Demps," he whined. "I and you ain't got no quarrel. I only wanted in on some the business here."

"You'll git the business, if you're not off the Hurricane in ten minutes," Demps said, his voice suddenly harsh. "Nor I ain't saying any more."

Sundance started to say something, then thought better of it, and was quiet. He tried to smile, but the smile wouldn't come up. He looked at Jeff, as if asking him for help. Jeff stared coldly back at him, and after a while he hitched his shoulders and slouched off toward the house. Shortly thereafter, he reappeared, carrying his bed and warbag. All the while he readied his horses, he moved like a man who is walking on eggs. When he was mounted and ready to ride, he turned his sneering eyes on Demps.

"What do I tell the boys about these skates?"

"Tell the boys to come and git 'em, and never to fetch no more," Demps said roughly. "When they took you into their company, they let me out."

"I'll tell 'em," Sundance said softly. "But I guarantee they won't like it. Not one little bit."

Jeff and Demps stood together, watching the devil's advocate depart, saying nothing so long as he was in sight. Jeff was relieved and glad to see him go. Already, the air around seemed clearer, somehow purer to inhale. But he didn't get to enjoy it long. Almost as quick as Sundance was out of sight down the creek trail, Demps turned on him the way he'd turned on Sundance.

"All right, Tex. It's your turn, now. Saddle up your dun, and pack your mare, and light a shuck. You been here too long, too."

If Demps had hit him with a neck yoke, without a word of warning, Jeff couldn't have been more staggered. He swung around, and found Demps's eyes waiting, hard as bullets. He started to know then that Demps meant what he had said.

"Demps," he heard his voice saying, "you going to give me any reason?"

"I ain't got to give you any reason," Demps said crossly. "Maybe you just plain wore your welcome out." But he didn't look at Jeff as he said it, and Jeff took a little hope from this.

"Dammit, kid," Demps went on aggrievedly, his face a little kinder, "you been on my back ever since you hit this country. Why not git off and stand on your own laigs awhile? Forgit that stuck-up little Garrett piece, and light a shuck out this country like you done before, only keep a-going this time. Git so far from here you'll never hear of Rustler River again. Git you a plump, black-eyed gal and settle down to raise hell and fat horses on your own. Pay me back for what I've did for you, by making something of yourself."

Demps had shifted ground so fast that Jeff was left off balance. He'd started out abusing Jeff as he'd abused Sundance. Now he was practically pleading. Jeff couldn't get the lay.

"Demps," he said, "what's eating you? What'd I do, to bring this on?"

"You didn't do nothing," Demps answered, the harshness in his voice again. "It's what I've done, letting you mix in my fight with Garrett. But I'm a-fixing that up quick. I'm sending you packing, kid."

Jeff saw the nightmare breaking, saw daylight come at last. He laughed in sheer exhilaration.

"Hell, Demps. For a minute there you had me worried. I thought it was something serious."

"It's serious, Tex," Demps said. "I wasn't going to show you. But there ain't no handling a porkypine like you."

Reaching up to one pocket, the homesteader brought out a piece of folded brown wrapping paper and forked it over. Jeff took it and spread it in his hands. An unartistic hand had sketched a crude skull and crossbones on it, with what looked to have been a piece of charcoal. Down below the death's head, the same rough hand had scrawled the numerals

3—7—77

"It was tacked to the stable door, when we got back just a while ago," Demps said. "I got it off before you and Sundance seen it."

"But what's it mean—the numbers?"

Demps smiled, but not at anything that was funny. "Once, in my colorful career, I dug graves for a livelihood. Standard dimensions are three feet wide, seven feet long, seventy-seven inches deep. That's what it means, Tex. My grave's been ordered, unless I drag it out of here."

Jeff continued to stare at the paper, trying to comprehend that it was anything but a clumsy joke.

"It's the same valentine the Vigilantes used to send just before they closed somebody out, up around Virginia City, in the early days," Demps went on. "I wasn't there. But I've talked to some that was. I've heard said that Garrett was there, one the big wheels in the companies. One the exterminators, too. I heard it said that the committee was hardest on them that got in the companies' way."

Jeff glanced over at the stable door, as if expecting to see some clue that would clear the mystery. "Who you reckon left it?"

"I purely wish I knew," Demps said fervently. "Strap Bowman, maybe. But I don't see no tracks around."

All at once, Jeff was remembering Sundance and his odd behavior; the digging and insinuating, the constant prying into his and Demps's affairs. Once more, he started to see the light.

Excitedly, he blurted the whole story of Sundance's conduct toward him. Of the oblique warnings and accusations, the unsolicited advice on this and that. Demps watched him intently, comprehension breaking on his face.

"He could have done it. He rode up here ahead of us, didn't he—then made like he'd dropped his rope, and had to ride back. That's when the bastard planted it!"

"But what's his angle? He working for Garrett, the way he did for Matador?"

"I wouldn't be surprised," Demps said. "Maybe for the Stock Association. That's how them so-called range detectives work. Ride into a man's camp, posing as something they ain't, baiging for help and favors. Eat your grub and sleep in your house, then watch their chance and shoot you in the back. They're a brave and moral lot, them cannibals!"

Jeff said nothing. Jeff was still trying to realize the thing was bona fide. Demps went on talking, staring at him moodily. "That's the lay, sure as such stuff stinks. Hell, I should of thought of him, right off. But I couldn't believe he'd take Bad Water and them other boys in the way he done. That bunch, they're old hands."

Jeff shook his head, not understanding all he knew about the setup. "But why is Garrett after you? You haven't been bothering him up here—have you?"

"Garrett wants this homestead, Tex," Demps answered him. "He needs it, now he's got caddle on the mesa. There ain't no trail up Cat or Paint Crick. There's a big dry canyon, west a ways, but he wants a watered trail. He sent Bowman up, last fall, to buy it off me. I told Strap no dice, and he warned me then they'd move me one way or another. Wate prides hisself on being fair, and giving a man every chance. First, he offers money. Then he sends a warning. After that, his exterminators take over."

Jeff scowled, impressed but not convinced. "But if Sundance was here to git you, why did he leave without?"

Demps laughed through his nose, sounding like a stud horse that is all hot and ready to go. "I expect he was like the Haw-Haw that was hunting bear. Found a track and followed it all day— then quit and went back to camp, because the track was getting too fresh! I expect Sundance figured he had found a bear track up here."

"But he had plenty chance, while he was here. Why didn't he take you from behind?"

For answer, Demps picked up the Winchester that leaned against the bars. A wide-winged marsh hawk was floating in lazy circles above the meadow, and Demps drew a bead. The rifle spanged, and the hawk jerked up in flight, then started a crazy dive for earth, streaming feathers out behind.

"I expect maybe that's why," Demps said punitively.

Jeff stood awhile, trying to think. No matter how he turned things in his head, they still looked bad.

"Well," he said, "if it comes to hauling freight, why don't you take your own advice? I'll go, if you'll go with me."

But Demps just laughed his stud-horse laugh, and took the paper back, crumpling it savagely in his hand.

"I'm staying where I goddam am!"

"All right. Then I stay."

Demps shook his head. "That's just what you ain't going to do. I . . . " *Bee-yowww!*

The high, whiny scream drove a hole through the valley silence, through whatever it had been that Demps had started out to say. Jeff saw the dust fly from Demps's shirt, as if someone had flicked it with a willow. Jeff heard a wet, meaty *plop*, and saw Demps knocked backward by an invisible fist. He saw Demps right himself and drop to one knee, the rifle in firing position.

117

Bee-yowwww. . . . bee-yowoweee. . . .

The savage cannonading there between the bluffs, the snarling scream of lead, the terrible unreal reality of it all, struck panic into Jeff that blotted out the world. When he found himself again, he was standing in the stable door, his unfired pistol in his hand. He was watching Sundance fall from the bluff across the corral, arms flapping like the wings of a great ungainly bird. He was watching Demps fold slowly over his now-silent rifle, settling slowly toward the ground.

9: The Hunted

By the time Jeff got to where he was, Demps was sprawled face down upon his rifle, his mouth open against the powdery manure that carpeted the corral. Jeff turned him over, and opened his shirt. There were three ragged wounds in his chest, two on the right side, one on the left side, close to where a heart as big as Demps's would have to be. A piece of pinkish rib bone protruded from one wound, and the flesh around was whitish, turning blue. All three holes hissed and bubbled as the hairy rib cage rose and fell.

"The son of a bitch," Demps said through clenched teeth. "He sure made a sieve out of me."

"You made snake meat out of him," Jeff answered. He found himself speaking between clenched teeth, as Demps was doing. There was an awful sickness in his stomach, a scalding shame that he had not been more account in the unexpected fight.

Demps's eyes were open now. He was breathing shallowly and watching Jeff with a strange expression of appealing trust. It occurred to Jeff that Demps was dependent on him for the first time in all their long association, and he tried desperately to chart a course of action. There was a canteen on the fence, and to start with, he fetched it. He held Demps's head up, so he could drink. But one of the slugs must have punctured the stomach, because water came out the hole, colored with blood.

"Can't even hold my water!" Demps said in measured, calm despair.

"Demps," Jeff said, coming to a decision, "I'm heading for Quadrille, to fetch a sawbones. You want I should git you up to the house first?"

Demps shook his head. "I need a sawbones about like a hog needs britches. Just leave me be a minute. In a little while, it won't matter what you do with me."

Grief weighed on Jeff until he couldn't breathe. This couldn't be happening. Not to Demps.

But it was.

"Hell," he said huskily, "you'll be all right. You're too damn tough to kill."

"In a hog's butt," the hurt man retorted with a ghost of his old profane vigor. "That sidewinder drove my tack. I'm dead from my ribs down, right now. . . . Go through him, would you, Tex? If you can find out what he is, I'd sort of like to know."

"We already know what he is," Jeff said. But he did as requested, glad to escape the intently watching eyes, glad to shuck the feeling of awful impotence that went with doing nothing.

He would leifer have touched a live rattler than the sprawled body at the foot of the bluff. But Demps was watching, and Demps was dying. He turned the body over with his foot, and saw the blood-matted clothes, the head that lolled grotesquely on one shoulder, the twisted gargoyle features, frozen forever in a snarling grimace.

The lifeless, colorless lumps of jelly which once had been eyes were upturned. Jeff looked away from them, held his breath so as not to inhale any of the smells, and made a quick but thorough search. All he found was a jackknife, a tobacco sack, and a whetstone.

Whoever he was, Sundance had traveled light.

"Look under his belt," Demps called. "If he's one of them Association animals, he's bound to have a badge somewhere."

Jeff unbuckled the belt, and pinned to its under side was a small metal shield. It was so worn he had to look close to read the raised lettering: *Inspector, Wyoming Stock Growers Association.*

He unfastened the badge and carried it back to Demps. The

hurt man inspected it, and loosed a dismal stream of invective upon all the dead man's kind.

"Wish I hadn't killed the fornicator! Wish I could kill 'im now —knowing what he is!"

The sun was hot, and Demps was sweating bad. He'd stopped bleeding outwardly, and there seemed only one thing to do. Jeff knelt and wrestled the hurt man up into his arms.

Demps swore at him, and begged to be left alone. But Jeff staggered down the path to the house, shoved open the door, and got him onto his bunk. Then he found a towel that was halfway clean, and started tearing it into strips.

"It's a waste of time and towel," Demps protested. "But if it will make you feel any better, go ahead."

Jeff bandaged up the wounds. Then, at a loss for anything else to do, he rolled a cigarette and started to put it in the hurt man's mouth. Demps shook his head. "Not now, Tex. It wouldn't help a bit."

He was silent awhile, his breath coming in irregular gasps. There was a blueness under his eyes and on his lips. Jeff knew that death was bereaving him again. Yet, while Demps still breathed, his mind refused to know it.

"I hate to mention this, Tex," Demps said in a minute. "I hate to wish a job like it on anybody. But you got to hide that thing down at the corral. They'll blame you for killing him, if you don't. I'll be where they can't git back at me, and they'll be for gitting at somebody. You're in the way around here, almost as much as I am. They'll hang you, Tex, if you let 'em find that stiff. They'll follow you to the end of the earth. They don't like people killing their exterminators and gitting by with it. That ever starts, it would ketch on big, you know. They got to nip you in the bud."

"Where'll I hide it, Demps?" Jeff asked dully.

"You could put it under right up there in the corral, with all the rest of it," Demps answered weakly. "You could move the manure pile a bit, and they'd never find the grave.

"You better do it, Tex," he went on, with rising, desperate urgency. "Your life ain't worth a nickel, if they find him. A jury in Colorado acquitted a fella two, three years ago, for killing one

of them cannibals. 'Quitted him, and handed him a vote of gratitude, for rendering a public service. But this ain't Colorado, kid.
They put high price tags on their hatchet men, up here!"

Jeff didn't see how he could bring himself to such a job, even
knowing that Demps was right. But Demps was fretting, so he felt
compelled to go along.

"I'll tend to it, Demps," he said.

Up at the stable, he found a round-bitted shovel and—without
a glance at the obscene thing that had been a man—scraped the
manure back from the ground, in close against the great heap
that had been shoveled from the barn in times past. Then he
started digging in the rich, black earth, finding it soft and easily
moved. He must have been six feet down before he struck bed-
rock.

Climbing up out of the oblong hole he'd made, he backed up
to the repulsive thing, took a boot in either hand, and like a horse
working between shafts dragged it to the grave. The killer had
pulled heavy woolen sox on over his boots, presumably to muffle
his footsteps and leave no tracks. One pulled off in Jeff's hand,
and it was the kind dispensed at Man Head.

The body was starting to stiffen, so he had no trouble toppling
it into the hole. The dead man's rifle and dropped pistol followed
the body, together with the pulled-off sock. He was starting to
shovel in dirt when he remembered the rest of the dead man's
outfit, wherever his horses were.

It was the hardest thing he'd ever done, just to walk away and
leave the grave unfilled, exposed to view. But he was playing for
keeps from this point on, and there seemed nothing else for it.
His dun was in the stable, and he didn't stop to saddle up. He
rode bareback down across the meadow, followed the tracks into
the breaks, and came upon the horses tied to the bars, switching
and kicking at the flies.

On the way back up, with the dead man's horses in tow, he
stopped in at the cabin. Demps was still alive, but not very much
alive.

"How you coming with your chores?" the dying man inquired.

"I'm still at 'em," Jeff confessed. "And it strikes me as a lot of unnecessary work. I could of just throwed him on top of that pile down there, and nobody would never have noticed. But, long as I got the hole dug, I figured I better heave his bedroll and warbag in. He'd left his horses at the bars, to circle back."

Demps smiled weakly. "Tex," he said, "you're still my candidate for Gov'nor, and Injun chief!"

The grave was two-thirds full of duffel, before he ever started to shovel in the dirt. After every dozen or so shovelfuls, he stopped and tamped the dirt in tight. Even so, he had almost half the pile left over when the hole was full. But the stable hadn't been cleaned for a good many months, and Jeff was a pilot from away back. By the time he'd got the place shoveled out, the pile had been enlarged sufficiently to hide the grave and surplus dirt.

He looked at the sun, and was surprised to find it still well up in the sky. You could still see where the manure pile had been recently enlarged, but the added portion had two or three hours yet to weather before the sun went down. And dung dried quickly in the sun.

Back at the cabin, he found Demps still living, but by a margin so narrow that it hardly counted. The handsome, square face already was white as Sundance's had been, the flesh sunk in around the bone. His voice was so hoarse and whispery that Jeff had to bend close to hear.

"You git Sundance under? . . . Good boy. Now I got another favor to ask, . . . Favor to me—favor to you."

The awful clawing urgency was in the tawny eyes again, and Jeff now felt up to anything.

"Name it," he said stolidly.

"I ain't got but a little longer, Tex. You're going to have to do something with this carcass, too, when I'm done with it. Authorities find it, it will start them thinking, nosing around. You got to hide me, too, kid, if you're going to be in the clear."

Words of assurance and malarky came to Jeff's tongue. But he didn't let them past his teeth. They both knew that Demps was finished. It seemed craven not to look at it.

"What you want me to do, Demps?"

"I'd like it," Demps said wistfully, "if you'd put me under down at the head of the meadow, where the salt lick is. I always liked it there, better 'n anywhere. You could move the salt trough, to cover up the scar, and the horses would tromp the dirt down. . . . Salt lick's almost as good as a corral, to hide a body you don't want around. I know, kid. I've used 'em once or twice, in my time. . . .

"Tex, I don't hanker to be buried in no corral."

"You won't be buried in no corral."

It was all said then. They looked at each other a time in silence, waiting for what had to come. Jeff suddenly felt impelled to say a thing that had been on his mind for hours.

"Demps, I'm sorry I didn't have the sense to tell you, when that bastard started nosing around me. I didn't figure you'd like it, if I said anything. If I had—"

Demps's face lighted with a pathetic shadow of his old smile. He laughed through his nose in the old Demps manner.

"Hell, Tex. Git shed of that sub-conscience mind you got. We don't count the ifs. If the dog hadn't stopped to piddle, he would have caught the rabbit. . . ."

The whispery voice strained as final tension filled the ruined body. The tension passed. Almost imperceptibly, the lights behind the tawny eyes went out, and Demps died as he had lived, unregenerate and defiant of the unfriendly world with which he'd ever been at odds, a ribald joke upon his lips. In a minute, it all was over, and Jeff stood looking down at him across a void the living mind could never bridge.

Feeling lonelier than he'd known a man could ever feel, moving like a sleepwalker, Jeff wrangled a couple of the horses and hitched them to the training cart. He pulled the cart up in front of the cabin door, then went inside, wrapped Demps up in his bloodstained quilts and roped him like a bedroll. After that, he stood awhile, trying to think of a prayer.

The only thing that came to mind was a kind of blasphemous parody of a prayer remembered from his boyhood. It was irreverent, and not a prayer at all. But it seemed somehow more appropriate for Demps than any real prayer, and Jeff didn't feel wicked letting the words run silently through his mind.

123

Our Father which art in heaven,
Hallowed by Thy name.
Thy kingdom come
On a big base drum.
It's high, low, jack, and the game. . . .

Digging was much harder at the head of the meadow, and the sky was starting to grow light to east by the time he'd filled in the second grave and placed the salt trough over the scar. Like the other trench, this one had been almost full before he'd started shoveling dirt in, and he had considerable surplus left over. This he loaded on the cart and hauled to the creek and dumped in a shallow. After that, he carried grain down from the stable to bait the horses around the trough, so that they would tromp the ground and give it a natural look.

He had unhitched the horses and turned them out and was just wondering if it would be any good to try to sleep when he saw two riders coming up across the meadow on the jump. His heart leaped up into his throat, and he started quickly to the house where his pistol was. Then he recognized the pair as Bad Water and Bitch Crick, of the horse gang, and his labored breathing eased. But, as they drew nearer, he was put back on edge by the sight of their drawn faces and hollow eyes, their winded, sweat-caked horses.

"Howdy, kid," Bad Water greeted with constrained urgency. "Where's Demps? Where's Sundance?"

These were questions Jeff had readied an answer to. He was pleased that he was able to speak it steadily. "They left here yesterday, on a ride down to the Platte. Sundance had some switchers spotted there that they figured to scout."

The two men exchanged a look. Bad Water shook his head. "Kid, if Demps left here with Sundance, you better not look for him back. We found out, a couple weeks after leaving here, that Sundance is a law spy. Had a posse waiting for us, up in the Big Horn, where we figured to unload the horses. Killed Pickens and Hard Pan and Mon Tan. Us and Dabs skun out. We grabbed one the posse, and sweated him some. He told us Sundance's real name is Hapgood. Spies for the Association, and works for Garrett. We hoped to find the snake still denned here."

Jeff stared blankly, scarcely hearing. Intelligence told him he should react for them, show surprise and horror at the revelation. But he was too wrung dry of feeling to make any show for them. He could only shake his head.

"Sundance acted awful queer, around here. But Demps didn't seem to notice."

"Demps was too damn trusting," Bitch Crick observed. "Big-hearted, to a fault."

"Demps didn't bring that piece of dung in here," Jeff said bitterly, finding feeling in him at last. "Sundance wasn't Demps's mistake!"

"That's right," Bad Water nodded. "He's our snake. We took him on at Rosebud. I didn't know him from Adam's ass. But we'd been seeing Stock Growers' dodgers on him, all the way from Yellowstone. Then Pockets got shot up, and left us short-handed. When that big rattler wanted to throw in with us, we figured he toted square."

"Stock Growers had a bunch of dodgers printed, and planted them on us!" Bitch Crick agreed, savage in his self-denunciation. "The oldest trick in the book, and we fell for it! God, I'd like to have the pimp in my sights for a minute!"

"Well, I wish you'd come a little sooner," Jeff said heavily. Then he caught himself. "They might come back, if you got time to wait."

Bad Water wagged his head. "They won't come back. I know how them buzzards work. Demps is rotting in some gulch by now, I reckon. Anyhow, there is a posse behind us."

Jeff stiffened. "A posse?"

Bad Water nodded, apologetically. "We done everything we could to lose them. But they wouldn't lose. They swung off to Man Head when we hit the Rustler—I expect to git fresh horses and maybe to notify the local sheriff. I reckon they'll be right along."

That news gave Jeff a bitter cud to chew on. He had fixed things there so he might have faced things through, with a little luck. But these two had to go and bring a posse in on him!

125

"Well, take your switchers with you, when you go," he said sharply. "We don't want them here."

"Ain't you coming with us?" Bitch Crick asked him in surprise.

Jeff laughed like a stud horse, through his nose. "I'm staying where I goddam am!"

The drovers didn't bother with taking their horses, as Jeff had ordered them to. They stopped at the house just long enough to fix a bait, then they rode down on the meadow, changed their saddles to fresh horses, and lit out along the upper trail. Jeff watched them from the cabin, and called them a hard name. But he didn't really care. He had no notion of trying to stay on at the homestead. His brag to the thieves had only been a dodge. He didn't figure to stay, and taste any more of Garrett's justice. But he didn't figure to ride with the fugitives, either.

The way Jeff looked at things, no one but Drake and the two drovers knew that he had been with Demps that summer. As quick as the thieves were gone, he intended to light a shuck himself. If he was crafty and hid his trail, he might get clean away and never even be thought of in connection with the horse ring.

The minute the thieves were out of sight, Jeff took a bait of grain from a sack in the stable and caught his dun and one-eyed mare. He took them to the corral and divided the rest of the oats between them, to build them for a grind. While they ate, he went down to the cabin to get his stuff together.

He'd gathered from the drovers' talk, from the leisurely manner in which they'd stayed to cook and eat a meal, that he had plenty of time. But he'd no more than got his bed rolled and roped when he heard voices down on the meadow. He jumped to the window, and his heart shriveled up to see ten men riding up across the bottoms, three of them leading pack horses. The foremost two looked like Gut Desmond and Wate Garrett. Strap Bowman was there, and a deputy of Desmond's, named Harper. The others he didn't know.

For a long minute, Jeff stood paralyzed, unable to move or think, his breath burning his lungs. He thought wildly of breaking from the cabin, of running up to get his dun and trying to make a break. But the posse was so near, he knew it would be suicide.

126

He knew, when he could think at all, that there was nothing for it now but to face things out.

Once he had made the admission, once he was resigned, a kind of calm came over him, and he set methodically about putting the place to rights. He unroped his bedroll and spread it, and set his warbag in the corner. Having thus destroyed all evidence of planned flight, he kicked dirt over a couple of bloodstains on the floor, and made certain there were no incriminating stains upon the bunk. Then he took up position by a crack in the shuttered window and began to wait.

The wait was not a long one. The possemen showed considerable interest in the horses on the meadow. But they kept riding, straight toward the cabin. Desmond's horse was almost against the door before he pulled rein. The others fanned out around him, and when all were set, Desmond rested his rifle across his pommel in such a way that it pointed straight at the door, then kicked on the cedar with the toe of his boot.

When Jeff pulled the door open, he found himself looking straight into the rifle's small black muzzle, inches from his face. The coldness in the mud-brown eyes above it put his skin to crawling. Knowing that he must not let his fear be seen, he feigned surprise.

"Well, howdy, men. What's this?"

"So you're still in the country, eh?" the sheriff said, obviously deriving no pleasure from the discovery.

"Any law against being in this country?" Jeff inquired.

No one answered him. To Jeff, it seemed that hours went by while the ring of hostile eyes probed and sounded him, as if looking for his fear.

"Is this the rider you fired, along with Rae, for mismarking cows?" Desmond asked finally.

"He's the one." Bowman nodded. "I advised him to make tracks out of the country. But some people can't take advice."

"This one can't," Desmond agreed. "I advised him the same way, when I had trouble with him in town, over the Pinkerton man that was killed two years ago."

Two men that Jeff didn't know edged their horses up to look him over.

"Looks ornery enough," one said.

"Yeah," the other nodded. "Kind of like he'd steal a horse."

It was unnatural, almost eerie, standing there and hearing them talk about him, as if he were a horse or cow that didn't know what was being said. It was worse to have them say things that made him sound like a Younger or Jesse James, and not have anything to say back.

"What you want?" he asked at last, his voice as strong as he could make it.

"Want you for one, I expect," Desmond answered. "We want Rae, too, and the rest that horse-thief outfit. Where-at are they?"

"What horse-thief outfit?" Jeff stalled.

"You know damned well. Where's Dempsey Rae?"

"I couldn't say."

Desmond glared at him. "You ain't learned a goddam thing, have you? Well, you better learn. We're looking for Rae. And we're looking for a Stock Association man, by name of Cis Hapgood."

Jeff shook his head. "I don't know no Cis Hapgood."

"Then you're a ignorant son of a bitch," the sheriff declared learnedly. "Hell, you had a fight with him, the day you tied on with that Texas trail herd, out of Quadrille. He would of made you hard to find, but Rae jumped on him while he was down. Liked to broke his neck."

"That wasn't Hapgood," Jeff disputed, playing out his hand. "That was an ornery-eyed Montanan, name of Sundance. He wasn't down when Demps jumped on him. He had a gun. I didn't."

Desmond let out his breath in a kind of wheeze. "If you're as ignorant as you let on, it ain't any wonder you're always in trouble to your haunches. Sundance is the name that Hapgood used, posing as a rounder to see what you cats was up to here. When was the last time you seen him?"

"That day out on Trail Crick, when they threw him on the wagon to take him into town."

Desmond glowered. "Look. We're after a horse-thief ring we know hangs out here. Horses are right down there in the field, and you're up here. Where you think this lying will git you?"

128

"I don't know nothing about no thieves," Jeff insisted. "I don't know where Demps is, nor nobody else. I only got in here last night. There wasn't nobody around."

"Got in from where?"

"Nebraska, where I spent the winter and part the summer, working and looking for work."

"You mean you did leave the country—and didn't have sense enough to stay away?"

Jeff looked at him and didn't answer. Desmond turned to Bowman.

"Does that square?"

Bowman nodded. "He was out around there, some. Mostly in jail and riding grub line. They run him out of every place he tried to stop."

"Tell him why, now!" Jeff challenged.

"Because smart cowmen don't hire no known thief to work for them. That's why."

Jeff stared the sneering green eyes away, but the victory brought no sense of triumph.

"Let me git your story straight," Desmond said craftily. "You say you didn't git here until last night. Everybody was gone, and you ain't seen nobody since."

Jeff started to nod, but his mind detected the trap in time. The posse had tracked Bad Water and Bitch Crick to the valley. Their jaded horses were down on the meadow in plain sight.

"Well—there was two men passed here, an hour or so ago. Said somebody'd stole some horses from them, and they were on the track. They asked for a meal and fresh horses to keep up the chase. I was here alone. I couldn't see no way to refuse 'em."

Desmond's eyes were baleful. "You're either ignoranter than I figured, else goddam smart. I expect we'll find out which. Harper, git down and have a look inside that robber's roost."

Harper stepped inside the cabin, and soon reappeared. "Story seems to square, far as it goes. A dozen bunks in there, but only one bed and outfit. Stove's been cooked on lately, and three men ate since the dishes got washed."

Desmond looked around at Garrett. "I don't git the lay. Didn't Hapgood say he'd hold Rae here?"

Garrett nodded and spoke for the first time, though his eyes had been busy from the first. Busy with Jeff and other objects around. "That was the plan. Apparently it didn't come off."

Jeff stared lingeringly at the man who by his words confirmed that he had sponsored the murder of Dempsey Rae.

Desmond grunted. "Well, we all better light, and snoop around. Keep a eye peeled for any gear that might be Hapgood's. And watch for places a man could hide in—alive or dead. There's something rotten here, and I aim to find what. Strap, how about you watching the prisoner?"

"It ain't a easy job for eyes," Strap said cheerfully. "But I guess somebody got to do it."

With the exception of Strap, the possemen all moved off to search. Even Garrett swung down and poked inquisitively around the place he evidently had not visited until that day.

Jeff almost suffocated when they first started snooping around the corrals, even though the manure pile looked natural to his eye, and Bad Water and Bitch Crick hadn't noticed anything. When Desmond shouted something from the stable, his knees went too weak to hold him, and he had to lean against the wall behind him. But when the sheriff came moping back, he only had one question.

"I noticed you just grained your horses. Like maybe you'd figured some on pulling out."

"I always keep my horses ready for riding," Jeff told him.

Desmond sneered. "I'll bet by-God you do!"

Strap Bowman had untied a coil of rope from his saddle strap and was fussing with it. Jeff tried not to notice the hangman's knot he fashioned.

"Today, you're going to wish you'd took the advice I give you, when I amputated you from Man Head," Strap predicted, when the noose was ready.

Harper drifted back to join them. He looked at the loop in Strap's rope, and quickly looked away. Even Desmond pretended not to notice the hanging knot, and Jeff began to comprehend that it was a Man Head posse, strictly. If Garrett and Bowman meant to hang him then and there, the law would not attempt to interfere.

130

"Nothing much around," one of the strangers told Garrett. "Saddle and some harness, up in the cave they use for a stable. Nothing that looks like Hapgood."

No one seemed to think it strange that the stable had been freshly cleaned, the manure pile lately enlarged. But Jeff didn't dare to hope. The posse was reassembling at the cabin, and Strap kept tossing his noose down to the ground at Jeff's feet, and jerking it back.

Old Man Garrett seemed more interested in the homestead than in any thieves or missing spies. Long after the others had all congregated back at the cabin, the ranchman kept poking around with a casual air of proprietorship, calling attention to this and that which took his eye: the natural corrals that opened into each other as neatly as if engineered by man; the stable that could be enlarged to any size and still be warm; the way the ringing bluffs made fences unnecessary.

"Odd how a man can be sixteen years in this country, and miss a place like this," he remarked almost cordially to Jeff. "How did Rae happen to stumble on it?"

"It's right cozy," Jeff answered him, only vaguely aware that he was quoting someone else. "Only one trail out, and one trail in. Demps has got bars across them both."

"I asked you a civil question," Garrett growled. "I expect a civil answer."

Jeff looked at him steadily. "The only civil question I ever heard was how-de-do."

Desmond struck him an open-handed blow that knocked his head against the log wall. Jeff swore at him, and Desmond would have struck again, but Garrett interfered.

"No need to manhandle him, Gut. I don't object to a man with spirit."

"Well, I object to this one here," Desmond complained, looking like a dog that has been scolded. "I still don't git the lay. There any chance Hapgood was wrong—about this being the hideout?"

"Damn slim chance," Strap answered. "Cis is an old hand at this game. He don't make mistakes."

"I'm not too sure," Garrett said softly, his beady eyes on Jeff.

"I'm thinking he may have made a *big* mistake here. His last one, maybe."

Jeff looked at the ground, for fear his eyes would betray him. The others stood around, watching him. Bowman kept tossing the hangman's knot down by his boots, and jerking it back again. There got to be a kind of hypnosis in its regular fall and pull. Jeff found himself wishing they would get on with whatever they figured to do.

"Well," Garrett said finally, "we're kind of falling down on the job. We know two of the gang are somewhere ahead of us. We've wasted a good hour here already."

"Strikes me we got a job right here, before we go on to any others," Strap said, tossing his rope again. "Any them cottonwoods down yonder by the crick would do just fine."

Garrett shook his head. "We are law-abiding citizens, Strap. Besides, we may want that boy as a witness, before we're done. Harper can take him to Quadrille, while the rest of us ride that trail."

Bowman didn't look pleased. But neither did he argue.

It didn't seem that anyone argued with Wate Garrett.

10: The Informer

The Quadrille jail was a little stone block with heavy walls and small barred windows. The cells inside were formed of two-by-six planks set broad-face-to, forming a solid partition six inches thick. Jeff's window was too high to look out of, and there was only a little peek-hole through the door. His cell furniture included, exactly, a bunk, a blanket, a broken chair, a bucket for his body wastes. The room was on the south, sweltering hot by day, too cold for just one blanket at night.

Jeff spent his first two or three days of confinement trying to contrive methods of escape. But the jail was built on a different order from the one he had dug out of in Nebraska, and Harper took no chances when bringing him food. After a while, he stopped thinking about escape—and all else. He spent as much of the time as he could in sleep, and in his waking hours he found that he could suspend all thought processes and be conscious in his body only. Thinking was a migraine he could not endure, and once he'd mastered the trick of wakeful sleeping, he managed to pass the days and nights without flying his track.

One breathless afternoon during the second week of his incarceration, he heard Gut Desmond's cawing voice, out in the corridor between the rows of cells. "I'll fetch the bronco out. We'll see what he can tell us."

The bolt was shot, the door swung inward. Desmond's pear-shaped form was revealed, pistol in one hand.

"Come on, Cocky. I want you to look at a couple men, and tell me who they are."

Jeff stood up, welcoming any diversion from his cell. Desmond snapped steel cuffs upon his wrists, then shoved him down the hall toward the office. His heart went down into his stomach when he saw Bad Water and Bitch Crick chained together, guarded by Harper's rifle.

Both thieves looked at him the way the brakie had looked at him in the train station an eternity ago, and the look angered him now as it had done before. They didn't need to be afraid of him.

Jeff felt Desmond watching him narrowly, and turned his eyes to objects on the street outside the open door. Desmond cleared his throat.

"Well? You ever see that pair before?"

Jeff shook his head. "Not that I remember."

Desmond swore in exasperated anger. "By God, if you ain't the hidebound little diehard! Well, I'll tell you something. I'm putting the three of you on bread and water till I find out what happened to Cis Hapgood. . . . You're going to git awful sick of bread and water."

The sheriff's prediction didn't exactly pan out. After three days on the diet, Jeff wolfed his two slices of bread night and morning like a hungry dog, and would have begged for more if he'd thought begging would have got him more.

By the fourth day, hunger was a clamor in his gut that reduced his status to that of a ravening animal—nervous, unsleeping, savagely fretful. By the sixth day, hunger was dulled, and he felt

133

weak and listless, but less restive. Nor did anyone come to bother him. After the one interview in the office, Desmond left him strictly to himself. He saw no one but Harper, and Harper only at mealtimes. In all six days, he never got a word out of the deputy, and finally he gave up trying.

It was sometime on the seventh day that he heard the sheriff's voice out in the corridor again. "This here is the bronco's stall. If Harper will hold these trays, I'll let you in."

The lock creaked, and the door pushed open, and the smell of good cooked meat took him by the throat like a hand. It tied his stomach in a quivering knot, and he would have vomited if he could. Never before in all his life had he smelled a smell so sickening good.

A man he had never seen before came into the cell, and as the door swung shut behind his caller, Jeff had a glimpse of Desmond and Harper, the latter holding a steaming food tray in either hand. The food smell lingered in the hot, dead air, and Jeff closed his eyes, too ill in mind and body to have any interest in his visitor.

"So you're Jeff Jimson!"

Cigar smoke was driving out the smell of food. For a minute, it made Jeff sicker than ever. He didn't open his eyes or try to answer.

"I'm John Poe, attorney for the Man Head company. I want to talk to you."

Jeff continued to lie where he was, eyes closed, the sickness alternating from his stomach to his mind. He heard the chair creak as his visitor sat upon it. The cigar smoke got thicker, more nauseating.

"Don't you think it's about time you got next to yourself, kid, and come clean on this Hapgood business?"

Jeff closed his eyes tighter. "Go to hell," he said, emphatically as he could.

There was a kind of swallowed chuckle. "Sure. I know. My old man can lick your old man. I can spit farther 'n you or any your relations. I ain't forgot, kid."

Jeff opened his eyes and looked at his visitor with stirring interest. He wore wrinkled store clothes and had an ageless, wrinkled face. His hooded eyes looked bored and cynical; his full-lipped mouth was shaped to a perpetual leer. A stiff whiskey breath explained the congested network of blue veins about his nose.

"I'm here to offer you a deal, kid."

Hope surged up in Jeff, only to die a-borning. His voice sounded like a crow's.

"A deal?"

"I been talking with Garrett. He's got some kind of interest in you—God knows why. Thinks you're a square toter that just got off on the wrong foot. Says you rode for him once, out at Man Head, and done good until you got in with the wrong kind of company. Says he'd like to reinstate you, give you back your job and take you off the blacklist—if you can cut the mustard."

Jeff's breathing went all loose on him. Hunger struck at him again, and somewhere in it was the picture of a heart-shaped face with blue eyes. It was a face—a hunger—he had kept out of his consciousness ever since his return from Nebraska. This was like a last-minute reprieve to a man sentenced to the gallows. He was afraid for a minute he was going to blubber.

"What's his price?"

"Just that you do your duty as a citizen, and tell us the straight of this damned Hapgood affair that's got the whole territory in an uproar with the Stock Growers. That's the sum and total of what he wants, just to git that settled. Wants you to prove you're in the clear, so he can take you on again."

Jeff closed his eyes and let the awful weakness fill him. Let the hunger rise and ravage him like fever—the food hunger and the whole bigger hunger that eating had never appeased. He let his mind tell him that this was Abby's work, that she had pressured her father into freeing him. He pictured riding at the ranch again, riding with Abby, racing her across the meadows, dancing with her at the dances. He let the whole dream flower for just an instant, then snapped the curtains together, obliterating the picture as he would snuff out a candle. He was wet with perspiration, and wished that he were dead. They wanted him to take a knife and cut out of himself the one thing he'd managed to keep unsullied. He wanted to do the same thing. But there was a fence before him which he could not scale. A line in his mind he could not cross.

135

He groaned and took a breath. "I've told 'em all I know."

Poe sighed. The chair squeaked as he stirred. "Come on, now, kid. Take the advice of somebody who's been through the mill, and climb down off your high horse. If your friend Rae is alive, and if he killed Hapgood, you'd better tell us how and where he is. Loyalty's a fine thing, but you're in trouble, and it's high time you started thinking of yourself. Garrett knows you been used hard. He sees you're young, and wants to give you another chance. But he can't help you, if you won't let him. . . . And if Dempsey's dead, why not come clean? Save your loyalty for yourself. Don't waste it on them carrion birds at Ekard, or in that other cell."

Jeff could see the fairness, the logic in the lawyer's argument. But the line in his mind remained. They didn't have anything sure on Bad Water and Bitch Crick, or they wouldn't be sweating him this way. He couldn't tell about Demps and Sundance, without telling the whole yarn. It was all one or all the other. He wouldn't pull a Roddy, no matter what they did to him. They could even hang him, like they'd done Rebel Jimson. They wouldn't make him sing.

"I told 'em all I know," he repeated, his voice sullen now.

Poe sighed again, and stood. "I'm sorry, if that's your decision. You don't leave us any choice. We're charging you with murder, kid."

"Go ahead and charge."

"We will, but we don't like it. We don't think you done it. But all the evidence points your way. You won't let us help you. So the law will have to take its course."

"Evidence?" Jeff sneered. "What evidence?"

"To start with, we have the word of that pair of deuces in the other cell that you are lying about the date of your return from Nebraska. They say you were in on the horse-thief ring, with Rae, and were there with him at the hideaway all summer. They say that Hapgood stayed there with the two of you, when they headed for the Big Horn with the horses. They say they found out who he was, and came back to kill him. They say you told them you'd already took care of him."

Jeff felt the blood draining from his head. He stared at the leering face, incredulous and stunned. Then fury flamed in him. He started up from the bed.

"You mean them tinhorns blabbed?"

Poe shrugged vastly. "Why, I thought you knew. Where you think Harper was bound to, with them platters? They're eating beefsteak right now, with hot potatoes, and gravy, and bread with lots of butter."

Jeff stood up slowly. Fury was a fire that consumed hunger and reason and everything but rage.

"They are lying sonsabitches! I never told them no such thing. I told them the same as I told the posse. I told 'em to take their damned horses, and never bring no more. But they wouldn't even do that much. They left me up against the blaze. Now they're telling lies to git me hung. Well, I can sing as loud as they can. But I can tell the truth. I can prove what I say, too, 'cause I know where the bodies are."

Poe leaned back in his chair, and took the cigar from his mouth. "Tell me all about it, kid," he said gently.

Jeff told him. Told everything, starting with his first meeting with Demps and Sundance. He told about getting fired from Man Head, and about leaving the country, about what he'd run into, trying to get work elsewhere. He told of going back and finding Demps with the horse herd, of the gang's coming—Bad Water and Bitch Crick with the others. Of the warning note pinned to the stable door, and Sundance's bushwhack try. He told how Demps and Sundance killed each other, and about Demps advising him to hide the bodies. He told how he'd done it, and where, and how.

"I didn't know what else to do," he finished in a whisper. "Demps said you'd hang me, if you found the bodies. I figured he was right, after the other treatment I got here. Maybe I done wrong. But I didn't know nothing else to do. I figured to quit the country, but that posse got up there too soon. Now you can string me up or any goddam thing you want, and I won't give a good goddam!"

Jeff was in tears before he'd done. He sat on the bunk and hid his face in his hands. Poe rose and walked over to clap him on the shoulder.

"Ain't nobody going to hang you, kid. Not now. Wate Garrett is heavy-handed in his ways, and sometimes thinks he's God. But when he says a thing, you can put his word in the bank and write checks on it. He offered you a deal, and it stands. He didn't want to hang you, or I wouldn't be here. I just need to git your statement down in writing now, is all."

The lawyer sat beside him on the bunk, produced pencil and paper and wrote rapidly, questioning Jeff from time to time to clarify his memory or an obscure point. Sometimes their glances would meet, and it seemed to Jeff that behind the lawyer's sneer he could see something of kindness, something of understanding and good will.

"Just one other thing," the inquisitor said when the story was all on paper. "I'm not quite clear what the relationship was between Rae and Drake, when Rae was mavericking."

Jeff's voice hung fire. It didn't seem quite right to inform on Drake, too. But now he'd started spilling, he found a kind of hateful pleasure in the process. It was like squeezing pus and poison from a badly festered wound.

"Drake paid Demps ten dollars a head for everything he branded in the Flying D."

"Where did Drake market the stuff?"

"Railroad camps, and butcher shops, wherever he could. Sold a lot to Mercer's shop, right here in town. The Drovers House bought Drake beef, and the Warbonnet, too. They'd send buggies out to Ekard, to pick it up."

Poe wrote some more, then stood up. "Good boy, Jimson," he said. "We'll have you out of here, as quick as I git these notes wrote up and your John Henry on them. In the meantime, I'll have Desmond bring you in some chuck."

His voice was hearty, as was his smile. But the eyes that looked at Jeff were coldly contemptuous again. Oddly enough, his scorn seemed directed at himself as much as at Jeff.

"I'll git the word to Garrett right away," he said. "You'll git your meal and cowboy job, and old John Poe will git a nice pat on the head. Ain't people bastards, though?"

Long after the strange cynic had taken his leave, Jeff sat on his bunk, staring blankly at the floor. The lawyer's odd, inverted scorn notwithstanding, he couldn't find it in himself to regret the thing he'd done. The dream in whose name he had turned informer wouldn't come convincingly to mind, but he felt somehow revenged on an unfriendly world, as on two peaching tinhorn thieves. He also felt vaguely that his act had changed him radically, had somehow made him over into a different person. He now felt a stranger to himself, a man whose behavior he could never again predict.

It was another week before he learned that the whole matter of the thieves talking had been put up—that Bad Water and Bitch Crick hadn't told the law a thing, that the food trays shown him through the door had only been a part of the frame.

But, by then, it didn't seem to matter.

part 2

11: Rifle Mountain

The day Jeff Jimson left the county jail, a free man, was a day he didn't soon forget. He'd been allowed to shave, and Harper fetched him some clothes the county apparently had inherited from some earlier nonpaying guest. They weren't new, and they didn't fit any better than the law allowed. But they covered a man's nakedness, and Jeff was glad to have them.

The few townspeople on the street looked at him curiously as he walked down the all but deserted thoroughfare, in company with a now tolerant if not benevolent Gut Desmond. But his stomach was comfortably full, and the morning sun was warm. And, for the first time in two years, he felt like a respectable human being—a law-abiding citizen with a future whose promise seemed to make life worth living.

He did feel low and crawly minutes later, inside Poe's dingy office, when Strap Bowman sneered at him, and he didn't even dare return the look. But Garrett was more civil, and that made up somewhat for Strap's insolent, bracing grin.

"So you want to come back and ride for us again, eh?" the old man said, breaking off a conversation with Poe as Jeff came in. "You think you've learned a bit since last time, and would like another chance."

Despite the kindness of his tone, the magisterial scolding struck a spark of the old defiant obstinance inside Jeff. But the fire was quickly quelled. Old Garrett had called the turn. Jeff had learned a bit, and learned it well.

"I'd like another chance," he agreed tonelessly, careful not to look at Bowman.

"Well—" The old man's gaze was thoughtful. "Mr. Bowman and I are bound for Cheyenne on business that will keep us for several days. But they're readying things for the roundup out at the ranch, and I suspect they could use you right away. I'll give you a note to hand to Powers. He's the man in charge of things, while Strap's away. Do you know the way out?"

"I can find it," Jeff said reverently.

The ranchman borrowed pen and paper from the lawyer, and scribbled a few words. He borrowed an envelope, and sealed it before passing it over. Jeff tried not to snatch at it, but lost no time getting it in his hand.

"Any personal items you might need you can draw at the commissary," the old man went on. "They will be charged against your account, and paid for in installments up to one-half of your check. Any other questions?"

Jeff hesitated awkwardly, wondering about transportation out. It was on his tongue to request permission to ride his dun out and send him back in to Hitch's right away. But after he'd considered it, he decided not to give Bowman another chance to dress him down.

"No questions," he said levelly.

But Garrett seemed to read his mind, and glanced at Poe. "John, you'll be driving out today, to pick up those land papers, won't you? Why don't you take the boy along?"

"I'll be leaving in an hour," Poe said to Jeff.

"I'll be down at Hitch's, where my stuff is," Jeff informed him. Then, anxious to escape Strap's leering gaze, he thanked Garrett with as much grace and dignity as he could muster, and walked outside—down to explain his release to Hitch, and to arrange to have his horses boarded at the livery corral until he could make other arrangements for them.

"Why not git shut of them—long as you don't need them any more?" Hitch demanded. "Or do you figure on gitting the can again?"

"I don't figure on gitting the can again," Jeff told him. "But I'd hate to be without a horse. Old Clay there is a Texian. I'll pay you by the month—if that's all right."

Once the town had sunk into the tawny sea behind Poe's high-strung team, the rutted road snaked north across rolling plain and prairie toward a long black mountain climaxed by twin black peaks, which Poe identified as Rifle Mountain. Gunsight Pass, he said, was in the V between the peaks, with Laramie River and the Medicine Bow beyond.

The road crossed Rustler River at an easy ford, then angled west toward the mouth of a narrow flank valley watered by a tributary which Poe identified as Little Rustler. Jeff thought wryly of Demps's allegation that Garrett was the biggest rustler around, and wondered if the name were not something of a joke. But he cannily refrained from voicing such a heresy.

For some time the terrain had been altering perceptibly, and here, where the Little Rustler Valley opened, it was such country as he had never seen before, not even in imagination. Unrelieved by foothills or tableland, mountains rose massive and black with pine, shaggy with aspen and smaller brush on the lower slopes and in the draws. The valley itself was about three miles wide at its mouth, and extended back into the rocky uplift five or six times as far. On either side, the black pine slopes leveled onto gray sage flats that gave way in turn to endless string meadows at the center —spreading out in two directions from the dense tree and brush hedge that marked the course of the Little Rustler.

High above the sheltered basin, sweeping timbered slopes were capped by sawtooth peaks that pierced the sky like fangs. Excepting only the hidden valley on Hurricane Creek, Jeff had never seen land that so took his eye.

Passage in and out of the land-locked reserve was blocked by a high, taut, barbwire fence, pierced by a narrow fenced lane that ran to the ranchstead proper, a mile or so away. There, deep among the pluming cottonwoods, stood a great white stone-and-lumber house, surprisingly similar to mansions Jeff had seen in Kansas City, complete even to curlicues and gingerbread trimmings. Around the house, partly hidden by the trees, clustered a small city of outbuildings, the whole surrounded by an elaborate system of stout and stylish pine-pole corrals. On above, still other wire and buck-pole fences divided the valley bottom into fields and pastures where horses and cattle grazed.

"That house," John Poe announced, continuing his role of teacher-tourist guide, "was Wate's concession to the actress girl he married back East and fetched out here to sleep with. Hired an architect from New York and turned him over to Abigail the First, and told him to give her what she wanted—and to hell with the cost. Shipped wood and rock here from all over the country, and hauled it from Quadrille with mule teams. Took two years to build it, and his wife sickened and died almost before they got moved in. Some people call it Garrett's Castle. But a friend of mine has no respect for nothing. Calls it Vulgar Manor."

Jeff looked at it in awe and envy. Including Kansas City, even, he didn't think he'd ever seen anything so grand. The fact that it was Abby's home, the house in which she had been born and reared, gave it an aura of holiness—like a temple of some kind. He felt a strong desire just to walk up and touch it. His mind could scarcely conceive of its being made of just ordinary wood and stone.

The road passed through a high portaled gate whose crosspiece was conspicuously marked with the Man Head emblem, and entered a yard which was the scene of a bewildering bustle—an industry as varied and intense as that of a cavalry post readying a regiment for war. A dozen wagons stood around, some canvas-hooded, some with hickory bows in place but covers off, some blocked up with wheels off, some with boxes removed to permit repairs to the running gears. The smoke-grimed blacksmith shop in the center of the yard clanged to the ring of iron on iron. From every direction came the sound of carpentry, and in the dusty corrals horses were being roped and shod and roached.

143

In all, Jeff reckoned a hundred men were there, hard at it, and not an idler in sight.

Poe pulled up at a hitching rail near the dooryard gate, and ordered Jeff to secure the team. Jeff complied, and by the time he'd finished, the lawyer was through the gate, closing it behind him.

"I imagine you'll find Powers somewhere around," he said by way of farewell.

Jeff wistfully watched him go up the graveled path, onto a wide veranda that extended the whole width of the house, and into a door at which he did not bother to knock. When the door slammed shut without bringing sign of Abby, he turned reluctantly back to the scene of industry. No one paid him the slightest attention as he drifted about, and finally he approached an elephantine, red-faced man who was repairing a cupboard in the back end of a wagon box.

"Excuse me, mister," he said humbly. "I'm looking for a man named Powers."

The perspiring carpenter turned, removed a dozen nails from his mouth, and nodded at a tall, gray man just emerging from the blacksmith shop. Then, still not having uttered a word, he put the nails back between his teeth and resumed his labors.

The tall man read Garrett's note, pushed it back at Jeff, and pointed at the carpenter Jeff had just accosted.

"Report to Hambone Hawley, over yonder," he said shortly, not once having looked squarely at Jeff. "He needs a nighthawk."

Jeff returned to the cupboard builder and announced his identity and assignment. The fat man straightened from the sawhorse he was kneeling on, looked him over without interest, and spoke with the nails still in his mouth.

"Find a jack and some dope, and grease these wheels. Then oil the harness in the box and see what it needs doing to. After that, we'll check the tents and tarps, and you can grind my axe and knives. Don't just stand there like we didn't have more to do than six men could do in the twice the time."

Must be a cook, Jeff remarked silently, turning to start his labors.

When darkness put an end to work, Jeff supped with the others by lantern light in the big cookhouse, and was served such a meal as he'd always thought the bullionaires would reserve for their own tables, strictly. Afterward, he was tapped to help wash the mountains of dishes and pans that had accumulated on the table by the stove. When he'd finished, he stepped out into the yard, and found a big fire going down beside the river, with thirty or forty of the crew around it. He started over and had reached the outer fringes of the circle when he was brought up by the talk.

". . . Well, I'm plumb sure he's the one. Him and Strap got into it at that benefit dance—and over Abby, too. He hit Strap like I never seen no man hit, never. Knocked him ass over appetite, and wrecked the table where all the ladies' suppers had been set. We ganged up to throw him out, and danged if he didn't clean half the crowd before we fixed his clock."

"Well, if that's the case, what's he doing working here? Ever I knock Strap on his one-spot, I'll either run for pres-i-dent or hook the next boat for South America."

"Aw, this kid's horny. He rode for the outfit once, two, three years ago. Him and that longhorn, Dempsey Rae, they got to burning brands on Man Head calves, and Strap tied the can to them. Then they joined the horse-thief gang that knocked off the Stock Growers man this spring. The kid put the finger on them for that, and killed his pardner, Rae. Story is, he was working for Garrett the whole time, just to spy them out. So, his mavericking and that fight with Strap was all put up . . ."

Jeff heard no more. The blood was pounding in his head, and the breath he breathed was fire inhaled. He started headlong for the center of the circle, but his arm was caught from the side in fingers that seemed made of iron. He fought with all his strength to tear himself free, but all his strength was not enough. The arm was twisted into a hammerlock, and his neck was caught in a kind of vice. Helpless, he was shoved out of the firelight, over toward the bunkhouses. After a while, he was allowed to stop, and Powers' voice spoke laboredly at his ear.

"I've heard of you, Jimson, and the kind of name you've got. That note from Garrett said to give you a try, and so I've got no choice. But you start any trouble around this outfit, and you've had your try. Now I hope a word to the wise is sufficient."

Jeff was tense a minute, all his muscles and all his innards tied into aching knots. Then he caved, and went loose all over. "All right," he said. "You can let me go. I won't make no trouble."

The bunkhouse being overcrowded, he spread his bedroll by the creek that night, and the stars were growing dim before the burning in his stomach cooled enough to let him sleep. But he was among the first in the cookshack in the morning, and while the latecomers were still at table, he was at the commissary by the granaries, fitting himself out with clothes. The clerk put no limit on the purchases he could make, on tick, and once again he made the most of an opportunity. Into the new warbag went three blue flannel army shirts, three pairs of brown checkered hard-weave wool pants, four red wool union suits, a dozen pairs of sox, and two bright red scarfs. For a hat, he chose a fancy fur-felt sombrero, not flat-crowned like the Texian hats but tall and pointed, like the peaks.

The only pair of boots in stock that he would have been caught wearing were flashy handmade, hickory-peg Hyers with Morocco tops and fancy stitching. They were about a size too small, and he couldn't get his feet in them with sox on. But no others would do him, so he pulled the sox off and greased his feet with wagon dope, and shoved them in, bare. Compared with the rest of his equipment, the old gun and belt he'd inherited from Demps looked shabbier than ever, so he bought a big bone-handled .45, with elaborately tooled holster and belt to match.

The clerk tallied his bill and whistled. "You'll be a long time working this off, doc."

"So what if I am?" Jeff shrugged. "I ain't going no place."

He shaved in the bunkhouse, and emerged minutes later smelling of camphor and looking the way he figured the well-dressed cowboy ought to look: booted and spurred and scarfed—his pants so tight that wrinkles in his drawers were visible. But his spirits went down somewhat when catcalls started coming from the filling yard around him.

"Hey, by God! Do you see that!"

"Yeah. Ain't that purty?"

"Where in hell's the dance?"

"We got no chance with Abby now!"

146

Jeff realized as the hoorawing went on that the clothes were a social error, and he suddenly wished them all at the bottom of the Little Rustler. But, being committed, he set his face against his tormentors and tried not to let his feelings show. At this, he was tolerably successful until Hambone Hawley looked up from his resumed carpentry at the chuck wagon, and stared wide-eyed.

"Well, you sure do cut a rusty this mawning, boy. You still a-courting the Old Man's chick?"

Jeff glanced in the direction of the house in spite of himself, and then had added cause for grievance. "What the hell is it to you or anybody else around here what I wear for clothes?" he flared. "Why don't you just leave me be?"

Hambone looked at him awhile, then shook his head as if bewildered by what he saw. "It ain't nothing to me, son, what you wear. Fine feathers make fine birds. But I don't misdoubt you'll be the best-dressed jinglebob at the roundup."

Hating him, Jeff turned away.

Hawley said no more about his clothing, but the others kept up a desultory badgering until Powers put an end to the pastime with a few brief remarks of which Jeff caught the gist but not the words. After that, he was discussed in undertones, and only a few snatches of the talk reached his ears.

"What you say his name is?"

"I dunno. Texas River, somebody said."

"Sounds like a name he just assumed."

"Well, he sure assumed some duds."

Throughout most of the day, Jeff and Hambone were kept busy resetting their wagon's tires at the forge in the smithy. Jeff had now perceived, in a vague but surely felt fashion, that his mistake in the matter of the clothes was simply one of having made himself conspicuous at the wrong time. He guessed the damage was done, but the smithy was an ideal place to take the shine off bright new shirts and pants. By night he didn't look so fine.

All day, off and on, he watched the house for sign of Abby. But there was no sign. Shunned by everyone in the yard, ignored even by Hambone except when there were instructions to be given, he felt himself as much alone, as much an outcast, as on his long and lonely ride the year before. The feeling grew on him

147

as night advanced, and when he'd swallowed a hasty supper and was sitting alone on the creek bank, listening to the water's worried mutter, a feeling of homesickness came over him. A loneliness for Demps and the place on Hurricane—even for Drake's place and the drinks and girls. For almost anything but this.

The fact of Demps's death now struck him fully for the first time. Before—at the homestead and in the jail—he'd been too much concerned with his own difficulties to really take it in. He tried to conceive of that robust body as being void of life, the tawny eyes unseeing, the lewd tongue stilled forever, and such desolation descended on him that for a time he couldn't even hate the men who had brought about the death.

"He was the only friend I ever had," he said aloud, seeing the truth so clearly that he wanted to die himself.

After a while, he heard a step beside him, and looked up to find Hambone standing over him, his big bland face oddly similar to the moon which revealed it.

"What you setting off here all by your lonesome for, son? Why don't you come on over and join the sociability?"

"I'm in good company," Jeff said gruffly.

Hambone sighed and turned back toward the yard. "You might be. But there is a difference of opinion, you know. You could be right and all the rest the world wrong. But there's odds against it."

The next morning, Powers met Jeff just outside the cookhouse and took him to the corrals to point out a bunch of horses. "That there is the string that goes with Hambone's wagon," he explained. "Six head for each the riders, a four-up team for both the Bains, and two horses each for you and the day wrangler. Seventy-two head in all. You'll ride that little stockinged black and the old rat-tailed Appaloosa over there by the fence. Now I figure we'll be shoving in the morning, so you better be gitting acquainted with the string, gitting them bunch-broke, and so on. So fetch your saddle and take them out to pasture. Stay with them all day, and see how they hold together."

The Appaloosa looked a sight more cordial than the little black, but Jeff didn't feel he could afford to admit that the black had him scared. So when he'd got his gear collected, he took his rope inside the corral, built a loop and kept the band milling until the black worked out of the circle, giving him a favorable throw. He made the cast free and easy, and the loop flew true.

There were saddle tracks on the pony's sides, but he was snaky and touchy about the head. So when Jeff had him snubbed, he used his new bandana for a blindfold while he applied saddle and bridle. Then he tied up one foot, the way Demps had shown him, while he climbed aboard. Once the rope and blind were off, the pony went into executive session and blew the lid. Jeff was put to it to stay in the stirrups.

"Pour the bud to 'im!" Powers shouted irately. "Straighten the mother-lover out, before you stir the whole bunch up. This here ain't any fairground!"

Jeff set his spurs and fought the reins. The black's response was to throw its head up and strike him in the face. Angered, he spurred again, and worked the rebel down the hind legs with the ribbons. After another moment's desperate struggle, the black yielded, acknowledging another master.

Jeff felt he'd acquitted himself with honors, and expected to find himself the center of attraction at the ranch. But when he looked around, Powers was opening the pasture gate, and no one else seemed to have noticed him at all.

"Come in tonight, in time to eat," Powers yelled at him, ducking back from the stampede that roared out the gate. "This'll be the last night's sleep you'll git in weeks."

After a time, he was joined by a wrinkled, word-stingy old cowboy who introduced himself as the day wrangler assigned to Hawley's wagon. He explained that each rider used the same string of horses year in and year out on different ranges, and it would take some time to get the ponies accustomed to staying together, because each string tended to form a separate unit and drift off by itself. He said that the thing to do was to spot the leader in each string, and bell it when they got out on the plains.

"It'll be new moon in a night or two," he warned. "And the only way you'll be able to keep tab on them will be by sound. Keep track the leaders, and you got them all."

The day passed slowly, and late that afternoon Jeff was still lazing around the grazing herd, still watching to find the leaders and commit them to memory, when he saw the Morgan pony, Mouse, approaching at a gallop, bearing an agile rider. Stricken by a sudden painful shyness, he prayed silently that the girl would not recognize him and pass him by. But he quickly sent out another prayer that the first would pass unanswered. And when the girl pulled up near him, smiling warmly, he felt himself the most favored man in all the world.

"Hello, Jeff!" Abby was saying. "My father said you were back with the company again. I'm glad."

Jeff swept off his new sombrero, and answered her smile. "I'm glad, too, Abby," he said, meaning it as he'd meant few things he'd ever said. "It took me a while to make it, but I did."

"You're face is bloody," Abby said. "Have you been fighting— again?"

"Just this bronc," Jeff answered, abashed. "He hit me with the top of his head. But I won the last round."

The girl was wearing a blue riding habit that emphasized the blue of her eyes. She looked so dauntingly radiant that Jeff squirmed in discomfort, remembering his reckless boast to Demps that he would someday marry her.

"I see you have a different horse," Abby remarked, a challenge in her eyes. "Can *that* one run?"

"I'd like to find out," Jeff told her. "But I have to watch those horses, and learn which ones belong together."

"I can tell you that—if you'll race me, after."

Jeff nodded. "It's a deal."

Fulfilling her commitment, the girl astounded him with her knowledge of the horse string and the ranch itself. She not only identified the different cliques, she knew each animal by name, and by the man who used it. She pointed out each string leader, and named the bunch-quitters for him.

"What's a bunch-quitter?"

"It's a horse that won't stay in the herd, where it belongs. They cause so much trouble we usually get rid of them unless they are awfully good animals. Strap doesn't want to keep any of them, but my father sometimes is sentimental about horses."

" 'Bunch-quitter,' eh?" Jeff repeated. It was a new epithet, and he'd thought by now he knew them all. Something about this one got under his skin. He didn't know why. He hadn't quit any bunch. The bunch had quit him. After Demps had died, there was no one to quit, no one to whom he owed loyalty any longer. But he couldn't help wondering what Bad Water and Bitch Crick might be calling him. Harder names than that, maybe.

"And Strap's all for gitting shed of them, eh?—bunch-quitters, I mean," he went on, unable to leave it alone.

Abby nodded gravely. She knew horses, and liked them, and took all talk about them seriously. "He says that's born in them, like some being outlaws and killers. He says they can't be pampered into staying put, and you surely can't beat them into it. He says if you let them choose their own time to pull out, they'll go just when you need them worst and usually they'll take others along with them out of the herd. So, he favors getting rid of them the minute they show the tendency."

"But your dad is soft-hearted about them?"

"Dad's weakness is horses. Good horses. If he takes a liking to one, it can do anything to him, and he'll still swear by it. Did you ever hear about the big American saddle-horse stallion that got away from him?"

"And took his saddle along?" Jeff nodded. "I've seen him. That's an animal to swear by!"

"But not the way Dad does. He's already spent more money trying to capture him than he's worth. This last trip to Cheyenne, he bought another horse to run him with. A big ugly blue with some thoroughbred blood that's supposed to be able to run forever and not get tired. Strap says he paid five hundred dollars for this one, and I know of four others he paid more for. He broke them all down, and he still hasn't caught the stallion."

"Maybe your dad just don't like the notion of the stud gitting the best of him," Jeff suggested, still oddly fascinated by the talk— still remembering his and Demps's talk about horses and riders that spring.

"That's what some people say," Abby conceded. "But they don't know Dad. It isn't that so much as it's knowing that there's a horse like that around that won't wear his brand."

"Then why don't he have him shot, by some Hapgood or other?" Jeff asked, speaking through set teeth.

"Oh, he wouldn't do that," Abby exclaimed. "I told you, he's sentimental about horses, and— Why, what's the matter? What did I say wrong?"

"Nothing," Jeff said tonelessly, refusing her eyes. "Let's have that race."

As with the dun, the Morgan won the contest, going away. But the strenuous exertion of the wild ride gave Jeff the opportunity to work off the poison of his mood, and this race too ended with taunts and laughter.

As they rode back to the horse herd, their talk drifted to other less touchy subjects. They reminisced about the benefit dance, about the fight, and the damage done to the pretty boxes. Jeff was profuse and sincere in his apologies, but Abby snipped off his regrets with the bright laugh he loved to hear.

"You shouldn't have started a fight inside—as my father said. But I was glad you hit Strap. I heard what he said to you. I hoped you would hit him. I hoped you would hit him hard!"

Jeff's spirits rose wonderfully, and he broached another subject that he had been speculating on for days.

"I didn't expect Strap would ever hear of hiring me, after I hit him that way."

"He didn't approve. But, for once, he didn't get his way."

"Whose idea was it?" Jeff pressed recklessly, staring straight ahead. "Springing me from jail—and giving me a job?"

"Oh, they knew all the time you didn't kill Hapgood," Abby answered carelessly. "But the Association was raising such a fuss, they had to do something. I think Daddy intended to offer your job back, all the time."

Jeff caught the evasion in her reply, and the blood started singing in his ears. It seemed incredible that only last night he had been feeling sorry for himself. . . .

It was coming on for evening then, and they started back to the ranchstead in silence, their talk exhausted, a sudden restraint between them.

On the hard-packed trail leading to the corrals, the rhythmic beat of their horses' hoofs merged to form a patterned tattoo of sound that was very close to melody. The sun was setting, pulling the crimson sky down upon the peaks. The atmosphere was heavy with the ripe, burned smells of autumn, and overhead the nighthawks beat the air with strong erratic wings.

Once more, in the magic of a moment, Jeff sensed the opening of a door that guarded all the riches of the world. Nor had the feeling left him when he said good-by to her at the stables, where she cared for her own pony as was her custom, and set off toward the house, speaking warmly to all the men she passed, calling each by name.

He was standing motionless, looking after her and marveling again at the miracle of a cold-blooded lizard like Garrett begetting such a child, when a hostile voice spoke harshly at his back.

"This here is a roundup git-ready, Sugarfoot, not a square dance with the ladies. What you supposed to be doing to help out?"

Turning, he looked into Bowman's cold triangular eyes, and read their challenge—their enduring animosity. But he called certain things to mind and was able to keep his blood pressure down.

"I been bunch-breaking my horse string, out in the pastures," he said, more humbly than he felt. "I'm nighthawking for Hawley's wagon, and Powers said I better start gitting acquainted with the string."

"I noticed your gitting-acquainted activities," Strap growled. "But that particular filly ain't in your string. The quicker you git that in your head, the longer you'll last around here. You been warned twice now. Third time is the charm."

Jeff understood fully what lay behind the foreman's rancor. He recalled certain words of Abby's, and savored the sense of advantage that went with recalling. But he remembered other things, too, and knew that the advantage wasn't strong enough to put to the test.

"I know what's in my string, Strap," he said, looking at the ground. "There won't need be no third time."

Strap turned and stalked away, mouthing words Jeff didn't catch. But he did look mollified, and Jeff knew then that boot-licking paid off with the Man Head foreman.

Jeff knew, too, that he could lick boots with the experts, when the prize was big enough.

153

12: Stool Pigeon

The Man Head company fielded eight roundup crews that fall, to gather and separate the mature steers and dry cows and heifers for marketing, and to brand any unmarked animals the drives turned up—the young calves following Man Head mothers in the Garrett iron, mature unmothered "mavericks" in the Association's M brand.

Each crew consisted of six Man Head riders counting the subforeman or wagonboss in charge, plus an Association inspector to supervise all branding, plus four or five riders from neighboring companies, on hand to protect their employers' interests; plus a cook and a day wrangler and nighthawk. A chuck wagon and a bed wagon were assigned to each outfit, just as the Texians had had things on the trail. And when Powers' layout shoved off shortly after sunup on the morning after Jeff's ride with Abby, Jeff was driving the bed wagon, while a couple of the circle riders helped the day wrangler whoop the horses.

"Flash," Hambone Hawley had told him cheerfully at the outset, "you got nothing to do this roundup, but drive the hooligan all day and herd horses all night. It don't matter when you sleep, so long as it ain't while you're driving team or watching horses, or doing chores around the camp. You got the best job in the outfit."

Once they had reached their part of the range and had the gather under way, there wasn't much driving of the bed wagon, except on moving days. But with fourteen men to feed and do for, Hambone required a lot of help around the camp. Inevitably, the work was of such a nature that most of it had to be done by daylight, when the day wrangler was out with the horses and Jeff was doing nothing but lying around the camp. So all the sleep he got was when he could crawl away unnoticed and grab a cat nap on the sly.

"My luck is poor," he complained to Hawley one day. "Once I had a job day wrangling. But it was in the summer, when the days was sixteen hours long, and scarcely no night at all. I used

154

to think then how good the night herder had it. Now I got the night job, and what's the season? Fall—with the nights sixteen hours long."

"You ain't got it so hard," Hambone told him, unsympathetically. "Long as this clear weather holds, there ain't none of us going to spoil. Thank God for small blessings, I always say, and the big ones in proportion."

It being a beef roundup, there wasn't a lot of branding or altering of bull calves to do. The wagons followed the riders, and camp was wherever they made a big enough gather to make a cut worthwhile. After a cut, the beef stuff was thrown into the market or hold herd, while the wet cows and young she-stuff and sire bulls were whooped back where they wouldn't be gathered in again.

By the end of the second week, the newness was off Jeff's clothes, and his cheeks bristled with a stubby beard. But Hambone still called him "Flash," and the name roweled him like a spur. But he kept the rankle hidden, and stood off from the others as they stood off from him. And if he made no friends, he did succeed in making a right impression on those he had set out to impress.

"That Flash keeps on the way he's going, he's going to make a hand," Hambone said one bright afternoon when Jeff was thought to be sleeping on his roll beneath the wagon.

"He's as good a hand as they is in the crew right now," Powers said stoutly. "If everybody tended to business like he does, we'd have this gether over with, and the beef all carred in Quadrille."

To Jeff, flushing pleasurably in his soogans, the approbation of those above him seemed to compensate for the slights and animosities of those whose lot he shared.

There were additional opportunities to prove himself, as the gather progressed to its end. One windy day when he was scouting wide for firewood, he came upon a green cowhide, tightly rolled and hidden in a stand of brush. Swinging down, he spread the hide, and found the Man Head brand. A further search turned up no head or feet, but he rolled the hide again and tied it to his saddle—carefully, as if it were an item of great worth. And when he arrived in camp that afternoon, snaking a dry cottonwood snag at the end of his lariat, he displayed his find with an odd, excited pleasure.

Powers happened to be in camp, acquainting Hambone with some emergency change in the eating schedule for the night. But neither the wagonboss nor the cook displayed much interest in the find.

"Likely, Horgan's wagon run out of beef, and didn't have no fat stray handy," Hambone theorized. "It's standard practice, when you do something like that against company policy, to ditch the hide in another wagon's territory. That way, if it gits found, it's somebody else's tail, not yours. I've did the same thing, myself, plenty times."

Jeff looked at Powers, and received a nod. "Yeah. It's one the wagons—Horgan's likely. Wouldn't be no outsiders butchering right under our noses. If I was you, I'd just ditch it, and forgit I'd seen it. The company can afford to feed its help."

The point of view was a familiar one to Jeff. At one time in his life, he would have shared it. But that time was not now. For one thing, Jeff resented the way he was treated as an outcast by the rest of the crew, and welcomed an opportunity to strike back. For another thing, it had been this same Horgan who had branded him as a Garrett spy that first night by the fire. More important yet, he figured Garrett would appreciate knowing about the hide, and these days Jeff was looking out for Jeff.

"I don't see where it's any different for Horgan to beef a company animal, against orders, than for a homesteader that's got no cattle of his own to butcher," he remarked argumentatively.

"Then you don't see much," Powers said shortly. "Just ditch the hide, like I said, and forget about it."

Jeff ditched the hide—in the bed wagon, at the bottom of everything—but he didn't forget it. A couple of days later, Old Man Garrett rode around with Strap Bowman to check on the size of the hold herd. And that evening, just before time to take the horses out, Jeff produced the hide again.

Unlike Hambone and Powers, Garrett attached importance to the find. "Why didn't you report it to Powers here?" he asked sharply. "It should have been looked into, at the time."

"I did report it," Jeff said steadily.

A silence ensued, during which everyone but Jeff looked over at the wagonboss. Jeff kept his eyes on Garrett, and saw the old man's features sharpen.

"Ah? And what did Powers say?"

Jeff had been holding his breath, choking down the feeling that kept wanting to rise in him. This time, his voice didn't sound so steady.

"He said Horgan's wagon likely had got hard up for beef. He said it was a common thing, and for me to forgit I'd seen it."

The silence this time was hollow and unstirring. Garrett's eyes remained on Powers.

"How about this, Tom?" he asked.

"Let that flannel-mouth tell it," Powers growled. "It's his story."

"I don't hear you denying it," Garrett persisted.

"Of course I don't deny it," Powers said angrily. "I said it. I'd say it again. But maybe not around a parrot."

"Then you're hardly the one to have running a wagon," Garrett said regretfully. "We don't have rules in this organization just to give me a talking point, when things like this come up. Rules are rules, in any organization. Enforcement has to come from the top."

"Horgan's a friend of mine!" Powers burst out, his voice still touched by that same futile, defensive anger.

Garrett nodded readily. "Friendship is a great thing, and should be cultivated. You can develop it further, you and Horgan both, circle-riding for Jock Snow's wagon, over on Hurricane—provided you're there in time to start the day tomorrow. Strap, find someone to take over this wagon, and Horgan's—tonight."

The old man had to speak twice to get Strap's attention. The foreman was looking at Jeff, absorbed in something he was thinking.

"And you, Jimson," the ranchman added, turning toward his horse, the rolled hide under one arm, "if you hear any more about this from anybody that doesn't like it, you let me know. We'll see what can be done about it."

That night, out with the horses, Jeff suffered from remorse and self-recrimination at what he'd done. Shame washed over him in

157

waves as hot as the night of the dance, when told he stunk. He told himself he wouldn't have done it if he'd known Powers would be demoted over it. It had been Horgan, not Powers, he'd wanted to get even with. But even as he suffered, he felt an inner glow of satisfaction. Regardless of what the others thought of him, regardless of what he thought of himself, the fact remained that he'd made a good impression on Garrett. Garrett had called him by name, and had served notice on all the crew that they better not tamper with him. That was all that mattered.

All through breakfast the next morning, Hambone ignored him as if he were not around. But when the riders had all roped their morning mounts and ridden out, when the day wrangler had trailed the other horses out to grass, Hambone turned on him with accusing, reviling eyes.

"What kind of game you think you're playing, Flash? You must feel plenty proud of what you pulled last night."

"I work for the company," Jeff said shortly. "Garrett sprung me out of jail. I aim to make it up to him."

Hambone spat, so angry he could scarcely talk. "You think that stunt you pulled made him think any more of you? You think he likes a snot-nosed stool pigeon any better than the rest of us?"

"He didn't demote me and send me to another wagon," Jeff answered smugly.

"Powers was the best friend you had in the outfit!" Hambone went on accusingly. "And you play him a trick like that! What kind of animal are you, anyhow? How many friends you think you'll keep that way?"

"I didn't hire out here to earn friends," Jeff retorted, touched where he was tender. "The only friend I ever did have was killed, for doing less than Horgan done. You got any idea I'm going to set by and see these stuck-up bastards git by with the same thing that got Demps Rae shot, you better think again!"

"I bet if your friend was alive today, he'd be mighty proud of you!" Hambone sneered.

"If you don't like it, you can lump it," Jeff said coldly, walking away. "I know what I'm doing."

Ignored before around the wagon, Jeff was now pointedly

158

shunned. Jase Charter, the new straw boss, treated him with oper. if wary contempt, as did the riders. But Jeff didn't let it bother him. He knew what he was after, and he was getting it. He told himself that, carefully and frequently. It was a thing he would not and could not forget.

Hambone drove him savagely at the chore work—deliberately inventing work at times to keep him occupied, away from sleep. Deliberately driving him, Jeff suspected, toward some act of insubordination that could be reported to Garrett, in retaliation. But the weapons were of Jeff's own choosing, and he would not be driven to thus exposing himself. Roddy had taught him long ago that the way to defeat an informer was to be exemplary. And throughout the rest of the cow gather, Jeff was exemplary, even though most of his sleep was of the cat nap variety, much of it snatched while in his saddle with the horse herd at night.

But the roundup was soon over, and when the beef herd was pointed south to Quadrille, for shipment, Jeff was promoted to drover and assigned to a different crew engaged in relocating the seed stock on the winter ranges. His new associates were all from other wagons, and disposed to be more friendly.

One day he was tapped to ride into Quadrille to pick up horseshoes for a couple of the wagon teams that were going tender. Distance in from the camp was only twenty miles, and it was reckoned that with an early start he could be back by night.

"We'll have to be moving on, in the morning, so don't git likkered and forgit to come back," Orse Peters, the crew boss told him sternly.

Jeff roped a classy little sorrel he'd been riding on the new job, and appropriated a pair of saddlebags in which to fetch back the iron. While the boss was looking the other way, Lob Tobin, the day wrangler, took up a collection from among his compatriots, and when Jeff rode out of camp, Lob rode with him. When a safe distance from headquarters, the wrangler proffered a handful of folding money.

"Here," he said. "You'll have room in them bags for a bottle or two. The boys said to give you this, and they'll dance at your funeral."

"Not my funeral," Jeff corrected. "It's against company rules to bring liquor to a wagon. You know that without me telling you."

Lob looked at him, unbelieving at first, then angering. "Well, ain't you the holy joe! Listen, we know the rules, and we know how to fracture 'em. You can cache the stuff out of camp, and lead us to it after dark. Orse won't know nothing about it. Ain't a man in the outfit can't handle his drink."

Jeff shook his head. "Put your money in your pocket. I ain't packing liquor to the job."

He turned from the ugly antipathy on the swart face and rode on. Lob shouted a warning.

"Then the stuff is on you, boy. You fetch it, or take some advice and don't come back!"

It was only slightly past noon when Jeff pulled up at Hitch's corral, and he was highly flattered by the stableman's expression as he eyed the company pony and the high-powered outfit that was Jeff's own: the comfortable saddle with rifle and boot attached; the spurs and chaps and bone-handled pistol. But his good feeling was knocked out of him by his friend's first words.

"Well, some people have come up in the world, now!"

Jeff winced inwardly, remembering how he'd said the same thing of a toady hobo, something like a million years ago. But outwardly, he was casual and debonair.

"Well, they say you can't keep a good man down!"

"Well, you sure done yourself a favor when you crawled outen that horse-thief deal," the stableman informed him pleasantly. "You hear about the trial the other day?"

Jeff shook his head. He had to force himself to speak. "What happened?"

"Jury found 'em guilty—naturally. They're both in Laramie now. Both got life."

"Life?" Jeff repeated skeptically. "Can they send a man up for life, just for stealing horses?"

"Wasn't just for stealing horses. They was hailed for being accessories to that Hapgood's murder. Charges stuck, too."

Jeff stared in horror. "Why, they can't do that. Them two didn't have nothing to do with killing Hapgood. They wasn't even around that day."

"Well, they done it," Hitch pointed out. "Ain't nothing Stock Growers can't do."

"But they can't make it stick," Jeff insisted. "I told 'em who killed Hapgood. Why didn't they call me as a witness?"

"Don't tell me," Hitch shrugged. "Tell Garrett's judge."

"By God, I will!" Jeff said indignantly.

"Will you?" Hitch leered.

"You're goddam right I will!" Jeff vowed, stomping up the street.

But once away from Hitch's knowing, leering eyes, he began to wonder if he should do it—if he'd only prove himself a fool.

He looked into a whiskey glass in the Longhorn Bar, but found no answer there. Nor was there any inspiration in the dinner he treated himself to, in the Warbonnet Café. But the waitress was nice to look at and talk to, and there was immense satisfaction in paying his bill in the coin of the realm, and receiving cash change in return. Feeling himself a man of means, therefore of integrity, he walked into the courthouse and through a door lettered *Judge Theodor Coates, Third Judicial District.*

The room beyond the door was large, and smelled of the books that lined the walls, of cigar smoke and varnish and peppermint whiskey—the stale breath of the law. Its only occupant was a short, rounded man in black broadcloth suit, white linen shirt and black planter's tie spangled with egg yolk from breakfast. His iron-gray hair was combed straight back and banged off straight at the shoulders, like a gelding's tail. His mouth was small and secret, as Aunt Emma's had been.

"How do you do, sir? How can I help you?"

Jeff took the speaker to be the judge. He didn't think the judge had ever seen him, though he might have heard of him during his sojourn in jail. The jurist seemed to think that he should know him, however; the secret mouth was smiling tentatively, though the brown eyes were searching. One hand was poised to be offered, but was as yet withheld.

"Judge," Jeff began huskily, "my name is Jimson. I work for Garrett."

It was plain that his own name meant nothing, that Garrett's name was a password. The cautious eyes warmed. The hand and the held-in smile came out together. The hand was soft and warm as a woman's. Jeff was embarrassed to hold it.

"Why, of course. Of course. I remember you, now. Glad to see you again. Won't you sit down, Mr.—ah—"

"Jimson."

"Of course. Mr. Jimson. Now, how can I be of service?"

Jeff sat uneasily on the edge of the uncushioned armchair, and inspected his boots. "Judge, I just heard that them two horse thieves that were tried this fall got sent up for life."

"That is right, Mr. Bimson. They were found guilty on all charges. Justice was tailored to fit the crime."

"What was the charges?"

"Grand larceny, committing public nuisance, being accessories to a murder that shocked the entire territory. The charges were various, my boy."

"Well, that's what I wanted to tell you," Jeff blurted. "They didn't have nothing to do with killing that—that range detective. I know. I was there and seen it. Hapgood and Dempsey Rae killed each other. Them others, they was a hundred miles away."

The judge was looking at him with kindling interest, but with no favor. "I place you, now," he said, not happily. "You're the— the man we held on open charges in that case."

Jeff nodded. "I'm the one. I didn't say nothing in that statement I signed about them other two being there at the time Hapgood was killed. If anything was in there about that, John Poe must of put it there."

The judge looked very distressed. He gazed long out the window. He drummed on the desk with his clean-nailed hands.

"May I ask, Mr. Binsom, in whose behalf you are coming forward right now?"

Jeff smiled faintly. "Them convicts' bee-half, I expect."

"Yes, yes. Of course. But you miss my meaning. Who encouraged you to intervene in the case?"

"Nobody encouraged me. I come on my own. I thought you would be interested—"

"It took you considerable time. The trial was several weeks ago."

162

"I know. But I just now heard about it. I been out on the range."

"Did you consult with your employer, before coming?"

"No—"

"Might I ask why not? I should think it would have been a most natural procedure—Mr. Garrett being the chief complaining witness in the case."

Jeff was beginning to perceive his meaning. "I only thought there likely had been some mistake," he mumbled. "I thought you both would want to see the right thing done."

"Yet you did not mention the matter to Mr. Garrett," the judge insisted, as though that were the crux of the whole problem. "Instead, you come directly to me, and accuse me to my face of being derelict in my duty—of malfeasance in office. I could hold you in contempt, you know."

Jeff saw his bet called and raised too high to meet. He scowled and felt his face redden. He could think of nothing that would do to say.

"Did you think, Mr. Bimson, that on the basis of the oral testimony of one man I could reopen a case that has already been tried and closed—at great expense to the county? Did you think the case could be tried again, on the basis of your testimony, and your part in the affair kept secret from your employer? Aren't you being extremely unrealistic?"

Jeff continued to sit silent, staring at his boots, seeing no way out of the pitfall he'd been nudged into. The judge smiled tolerantly at his distress, and stood up to place a fatherly hand upon his shoulder.

"You did right to come and see me, if you had any doubts—instead of speaking them to others, to my back. I'm glad that you did come, because I am certain we've cleared those doubts up adequately. Your accusation against me was of the most serious nature. But you are young, and I detect liquor on your breath. And I like the looks of you. I'm sure you see your coming as a mistake, but it has been rectified. Just be more discreet in the future. . . . And now, I know you'll understand that I'm a very busy man. . . ."

Back out on the courthouse steps, Jeff stood in the thin autumn

163

sunlight, feeling defeated and helpless. He could go to the Governor, he guessed, down in Cheyenne. But Demps had said that the Governor was one of Garrett's crowd, too. All he'd accomplish that way would be to make trouble for himself, without helping Bad Water and Bitch Crick any.

The longer he thought about it, the more he was convinced that the judge had called the turn. The horse thieves were already in jail, and nothing he could do would shorten their terms any. And, when you got right down to it, it wasn't Jeff's fault that they'd been sent up for life. His testimony probably had convicted them of the larceny charges. But he hadn't implicated them in the killing, and he'd done his best to get them cleared. He had tried. He had done everything within his power.

The door opened behind him, and he turned to see the judge coming out. He readied a smile and a nod, to demonstrate to his adviser that they now were of a common mind. But Coates walked briskly past without a flicker of recognition, leaving him cut and alone and estranged, puzzled and not puzzled, hating the judge and not hating him, all undecided again.

Then he heard his name spoken by a voice he knew, and saw Abby Garrett across the street, smiling at him, waiting for him, looking prettier than he'd ever seen her.

For about the time that was required to draw in and let out a long breath, he stood in wavering indecision. Then he answered her smile and stepped down in the dust of the street, to join her.

It was long past dark when he arrived back at the cow camp, with the horseshoes. Orse Peters, the wagonboss, was nowhere in evidence. The others watched him expectantly as he swung down by the fire. As that morning, Lob Tobin took upon himself the function of spokesman.

"Well, did you fetch what I told you to?"

Jeff unstrapped the saddlebags and dropped them to the ground. "The horse iron is right in here," he said.

"Where's the bug juice I told you to fetch?"

Jeff flipped a stirrup up over his warm saddle seat, and tugged at the cinch. "The bug juice is all in town."

In the silence that followed, he stripped the saddle from his

164

pony's back, and placed it carefully astride the bed wagon's front wheel. He picked up an empty gunnysack that would do to rub the horse down with. As he turned he saw Tobin straightening up from the open saddlebags.

"The son of a bitch ain't just a-woofing," the wrangler announced. "He didn't fetch a drop."

Jeff paused, sack in hand, and looked around him. What he saw was plain trouble. Tobin was looking at him, hands on hips. The others were coming around the fire to take up position by the wrangler. There were five of them, and they all were big men.

"Ain't you the teacher's pet, though?" Tobin said. "You're all for the company, ain't you?"

"I work for the company," Jeff said reasonably. "Why shouldn't I be for it?"

"His old lady must of been scared by a preacher," a thick-built stomper by name of Hobbs put in. "We'd ought to tie him to that horse's tail, and start 'im back. Maybe next time, he would fetch it."

"Well, it's a chaps' case, anyhow," Tobin opined, watching Jeff narrowly. "What you say, boys? Do we work 'im over?"

"Give me a chance at the bastard!"

They started coming at him. Four were empty-handed. Hobbs carried the heavy leather chaps they intended to spank him with, once they'd ripped off his pants. Jeff backed off slowly toward the wagon, keeping them against the firelight, himself in shadow where distance was difficult to judge. When Tobin was near enough Jeff jumped forward and kicked out hard. His boot connected where it did the most good, and Tobin bent double, roaring in pain. Jeff struck him once on the back of the neck, a chopping slice with the edge of his open hand. Tobin went down like a beef, and Jeff whirled in time to catch a driving shoulder blow from another, while hands tore at his throat from behind.

Reeling, Jeff drove his head back like a maul. He didn't know at the instant whether the bone he felt snap was in his head or someone else's face. But the hands fell away from his windpipe, and his own fists were free to combat the head that drove against him, bull-fashion, jamming him back against the wagon. Hands joined together, he clubbed down hard.

The clincher fell just as a fourth man jumped in at him. Jeff dodged a kick that had death in it, and smashed a fist into the attacker's face, striking it from view.

Having won a breather, Jeff planted his back firmly against the wagon, and looked around. Besides himself, Hobbs was the only man in camp still on his feet. Hobbs stood back stupidly, holding the chaps. Jeff was debating whether to carry the fight to him or seek a truce when a familiar, strident voice took his eyes to the fire.

"What in the gee-hell goes on here?"

Of all people in Garrett-land who might have ridden up in the dark just then, two of those who had were Garrett and Strap Bowman. The other was Orse Peters, the straw boss. Their horses' eyes were pools of liquid fire, and they were still in their saddles, staring at Jeff across the flames. Jeff's vast upsurge of pride at being apprehended in the instant of victory over odds so impossible was watered down with anxiety at the expression on Bowman's face.

"I said, what in hell goes on?" Strap repeated ominously.

"Aw," Hobbs said sheepishly, showing the chaps, "we was just having a friendly scuffle."

"It don't look very friendly, from here," Strap said, watching the four pick themselves up off the ground, two of them bleeding freely about the face.

The foreman's gaze came around to rest on Jeff, and Jeff felt constrained to speak. His first impulse was to keep the brawl a private one, to stand with his attackers against a common threat. But he quickly smothered the inclination. He was finished with playing the fool.

"I rode into town today, to fetch some horseshoes, and they wanted me to fetch some whiskey out. When I didn't, they got rasped."

A short, shocked silence ensued. Then, as Bowman swung down to stand in the firelight, his anger was directed at Jeff, not at those who'd conspired to ignore a company ruling.

"By God, Jimson," he began, "until we took you on, we never had no trouble around the wagons. Since, we ain't had a thing but trouble. I figure we've had about enough. Now . . ."

166

"Did you bring the horseshoes you went after?" Garrett's voice intruded quietly, cutting Bowman off.

Jeff looked at the old man for the first time, and tried unsuccessfully to read the graven face. He nodded emphatically.

"They're there, in them saddlebags."

"Well," Garrett said, overreaching his foreman further, "he did the job he was sent to do, and he got back to camp sober, which is more than you can trust the majority to do. And he left the whiskey in town. The way I see it, he saved his job, and these others their jobs in the bargain. They'd ought to thank him for the service, instead of trying to kill him."

Jeff didn't risk looking at Bowman just then. He figured trouble was coming fast enough without any help on his part. Instead, he showed his appreciation of the old man's patronage by taking the lead in unsaddling and tending the newcomers' horses, in unpacking the two bed horses, and hobbling the whole bunch out to graze. After, in the cook's incapacity, he stirred up the fire and fixed the late arrivals a bait of supper. Still later, basking in his employer's obvious approbation, he washed up the wrecks and chopped more wood for morning.

All the while, he felt Strap Bowman watching him lingeringly again. He tried to demonstrate a lack of concern by yawning and seeking his bed. And, lying wakeful in his quilts beneath the wagon, he overheard another conversation not meant for his ears.

"Wate," Strap was saying, respectful but rueful, "it's your company, and I'm not trying to tell you how to run it. But we've had troublemakers around here before, and I know what it generally leads to. I think you're making a mistake, keeping that mouthy pup terrier around."

Garrett was silent so long that Jeff almost suffocated, holding his breath to hear.

"You may be right—within limits. He doesn't seem to get along in the crews. But I'm not convinced the fault all lies with him. He's got a talent I think we should use."

"Use—how?"

"I think he'll make us a watchdog. I think we'll bring him in to headquarters, and put him to work as outrider. He won't be in close contact with the others, that way, and should get along better. As far as the rest of the men are concerned, he can be breaking horses or packing supplies to the line camps, or anything you can figure that will get him around the country. His real job will be to circulate and keep an eye on things—to let us know what's going on."

Bowman grunted distastefully. "Have things got to the point where we have to start spying on our own help?"

"Seemingly, it has," the old man answered mildly. "He's turned up a couple of things here lately that I didn't know was going on. I'd like for you to see to that, right away."

Jeff smiled into his quilts, and tried to believe in his continuing, improbable good fortune. He shuddered to think how near he had been to shucking the whole business in town, after talking to the judge. Remembering, he wondered how he could almost have been so big a fool.

13: Hatchet Man

Abby had departed for the East to resume her schooling before Jeff returned to Rifle Mountain, so he was deprived of the association he had looked forward to with much anticipation. But he was comfortably installed in the warm log bunkhouse for the cold months, and had his pick of the horses and gear for his frequent unannounced scouting trips to other ranches. Also, he had access to the Garrett library, and—painfully conscious of his lack of formal education—he set about the business of self-instruction in book learning with the same dogged persistence that he had brought to his job.

Topically, he was most interested in history and animal breeding and husbandry. But he was aware that knowledge in these fields alone would not qualify him for making talk with a highly cultured young lady. So he broadened his range and pastured on Gibbon and Poe's stories. He even tried poetry when he'd gleaned the other fields, but it struck him as artificial and hard to make sense of. And the sense, when present, was not very palatable:

168

Just for a handful of silver he left us,
Just for a riband to stick in his coat. . . . .

"'Smatter, Flash?" Hambone inquired, looking up from his solitaire game when Jeff snapped the volume shut with a crack. "You look like you'd swallowed something that upset your stomick."

"I guess maybe that's what I done," Jeff admitted ruefully.

Jeff told himself emphatically that the poem did not apply to him. He hadn't left anybody. It was just the other way around. Everybody else had left him. But the lines continued to eat at his peace of mind. Idly, he picked up the Browning again and thumbed the pages until his eye was taken by another pair of lines that some reader had underlined in ink:

Ah, but a man's reach should exceed his grasp,
Or what's a heaven for?

But, strenuous as he made his mind-improvement program, he was careful to see that it did not interfere with the more important business of succeeding at his job. Breaking horses, scattering salt, supplying the outlying ranches and line camps by pack train, he became a familiar figure over most of the company range that winter—warmly and handsomely clothed in fur cap, red mackinaw, sheepskin chaps, fleece-lined boots. On all his expeditions, his saddlebags were well-stocked with books for evening perusal by lantern light in camp. But, by day, his eyes read the country only. If some secure-feeling line rider spent his waking time visiting neighboring camps or on his bed while cattle drifted into death-trap ravines, Wate Garrett heard of their remissions at far-away headquarters, and the slackers were promptly amputated.

Jeff never had been accepted by the bunkhouse crowd—never was invited to sit in on the stud games or bull sessions, to join the Saturday night blowouts in town. But it was known that he enjoyed Garrett's favor, and no one at first offered to risk the old man's displeasure by bringing hostilities into the open. Jeff was merely ignored, as he had been around the branding wagons in the fall; treated as if he did not exist. But he was accustomed to being shunned by now, and accepted the crew's animosity as fair fee for advantages he had gained. He'd found his second million as hard as the first, to garner. But the third seemed to be coming in right nicely. He now was making fifty a month, ranking second only to Bowman himself in pay, in privilege, in prestige.

Garrett had made it clear from the first that his function must be kept secret if it were to be effective. So he'd been circumspect in making his observations and reports. But it wasn't long before his associates began putting two and two together, and their enmity began taking more aggressive forms. Water was poured in his bunk one night when the temperature dropped to fifty below, and he spent most of the time in a chair by the stove. On another occasion, his blankets were tarred. Currycombs were thrust under his saddle blankets to make his horses buck and rub back sores. His better clothes had a way of disappearing, to turn up in the frozen horse trough in the yard.

Jeff figured the crew's strategy was to crowd fights, and thus give weight to Bowman's charge that he was an ingrained troublemaker. So, at first, he took the hazing in good part, and laughed off the pranks. But the morning he awoke to find that his new boots had been filled with barley and water poured in to swell the grain and break out the stitching, he figured the practical jokes were getting too practical. That night, every bunk but Jeff's collapsed owing to the circumstance that someone had sawed the crosspieces all but through, and all the lanterns, mysteriously, had disappeared.

Lob Tobin, still nursing an old grudge, undertook to smash Jeff's bunk in the dark, and the resulting difficulty smashed almost everything in the room that was smashable, including Lob's oft-smashed nose.

A couple of nights later, as Jeff thrust open the bunkhouse door, a bucket wired to the top of the frame was tilted by the door's action to spill fresh cow manure down on Jeff's head and shoulders. His audience applauded gleefully, and the compliments paid to Hambone identified him as the perpetrator.

Hambone was not as young as he'd been once. But he was big as a horse and half as strong—as Jeff learned when he'd got hold of him. The resulting racket brought Bowman down from the cabin where he lived by himself, alert for just such disturbances since the previous brawl's property damage had been assayed.

When he saw Hambone beaten and bloody on the floor, wearing the green-plastered bucket like a helmet, the foreman looked at Jeff with jaundiced eyes.

"How come you're picking on poor old Hambone?" he wanted to know. "He's a bit out of your age class, you know."

"I wasn't picking on him," Jeff panted, peeling off his soiled clothes. "I'm just taking them in rotation. He was next."

"Well," Strap said thoughtfully, "they git bigger and tougher, as you work up. Keep it going, and it will git more interesting."

"Practice makes perfect," Jeff shrugged. "And I'm gitting the practice, seems like."

In all his riding, Jeff managed to avoid the hidden valley on Hurricane Creek. He was on the mesa several times, salting the licks and supplying the men in the line camps on the far edge of the tableland. But he rode the dry route to the south of Hurricane Creek, telling himself it was shorter and therefore saved time, even though the trail was much rougher. Similarly, he always gave Ekard a wide swing, telling himself there was no one at the road-ranch he ever wanted to see again.

Frequently, up on the mesa, he caught brief glimpses of the out-law red stud and his mustang band. And the notion of the big renegade running free there on the plateaus with the remnant of Garrett's saddle still on its back continued to hold fascination for him. Once or twice, he even let himself remember a thing Demps had said.

You and me ain't never had a rider, Tex. I expect it's a little early to say how we'd be.

Well, it wasn't so bad, having a rider. And Demps had missed it some when he'd said it was envy alone which made a mounted horse want to corral everything in sight. Sometimes, Jeff figured, a horse just wanted to be the head horse in the string.

Jeff wanted to be head horse in Garrett's string, and he worked hard toward attainment of that goal. He was a man with a mission, and that mission was serving the company—as eyes, ears, and fist. He turned up thieves, actual and suspected, in the crew and on the outside. He kept a sharp eye on encroaching settlers, and destroyed section-corner markers with religious zeal, to promote imperfect entry on the part of homesteaders and thereby simplify eviction.

One day, on Cat Creek, he saw a ramshackle wagon pulled up in front of the dugout he had shared with Demps the year they had trapped for a living. A bony, moth-eaten team was hobbled out to graze on the meadow, and when Jeff rode over for a look-see, he found a couple of spools of new barbwire in the shabby box, along with the tell-tale plow.

Smoke was rising out of the rusted cabin chimney. There still was no window, so Jeff concluded that his coming had not been witnessed. He put his pony over close to the door. He rested his rifle across his saddle in such a way that it would point straight in the face of anyone opening the door, and kicked at the frame with his boot.

There was a shuffling inside, and the door opened. A squat, hefty man with whiskery face and colorless hard eyes looked with amazement into the rifle muzzle, then inquiringly up at Jeff. A thin-faced, unpretty woman stood close behind him, a bundle of something held to her breast. Jeff carefully avoided looking at the woman or the bundle she held.

"Yes, mister?"

The man's voice was hard and edgy as his eyes. His lowering gaze would not be driven away by Jeff's threatening stare. For just an instant, the unarmed man had the upper hand of him, though Jeff didn't quite know how. Anger burned in Jeff—vague and undirected, but hot enough to sustain him. Hot enough to put confidence and authority in his voice, at least to Jeff's own ears.

"You just stopping here overnight, friend?"

The man in the door lifted a hand and let it fall. "We figured to homestead this crick bottom," he stated, looking at the rifle. "We been told it was open to filing."

"You got told all wrong," Jeff snapped. "This here is Man Head ground. You're here in trespass. It ain't safe practice to trespass on Man Head."

"Is the ground already deeded?" the other asked. "Or is it public land?"

The man wasn't defiant. He didn't even look stubborn. He was just immovable. Jeff was angered again.

"It don't make a nickel's worth of difference. Deeded or undeeded, it's Man Head range. If you can take good advice, you'll be off it—today."

"Why?"

It was a puzzling question, still not challenging, but challenging in a way. From the tail of his eye, Jeff saw a broad-winged hawk wheeling in lazy circles above the meadow, a hundred yards or so distant. Turning the rifle on impulse, he lined his sights, led the bird properly, and pulled the trigger.

A miss would have made him look foolish. But he was confident that he wouldn't miss. The bird jerked sharply up, just as many birds had done before, then started a crazy glide to earth, trailing feathers behind it.

Jeff levered another cartridge into the firing chamber, and looked back at the watching eyes.

"I expect that's why," he said, reining his horse around. "I'll be back this way tomorrow. I hope I don't see you around."

True to his promise, he rode past the dugout again next day, and was torn between shame and triumph to find it abandoned again.

Jeff was scrupulously constant in reporting all such accomplishments and triumphs at headquarters, always to Garrett, never to Bowman. Strap made no effort whatsoever to conceal his hostility any more, and Jeff avoided him as much as was possible, knowing that an open clash could still bring disaster. But he refused to slight his work out of regard for Strap, and the day he got two men fired for deserting a maternity corral early in the spring and spending the week at Ekard it looked as if matters might move to a head.

The culprits were old friends of Bowman's, and news of their dismissal brought the foreman in from another ranch. When he emerged from Garrett's office, he looked like a man who'd been eating fire.

"It's about time I and you plucked a little crow, Jimson," he began, crossing to where Jeff stood readying his packs. "Maybe you got the notion you're the foreman here. Maybe somebody told you you was running the layout."

Jeff turned slowly to face him. Twenty-one now and split up the middle almost as far as Strap himself, Jeff no longer had to look up to meet his eyes, though Strap cast the heftier shadow.

Jeff had never seen a man so full of fury, never a fury so cold and so well controlled. He figured this was trouble, and knew he'd best speak sweet and low.

"Why, I ain't trying to run the layout," he disclaimed mildly. "Garrett hired me to do a job. I'm only trying to earn my money."

"Well, you're trying a mite too hard," the foreman growled, only partly mollified to see him crawl. "And, as of now, I'm cutting you in on the know. You keep out of my territory and off my toes, or by the big God one of us is going to lose some hair!"

Bowman's voice shook dangerously, and Jeff accepted the ultimatum without retort. But his meekness did not extend to the two discharged riders who stood nearby with their saddles and bedrolls and gear, waiting for the buckboard Strap had arranged to haul them into town.

"If you ain't a hundred-proof, twenty-carat, gen-u-wine son of a bitch!" one of them snarled at Jeff, emboldened by Bowman's presence. "The way you're going, you ain't going to live long enough to marry the boss's daughter—"

This time, Jeff's fist answered for him. The surprising fist that struck faster and farther and harder than was expected. The speaker took half the yard to fall in, and Jeff kept him in view, while watching the other, ready to draw a gun, if need be. But Bowman intervened, and saw to it there was no shooting.

"Pull in your horns, boys. His hand's best, this bet. But his luck is running out."

But Strap's prediction appeared to be wishful thinking. Jeff was promoted to wagonboss for the big spring calf roundup, and demonstrated to all that he was qualified in the executive department, too. He drove himself and his crew without mercy, and earned even a deeper enmity from most with whom he dealt. But his wagon tallied and branded more calves than any other, and he was personally commended by Garrett for his accomplishment.

174

He didn't get by without trouble from his men. But he handled all difficulties without help from above. And when there was fighting, it was usually the other man who carried the souvenirs of the clash.

He'd heard no word from Abby since her departure for the East the fall before. At various times he had asked leading questions of and around her father. But Garrett invariably turned the talk to other things, and Jeff didn't learn much. However, he continued optimistic and patiently awaited the day of her return —building in the meantime a vivid fantasy-life around her, seeing her this way and that, hearing her laugh, tasting her kisses, lying at her side through the long hours of night. And if his dream was only one-dimensional, like a painting, he was pleasantly unaware.

He did realize, in a vague sort of fashion, that his feeling for her transcended the usual male ambitions toward a female. But he put that down to being in love with her. And if he hungered for the wealth and position that were hers to offer, he didn't clearly see the circumstance as cheapening his love. She was divinity, and he worshiped devoutly at her shrine. The fact that he too aspired to divinity did not make his prayers less reverent.

He was up on Hurricane Mesa, investigating rumors of rustler depredations to brood stock there, when he heard from a packer that she was back at the ranch. He pretended to receive the news casually. Painfully aware of the covert stares and hidden smiles of the line riders with whom he was camped, he spoke easily of an unexplained cow trail he had found leading off in the direction of Ekard, and announced an intention to ride to Drake's next day. But, once off the mesa, he turned his horse toward Man Head and rode in a fidget—fretting that the miles passed so slowly, wishing at the end that there were more miles, to delay a little longer the encounter whose prospect frightened him unreasonably.

For always in his mind there lurked the awful fear that Abby would meet some dude back East who'd sweep her off her feet and win her love before he was in position to declare his own. Surely, he thought when he could endure such thinking, the East was crawling with rich and handsome young men who'd bid high for a prize like Abby, whenever her father placed her on the block. Now that he considered it, he wondered if the same thought hadn't occurred to Garrett, if that weren't the reason the old man kept shipping her back away from the ranch and its hungry-eyed male population. And what chance would he stand in competition with the Boston Bean Boys, as Demps had called them, when showdown poker was played? What chance would he stand even with Strap Bowman, if Garrett should select his foreman as the man to take over his interests and inherit his kingdom?

Throughout the long ride, he tortured himself with these and like questions, trying deliberately to steel himself for bad news. By the time he'd arrived, he had practically convinced himself that the worst awaited him, that the dream was over with—busted. Almost shrinkingly, he rode through the big portaled gate, and looked apprehensively around him. The place appeared strangely deserted.

"Where's everybody?" he asked of Dolly Bart, the home ranch wrangler, whom he found stretched out on his bed in the bunkhouse, studying a mail-order catalog.

"Garretts and Bowman are in Quadrille," Dolly said, never looking up from his reading matter. "The boys all left for Cow Crick, a little bit ago. They finished that new bridge there this week, and they're holding a big dance on it tonight, to raise more money for the skule. The Old Man donated a beef they're going to barbeque. They'll be a hot time on the new bridge tonight!"

Jeff wanted to ask if Abby would be there, but restrained himself. For one thing, he doubted that Dolly knew any more than he knew of the Garretts' personal plans. For another thing, he shrank from the knowing leers that always came his way with the mention of Abby's name.

Dolly's face was slick, and he smelled of bay rum, though he wasn't yet dressed.

"You going to ride over for it?" Jeff asked him.

The wrangler nodded, eyes still on the book.

"Well," Jeff said carelessly, as if just making up his mind, "I'll catch a dip and a shave, and ride with you."

The night on Cow Crick was sultry, threatening rain, so a

176

canopy of tarps and wagon covers had been fitted on the bridge, stretched between small pole uprights wired to the railings on either side. The long, narrow house-bridge thus formed was open at each end, the interior dimly lighted by a dozen lanterns. The fiddlers were lined up side by side about midway of the narrow tunnel, backs to the rail, so as to be out of the dancers' way. On either bank, bonfires blazed brightly, casting flickering light over the assembled teams and rigs. On the ranch side, a yearling beef turned slowly on a spit operated by the cookhouse helper from headquarters, while Hambone Hawley presided ceremoniously, his ponderous stomach ballooning a greasy, once-white sacking apron.

Arriving early, Jeff helped ready the chuck wagon plates and cups, and otherwise assisted with arrangements. After the chore work was done, he stood about the fire, inhaling the prosperous odors, joining Hambone in an occasional "stirrup cup" from the big stone jug the boys had fetched from town. When the fiddles started sawing, he screwed up his courage and presented himself to one of the town girls, as a candidate for the waltz.

The girl was dumpy and a sloven. Her face was painted like a signboard, and she wore a moth-eaten bobcat pelt around her throat, even though the atmosphere beneath the canvas was hot and sticky. But Jeff had never danced, and he felt the need of practice if he were to challenge Abby to a contest later. So he led the girl onto the rough-plank platform and faced her uncertainly. She smiled a terrible smile as she gave herself to him. She pressed her soft body against his, and his flesh recoiled from the contact. Concentrating on the fiddles' rhythmic scrape, he stepped off, thinking of a hog on ice.

The experiment was notably unsuccessful. His high heels kept catching in the cracks, tripping him up and throwing him off balance. Every time he tried to place a foot down, the girl's foot was already there. Frustration tensed his muscles, and the tenseness wearied him; perspiration drenched his clothes and ran down in rivulets into his eyes. The bobcat pelt had not been properly tanned, and the dead stink took him back to another benefit dance in another hall. Frustration blossomed into panic, and he trampled the town girl like a stampeding horse.

"You're nice, cowboy," the girl said when the ordeal finally ended. "But you really ought to take your spurs off, when you ride."

Out at the cooking fire again, Jeff took a long, hard pull at Hambone's jug. Then, ridden by a restlessness that bordered on frenzy, he left the fire to walk in the dark among the horses and rigs. He considered getting on his pony and leaving right then. But he didn't leave. And when he returned at last to the bridge, he saw that the Garretts had arrived. Abby was dancing with Strap, and wearing the same spangled gown she'd sported at the other dance. Jeff's heartbeat slowed to see how gracefully she handled herself, her feet seeming not to touch the floor. He saw the town girl, jigging with Dolly Bart. He looked from one girl to the other, and—remembering

> The colonel's lady
> And Judy O'Grady
> Are sisters under the skin . . .

—felt his mind rebel against all poetry.

Still smarting from the humiliation of the first dance, he did not intend to approach Abby at all. Even if he had wished to risk his dignity in so reckless a fashion, women were so scarce that the cowboys were dancing with one another again, and Abby was the center of an all-male riot each time the music stopped. He thought he was standing back where he would not be noticed, but once she danced close to where he was, and dazzled him with an inviting smile. When the fiddles paused again, he forgot that he would trample her like a stud horse, and went to her as the fluttering moths went to the hanging lanterns.

He was ahead of the stampede, and Abby was waiting for him. Bowman was at her side, but she turned her back on her escort to welcome Jeff. Jeff was aware of the green, inimical stare—but only momentarily.

"Hello, Jeff!" she said in the old special way that always put the blood to singing at his ears. "I was wondering if you would be too busy to come. Dad tells me you're working hard."

"I've got a lot to work hard for," he answered boldly, and was pleased to see her blush. "But I decided to take time out."

"Well, I'm glad you're here, because I saved you the next dance," she went on loudly, causing him to believe that she meant the words as much for Bowman as for him. "I believe it's a Virginia reel. We'd better find a set."

It was a reel, just as Abby had foretold, and after the first few maneuvers Jeff was relaxed and confident, smiling when Abby smiled, clapping and stepping in time to the tune, going through the patterns as easily as if he'd done it many times before.

All too soon, the set was over, and he started reluctantly to lead her back to Strap. But Abby had different notions.

"It's so warm!" she complained. "Do you suppose Hambone would make us a sandwich, if we asked him nice?"

"It would sure be worth a try." Jeff grinned, fighting his eyes away from the place where Bowman waited.

The beef was rich and tasty, and coffee better than any Jeff had ever drunk. When they had satisfied their hunger, they started back, but somehow missed the bridge and crowd, somehow wound up all alone down on the creek bank. The clouds had broken overhead, and the sluggish stream glimmered silver in the moonlight, then crept silently into darkness.

It seemed a proper moment for poetry, and Jeff searched his memory for a fitting rhyme. But all that would come was "The Colonel's Lady and Judy O'Grady," and that was blasphemy.

So there wasn't any poetry, but their talk was unstrained and spontaneous, of things both important and trivial. Jeff could never recall later the words she used, but Abby told him simply that she was glad to be home again, that she had missed him while away. After a time, their talk was exhausted, and they stood in silence, staring at the stream. There was much that Jeff wanted to say, now that the chance at last had come. But he could only grope for Abby's hand. When he'd found it, he turned and found her waiting.

He didn't know, at the time or later, exactly how it came about. It just happened, as naturally as breathing. Abby was close against him, her mouth seeking his in a strange and ancient quest that did not seem strange at all. Once again, his arms and hands and all his body knew the appalling softness of woman. But this softness was not the coreless, spongy soft he had known with the town

179

girl on the bridge. This was the softness of sheathed steel, yielding and unyielding. The softness of moss on stone.

. After a second or an hour, a footfall sounded thinly somewhere. Both heard it, and started back, the kingly thing that they had shared shattered like broken glass. A shadow stood near them, and after an instant's silence it spoke in a voice that was calm—genial, even, yet menacing as a raised whip.

"Come, Abigail. It's time we were leaving. I have the horses hitched, and it's a long way back."

The girl stood stiffly motionless throughout a dead, unreal moment. Jeff thought wildly for an instant that she was going to defy her parent and stay with him. He was both exalted and numbed by the possibility, and into his mind there came a picture of a super-Jeff who placed a protective arm about her waist and stared the horsewhip-father down—who then and there laid firm claim to the prize he'd won, defying any and all to challenge his proprietorship.

But the horsewhip voice spoke wheedlingly again, and the super-Jeff remained a picture only.

"Come. I'm leaving now. You wouldn't want to stay behind."

Abby bowed her head and left Jeff's side without a glance at him. She joined the shadow, and as Jeff watched, became a shadow too. . . .

14: Heir Apparent

Jeff did not return to the lighted bridge, where the sound of fiddles and talk and laughter went on, the same as if an earth-shaking catastrophe had not just struck. When he finally left the stream bank, it was to saddle his horse and ride, holding to the shadows like a fugitive. A craven part of him considered flight out of the country, that night, before the lord of Man Head could arrange whatever punishment was meted out to lowly men-at-arms who profaned princesses by moonlight, and were discovered in the act by the lord himself. But when he rode, it was to take the Man Head road.

The big house was in darkness when he arrived, but the buckboard was in the yard, the warm team just through the pasture gate. Jeff unsaddled and let his own horse through the gate, then went straight to the deserted bunkhouse and sought his bed. He surprised himself by sleeping well, and when he awoke next morning it was to a somewhat detached speculation on the mode of punishment that awaited him: whether he would be gelded in secret and whipped out of the country, or just told to git and not leave any forwarding address.

But when Abby showed up for her customary morning ride, she looked more glowing and animated than he'd ever seen her. And though she rather pointedly did not invite him to join her, she did whisper a message that took his breath.

"Father and I talked last night, about—you and me. He wants to speak with you, tonight. Supper will be at nine—if you will come."

If he would come!

"I'll be there—with bells on!" he promised, when he could speak at all.

It wasn't exactly bells that Jeff was wearing when he let himself through the dooryard gate for the first time that evening, and took a long time shutting it behind him. But it was good black broadcloth, as fine as money could buy—a suit he'd purchased in town almost a year before, and hadn't had occasion or courage to wear before—together with boiled shirt and black bow tie. The man he'd seen in the bunkhouse mirror had little to do with the embittered and bewildered younker who'd been thrown out of a dance in Quadrille because he smelled bad, scarcely more than two years ago. And the taunts and catcalls of the bunkhouse crowd still rang in his burning ears.

"Hey, look at the Prince of Wales."

"My God! Ain't that handsome?"

"Wish I could be a prince, and marry a princess, and live happy ever after!"

"Hey, Flash—! Which fork you going to use first?"

"He better take a pitchfork. He knows what they are for!"

The gate closed at last, he felt unalterably committed, and

squared himself like a man about to meet his doom. "Just like a ram to the slaughter," he said aloud, in a feeble attempt at bravado.

Old Garrett himself admitted him, and once he was free of his hat and seated on the great black leather divan in the parlor, his uneasiness began to wane. The room was big enough to hold court in, and furnished like a picture in a book. But instead of the ogre he had conjured up in his mind, his host was a cordial and gracious gentleman whom Jeff felt he had never met before.

"Abby will be down directly," the old man told him, giving an unaccountable intimacy to the words. "In the meantime, I believe Sing is fetching something wet."

The whiskey and the old man's warm civility were wonderful stimulants, and when Abby came down the big open stairway, looking fresh and lovely as a flower, Jeff suddenly was daunted again by the brazen gall of his aspirations. For an awful instant, he wanted to set down his glass and flee. Then Abby was standing before him, smiling as he rose to greet her.

"Good evening, Jeff. I'm glad you came. . . ."

The supper was a fine affair, a fitting climax to what had gone, an eloquent expression of graceful living in a land where the wickiup had been the standard habitation not twenty years before. An expression of a way of living that was as alien to Jeff Jimson as life on a distant planet.

The long mahogany table would have seated a dozen comfortably, though there were only the two Garretts and Jeff to sit down. The vaulted, oak-paneled dining room seemed smaller than it really was, the only illumination coming from the branched silver candlesticks on the table, the room's high ceiling and corners being lost in shadow. The flickering mellow light fell in golden pools upon the white linen cover; it flattered Abby wonderfully, enriching the soft ivory texture of her skin, glowing on her coppery hair.

The old man presided, at the table's head. Dressed in black, with board-front shirt and high collar, he filled to perfection the role of country squire, as—half-drunk on Bourbon and arrogance—he harangued his daughter and his guest on such timely topics as states' rights, the tariff, and the homesteader threat. The dereliction of the territory's delegate to Congress, who was supposed to safeguard the interests of his constituents. The blind and wasteful politicking of the mining and Granger cliques who sought to control the territorial legislature.

"Those people can't legislate for me! I was on this river, fighting Indians and drouths and thieves, before there was any territory. A man gives the best years of his life to building a new country, and what happens? The festive Granger comes flocking in, to glean our fields ahead of us. . . ."

The strident, scratchy voice rose and fell at the edge of Jeff's consciousness like wind outside a house whose interior was light and warm, given to revelry. His new clothes seemed to fit him better, and as his eyes communed secretly with Abby's eyes across the table, he found himself feeling wise and debonair, somewhat arrogant in his own right. Looking at the linen and candlesticks and eating silver, he had a vision of Jeff Jimson someday sitting at the table's head, ably and destructively discoursing upon the topics of the day.

And, through it all, there was a place in his memory where a gawky and bad-smelling bumpkin stood trustingly and insufferably ridiculous, naïvely offering two dollars for the company of a girl whose society was eagerly sought by every unattached man in the country. Even yet, whenever Jeff permitted himself to recall the ghastly affair at the first benefit dance, he writhed in torment so agonizing that life itself seemed unbearable. Even yet, whenever he thought of success or full living, he thought in terms of clean-smelling work and good clothes and a full wallet. Of money so abundant and so casually come by that he could carelessly bid a hundred dollars for a lunchbox, and enjoy the breathless incredulity and envy of all who witnessed his extravagance.

"This present policy of the government's—of encouraging the settlers to come in and break the soil with plows—is not to be tolerated. One way or another, we'll stand them off. . . ."

The slashing, cawing voice nagged at his attention, and Jeff listened, not listening. Jeff just now was preoccupied with the discovery that Abby's eyes by candlelight were like stars in a dark winter sky. He was only dimly aware when the old man began addressing him directly.

"Old Desmond is getting too chair-bound to run his office the way it must be run. With land filers coming in the way they are, we're going to have to have an able-bodied man in that office. The board of county commissioners has voted to give him a deputy. As chairman of that board, I'm recommending you to fill the position."

Jeff turned to look at him in numbed surprise.

"Me?" he blurted, lifting a hand to his chest.

Garrett nodded, and smiled benevolently.

"You," he confirmed, obviously misinterpreting Jeff's expression. "You've shown an aptitude for the work, and you've earned a chance to show what you can do. We'll pay you a hundred and fifty dollars a month, and furnish board for your horses at the livery barn in town. And, just between the two of us, Desmond is about through. I shouldn't be surprised if he'll want to retire, next election. We'll want a man ready to step in and take over. I think that man is you."

Jeff sensed that he should rise to the occasion and in some fashion express his gratitude. He sensed that he should feel grateful, not grudging and somehow defrauded. After all, he would be doubling his pay, and there would be opportunity to increase it substantially again, when he succeeded to the sheriff's chair. On sheriff's pay, a man could support a wife—an ordinary wife at least. And right there, it seemed, was the whole basis of his feeling that he'd just had the world jerked out from under him: For if he were ever to take over the management of the Garrett holdings, as he'd had been brash enough to hope, it didn't seem logical or even sensible that he should be going to the sheriff's office now, leaving the ranch to Bowman's continued stewardship.

"I appreciate your thinking of me, Mr. Garrett," he heard himself saying, though his voice sounded strange. "More than I can say."

He didn't dare look at Abby again, and throughout the remainder of the meal the old man's words ate at his mind like acid: You've shown an aptitude for the work. . . .

By the time the meal was done, he was ready to believe that he

184

was being punished for last night's indiscretion, after all—that he'd had his question answered before he'd got around to asking it. But he was resolved not to leave the manor without knowing the worst for certain. So it seemed especially providential when, after dessert, his host invited him to take wine and cigars with him, in the privacy of the big study-office, off the parlor.

Minutes later, in the richly appointed sanctum where he'd never been before, Jeff looked unseeing at the great oak desk with its litter of rusted Indian knives, pottery, and other mementos of an earlier era, at the Indian clothing and old firearms that decorated the walls.

In light of Abby's whispered message at the stable that morning, he kept hoping, almost expecting, that Garrett would broach the big subject himself. But Garrett did not bring the matter up, and now that the time had come when he must speak out, the question which had been so easily phrased all day seemed impossible to put in words. In the yellow glow of the ornate lamp on the big desk, his host's narrow face became a mask of such daunting formidability that Jeff's tongue lay heavy as a stone at the bottom of his mouth.

Garrett noted the direction of his gaze and graciously offered to explain the various souvenirs, and Jeff grasped thankfully at the reprieve. While the old man talked, Jeff drank deeply of his wine and desperately sought words in which the question might be put.

"It is my intention someday to enlarge the collection. Make it something of a museum. Of course, I'll need a larger room in which to house it."

"It surely can be arranged," Jeff said vaguely, thinking of Abby.

The old man sighed. "It's the only real diversion I have any more. The collection, and running the red stallion that escaped me three years ago. That pistol on the wall belonged to Wild Bill Hickok. The cavalry carbine was picked up at Little Big Horn."

"That one?" Jeff said politely, reaching his glass again.

"But I'm boring you," the ranchman apologized. "And your cigar isn't lighted."

"Not at all," Jeff protested, leaning forward to accept a light. "But there is a matter I would like to mention. I"—puff—"well, that is . . ."

"Excuse me," Garrett interrupted, "but I believe your smoke will be more satisfactory if you remove the wrapper—"

Jeff was mortified to discover that he had lighted the cigar with the wrapper still intact, and the paper was ablaze, curling slowly toward his fingers. Flushing, he crushed the fire out, and removed the charred sheath to dispose of it.

"Now, then, you were saying . . . ah, did you really intend to drop that paper into your wine? The tray is at your left. I only mention it—"

Face aflame and jaw set grimly, Jeff wallowed through confused embarrassment to put his question, while the perspiration gathered on his face and neck. "What I wanted to say—to ask—is, well, I wanted you to know—I think you ought to know—that Abby and I—well, we would like your permission to . . ."

"My daughter and I have already discussed the matter." The old man smiled. "I am glad you mentioned it. I wanted to discuss it with you."

Jeff sat staring dumbly, feeling somewhat as if he had lifted a foot to mount a stair and found the step not there. The acrid blue eyes were laughing at him, but he scarcely noticed this. At least, his host and benefactor had not ordered him from the house and ranch for his brazen cheek. Weak with relief, he produced a folded new white handkerchief and wiped his face.

"But before we come to personal matters, there are a few items of business I would like to have settled. In the first place, your duties as deputy sheriff will commence tomorrow. And I'm afraid we're headed for more trouble over that homestead up on Hurricane, where you hung out awhile with Dempsy Rae."

"Trouble?" Jeff echoed.

Garrett nodded. "There is a fellow around, I hear, who claims to be a brother of Rae, from Texas. He's trying to file on that ground his brother lost. The land office agent in Quadrille stalled him, and got word to me. We can make our filing first, if we have the papers to him sometime tomorrow. I have the form right here, all filled out but for signing. I should explain perhaps that I'm filing in your name. You see, I used my homestead right when I pre-empted these bottoms, years ago. My wife's right, and Abby's, was used, too. Strap has used his, and just about everyone else I could trust not to double-cross me after the patent has been granted."

The paper was a filing form, completed for all but signature. Long after he had finished looking it over, Jeff kept up a pretense of reading, delaying the moment when he would have to look up, the moment when he would have to give his answer.

"We have to have that ground up there," the old man went on impatiently, as if reading the reluctance that Jeff was trying to conceal. "Now that we're grazing the mesa, we have to trail that way. The other trail is dry. If someone who could keep it were to get hold of it, he would have us where the hair is short. This Rae already has made the statement that he intends to shut us off the Hurricane trail unless we pay a toll. He could break us, if he made it stand up."

"What does he look like—this Rae?" Jeff asked, eyes still on the paper.

Garrett grunted. "Just another longhorn. Tall, and red-haired. Calls himself Barley, or some such name."

"Harley," Jeff corrected.

"Harley." Garrett nodded. "Harley Rae. You know him?"

Jeff hesitated, then inclined his head. "Yeah. I know him. I trailed cows with him."

Garrett waited, watching him, expecting him to say more. But Jeff had no more to say.

"We can't risk having that ground pass into hands that might be turned against us," Garrett went on finally. "Naturally, I thought of you when it came to filing. Your record here has been the best. Then, of course, there is Abby and the way you feel about her—"

The voice trailed off, suggestively, and Jeff suspected he was being reminded that his request to pay court to Abby had not yet been granted. Improbable as it seemed, he halfway believed that Garrett was offering him a deal—permission to keep company with his daughter in return for his signature on the papers. He could not believe it wholly. But people did strange things for land.

"Have you a pen?" he asked, still without meeting the watching eyes.

The ranchman looked on benignly as Jeff signed the document.

187

Then he leaned back in his swivel chair, his expression thoughtful.

"Now, as to this business of you and Abigail. I've certainly no objections to your having an understanding, since she assures me that she returns your feeling. But she has another year of schooling left, and I'm sure that—like myself—you would want to see her finish. . . ."

The old man said more. He said friendly and fatherly things that seemed of small consequence in light of the head-filling and heart-filling fact that he accepted Jeff as a prospective son-in-law. Jeff was stricken at the requirement that they wait a year. But he could see the justness of it. And a year was not a long time. Not to wait for a prize like Abby. According to the Bible, Jacob had labored seven years for his wife.

". . . I believe you'll agree, too, that it will be better if you do not see too much of one another in the time of waiting. Abigail will, of course, spend the winter in the East. She has already granted my request that you'll not exchange letters in that time, and I must require that you agree to honor the arrangement. Also, in light of everything, you must agree that you'll not try to see her, unchaperoned, while she is here."

Jeff's heady exultation palled at this. But no limiting condition could alter the incredible fact that Wate Garrett did not actively oppose the match. The comforting thought occurred to him that this must be the way such things were handled by the upper crust —that if he aspired to be upper crust himself, he must accept its ways.

"You have my word—on everything," he said humbly.

Now that the painful interview had ended, he was impatient to return to Abby and break the news to her—to hear her speak the pledge he had read so plainly in her eyes at supper. But Garrett's manner had turned brisk, and the next thing Jeff knew, his host was at the door that led outside, was bidding him good night.

"I may not see you in the morning. If not, Desmond is expecting you, and you had better start in the first thing. You won't need to bother with the filing papers. I'll deliver them myself. And now, I believe it's time all honest people were asleep. . . ."

Jeff was confident that the stipulation requiring that he not see Abby without a chaperon would be waived for this one night, in

188

deference to the occasion. He hoped and half-expected that his promised bride would be waiting for him on the porch—there to seal the contract in the old, old way.

But Abby wasn't waiting for him on the porch, and though he lingered hopefully for what seemed an eternity, she did not come. Jeff still felt wonderfully warm inside as he contemplated the night's astounding developments. But when the last light inside the house flicked out, and Abby still did not come to seal her pledge, the night wind suddenly felt cold against his skin.

Even Gut Desmond appeared to appreciate the irony of acquiring, as deputy, the dubious piece of driftwood he had arrested twice in the past: once as a mouthy juvenile delinquent and again as a hardened horse thief—both times suspected of involvement in murder. But it was not the lawman's way to question the doings of the lord, and he greeted Jeff that day with glum resignation. But when the new deputy had raised his right hand in front of Judge Coates and recited the oath that he would do his best to become all that he despised in mankind, the old sheriff could not restrain a wry comment.

"Well," he twanged dryly, producing the tarnished metal shield that went with the job, "I never figured, that day we fetched you in from Hurricane cuffed to your saddle, that I'd ever be pinning one of these to your shirt."

"Yeah," Jeff agreed ironically. "Life's plumb full of surprises. I was like you. I figured I'd sunk about as low as a man could, that day. I sure didn't see nothing like this coming."

Old Hitch saw the anomaly of it, too, and was even more direct than Gut Desmond had been in commenting on it. "There sure ain't no halfway with you, kid," the stableman observed, when Jeff appeared at the corral wearing his badge, to leave the Man Head horses until called for, and to announce that henceforth he would be using his own two animals again, at county expense.

"You got to be whole hog, or none. With you, they ain't no middle way. Either, by God, you're shooting at badges, or else you're wearing one! Which side you on, anyhow?"

"I'm on my side," Jeff told him curtly. "And if a man has got to be a son of a bitch to git along in this world, he's got no call to be half-assed. Whatever a man is, I say he's better off to be a good one."

"Well, you'd ought to know," the stableman told him, grinning. "You git around, seems like."

But in his first encounter with Harley Rae, Jeff did not explain himself so well. It was on his seventh day as deputy, and he was drinking alone in the Longhorn Bar where he was coming to spend more and more of his leisure, shoulders hunched against the rest of the world. As a habit, he didn't often look at a mirror any more. But as he put back his head to drain his glass, his eyes touched the glass back of the counter, and he froze in the act of drinking. A face was looking at him out of the mirror, and his first thought was that he'd had one glass too many—that he was losing his mind.

Jeff's worst nightmares in more than a year had to do with meeting up with Dempsey Rae, in the flesh or otherwise—with trying to explain to Demps the thing that had happened to him, the thing he had become. During his waking hours, he generally managed to avoid such thoughts. But, in sleep, his fancy could not be ordered, and more and more of late he had been hailed before Demps for judgment. Always, in such dreams, his tongue was gripped by the same paralysis that held his brain and his limbs, and he could not answer the terrible accusation he saw in two tawny eyes.

He knew he was not sleeping now. He knew the face could not be there, but it was. The same accusation was traced in its every line, and the same nightmare held Jeff helpless and silent—a man on a gallows, a man in a grave.

"You're Jimson, ain't you?"

Jeff heard the voice faintly, still as in a dream. But the sound did something to him. It wasn't Demps's voice that he heard. The eyes weren't Demps's eyes. The hair wasn't Demps's hair. The hair was red. Red as that of a blood-colored horse.

The paralysis passed so abruptly that the liquid in Jeff's throat choked him. He suffered a spasm of coughing that added further embarrassment to his unmanly seizure. Mentally, he swore at himself for a disgusting lush. It seemed an added ignominy that he had to brush tears from his eyes before he could face his accoster.

"My name is Rae," the voice was saying when he heard it

again. "Harley Rae. Maybe you remember me. You joined a cow drive I was on. The time you hooked onto my brother, Dempsey. You remember?"

"Hell, yes." Jeff nodded, trying to sound cordial. "How are you?"

He put out a hand as he spoke. The hard blue eyes glanced down at it, then moved back to Jeff's face. The hand was not taken. Jeff pulled it back, looked at it searchingly, then dropped it to his side.

"I just heard about Demps," the hostile, held-in voice went on. "I come up here to find out what happened to him. From all I hear, you're the only one that can tell me."

Jeff turned back to his glass, wishing he were better fortified, but somehow unable to drink with Harley looking on. He tried to get angry, but couldn't.

"Harley," he said in a voice that was strained and off-key, "everything happened up there just like I said in the statement they made me make at the time. Goddamnit, it just happened that way. I know. I was there and seen it."

The hard eyes didn't soften. They looked him up and down. "You appear to have come off whole-hided."

Jeff bridled, or tried to. It wouldn't come off. "I had no chance to mix in it. They had each other down before I could git to a gun."

Harley sneered. "And only you lived to tell the tale!"

Jeff nodded and said nothing. Harley's manner didn't soften. "How'd he git in bad with the association?"

Jeff told him, as best he could. Told the whole story, commencing with their mavericking, and getting fired. Unmindful of the intent listeners around, he told of leaving Demps, and looking for work elsewhere. He told of returning, and finding Demps set up on the Hurricane homestead.

"I never did git straight on everything. Demps was close-mouthed, and wouldn't talk about the horses. I was told after that this horse-thief ring was stealing switchers up in Montan' and driving them to that place on Hurricane to fatten and twist out. I was told Demps found the hideout, and filed on it, then offered to do the twisting—for a cut. This Sundance tied on with the

191

gang and rode in with the others. That's why we didn't suspicion him."

Harley's eyes were unrelenting. "And when it was all over, Garrett felt so sorry for you he handed you a riding job and hung a deputy badge on you!"

Jeff tried to make his eyes stand to the eyes of his accuser, but couldn't do it. This was the nightmare, after all. This was facing Demps and trying to explain a thing that had no explanation.

"Then you felt so grateful to Garrett that you filed on Demps's homestead, to hold it for the syndicate—after the agent tipped Garrett off about me!"

Jeff looked at the speaker's knees and said nothing. He wouldn't look lower, but he couldn't look higher.

"I been hearing a lot of things about you, Jimson. Far as I can find out, they never was a man had anything to do with you that he didn't git et up at the end. Well, I wanted to tell you. I'm here to find out how Demps was really killed, and when I do, it's going to be all day for somebody. . . . And about that homestead. You can tell Wate Garrett that I don't recognize his proxy filing. You can tell him if he undertakes to move me off that ground, he better send his men, and keep his lap dogs to home."

In the silence that followed the Texian's departure, Jeff stood hunched over his drink, aware of the score of faces that were still turned attentively toward him. There had been a time when the knowledge that so many eyes and ears had witnessed his degradation would have made him ill. Now he could shrug it off as just another bad time. After a while, he became aware that Hog Muldroon, the paunchy barkeep, was eyeing him in sour distaste.

"By God, if I wore a law badge, I wouldn't take talk like that off no man!"

Jeff met the lowering gaze, and smiled a smile that had no meaning. "Hog," he said, "if you wore a law badge, there ain't nothing you wouldn't do."

As Desmond's deputy, Jeff enjoyed free rein in all things. The sheriff made no pretense of approving his appointment, and offered no direction.

"The county board hired you," he growled on one occasion

192

when Jeff had asked for orders. "Let them tell you what to do."

Jeff understood by now that the county board was Garrett, so he went on doing much as he'd done before—headquartering in town, but policing the range for Man Head. Discouraging settlers and thieves and would-be thieves, reporting on grass and water conditions, shooting predators and trying generally to earn his wages.

In the course of it all, he was a frequent caller at the headquarters ranch, an attentive suitor paying court to his promised wife— pretending all was as it should be. There were Sunday dinners in the oak-paneled dining-room at the big house, and evenings spent in talk of trivials with his prospective father-in-law in the chandeliered ballroom-size parlor, while Abby played the organ and sang in a sultry langorous voice that made him frantic with impatience. There were a few rides together, at which Dolly Bart or someone of the ranch hands always accompanied them in the role of servant-guardian to the master's daughter. Usually, by common accord, they would manage at some point in the course of the ride to elude the chaperon. Then there were hurried embraces in which Jeff kissed ice and fire, and wondered painfully how much longer he could deny the hunger that was rising in him like fever.

"Don't, Jeff. Not so hard. You're hurting me!"

They had pulled their horses close together in a cottonwood stand out of sight of their escort, and Jeff had lifted her almost out of the saddle, to bruise her mouth with his.

"I want to hurt you!" he said between set teeth, when his mouth was free again.

"But—why?"

She pushed back in his arms to look up at him. They both were breathless from the long, demanding kiss. They both were breathing hard, and there was a darkness in Abby's eyes, like hurt or fear.

"Why, Jeff?"

Jeff couldn't answer. He could only release her, and start his horse, and ride along in silence that was half-sullen. Abby rode beside him, her questioning eyes on his face. After a while, he managed to smile.

"I don't know. I expect because I can't ever ketch you."

193

It was an old joke between them. Abby tried to answer his smile, but didn't quite succeed.

"But, Jeff," she said in small, sad voice, "you have caught me now. I don't want to go away again. I've been to school long enough. I want to stay home—with you."

Jeff looked at her through a rising golden haze, warmer and brighter than sunlight. The old kingly impulsion lifted him like a swelling wave. He was all radiance, all bitter gold inside.

"But Wate says . . ."

"I know what he says. But I've already told him I won't go."

Exalted, gleeful but deeply perturbed, Jeff looked away from her, out over the valley that lay rich and fertile before them. He smiled wisely and shook his head.

"That wouldn't change his mind, Abby. They tell me that nothing ever changes his mind."

Abby was quiet a minute. Then she spoke quickly. "Jeff—we could elope. I could meet you in town, and we could take the train to Cheyenne. We could be married there, and send Daddy a wire. He couldn't do anything then."

Elope.

The word struck him like a fist. Jeff turned and looked at her as at a stranger. His mouth tasted swollen and brassy.

"Elope?" he repeated blankly, as if the word had no meaning.

Abby was blushing. Her eyes looked penitent. But she stood her ground.

"I'm tired of waiting, Jeff. Aren't you?"

Jeff's head jerked up and down, but his mind was in a whirl. "Wate would hunt us down, with dogs."

"He wouldn't, Jeff. He couldn't. I'm of the age of consent."

Jeff rode along, staring into space, trying hard to think. The suggestion was so novel, so exciting, that he found it hard to get his breath. But he knew somewhere behind his agitation that he couldn't do things that way. From what he had seen of Garrett, he didn't doubt that the lord of Man Head would disinherit even his only child for such rank disobedience. And even if Jeff had a place to take a wife, he couldn't take Abby out of the Big House. She belonged there, with chandeliers and white linen and old silver. She was chandeliers and white linen and old silver. He couldn't take her to a dugout hovel in some cutbank, such as he'd lived in before coming to Man Head. He could do many things, but not that.

"The book law says you're old enough, Abby," he said heavily. "But Wate Garrett is the law in this county. He would bring you back, and lock you up in the tower room. He would hang me for—for—" the word *rape* would not pass his lips; not when it had to do with Abby—"for kidnaping."

"Not if he couldn't find us, Jeff. We could go somewhere, and stay for a while. He would be angry. But time would heal that. He would want us to come back—someday."

Jeff was staggered. He was weak. He was tempted almost beyond endurance. But he still knew it wouldn't do. He didn't know exactly why. But he did sense that his feeling for Wate Garrett was involved, as much as was his feeling for Abby. He had never known a father. There had been substitute fathers all along: McCord and old Hitch, and especially Demps. But none had quite filled the bill the way Wate Garrett filled it. Wate Garrett was security, was the supreme arbiter of men's fates, was God. Jeff's loyalty toward him was as intense and undivided as his earlier loyalty toward Demps. Wate Garrett had wealth and status and power. He wouldn't get hanged by the night riders or shot by a hired skulk, leaving Jeff to the mercies of a hostile and baleful jungle-world. Wate Garrett was a good father. Jeff wanted to be an obedient son.

"No, Abby," he said finally, looking straight ahead lest he should weaken again, "when we're married, we'll do it in style. We won't run off like—like a couple of nobodies."

The girl was silent a long time, and when Jeff finally looked at her again, she was riding along with downcast eyes, fingering the pleats in her riding skirt.

"I'm sorry, Jeff," she said finally. "I didn't mean to throw myself at you. I guess I must have just lost my head."

Jeff closed his eyes and groaned. "Oh, Abby—don't—"

He could say no more, and was spared the necessity by the timely arrival of Dolly Bart. It was the first time that he ever had welcomed the horse herder's presence, and instead of giving him

195

a cold shoulder as usual, Jeff spoke pleasantly to him, and even joked with him about not being able to keep up with them.

Throughout the rest of the ride, Abby was subdued and withdrawn. Her eyes avoided Jeff, and she didn't speak except when forced to. Jeff completed the ride in turmoil, and was saddened and alarmed when she told him good-by at the dooryard gate, instead of inviting him up to the house as was her custom.

"Abby," he said desperately, voice held to an undertone, "I'll speak to your pa again. I'll make him give us his consent—now."

She looked at him for the first time since their talk, and he was dismayed again to see how hurt she was—how proud and vindictive.

"It wouldn't do any good, Jeff," she told him brightly. "You were right about that. He says—he says it's the ranch you're interested in—not me."

Before he could say any more, she had turned and was walking quickly up the path to the house. Jeff started to call after her, but changed his mind, not knowing what he would say.

He saw her frequently, thereafter. There were other rides, other Sunday dinners, other parlor evenings with old Garrett's presence a restraint on them both. But things had changed since their conversation. Even when they were alone, the restraint was still on them. There were no more embraces, no more stolen kisses. Whenever he was demanding, she was elusive, pretending not to know what it was he wanted. When he turned sullen, her mood brightened to maddening gaiety. When he tried to talk of things that mattered, she turned his words into nonsense, and laughed at him for being solemn.

"Abby," he said one day in rising exasperation, "I tell you, I'll speak to Wate again. I'll talk to him tonight."

"No, thank you, Mr. Jimson," she said lightly, shaking her curls like a spoiled child. "I've changed my mind. I'm going back to school. When I finish, I'll join the sufragettes—and never marry any man!"

They were out in the stables, combing the mouse-brown Morgan. Jeff caught her roughly about the waist, and turned her face to his.

"Don't say that!" he said harshly.

She exploded against him, and with a strength that astounded him broke out of his arms. "I say anything I please! And I don't have to be mauled—by you or anyone."

Before he could shake his stupefaction, a step had sounded behind him, and he turned to see Strap Bowman standing long and lean as a horseweed, just inside the stall door. The foreman's hands were hooked into his gunbelt, fingers hanging down like skewered meat. His eyes bored into Jeff's like augurs.

"You having any trouble in here, Abigail?" he asked softly. "Is there anybody you'd like horsewhipped off the place?"

"If I'm having any trouble, it's nothing I can't handle for myself!" Abby answered, showing Strap the same startling anger she had turned on Jeff. Back of her anger, Jeff could see she was badly frightened. And that Jeff could understand, being frightened himself. Strap could not have appeared so quickly unless he'd been eavesdropping for some time. If he reported to Garrett what he had seen and heard, it would not be well for either of them.

"It would be a fine pleasure to heave him out of here, if you want it done," Strap insisted, his malignant eyes still on Jeff.

All Jeff's being clamored for violence, for a settling of an old enmity then and there. But his good sense overruled his emotions. He stood rigid a moment, giving back Strap's challenging stare. Then, feeling low and crawly again, he picked up his dropped currycomb and joined Abby in silently grooming the pony.

Jeff didn't see Abby often after that. Nor did he carry out his threat to speak to Garrett again. His intention was to do so, even in the face of Abby's opposition. But the right opportunity seemed not to present itself—or, when it did, he saw things in too clear and sane a perspective to risk the old man's displeasure. So the remaining weeks went by, and he didn't repeat his request.

Yet, in his way, he did renew his petition. In his way, he made a renewed bid for his employer's approval with almost every day that passed. He covered the range like a hunting animal driven by hunger. He drove himself from dawn until dark, hunting for evidence of trespass or thievery or incompetence. Some days his search was successful, and he had clear evidence to act on. Some

197

days the hunting was poorer, and he had to stretch evidence to have anything to go on.

When roundup time came again, he joined the wagons out on the range and, in the pretense of checking the legality of the various operations, lent valuable service as outrider and circle man, as watchdog at the branding fires. Bowman started out by ignoring him. But the day that Jeff personally cut a dozen heifer yearlings out of the hold herd and pushed them back with the stock to be retained, Strap pressed a showdown.

"Jimsie," he said through contained anger, "you're kind of overstepping your territory. You stick to your sheriff's job, and leave the running of the ranch to me, or one of us is going to go down the trail talking to himself."

Jeff met the hostile eyes, and for the first time since he'd gone to work at Man Head, he stood up to the foreman.

"I take orders from Wate," he stated coldly. "The way you run things, it's a good thing you got some free help."

"Have it your own way," Bowman answered inimically. And, within the hour, Wate Garrett sought Jeff out, looking fussed and bothered.

"Jeff," the ranchman started out, his eyes on Jeff's horse, "I hear I'm opening myself up to criticism, having a man on the county payroll out here riding my roundup. Besides that, I'm afraid you're neglecting your job. Gut Desmond has been under the weather the last few days. I understand there's been no one in the sheriff's office at all."

Jeff blinked at him, and felt his jaw come out. This was a defeat he could not afford. But he didn't know what to do about it.

"But why hang around the office, in town?" he said in protest. "Nobody ever shows up there."

"I don't believe you're in a position to judge," the old man answered more sharply, looking at him now. "I don't believe you've put in a full hour in the office since taking the job. And that's your first duty as deputy, you know. Just to be there, available, in case you're needed. Now, I suggest you leave this end to us, and start tending to business."

Tending to business. . . .

The words were so ill-chosen, so unfair and unreasonably blind

198

that Jeff could have wept in chagrin. Aside from the clear-cut triumph they afforded to Strap, the words seemed to confirm what he had suspected all along, but had steadfastly refused to admit: That his assignment to work in town was made in the form of exile, not as reward for work well done.

"Just as you say, Mr. Garrett," he sighed. "Not as I give a damn."

15: Stray Dog

Jeff didn't see Abby to say good-by to her before her departure for the East. Old Garrett merely remarked to him that she had gone, one day when Jeff returned from a two-day ride to Rustler Station, to investigate rumors that the station café was serving unblest beef.

"She said to tell you she was sorry to miss you," her father reported. "She said that she'll be seeing you, in the spring."

The words sounded more like Garrett's than his daughter's. It had been on Garrett's say-so that he'd made the ride to Rustler; there had been no evidence that stolen beef was being butchered, and Jeff half-suspected the old man of deliberately arranging his absence so there could be no farewells spoken.

"Thanks," Jeff said, eyes averted to hide his feelings. "I'm sorry, too."

"Now, Desmond's leg is plaguing him again," the old man continued with an abrupt change of subject. "That means you're the sheriff, when he's not on duty. And you're probably in for a lively time of it, with all these settlers flocking in, and nothing to eat but other people's cattle."

"Settlers?" Jeff repeated. "I haven't seen many around."

"I'm not surprised," Garrett snapped. "They have little business in the Longhorn Bar, where you put in your time. They're congregating up around Drake's hog ranch, in between us and Shoe. I don't know what they're going to live on, besides Man Head cattle."

The bright blue weather of fall curdled into blustery winter, and a part of Jeff rejoiced that he had a comfortable town job, keeping a chair warm in Desmond's office. But that part of him was whistling in the dark, and as weeks lengthened into months and still no letter came from Abby, the winter chill began to numb his mind and hopes.

He wasn't forgetting the terms forced on them, the night of their supposed betrothal. He didn't expect Abby to violate her pledge, any more than he would have broken his word on the matter of letters. But, in light of their quarrel and the way she had left without good-by, he expected some note from her, some assurance that things were still as they should be. If he'd been at the ranch, she couldn't have got a letter into his hands without her father knowing. But she knew that he was here in town. She could have written without fear of discovery. But no note came, and—imagining that he was becoming a laughingstock—he soon ceased haunting the little post office at the front of Gentile's store.

Then one day, a week or so before Christmas, the merchant came into his office, a small white envelope in his hand.

"This here came in today. I figured you might want it, right away."

Jeff thanked him in a casual voice, and tried not to seem to snatch at the missive. Once he had it in his hand, he waited impatiently for the bearer to leave, not bothering to conceal his anxiety. And, when alone at last, he looked at the neat purple-ink lettering which spelled his name, and thought how it resembled the writer—how he could have picked it as Abby's, out of a whole roomful of letters.

He was spoiling to know what was inside. But he was fearful, too. Besides, it was the first piece of mail he ever had received. He weighed it in his hand, smelled its haunting perfume, and tortured himself awhile. Then he took out his jackknife and made a ceremony of opening it.

But ritual and incantation were unavailing. The envelope held nothing but a card—an ornate card, with a brown-and-white picture of the three wise men on their camels, following a star that gave off light in rays as thick as wagon spokes. Across the top, in fancy scroll, was the legend: *Merry Christmas and a Happy New Year.* At the bottom, in the same purple ink as the address, the same neat, precise hand had inscribed five magic words: *With all my love—Abby.*

Hungrily, he turned it over. But the back was blank. He picked up the envelope again and peered hopefully inside. He turned the envelope in his hands, thinking he somehow must have missed something, somewhere. The envelope bore the printed words, *Boston, Mass.* But there was no return address. There was nothing but the formal and impersonal *With all my love.*

For a long time, Jeff sat motionless, staring at the painted scene, bitterness and disappointment building up in him. He had a ring picked out, over in Gentile's showcase. He had the money to pay for it, and had figured to send it on for Christmas. But he had no address. He couldn't ask her father for it. Not as things stood. As things stood, he could hardly send it if he'd had the address. Yet he sensed that if the ring were not sent now, it would never be sent. Would never pass from him to Abby, ever. So what was he to do? What was any man to do, having no Christmas star to guide him, like the wise men in the picture?

"Hell," he said, crumpling the card. "We could all be wise men, if we had a beacon light like that to follow!"

He saw Garrett frequently in town, and the ranchman's manner toward him continued cordial. Too cordial, it sometimes seemed to Jeff, in light of certain memories. At first, the old man generally had some little tidbit of news to pass on: Abby had been down to New York, to visit relatives there; she had been down a week with chills and fever, but was better now; she was doing well in her studies, and had won some kind of honor or other. But if she sent any personal word to Jeff, that word was not passed on.

As winter lengthened and their encounters became less and less frequent, the prospective father-in-law began to neglect even to mention his daughter's name, unless Jeff took the lead. In time, the answers became so evasive and unsatisfactory that Jeff finally gave up asking after her.

There were times when, reviewing the matter in his mind, he

was certain that the whole affair had been a put-up job—times when he admitted to himself that Garrett could not have been sincere in his agreement, or he would have held Jeff at the ranch to learn the business, instead of exiling him to town.

But his faith in Abby continued strong. He told himself convincingly that she was merely an obedient daughter, as was proper, that her failure to write was only added evidence of a bright, unsullied honor. But back behind conviction, there was gnawing doubt.

He didn't see or hear of Harley Rae for several months. But when the winds began to blow warm again, cutting the drifts from the draws and ringing the potholes with greening grass, the predicted settlers began to appear, in rattletrap buggies and wagons loaded with chickens and children, some with cows tied behind. Most didn't linger in Quadrille, but kept rolling north to Squatters' Row, up somewhere west of Ekard, where the early arrivals had a Grange organized and were helping latecomers to locate.

Jeff heard no direct news of trouble on the ranges. But one day an angry delegation came in while he was dozing at his desk. He counted six men, all obviously farmers by their look. They were headed by the sullen, thick-set man Jeff had scared off the place on Cat Creek some months before. The man seemed to find Jeff's face familiar, but not to place it immediately in his mind.

"My name is Mundy," the farmer began ill-temperedly. "I got a complaint to make. Us boys have all filed homesteads, legal and within the law. But that Garrett outfit is making trouble for us. We know our rights, and we want . . ."

The heavy voice trailed off as recognition dawned on the square, blunt face. A kind of horror filled the baleful eyes, much as if Jeff had turned into a tiger as they watched.

"Looks like our mistake, boys," the farmer said, backing toward the door. "Looks like we handle this ourselves—if it gits handled a-tall."

Jeff watched them leave, scowling and talking in undertones. Then he laughed mirthlessly and headed for the Longhorn to have another drink. When he returned to the office, he found Garrett and Bowman in long-faced conference with Gut Desmond. The talk broke off as he came in. Garrett nodded a greeting.

"Come in, Jeff. We're just talking about a friend of yours."

"A friend of mine?"

It was odd, but when Jeff tried to think of someone who qualified as such, he couldn't for the life of him bring such a person to mind.

"It's this fellow Rae," Garrett went on. "He refuses to recognize your filing on that Hurricane homestead he's squatting on. We've tried to move him, but he won't budge. I've taken the matter up with Theo Coates, and he's given us a court order telling Rae to pack his rag sack and vacate. We want the papers served, right away."

Jeff leaned against the door frame. To gain a little time, he produced his tobacco sack and tried to roll a cigarette. His hands were shaking so bad he spilled the golden grain all down him. He grinned apologetically and put the sack back in his shirt pocket. He put his hands in his pants pockets out of sight, and tried to look disinterested. He couldn't explain to Garrett how he felt about the homestead up on Hurricane. He couldn't make him understand why he had never been back since the day the posse had taken him away, almost two years ago. He couldn't tell his patron and benefactor that he wouldn't be able to go up now, on such an errand as the one proposed. Yet he knew he couldn't go through with it.

"Why not just let him wither on the vine?" he suggested weakly. "He can't last long up there, if we just ignore him."

Garrett laughed dryly. "Our vine is the one that stands to wither, with that bobcat, holed in up there. He stopped Strap at the lower bars the other day, and refused to let cattle pass, without a toll charge. We've got to convert him to Christianity."

Jeff smiled a little. "You mean one man bluffed the whole damned outfit?"

"He wasn't bluffing," Strap scowled. "The son of a bitch would of shot. Long as he's got no business being up there, I figured he comes in your department, not mine. You'd ought to do something to earn your keep."

Garrett nodded approval of his foreman's words, and thrust a legal-looking paper out at Jeff. Jeff stared at the ornate script, and felt helplessly trapped. All the while, he felt Bowman's eyes on him. And now as always he thought of a giant hunter-insect whose feelers waved incessantly to catch and register every sound and impulse that stirred the air. Now he sensed that the boring green eyes read his disloyal feelings—that, having detected his weakness, they would strike him through it.

"I'll see what I can do," he said with creditable equanimity.

During the days that followed, Jeff had it harder and harder to remember that drink was futile. Most of his waking time was spent in the Longhorn, quarreling with Hog Muldroon and anyone at hand, trying to get his courage up to make a ride to Hurricane, to serve a fraudulent paper on a man he couldn't look between the eyes. A man who likely would shoot him when he tried. A man he couldn't shoot in self-defense.

Trying to drown a thing that the whiskey didn't get to.

When Desmond began to crowd him on the matter of Harley's arrest, he took the coward's way and stayed in his bed at Mom Phlett's boardinghouse, pretending sickness that wasn't wholly feigned. Then, unexpectedly, he won reprieve.

"Just as well you didn't git around to serve that paper," Desmond told him during one of his infrequent visits, on the fifth day of Jeff's confinement. "That red-haired feather merchant is bringing suit against Wate and you, in district court, to have your filing nullified. We'll just let things slide now, till the case is called and decided."

"Don't he know any more than to go to court with Wate?" Jeff asked wonderingly.

"There's a heap that knucklehead don't know," the sheriff said aggrievedly. "Them kind just have to learn. Ain't no way you can tell 'em."

The news speeded Jeff's recovery, but the day he left his bed he received a shock that almost put him down again. Abby Garrett had returned from the East during his voluntary indisposal, and had not called on him. Strap Bowman had met her at the station in the ranch buckboard and had whisked her out of town. Guarded inquiry around turned up no evidence that she had even asked about him. And this was to have been the summer of their wedding!

At first, he toyed with the idea of riding out to see her. But the perversity he was nourishing for no clear reason intervened, and he stayed in town.

"She knows where I am, if she wants to see me," he told himself sullenly. "This time, the mountain can come to Mahomet." But day followed day, and Mahomet waited in vain. The mountain didn't move.

In the beginning, even while he sulked, his mind made up excuses for her. She was tired from her long trip. She was busy getting settled in her home again, giving her neglected pony needed exercise. She wanted to come, but couldn't be openly running after a man; the upper-crust ladies simply didn't behave that way. She had every reason to expect him to call on her, not knowing of the peculiar chain of events that rendered this impossible. She couldn't know of her father's coolness toward him, his exile from the ranch, the lack of news he'd had of her—of any of the thousand and one little incidents and looks and words, none of which was significant in itself, but which, taken altogether, did add up to something he could no longer pretend to be blind to.

Besides, he heard on every side that Wate was out in the badlands again, running the red stud. It was a safe bet that Abby was out at his horse camp, sharing in the sport. She wouldn't be at the ranch to see him, even if he should ride out.

But there was little comfort in the latter speculation. For almost two years now, Jeff had been ignoring the fact that he did not rate invitation to Wate Garrett's mustang-chasing parties. He had known, without admitting knowledge, that such invitation was the highest token of the old man's esteem, the ultimate in social acceptability in the county. Always before, he had told himself that his work was too important to the company, that the reason for this exclusion was that he had more important things to do. But now the long-sustained illusion was breaking down.

This spring, so far as he knew, there were no bigwigs or celebrities on hand as there had been on most occasions previously. No pink-cheeked company stockholders from New York and Boston; no monocled Haw-Haws from the English ranches on the Powder to the north. But Judge Coates who didn't know which end of the horse to bridle had been up to the camp for a two-day outing, as had Gut Desmond and the others in the courthouse crowd. John Poe had been invited, and Jim Gentile, and almost everyone that Jeff knew, except the homesteaders and the most lowly of the hired hands.

"How come you ain't out chasing horses, with the rest the club?" Hitch asked him.

"On account of us horses have decided to stick together, from here on out," Jeff answered shortly.

16: Bunch-Quitter

Jeff didn't even hear that Garrett had finally recaptured the red stud until morning of the day that the civil case of Harley Rae versus Jefferson Jimson and Wateman Garrett was to be heard.

The word had gone around that the Grange was backing Rae, and the farmers started coming in from Squatters' Row in time for morning court, apparently not knowing that the case had been set for afternoon, to give Garrett time to ride in from the tablelands. A few of the homesteaders rode horseback, but most were in shabby wagons and buggies, drawn by hungry-looking horses whose coats were still rough with winter hair.

Those who came in rigs almost invariably shared their seats with roughly dressed, wan-faced women, while the boxes behind were loaded with children—poorly dressed in cast-offs and dusty from the drive, but scrubbed to a shine beneath the dust. For the first time in Jeff's residence, the sun-blistered street rang to the sound of shouts and laughter, and the atmosphere was almost a gala one as more and more teams arrived.

The women, like their children, were on a holiday; but the men were cautious and sullen. While the women chattered and bustled in and out of the stores, the men banded together as if for protection, to stand in little groups around the courthouse, watching the street and rarely speaking.

Jeff stood alone in the doorway of the sheriff's office he someday would inherit, watching for a man with red hair and a Texas way about him. When at last he saw him coming in, riding the stockinged sorrel pony that once had belonged to Demps, he eased himself back inside the office and watched secretly from the window, like a fugitive.

Harley Rae had grown a winter beard that glistened red as his hair in the morning sun. He was wearing a pistol and carried a rifle in his saddle boot. He had a quiet, confident smile for his backers and well-wishers, a bold, challenging stare for the townsmen he didn't know. He pulled up in front of the Hat Saloon, swung down, and with a sweeping salute to all in sight, clanked swaggeringly inside.

Jeff was still at the window, still staring wistfully at the swinging doors of the Hat and trying to envision the scene inside when he heard other horses on the road and saw Strap Bowman and Dolly Bart come up at a swinging trot. Strap swung down at the tie rail, handed his reins to Dolly, and came inside. He was dusty and preoccupied, in one of his executive sweats.

"Where's Gut?" the foreman's voice rapped out.

Jeff shrugged. "He's around somewhere. Keeping an eye on the farmers, I guess."

The foreman turned on his heel and departed, scowling. Jeff watched him go, then stepped to the door and nodded at Bart.

"What's up, Dolly?"

"Wate and the boys are headed this way with that red stud and fifty, sixty broomtails. He wants the street cleared, so he can whoop the wild bunch down into the railroad corrals."

Jeff came out of the torpor that had held him all morning. "You mean to say he caught that stud finally?"

Dolly nodded. "We trapped him a couple days ago. Nothing to it, once he built the right kind of trap, and got a horse that could run. Why, that big blue devil could outrun a hawk!"

Dolly then went into an enthusiastic and detailed account of how the capture had been effected, with the aid of Garrett's new blue horse. But, though aware of the unrhythmic rise and fall of the boyish voice, Jeff didn't hear much of what was said. News of the stallion's downfall had hit him with an impact that was out of all proportion to its significance. Omnipotent though Garrett was, he had until this day been defied successfully by another living being, there in the country where he ruled as petty king. Jeff hadn't known how much comfort he'd taken in the knowledge until Dolly brought the word of the rebel's capture. Somehow it seemed a personal defeat—another and a final disaster to Jeff himself.

"What's he bringing him down to town for?" he asked hollowly when he could speak again.

"He's got a Army buyer coming up to trim the bunch," Dolly explained. "The ones the cavalry can't use he figures to ship as canners. Wate don't love a dollar no more than his right arm, you know."

When Jeff looked down the street again, he saw that Strap had located Desmond, and the two were clearing the street of rigs and horses. In ordinary circumstances, he would have resented Strap's snubbing him so pointedly, in work that concerned his office. But right now, he was content to be left out, even though the work was serving Garrett directly. It seemed a bit early to start pushing the farmer crowd around, and he was glad to be spared the taking of even a minor part in the confinement of the big red stud.

An hour or so later, Jeff was in the office doorway again, watching the wild horse band swing onto the cleared street, raising a dust that hung like ribbon fog in the hot, still air. The willow-legged colts were jackrabbiting one instant, staggering the next; the mares were rope-scarred and tender-footed, their nostrils closed by brutal tie-wire sutures that forced mouth breathing and broke their wind, rendering them easier to handle. All were wet with muddy foam, and all were panting hoarsely. Dry mouths hung open against the heat; tongues lolled like the tongues of hard-run dogs.

Behind them, flanking and pointing and whooping them up, came almost a dozen Man Head mustangers, dusty and unshaven and showing the grind of the ride.

"You can sure pick out that red devil's colts," Gut Desmond observed comfortably, down at the tie rail where he stood with Strap Bowman. "But they don't look much today. Army must be hard up for switchers, if Wate can unload that layout on them."

The thought came to Jeff that Wate must be the one hard up, to be handling horses as the ones in the street had been handled, just for the few dollars a head they would bring. But, naturally, he did not speak the thought aloud. Anyhow, the drag of the band had now hove into view, and when Jeff saw the red stud, all other thoughts were promptly driven from his mind.

The magnificent creature stood seventeen hands high if one, and his glistening coat was rope-scarred and lathering like the others. But his soft flaring nostrils had not been pierced by the punishing wire twists that choked the cayuses down. Instead, he wore a heavy leather halter and was being rop-led by two riders who kept the width of the street between their ponies, as if respectful of their captive's hoofs and teeth. His legs were sidelined in rope hobbles so that he couldn't take a full stride, but must mince along like a circus dancing horse, taking three steps to the others' one. But there was still ample pride and defiance in the arch of his head and tail, and back on the snaky torso was an eloquent memento of an old victory over the man whose brand he wore but whose mastery was yet to be acknowledged: two frayed hemp cinches securing a fine oak saddle tree from which all leather had long been scuffed, together with skirt and stirrups, leaving only the weathered wood.

"Ain't much left of that saddle, is they?" Desmond grunted.

"Not much," Strap agreed, his tone reverent. "But, such as there is, Wate finally got it back. He usually gits what he goes after."

By now, the mincing stud had passed the sheriff's office, and Garrett himself was riding up out of the dust, a week's growth of hair on his face, a week's coating of badlands alkali on his clothes. The blue horse he was riding was the nearest thing to a camel that Jeff had ever seen. The jubilant pride with which Wate bore himself put Jeff in mind of stories he'd read of the way the old Roman generals used to parade vanquished foes through the home city's streets at the close of victorious campaigns, to impress the homefolks. And, in the thought, he found the explanation of why the red stallion had been brought into town with the mustangs instead of being taken directly to the ranch—why the beat-up saddle remnant had not been stripped from the scarred back out at the mustang trap: It was here in Quadrille that the stud had humbled his owner in front of the town's population. Here it was, therefore, that the renegade was being exhibited in surrender, and on a day when the scheduled court trial had brought people in from all over the county.

Up on the tablelands, while its wearer was running free, the skeletal saddle had been an everlasting taunt to Wate Garrett. But, here in town, with the stud wearing bonds of a captive, the saddle became a striking emblem of defeat, an impressive token of the long-range futility of bucking the system.

Bowman and Desmond had stepped out into the street to offer their felicitations, and Jeff knew that it would be to his advantage to follow the example. But, without asking himself why, he stood firmly where he was, unable to do a thing he knew would benefit him in the end.

Standing there alone and aloof of activities in the street, he felt conspicuous and irreparably estranged, envious of those who fit well together and could painlessly render tribute where tribute was due, perversely incapable of making so small an investment in his own future.

Hale and vigorous at sixty as most men at forty, Garrett was pulling up in front of the Drovers House. He was smiling around at the crowd—his eyes somehow missing Jeff Jimson. He was nodding and waving at his congratulators, and simultaneously giving his mustangers instruction in the matter of confining the red stud in the stockyards at the end of the street. He was dismounting, and climbing the hotel steps, surrounded by retainers who competed for the nearer positions, wagging around him like eager dogs.

It was a noisy, high-powered group that swept up the hotel steps and into the lobby, leaving Jeff alone on the street with the silently watching farmers. He looked down at the tracks and saw that the stockyard gates already had closed on the captive stud and his harem. A gust of wind hurled a scattering of gravel against his face, and somewhere in the distance, thunder rumbled ill-temperedly.

His eyes, never still, kept raking the street for a sight they did not see. He had expected Abby to come riding in with her father behind the horse herd. But she hadn't shown up. He could only conclude that she hadn't been at the mustang camp after all. Yet it seemed unlikely that she would not be in town on this of all days, to share in her father's triumph.

He was standing in the office doorway, morosely staring out, when Gut Desmond appeared on the hotel steps, and beckoned urgently. Jeff crossed over to join him, and the old man spoke snappishly.

"Where you been? Wate's asking for you."

"I'm flattered as hell," Jeff mumbled, pushing through the doors.

A kind of council was convened in a little private dining room off the lobby, and the company if small was select. Judge Coates was there, already wearing his courtroom manner, as was John Poe. Bowman was there, and—of course—Garrett himself, seated at the table's head, a sheaf of papers in front of him.

The ranchman hadn't washed or brushed his clothes. He looked up as Jeff came in, and smiled cordially. Jeff tried to think of something he could say in the way of congratulation, but his mind was blank. It seemed a barbarous omission, but Jeff's first words had to do with business.

"You want to see me?"

Garrett nodded. "We have a little problem here, on the case this afternoon. As long as it's your filing Rae has challenged, I thought we should at least talk things over."

More and more of late, when thrown into company with his patron, Jeff was torn between reverence and contempt—humility and smoldering antagonism. He looked at the wall just beyond the old man's head.

"I've been thinking about that," he said, frowning thoughtfully. "I don't see how I can swear I've lived on that homestead the last six months. Everybody knows I haven't done. I couldn't very well have lived there, with Harley in the cabin."

"You apparently are not familiar with the law," Garrett said easily. "The residence requirement applies only in cases where the land is taken without payment. Where payment is made, at the rate of a dollar and twenty-five cents an acre, the patent is granted at the time of filing. That land deed is already in your name. I put the money down, myself."

"Then how can Harley challenge it?"

Garrett's smile was fleeting. "He has the idea that he filed ahead of you. Your filing is dated September 1, his application September 10. All you'll have to do over there is swear that you filed on the day your application was dated. The land agent will testify the same. The burden of proof will be on Rae."

Jeff inhaled deeply, and let the air out again, in dribbles. After all he'd done, the matter of swearing false oath in court was a small one.

"I don't know," he mumbled, looking at the floor. "What if the land agent says something else?"

"I can vouch for him," Garrett promised easily. "Question is— can we depend on you?"

Jeff stood like a wooden figure, neither co-operative nor defiant —groping for words of refusal that would dissuade without sounding mutinous. And all the time, he felt Bowman's eyes sounding him, reading his disaffection and taking pleasure in it.

"And—by the way," the old man went on, his tone confidential, almost wheedling, "Abigail said to tell you she will be in later this afternoon. She was out at the horse camp with us, but she wouldn't come on in as she was. She insisted on going by way of the ranch, to powder her nose. . . ."

It was the first time in months that Garrett had referred to his daughter in Jeff's hearing. His bringing her name into the conversation right at that point was so crude that Jeff was mortally affronted. He suddenly felt the necessity for getting out of the room before he said something he would repent.

"All right," he said, "I'll say what needs be said."

He had no thought of eavesdropping, once he'd stepped out and closed the door behind him. It was just that he felt bruised and shaken, and wanted to regain composure before going any further. He was mopping his face on his pocket handkerchief when Wate Garrett's voice came to him as clearly as if he'd still been in the room.

"How's our Jeffrey been behaving himself lately? Is he still up and coming?"

"Up and coming, all right," Strap Bowman's voice said sourly. But I don't know what to. Sometimes, I think you're raising a pup to bite you."

"Bite me?" Garrett laughed. "Our Jeffrey? No-o-o. I don't think so. He's big for his age, and knows it. A 'Goin' Jesse' as John says. But he's all for the company."

"All for Abby, anyhow," Strap said maliciously.

"I think I have scotched those ideas," Garrett said. "He's easier handled than the girl. She fancies herself in love with him, and she's headstrong as her mother was. But he's a different case. He only means to bleed me for what he can—I hope. Well, I've bought him off this long. I expect I can continue. Money to him is like meat to a dog."

Jeff didn't hear any more. Jeff was blind and deaf and dumb. His feet must have found their own way out of the hotel and down the street. The next he knew, he was standing at the counter in the Hat Saloon, where he hadn't been in years. A bottle and a glass were on the hardwood in front of him. But he was scarcely aware of them. He was staring at a face in the muggy bar mirror, trying to realize it was his own. It was old for its years, somehow misshapen and furtive and hangdog. It was a face he didn't know, and didn't want to know.

For the first time in his life, he was seeing himself as others must see him. For the first time in his life, he wanted nothing to do with himself.

His lowering eyes encountered the bottle and glass, and he poured himself a slug. As he did so, his ears started to register the talk around him.

"Paddlefoot, you sure ain't particular what you let in here no more."

"Naw. Been a bad year for snakes, all over."

Jeff was turning to retort when a scream of hate and defiance rolled up the street, shrill and prolonged like the blast from a locomotive whistle, ending in a grating crash that brought all eyes in the room together.

"That damned red stud!" somebody breathed.

Jeff found himself in the crowd of barflies that spilled out onto the sidewalk, there to see a sight he never would forget. Free now of hobbles and halter and restraining ropes, the big outlaw stud was on the loose again, hurling himself back up the canyon of the street, the skeleton saddle still strapped to his back.

213

The Man Head mustangers were diving for their tethered ponies. But Jeff saw at a glance that they wouldn't be in time, and no man was so foolhardy as to venture out into the street on foot. But Wate Garrett had been warned, and already was on the tall blue's back, a coil of rope in his hand. He was shouting to his riders, waving the rope in the air, spurring the blue to head off the charging monster.

But the tall blue geld seemed infected by the general excitement. Instead of closing with the renegade as its rider willed, it bellowed a protest to the bite of the steel and went high into the air, back arched like a cat's, all four legs pointed stiffly down. Then it struck the earth, swallowed its neck and kicked high, all in one twisting, gut-tearing contortion.

Jeff forgot to breathe as the rider lost both stirrups and fought desperately for one endless moment to keep his saddle. Then Wate Garrett was rolling in the dust almost at his feet, and the red stud was out of town. The big blue geld was leaving, too, still bucking the empty saddle so strenuously that the stirrups were meeting high up over its back at every jump.

Desmond and Strap Bowman jostled one another in their haste to reach their fallen master. But Garrett got back to his feet unaided and shook them off. He bawled frantically for another horse, and one of the late-arriving riders surrendered his.

"You stay here, and speak for me in court!" he yelled at Bowman. Then he vaulted to the saddle and departed in a flurry of hoofs and curses, calling his mustangers to follow.

The red outlaw and his tall blue accomplice now were at the river ford beyond the town. Running neck and neck, they hit the stream and knocked it dry, then raced off together toward the distant tablelands. Seeing that the pursuit stood no chance of overtaking them, Jeff let out the breath he unconsciously had been holding and inhaled again deeply—much as if he himself had just shaken loose an arrogant rider and was headed for the freedom of the mesas.

"Well," he couldn't keep from saying, "now Wate has been stacked another time. Now he's lost another saddle."

"It beats anything I ever seen," Gut Desmond conceded grudgingly. "He'd of turned that stud, if the blue hadn't acted up

214

right then. Traitor like that blue coyote ought be hung at sunrise."

"Maybe," Jeff said, knowing he should keep quiet. "Maybe not. Depends on how you look at things. The blue sure ain't any traitor to his own kind."

Desmond paid no attention to what he'd said, seemed not even to hear. But Bowman heard, and turned to look at Jeff, green eyes probing again.

"Just how do you look at things, Jimsie?" he asked quietly.

Jeff took another breath and stood to the probing eyes. "Why," he answered, "I'd say that Wate used spurs on the wrong horse at the right time. I'd say it looks like he would learn someday it ain't every horse will take his knocking around, the way some do."

"Meaning anything in particular?" Strap pressed.

Jeff nodded slowly. A cold, impelling fury was rising in him, and mixed in it was a kind of heady exhilaration. He saw Harley Rae standing among the farmers over in front of the Hat, the sun glistening on his red hair and beard, and the sight helped him to a decision.

"Meaning I won't stand up in Theo Coates's kangaroo court, and perjure myself," he said loud enough that a couple of listening farmers could hear. "Meaning that Wate better not even answer Harley's suit, or I'll take the stand and tell the whole truth about that homestead filing deal. The land commissioner in Washington gits hold of it, Wate could set in his own jail awhile, and think things over."

Bowman was silent a minute, looking amazed, but not displeased. Gut Desmond was wearing a thunderstruck expression. The farmers' mouths were open.

"I guess you know what that means," Bowman said finally.

"I know what it means," Jeff nodded, his voice just under control. "It means you can take this chunk of tin, and set on it until it hatches. You can pin all the little ones on the boys out at the ranch, and everybody can be a pimp. Me, I got enough."

Tossing the tarnished badge to the blinking sheriff, Jeff turned and walked away. He hadn't gone a dozen steps before his mind rebelled against the thing he'd done, bidding him reconsider. It told him he couldn't just up and throw everything over on a sense-less whim that would pass and leave him stranded.

Only the picture of a rebellious blue horse reversing the usual role of horses and stacking its rider to save one of its own kind from capture kept him from crawling back and reclaiming his badge and status while he could.

The same roweling memory carried him through the ordeal of packing his clothes and duffel, up in Mom Phlett's place above the harness shop. He had almost finished when he heard footsteps and a rap upon his door. He bade the knocker enter, expecting it would be Harley Rae. Instead, he smelled cigar smoke, and—turning—looked into the sneering eyes of John Poe.

"What's this I hear about you going broncky on us again?" the lawyer asked abruptly. "You lost your mind completely?"

"Go to hell," Jeff told him calmly.

"I likely will," the cynic said. "But I ain't quite as headlong hurried as some to git there. You're turning renegade, boy. You know where that word comes from? Comes from the word 're-nege.' You've reneged on just about everybody, now. Where you think it's going to git you?"

Jeff went on with his packing, and didn't answer.

"You think it will endear you to them farmers, you're in for disappointment," the lawyer persisted. "You're tarred with the Man Head stick, and they won't trust you. Know what Harley said when he heard you'd turned in your badge to keep from tak-ing the stand against him? Said it was another of yours and Gar-rett's tricks. Said he wouldn't touch you with a ten-foot pole. So where does that leave you? What you going to do for friends?"

"Do without," Jeff said shortly. "Like I've always done."

Poe shook his head. "That's what I come about. I've talked to Strap and Gut, and the judge. It ain't too late for you to change your mind. You can still take the stand in there, and keep your badge. . . .

"Well? What's your answer?"

"I can't put it into words," Jeff said. "You'll have to give me an emetic."

Poe clucked and shook his head. "You're making a big mis-take."

216

"My big mistake was in listening to you once before," Jeff told him. "Now, git out, before I help you out."

Even including the sack of oats, the pack that Jeff lashed down upon his mare's sway back down in the livery corral wasn't overweight. A bedroll and a warbag tightly filled; a camp axe and a tarp and two canteens; some cooking utensils and a little canned stuff picked up at Gentile's store. That was the full inventory of the pack. Together with the two horses, the rifle and saddle and pistol and the clothes he stood in, it represented the sum and total of his worldly acquisitions.

Even counting the twelve hundred dollars he was leaving banked with Jim Gentile, it didn't seem much to show for two years' work for a man who could have handed all that section of the globe on a silver platter. But it was too late to think of that now.

Maybe the fourth million would come easier. . . .

The horses had finished their grain, and he was ready to mount and ride when he heard a pony approaching at a canter. Even before he looked, he knew it would be Abby, riding the Morgan. But he looked anyhow, then quickly ducked his head and started fussing with his cinch, hoping she would pass without noticing him. But the patterned hoofbeat broke its cadence, as it neared the corral. As he listened, it slowed, then stopped entirely. By looking sidelong underneath his dun's neck, he could see the dainty stockinged legs of Mouse, the lucky pony, not fifteen feet from where he stood, and the familiar trapped feeling came over him, bordering almost on panic.

Somehow, in his sudden, savage resolve to break with life, he hadn't foreseen this encounter, hadn't provided against it. Now he wished futilely that he hadn't taken time to grain his horses. But he had. And intelligence told him that it was childish to go on hiding. But a craven part of him held him as he was.

"Hello, Jeff!" a voice that he remembered painfully called out gaily. "Do you remember me?"

Having no choice now, he raised his head and showed his face above the dun's back. This time his eyes went to the rider, not to the horse, and he tried to feign surprise. But surprise was not what he felt in looking at her.

Even in dusty riding habit and obscuring veil, old Garrett's only chick was still much prettier than any girl had right to be. Jeff would liked to have looked long enough to memorize everything about her. But he didn't dare. It was too late for regrets in this direction, too.

"Seem's like I've seen you somewheres," he admitted, entering into the mood she had set but speaking to his cinch. "I don't clearly remember where."

"It was at a dance," she told him. "You spoiled my lunch, and never so much as offered to pay for it."

She seemed to expect him to carry it on. But the picture her words called up to memory choked him like a rope. When he kept his face averted and did not offer to say any more, she spoke in a different vein.

"I had sort of been expecting you to come out, Jeff. I've been home for more than a week."

"I hadn't heard," Jeff said, more harshly than he'd intended.

His statement brought a silence. Then Abby spoke in yet another voice.

"Didn't you get my message?"

"Message?"

He risked another glance at her. For just an instant he grasped at the word like a drowning man at a piece of driftwood. Then he saw that it didn't signify. Even if she had sent him a message that was never delivered, it didn't mean anything now. It didn't mean a thing.

"No," he said gruffly, talking to his cinch again. "We must of had our wires crossed. We just got out of touch."

Abby started to say something, then changed her mind. When she did speak again, her voice was studiedly light and casual again.

"Well, I'm looking for my errant father? Have you, by any chance, seen him lately?"

"He was in town a while ago," Jeff answered, loosening the latigo he had just tightened. "But he lost a couple of horses. Last I seen of him, he was trying to run them down."

"Daddy and his horses!" Abby said. There was exasperation in her voice, but Jeff sensed that she was pretending, just as he was doing. When he chanced another look at her, he saw that she was studying his horses and outfit—the rounded panniers and warbag, the tarp-wrapped bedroll, the slicker and the big wet canteens slung down on either side of the packs.

"Is your trip going to be in the interests of the county?" he heard her ask, again determinedly casual. He couldn't restrain a dry chuckle.

"Strictly in the interests of Jeff Jimson," he said.

Then he gave up trying to hide, and walked around the dun to get it over with. Abby had pushed up her veil, and he noted with a kind of transient sadness that she hadn't changed a lot since her jealous parent had bundled her away to school the fall before, to put her out of his reach. As he looked at her, the empty months fell away, and he knew the winter had not changed her feelings either. Not unless they taught acting at the Eastern boarding schools.

The blue eyes clung to his in the old way. The tentative smile was there, the screwed-up look about the eyes, eager and vital and interested—in him. And Jeff knew all at once that things were not going to go off at all as he had planned them.

"You've lost your job!" Abby was saying, staring at his shirt. Jeff looked down and saw where the blue flannel had faded around the missing badge, leaving the shape of the shield stenciled there in darker blue, a carbon copy of the original. A shadow of the past.

"The job lost me, Abby," he corrected. "I quit."

"But—why?"

It was a question Jeff had not attempted to formulate any rounded and pat answer to. He didn't see how he could give out with any such answer now. He didn't see how he could explain his feelings when he saw the blue geld throw Wate.

"It just ain't any good, my being here, Abby," he began lamely. "Or maybe I'm no good. I've tried a lot of things, and it's always the same. I'm just a square peg, I guess. I don't fit in."

It was futile, trying to put it into words. His thoughts went again to the horses. To John Poe's words of a few minutes earlier.

To a thing Abby herself had said that day when he had met her, out with the horse band on the ranch.

"I guess I'm just a renegade. A bunch-quitter, as you say."

The girl was looking at him very carefully. Understanding was on her face, but there was protest, too. There was another thing that he didn't care to give a name to, and he knew it was going to take all his strength to see things through.

"You were doing well here," she said. "My father gave you every chance."

"Every chance but one," Jeff said bitterly. But he hadn't meant to bring that up. That was water under the bridge. He quickly changed the subject.

"I expect that's maybe more than half the trouble. He gives me every chance. And, around here, every chance is his to give. Well, there must be some place out here where a man can make his own chances, and not lackey all his life for somebody who thinks that God created the whole world just for his personal benefit. Chase his coyotes and come when he whistles, hoping for a pat on the head. Working against yourself the whole time."

The blue eyes continued to study him, without surprise or anger, only with protest and that something else he could not name. "You're not being fair, Jeff, either to my father or yourself. It's not like you to say a thing so wrong. Everyone has to start low, no matter what they do—"

Jeff laughed caustically. "Not as low as I started, Abby. And I guess that's mostly what I'm trying to say. I'm tired of looking up to snakes."

The blue eyes now looked withdrawn. The chin was set in the way he'd seen Wate's chin set, when faced with opposition.

"You never tried to fit in here, Jeff. You won't fit in anywhere, unless you try. Wherever you go, unless it's to a mountain peak to live in a cave the rest of your life and never see anyone, there'll be someone ahead of you. You'll have to accept the fact, and take things as they are."

It was the first time Abby had preached to him. He was in no mood for preaching. Turning, he caught his stirrup and swung up to his saddle. But the girl sat motionless and he did likewise— wishing to end it quickly, unable to see it end.

220

"Where will you go?" he heard her ask. And, once again, he found it necessary to face a question he had not faced till then. After a while, he shrugged and waved a hand.

"I don't know. Somewhere a good long ways from here. Some place where a man don't have to be so low to make a start."

Abby shook her head. "I don't understand you at all, Jeff. I don't believe you understand yourself."

Jeff looked at her, and wondered if ever again he would see eyes so intensely blue. He looked at the lips he had kissed and would not kiss again. He wished sadly that he could make her see, and knew that he could not.

He couldn't tell her how a young man felt, shut up in a country that was under the rule of one tight-fisted, tight-minded old man whose way of thinking and doing had brought on most of the wars of history. How a man felt in such a country torn by trouble that could end only in deadly strife, knowing himself to be in the wrong camp, traitor to all his kind, traitor therefore to himself.

"I guess it's just that I don't like what I see when I look in a looking glass—or the thoughts I think when I think anything at all," he said to her. "I—I guess I'd just like to be a horse that ain't afraid to buck."

The words made sense to him. It was plain that they made none to Abby. He felt he'd drawn it out too long.

Abby put out a hand, as if to stay him. "What about—us?"

Jeff scowled and looked away. "Things would never have worked out for us, Abby. You must know that, better than I do. We only make it harder on both of us, not looking at it. We only make it harder, with me hanging around where I don't belong.

"And, now," he said, "I believe I'd better go. Maybe I'll see you, someday."

"Maybe," Abby said.

And it was over, then. She didn't ask him to take her with him, this time. She didn't try to keep him, and she didn't ask if he would write. She too knew the future held nothing for them, while her father lived, and men like Garrett lived forever. She let him go without even a good-by, and that was the only way.

Emerging from the river ford, Jeff took the road's right-hand branch that led to Rustler Station and the north. As he did so, he felt a strong urge to look back, but kept his eyes doggedly on the road ahead.

It was the same road he had ridden out of Quadrille five years before, riding these same horses, on the drag of a Texas cattle herd. Traveling it again now brought back many memories which he had marked for forgetting, yet somehow had not forgot. Traveling it now was like moving back through time, even knowing that time's was a one-way road, and there wasn't any going back.

part 3

17: Road Back

Jeff camped the night in the Cat Creek cabin he once had shared with Demps, and dawn found him on the trail again, still pointed north. He had no plan in mind, no specific destination in view. His only idea was to get far out of Wyoming —so far he would never hear of Rustler River again. So far that he could erase the last five years completely, and start all over. Start building from the bottom again.

He didn't doubt that his name would go back on the blacklist now. But even that eventuality didn't seem important at the moment. Nothing seemed important, except that he get away. Get out and change his name, along with his way of doing. Bury his old name, his old self, along with the past. Disown his name as he had disowned all that the name had come to stand for. The thought that the world never again would hear of Jeff Jimson brought a sad comfort, a new courage that almost freed him of his burden of shame and guilt.

"Our big mistake," he told the inattentive horses, "was when we didn't change our name and just keep going, the first time we pulled out."

He struck Rustler Station about noon. Big Ben Hackett, the station keeper, greeted him cordially, and gave him the news that Judge Coates had ruled in favor of Garrett and the company, in spite of Jeff's failure to take the stand and testify for Man Head.

"That's right. Theo ruled that your filing stood, no matter whether you wanted it or not. But it wouldn't matter a whole lot if he'd ruled the other way. Harley's all shot to hell, and won't be looking after no place for a good long while."

"Harley—shot?" Jeff echoed.

"Why, godamighty, yes. Don't hear nothing that goes on? He and some the farmers got likkered up on losers' whiskey over in the Hat, and Harley run onto Strap out on the sidewalk. Strap had looked on the wine while it was red, but I guess Harley was the drunkest, because he ain't no slouch with a gun. Strap done cut him down."

"What are his chances?" Jeff asked slowly.

Hackett shrugged. "What's any man's chance, with a bullet in his brisket? Maybeso. Maybeno. They put him on a buggy and started out for Ekard. If he lived that long, on that road they got, I'd say he can't be killed. He's tougher 'n a mule's hind end, that boy."

"Why did they take him to Ekard?" Jeff persisted, trying to make sense of things. "They making sure he dies?"

Hackett produced a well-charred pipe and pouch. "Well, Harley cottons to Drake, same as Dempsey done. They knew each other down in Texas, I hear tell."

"But I'd think they would have kept him in town, where there's a doc."

"There's a doc on Squatters Row, in there close to Drake's. Dude by name of Woodrow. Seems to know his onions, too. Says he had a practice, back in Ohio, before the land bug bit him. Now he farms, and passes out pills on the side."

The speaker scratched a match and puffed thoughtfully. "This land fever is no respecter of persons or trades. Along with Woodrow, they got a farming preacher up there to pray on Sundays, and a part-time undertaker to plant the ones that Woodrow and the parson can't drag through. Besides these, they have carpenters and blacksmiths and blamed near anything you need in a community to git by. They all trade work back and forth, and help each other out. They're a-going to make it, too. Drake's going to be setting pretty in a year or two."

"Drake?" Jeff repeated, confused.

The station man's nod was profound. "Drake plays it smart. Long as this country was full of Texas snowbirds looking for a roost, he had one. Now it's them Bible-swearing Ohiowans, and he caters to them same way. He's married that Alice girl he used to keep up there for the cowboys, and joined their church. For a ten-dollar fee, he locates people on new ground, and let's 'em run a bill for what they need. That way, he ties 'em up. Keep 'em from going to Quadrille to trade, and gits a mortgage on the land, in the bargain. Another year or two, he'll own as much as Garrett uses for free. Give him time, he'll eat Garrett up."

"He's got quite a ways to go."

"Sure he has. But he's come a long ways, too. I first met him, he didn't have a pot. Now he's on Easy Street, and got more votes than Garrett ever had. Next 'lection, Wate will have to bring in a sight more Injuns and vote his ranch hands a sight more times that he did before, to git anywhere. Even then, they'll nail his hide to the fence, in time. The writing's on the wall right now. But Wate didn't never learn to read."

Jeff was thinking of a like prediction that Demps had made four long years ago. But, now as then, he couldn't feel any excitement about Duckbill Drake.

"You reckon Duck will be any improvement over Wate?" he asked.

"Could be, till he gits too great, and working strictly for himself." Hacket said thoughtfully. "He ain't any Abraham Lincoln. But there's one thing to be said for your small-bore politicians. Long as they're small, they got to run things to suit most the people, or they git it where Clancey got the axe. These little kings like Garrett, they forgit there's more people than anybody. When they finally do find out, the shock usually kills 'em—provided the people don't."

The news of Harley's shooting disturbed Jeff even more than quitting his job had done. That night he lay sleepless on his bed, staring into the dark with dry and smarting eyes, telling himself again and again that Harley was no skin off him, that it was all one if Harley should die of sudden death for blindly bucking a sure thing—just as Demps had died—as Rebel Jimson had died—as Jeff would die, if he did not clear out. . . .

He told himself that he was being a fool, that there was no connection: That Rebel Jimson died in the fight over states' rights; Demps because he'd mixed in with a horse-thief ring; Harley because he'd got himself liquored and crowded trouble with Strap Bowman. When you got right down to fundamentals, there was no similarity whatsoever. And yet there was a pattern. There was a thread, a continuity, too dim to see clearly, but too surely felt to doubt. A conviction you could reason out of, but could not escape.

"Well, I'm damned well out of it," he said aloud next morning, when he was saddled and packed and ready to ride. "I learned, even if some can't learn. I've cut the big gut. I'm G. T. Montana, or Canada, or somewhere."

But when he came to the fork in the road, the east branch bending off toward Deadwood and the Black Hills, the other west toward Ekard, he took the west fork.

"I'm damned well out of it," he repeated. "But I'll check on Harley, and talk things over. If he wants that homestead so bad, I'll deed the goddam thing over to him, before I go. We'll see what Wate and Theo Coates can do about that!"

It was nearing noon when he brought Ekard in sight, and if Hackett hadn't prepared him somewhat, he wouldn't have recognized the place. Duckbill had got hold of lumber somewhere, and had built a tall, two-story building that was labeled *Drake Hotel and Mercantile Store*. It was painted a kind of brindle brown, and there were curtains at the windows, upstairs and down. A long porch extended the width of the structure's front, out past a lean-to that was signed *The Drake Saloon*. The old log structure that Jeff remembered was still there, but converted to a livery stable: the *Drake Feed and Livery Company*. A couple of residences and a blacksmith shop had been thrown up, facing the hotel-store-saloon, creating the illusion of a street. There was even a freshly painted sign, the ultimate in civic aspiration: *Welcome to Ekard—The Greatest Little Town On Earth.*

"Well, some folks have come up in the world!" Jeff told himself wryly.

There were several teams at the tie rail, plus a single horse or so. Except for a couple of children playing beside one of the houses, no human being was in sight. But a committee of dogs assembled to bark a noisy welcome, and a woman's face peered curiously from one of the houses. Jeff couldn't have said for certain, but he thought the face belonged to Boxcar Alice. Married now, Hackett said. A respectful member of the community. Mother of the two healthy-looking children, maybe.

"Duckbill's bosom friend," he mused aloud.

Uncertain whether the welcome sign applied to him, Jeff swung down at the hitching rail, and climbed the painted steps. The buzz of talk ended as he pushed into the saloon. The silence that greeted him everywhere greeted him here. Then a familiar, unfriendly voice was speaking.

"Well, if it ain't Texas River. The Man Head Kid himself!"

Jeff's eyes found the speaker. Duckbill wasn't behind the whiskey counter, as in the good old days. He was sitting with the whittlers around the cold heating stove toward the rear. His once-black hair was iron gray, and his clothes would have looked at home on Garrett. His once-waxed and upcurling mustache now drooped with casual dignity around his mouth. He was growing a bay window. His unbuttoned coat revealed a flowered vest, spanned by a gold log chain.

"Hello, Duck," Jeff said with as much cordiality as he could muster. "Long time no see."

"Not long enough—for my tastes," the town builder said. "And the name is Drake. Mr. Drake, to you."

"Excuse me," Jeff said gravely. "Hello, Mr. Drake. Long time no see."

Drake made no response, and to cover a moment's uncertainty

Jeff walked to the bar and signed for a bottle. The bartender turned toward the cupboard. But Drake's voice intervened.

"Leave him go to hell, Buxton. He can't buy nothing here—but trouble."

"I'm not in the trouble market today," Jeff told him. "But git one thing straight, if you can. I'm not with Man Head any longer. I turned my badge in."

The black eyes gleamed. "Yeah. I heard tell you done Garrett like you done everybody else you ever tied to. Now you got no friends anywhere, and no tin badge to hide behind. That must make things tough. Shouldn't happen to a dog. But it did."

Somewhat to his own surprise, Jeff was able to take it all in stride. "I never tied to you, so you ain't out nothing. I come here to see Harley Rae."

"Well, you can't see him," Drake stated flatly. "He's about done for, as it is. Sight of you would finish him off."

Jeff looked around at the others in the room. He could make them all out plainly now, could see that they were farmers as he had expected. Some two or three he remembered seeing in town the day of his renunciation. But there was no friendliness in any of the faces. The cold reviling stares acted as a powerful stimulant, and all at once Jeff knew the real reason he had come around by Ekard.

"Well," he said, "when Harley comes around so's he can stand it, tell him he ain't got to worry about that homestead. Tell him I'll sign it over to him, when he's ready to look after it. Tell him that until then I'll camp up there, and look after it for him."

The announcement brought on a silence that must have been audible for miles. But the faces around the stove registered nothing but hatred and suspicion.

"I'll tell him," Drake sneered at last. "But I don't expect it will encourage him. Be like a coyote taking care somebody's sheep."

"You should know about that—the flock you're gitting around you!" Jeff sneered in return. "Just tell Harley I'll be there on the place, when he's able to tear himself away."

On his way out, his eyes searched unconsciously for a homely framed motto that once had graced the old saloon. But the only lettering in sight was on a piece of cardboard that hung from a

228

rifle nailed to the wall behind the bar. The gun was a rusted Winchester and had a vaguely familiar look. The placard seemed to identify the weapon as Demps's, though how it had got there Jeff could not guess:

This Is the Gun That Killed Cis Hapgood
Man Head Spies Beware

Out in the sunlight again, Jeff mounted and rode off toward the mesa. New purpose now had taken him, and for the first time since he'd seen a tall blue horse shuck its rider and race off to these same tablelands, he was able to see things for what they were. It was here on Rustler River that his unsavory name and reputation had been acquired. Here it was that both would have to be repaired, if any fixing was to be done.

"Drake'll eat his words, before I'm through," he promised the world aloud. "Garrett and Bowman, too."

The Hurricane homestead hadn't changed much in the time he'd been away. The cabin and stables were a little dirtier, but otherwise just as he remembered them. Demps's old iron-wheeled cart was still up at the corrals, and in the cabin there were many relics of the only real friendship he'd ever known: the blue granite plate Demps had always eaten off, the battered pewter cup he'd favored, the bunk on which he'd slept and died. A couple of old coats and the shapeless hat he'd worn when shot, hanging on a nail behind the door. The window shutter Demps had lowered religiously before lighting the stinking lamp. The barrel chair where he had sat. The old heart-and-hand bulletin, rolled up and wedged between the logs above the bunk where Demps had lain long hours in life, debating the advantages of this charmer, opposed to that.

It was dark at the time of his arrival, so he cooked a savorless meal and stretched out on his old bunk without exploring the valley itself. But in the morning when he stepped out into the newly risen sun and looked around, other ghosts were there to haunt him: the ringing bluffs and bottoms already green with new meadow grass. The muttering creek and the budding trees and brush. The upper canyon leading to the mesa, the lower trail up which the posse once had come to hang him. The salt trough at the meadow's head, where Demps lay rotting in the earth because he'd challenged one man's title to half the territory.

Jeff had heard at the time how the Stock Association had reclaimed its assassin's body from the muck to which Jeff had consigned it, reburying it with honors in the bone yard in Quadrille. But no one had been interested enough in Demps to pull him from the ground. As Jeff had heard it, the sheriff's men merely had dug down deep enough to verify Jeff's story that Demps was there, then had covered him back over and let him lie. When Jeff walked down that morning to look things over and pay respects, he found a newly hewn headboard had been set up, doubtless by Harley Rae, the letters burned by a hand skilled at free marking with a heated iron.

Dempsey Rae

Killed by Sons of Bitches

Jimson and Hapgood

With his jackknife, Jeff carefully obliterated the words *Jimson* and *Hapgood*. Finished with his labors, he stood a time in reverent silence, feeling that he was on hallowed ground, wishing as he had wished before that he could pray effectively. Then he considered the man that Demps had been alive, and felt abashed to have presumed that Demps might need his prayers.

I won't take a slap from God's own hand, he heard the drawling voice declare again, in memory. "Said he—his face beat raw from slapping!" Jeff said bitterly, aloud.

Someone had removed the bars from both the upper and lower trails, and Man Head cattle grazed the upper meadow. Jeff's first act after his visit to the grave was to whoop the cattle up the canyon toward the mesa. When he came upon a fat unweaned yearling steer with its muzzle in the flank of a bone-poor cow, he shook out his rope, dropped a loop around its neck, and left it tethered to a sapling. When he'd hazed the others through the gate and replaced the bars, he towed the captive back to the corrals and imprisoned it inside the stable.

230

"The Progical Son is back, and you're the fatted calf," he said apologetically, as he butchered it and dressed it out—inside the barn.

He cut the brand out of the hide to burn in his cookstove, and buried the head, hide and guts in the manure pile outside. "Little horse manure, spread in the right place, can cover a multitude of sins." He grinned.

He left the carcass hanging in the stable's cool, cellar-like interior, and made pan bread from a sourdough jar he found fermenting beside the stove, evidently set by Harley Rae. That night, he ate heartily of good, rich fare, behind a shuttered window, and commenced to feel at home.

"Thank thee, Harley, for the bread, and thee, Wate Garrett, for the meat," he said whimsically, by way of grace.

When first riding in from Ekard, he saw where Harley had made a start at digging out the narrow points along the lower trail, widening it to road-breadth. On the third day of his residence, time began to drag, and more to push back the loneliness than anything else he located a shovel and rode down to continue the work.

For most of the distance, the canyon already was wide enough to pass an ordinary wagon. It was only the points and the occasional overhanging banks that needed scaling back. Even so, progress was not rapid with just one shovel working. Two weeks had passed and the days were warm and long—the grass growing as if pushed up by some magic force—before he was satisfied with his dug road.

The groceries in his packs were soon exhausted. But Harley Rae had laid in a big stock of canned stuff, and since Jeff looked upon his role as that of hired man, he didn't hesitate to help himself.

On the morning of his first free day, he heard travelers coming up the lower trail. Thinking that it might be someone with news of Harley, he saddled his pony and rode down to meet them. Four men were at the lower bars, three on horses and one dismounted, removing the poles Jeff had rounded up and placed in position upon arrival. The man on the ground was Bowman. His back was to Jeff, and the soft earth muffled the dun's footsteps so that the foreman didn't hear Jeff's approach. He was talking in a scolding tone.

"I find who it is keeps putting these bars up and hacking at that dug road, I'm going to make him hard to find. Dab a rope on them poles, and drag 'em off where they won't be found."

The foreman's three companions had their eyes on Jeff. They looked embarrassed and did not move. Jeff rode leisurely, rifle resting on his pommel, hammer under his thumb. When Strap turned to see what the others were looking at, Jeff was pulled up some fifteen feet away, sitting loosely in the saddle, both hands on the gun.

"You're tampering with private property, Strap. I'd advise you to let that gate wood be."

Strap oggled him, his jaw hanging down. Jeff had trouble holding in a smile.

"So you're still around, eh, Jimsie?" the foreman said finally. "What you up to now?"

Jeff let his smile come out, let it close his eyes, as a remembered smile had used to do. "I'm looking after this here place, for Harley Rae. And Harley's a mite particular about his gates. If you're bound up for the mesa, you can pass through—long as you ain't got cows along. But put the gates up behind you, or you don't go through no more."

Strap shook his head, and spat. "You're talking through your hat, Flash. Harley Rae is dead. Dead men don't have no property rights."

"You're a goddam liar," Jeff said coldly.

"Not if you say so," Strap retorted.

Jeff sat woodenly, knowing that Strap was telling the truth—that Harley had died as Demps had died. That Jeff's own staying had been just another bad mistake.

Or had it?

"It wouldn't make no difference, even if Harley'd lived," Strap went on, sinking in his spurs. "He didn't never own this ground. The court settled all that, while he was still alive."

"That's what I hear," Jeff agreed slowly, starting at last to see how the thing was setting up. "The court decided the place was mine. Git off my ground, Bowman. And don't come back."

Strap's boring eyes seemed to grow smaller, to recede into his bullet skull. "Jimsie," he breathed, "you wouldn't dare."

Jeff discovered in that instant that life could be rewarding, after all. He knew then that it had not been useless and a mistake to stay. He knew that this eventuality, this encounter, had been somewhere at the back of his mind the whole time. He laughed suddenly, through his nose, like a stud horse.

"You never was wronger, Strap," he said. "And you had plenty practice. Or maybe you want to put things to a test."

Bowman didn't answer. Bowman seemed to be in trouble with his thoughts, and Jeff crowded his advantage.

"Like I said, I don't mind you boys riding across today. But when you start trailing cows, trail the other way, or come prepared to pay a toll. Fifty cents a cow, each way, is what this road costs."

Strap wagged his head slowly, as at a thing beyond his comprehension. "You're a bigger fool than I thought you was, Jimsie. But have it your way—for now. . . ."

As was his custom, the foreman turned his back while he was talking, and started walking toward his horse. Jeff eased the rifle hammer back to cock, and the dry metallic click brought Strap up short.

"Don't forgit them bars, Strap," Jeff counseled. "Whether you come through or go back the long way around, you know enough to put a gate behind you. I advise that's what you do."

Strap hesitated for just a moment, then resumed his walk toward his horse. "You're gitting plain impossible to live with, Tex," he grumbled. "We'll talk about this here again."

Before mounting his horse, Strap motioned his three companions through the gate, then replaced the bars he had ordered scattered not so long before. Jeff followed the quartette up across the meadow and through the upper bars, seeing that they closed the second gate also. The act brought a sense of satisfaction, of just retaliation. But once the four were through the bars and gone, and Jeff was riding the return trail alone, his back felt naked and exposed and vulnerable.

By the time he'd reached the cabin, he was commencing to see that his unguarded talk to Bowman had committed him to sticking with the homestead, no matter what happened from then on.

That, once again, his unbridled tongue had trapped him, and there was nothing for it now but to settle down and try to stay alive on ground that had claimed two lives already. That he had no other place to go to, anyhow. That, if he could figure a way to stay alive, Hurricane Creek was lonesome enough to suit him.

While trapping with Demps on Cat Creek, he'd once come upon an old dog wolf, toothless and senile, living in the carcass of a winter-weakened cow it had managed to bring down. Having made its kill, the predator first had devoured the viscera, then had denned up in the cavity created by its own digestive tract. Celibate and solitary, outcast from the pack, it yet had lived on in relative comfort, all its needs supplied by a single windfall.

Even at the time, Jeff had felt a strange kinship with the renegade—an affinity so strong that he'd sheathed his rifle and had ridden on, leaving the outlawed recluse in possession of its worthless life, inviolate in its hard-won hermitage. The details of the incident had never left his mind, and now he found an armoring comfort in the memory. He too had made a kill, had come into a windfall through Garrett's inadvertent gift of the homestead he had once deserted. From this point on, he would live as the old wolf had lived—unmated and withdrawn from all his kind, self-sufficient and self-sufficing, asking no odds and giving none. And if he couldn't register a brand and ranch as he wished, there were still animals around to be trapped when winter had primed the furs. In the meantime, there were bones around that he could gather up and haul to town.

He knew there still would be the stinks that once had sickened him. But, compared to the odors he'd inhaled at Man Head, he reckoned the dead-cow stench would be fragrant as Abby's perfume.

18: Recluse

From Hackett at Rustler Station, Jeff purchased a wagon and team and set of harness for a hundred and fifty dollars, complete. He made payment in the form of a check scribbled on a piece of wrapping paper, ordering Gentile in Quadrille to pay the specified amount from money he'd left banked at the store. He picked up enough lumber around Rustler to build a rack on the wagonbox for hauling, and—like a snake resuming a skin it had cast—went back to picking bones.

He worked as Demps had taught him to work: with all his feelers out, and rifle ever within ready reach; camping with his outfit on the flats to save long travel between headquarters and the job; assembling the bones in dumps in various locations, for later hauling in to town.

Unlike the first time he had done such work, he did not feel degraded by it, did not resent his having to resort to such employment to make a livelihood. There was a kind of penance in it, and this he needed as he needed food three times a day. He found a perverse satisfaction in tearing a weather-picked carcass apart—in hammering the bones upon the ground and seeing the fat bugs scurry, in inhaling the rank effluvium that once had filled him with fury and revulsion.

Instead of seeking the more isolated places where he would not be seen, he purposely worked in close to Rustler Station and to Ekard and the farmer settlements, and was unapologetic when the idle and the curious came out to look him over. With those who paused to talk, he discussed the finer points of the industry with an outward self-esteem that was not entirely feigned. When Man Head cowboys rode past to sing out tentative taunts, he was flattered by the caution exhibited, and refused to be affronted. When his supplies ran low, he made a trip into Quadrille instead of back to Rustler Station. To make the trip count double, he loaded the rack with bones and made his first delivery at the railroad. He didn't follow the back way in, as he'd used to do when hauling bones with Demps, but paraded his reeking cargo down

Main Street, taking a melancholy pride in the attention he attracted.

Old Hitch appeared while he was transferring his lading to the ground, and stood leering humorously. "I heerd you was still around, raising hell as usual. Still slapping Wate Garrett around the ears with your cowboy hat, yelling the Texas yell."

"You heard partly right," Jeff answered, not bothering to look up. "I'm still around, anyhow."

"Kind of back where you started, ain't you?" Hitch persisted, mischief in his gleaming eye. "Sticks in my mind you was picking bones four, five years ago."

"Well, I'm holding my own," Jeff answered temperantly. "That's more than I could say a year or two back."

Hitch shook his head, as if mystified by what he saw and heard. "Some people would do anything just to own a piece of ground."

"We only think we own the ground," Jeff said philosophically. "You come right down to it, it's the ground that owns the man. I expect that's why we do some the things we do."

Hitch leered again, derisively. "That ground up there sure owns them Rae boys—and plenty others that's tried what you're trying. Why don't you wise up, and quit while you're ahead?"

"Who's ahead?" Jeff asked mildly.

Sometime later, he stood in the long aisle between the counters in Gentile's store, running his eyes over the well-stocked shelves, inhaling the composite aroma of camphor and new leather and salt-cured meats. It was a bounteous smell, rich and soothing to the senses, sharply contrasted to the smells Jeff lived with on the range. It seemed pleasantly to saturate his clothing, to soak into his very skin. It seemed to hold all a man could want of comfort and security and full living. It reminded him of a boyhood ambition to someday keep a store. It filled him with a sad regret that the aspiration had not been attained.

"Well, well—" Gentile greeted him with unaccustomed cordiality. "If it ain't our newest homesteader, and looking the part! You got the lean and hungry look!"

"I got reason to," Jeff said easily. "I been working the homesteader's eight-hour day. Eight hours before breakfast, and eight hours after. Nor there ain't no Sunday, up on Hurricane."

"Well, relax a little. Set down, and take the weight off your mind. I been wanting to talk to you, ever since I heard you'd upped and told Garrett where to go. Come on back to the den, and growl. We'll open a keg o' nails."

The promised keg proved to be a tall, leather-covered bottle whose mellow content warmed a man and made him conscious of his blood. Then, once the formalities were over, the merchant's manner turned merchant-like.

"What I got to say, I'll say right out. I'm gitting along in years, and about ready to start taking things easy. I'm looking for a pardner that's young and full of beans. You got near a thousand dollars left in my safe there. Why not invest it here, before you pee it all against the wind, buying rattletrap wagons and broken-down horses? In time the whole business would be yours."

Jeff looked at him, and saw that he was serious. He inhaled the prosperous smells again, and wondered at the offer. He wanted to accept it, quickly, before it would be withdrawn. But he knew he wouldn't.

"What's all this?" he asked. "Why me?"

Gentile shrugged vastly. "I want somebody with enough git-up-and-go to take things over, and leave me free to loaf. Go back East and see some friends and relatives. Waller my dodger, and enjoy what time I got left."

"Why me?" Jeff repeated.

The merchant shrugged again. "Maybe I just like the way you tote. You don't let no grass grow under you. You don't stand around like most, waiting for a chance to hold Garrett's horse. I could use you in this store."

It was the first really kind thing anyone had said of Jeff since Dempsey died. He was flattered. He was grateful, almost to the point of tears. But he knew he had to turn the offer down.

"Thanks for the compliment, Jim. But I got a place to look after. Up on Hurricane."

"So I heard," Gentile wheezed. "But how you aim to do a thing like that? What can you raise up there, but cows? How can you raise cows, when you can't register a brand?"

"I'll stock Herefords. The color will be my brand."

"Where'll you git pasture for 'em?"

"Up on the mesa, with Garrett's stuff. Make us partners, in a way."

Gentile wagged his head. "You know Wate's no damned philanthropist. How long you think it would be until he put you off?"

"Till the time he can show me a deed signed by God A'mighty, witnessed by President Garfield, certifying he owns that ground."

Gentile grunted in disapproval. "You can't buck Man Head. Of all people, you should ought to know that."

"I reckon I should," Jeff conceded. "I been hearing it said, ever since I hit this country. You people been saying it so long you've all convinced yourselves and each other. And that's another reason I couldn't buy into this business with you. Another year or so, and you ain't going to have any business. You ain't even going to have a town. Drake's going to have everything up to Ekard, and leave you boys setting here on the railroad tracks, with your heads bowed down to Garrett. Comes the next election, they'll move the courthouse up there, too, and start running things to suit the people. Then you and Wate and Hog Muldroon will have the town all to yourselves. How'll you like it, then?"

"I ain't blind to what's happening, with all them farmers coming in," the merchant said cheerlessly. "And I don't doubt you're right, that the homesteader element will be taking over. But if it's just a matter of trading Wate for Drake, I don't see where we stand to gain."

"Why's it got to be a choice like that?" Jeff challenged. "Why don't some the rest of you talk turkey to Garrett, and tell him which way the wind is starting to blow. You could be elected to his office, if he would hear sense and resign it. You ever thought about that?"

Gentile grunted a negative. "I'm an old man. Country's been good to me, the way it is. It's you young bucks will have to make the changes, if any git made."

"Drake'll make some changes you won't like," Jeff predicted hopefully. "Country might not be so good to you, once he's calling the square dance."

"It's no skin off me, if Drake takes over," Gentile wheezed. "I got mine made. He can't hurt me."

238

"That's the hell of it," Jeff said sourly. "By the time a man gits big enough and smart enough that he's got a little influence, he's either old and fat and don't give a damn—else he's scared he stands to lose some of what he's piled away. Either way, the people git it in the butt."

"Wait till you git a few more thousand stashed away," the merchant laughed. "You won't be so hungry-hot for changes, neither."

Besides eatables for his camp, Jeff bought a scythe and a couple of pitchforks for use in harvesting his planned hay crop from his meadow. He had the groceries loaded in his wagon and was just stepping out the door when he heard a horse coming at a leisurely, ambling walk. Preoccupied with his argument with Gentile, Jeff cast a cursory glance in the direction of the sound, and froze where he stood. Wate Garrett was riding up the street, astride the tall blue geld.

For a second or two, Jeff stood rigid, stunned beyond thought or motion, the brassy taste in his mouth again. Then he backed inside the door again and watched furtively through the dirty window, unaware of anything but the once-rebellious geld's spectacular acquiescence, the once-stacked rider's offhand manner of dominance. Finding in the evidence of the blue's surrender the portents of an ignominious personal defeat.

After a minute, he heard a step behind him, and sensed the store man's curious, inquiring scrutiny. He started to breathe again, and tried to speak casually.

"When did Wate git back the blue?"

"Git back the what?"

"Git back the blue camel he's riding there. I seen the bastard pile him ass over appetite here on court day in the spring. Seen him throw away everything but his tail and light a shuck for the mesas, along with that red stud."

"Oh—" Gentile's laugh was short. "The blue didn't go far. As I remember, he did git excited that day, and wanted to run. But once he got it out of his system, he was ready to settle down. Wate says he's been a better horse since than he ever was before."

Jeff followed the merchant's words with shrinking fascination. He half-suspected Gentile of knowing all about his feeling of association with the traitorous blue. He sensed a deadly affront in

239

the store man's words, but there was nothing to put his finger on.

"What happened to the red stud?"

"Didn't you hear? Broke a laig, that last run. Wate had to have him shot."

Jeff's mouth clicked shut. News of the stud's death was even more demoralizing than the news of Harley's fate had been. The parallels were too close to be ignored.

"Just like Harley, eh?" he breathed.

"Harley? Harley Rae? Did Harley break a leg?"

"Didn't he?" Jeff flared. "Why else did Wate have him shot?"

"Garrett didn't have Harley shot," Gentile averred. "Harley got himself full of Renfro's whiskey, and started throwing his Texas weight around. He crowded that fight with Strap. He was in the wrong—and just a leetle slow."

"In a hog's eye!" Jeff snapped. "He got himself shot because Wate knew the court's ruling on that Hurricane place would never stand up. It was that homestead got Harley shot, same as Demps!"

"You could be right," the merchant conceded glumly. "You could be wrong. If you're convinced, I'd think you'd learn from the example. Why don't you git the chips off your shoulders, and make things easy for yourself?"

"Like hell I will," Jeff declared. "I don't doubt you're right, and I'll git laid in the end. But, by God, it'll be a case of rape— not willful fornication!"

Garrett was coming abreast of the store, and it seemed to Jeff that he must be aware of his hidden audience. He sat so relaxed and confident, so effortlessly astride the one-time rebel. The perfidious blue likewise seemed to know that he was passing in review. He singlefooted sedately, and permitted himself to be guided by his master's thighs, never requiring pressure from either rein. Jeff hated the animal for its weakness, and envied its sublime acceptance of the inevitable. He felt lonelier than he'd ever felt before.

With no visible direction from the rider, the tall blue turned in at the Drovers House tie rail. Ostentatiously, it seemed to Jeff, Garrett dropped his reins, and—swinging down—stalked up the wooden steps without bothering even to tie the renegade that had

240

humiliated him in front of half the county not a month before. The geld seemed to enter into the offensive performance with un-horse-like grasp of all expected of it. Once the rider was off its back, it sighed and slumped meekly, standing hipshot and dejected with unsecured head hanging down, the very picture of patient resignation—of penance, publicly proclaimed.

The affront was there, all right, demoralizing in implication if not in actual prediction. Unable to retaliate against the real offender, Jeff turned waspishly on Gentile.

"How long you been a horse, Jim?"

Gentile's face, while blank, was wary. "I'm not sure just what you're gitting at."

"I'm gitting at that big blue manure pile, over there in front the House," Jeff said in fury. "Take a look at him. Big enough to chaw Wate up and spit him out. But does he do it? Hell, no! Totes him around instead, takes his kicks and knocks, and comes back for more. Figures that taking a man's licks and doing his dirty work makes him part man, too!"

Gentile smiled wryly and stared out at the horse, probing his gums with a broomstraw. "Don't know as I follow you for sure, Jimson. But I will say this. A horse is a horse whether it tries to be a man or not. And a horse that's got a smart rider will git further than one without—provided it remembers it's a horse and don't fight the bit. But a horse that wants to be on both sides of the saddle, he's some mixed up."

"That why you offered me a saddle here, a while ago?" Jeff sneered.

"I ain't made up my mind which side the saddle you fit," the merchant confessed. "Nor I don't expect nobody can, till you decide yourself. All I say is you can't have it both ways. You can't ride and carry all the same time."

Jeff picked up his implements and started for the door. But the merchant's voice held him another minute.

"I don't git all this talk about horses and riders. But I don't like the sound of it. I only advised you to git the chips off your shoulders, so you put on whole wood blocks. You're the kind that goes through life expecting every minute somebody's going to take a swing at you. When they don't, you feel slighted, and set out to badger 'em into it. Why make things tougher on yourself than they already are? Why worry about which end of the horse is who, and who's astraddle of who? Why all this sweating about Garrett, when he'd ought to be sweating about you? Garrett don't count for nothing, except to Garrett. You're the one that counts, with you."

"I'll count with some others, too, before they've heard the last out of me," Jeff predicted warmly.

He was out on the sidewalk, almost to his wagon, when a cawing voice he recognized speared him in the back. "Well, as I live and breathe. It's my missing deputy!"

Jeff glanced over his shoulder, and saw Garrett stomping down the hotel steps. He had hoped to avoid the encounter, and the familiar trapped feeling struck at him again. He started to throw the degrading farm implements up into the wagon to get them out of sight. But a resurgence of the old perversity made him change his mind. He kept the implements in his hand. Garrett eyed them acridly.

"What's this you have there? Tools of your new trade?"

The crackling, scornful voice did more for Jeff than Gentile's bottle had done, inside. He discovered right then, all over again, that all he ever had to do when beset by weakness or uncertainty was to look Wate Garrett in the face. In that act, he would always find the strength and will to go on.

"We all have use for tools, Wate," he said with creditable calm. "You buy your kind. I buy mine."

"Be careful you don't get hold of a bad one," the ranchman said with irony. "That could cost you dear. . . . What's this I hear about you squatting on my homestead, closing it to travel?"

"Your homestead?" Jeff repeated, commencing to enjoy himself. "Sticks in my mind the judge ruled it belonged to me."

As Jeff was talking, he became aware that Jim Gentile was listening to their talk, from just inside his door. Several other townspeople, plus a few farmers, were loitering near, ears flared out to catch it all.

"Sticks in my mind we had an agreement about that," the ranchman reminded. "Is your word as worthless as all that?"

"I expect it's worth about as much as yours," Jeff thrust at him.

"As I remember, we made another bargain, that didn't come to much."

The jab touched home. For the first time in all the while they'd been exchanging looks, Garrett's eyes were first to fall. And Jeff was ready then to break it off. He dropped the implements in the wagonbox, and climbed up to the seat.

"All right," Garrett sighed. "You win. How much do you want?"

Something dark and hideous tried to possess Jeff's mind and body. He pushed it back.

"How much what?" he asked politely.

"How much money—for that damned valley. You know I have to have it. You know that if the price is right I would rather buy it than—well, I'd rather buy it."

Jeff surprised himself by laughing. "The homestead ain't for sale, Wate. You'll just have to hire me shot, the way you done with Demps and Harley Rae."

Jeff didn't look back as he drove away. He was beyond the river ford before he thought of the tall blue geld again. He was oddly impressed by the fact that the blue's base conduct had not influenced his own actions.

"I guess Jim was right on one thing," he said aloud, greatly uplifted by the thought. "That breachy bastard don't count for nothing, after all."

19: Down Wind

The encounter with Garrett in Quadrille gave Jeff a new slant at things, himself included. For the first time since he'd peered around a pile of ties and seen a bird-faced old man seated on a red-wheeled buckboard drawn by a team of high-stepping bays, he felt free of Wateman Garrett. Free of caring what Garrett thought of him. Free of wanting his approval and good will. Free of wanting to become what Garrett was. Free of an obstacle delusion—of the whole business of horses and riders and an entire false system of values. Free, in a manner, of himself.

In a way, Jeff even felt free of Abby. Abby was sunshine and moonlight and spangled silk. She was the softness of featherdown and the brightness of sky. She was all things a man aspired to. She didn't dirty her underwear, and her feet didn't stink. But she was Man Head, just as her father was. She stood for the same things, saw everything through the spectacles of wealth. She too believed in the divine right of bullionaires, and her ways weren't Jeff's.

> Wate Garrett's daughter said, before she died,
> "Papa, fix the brands so the rustlers can't ride.
> If ride they must, let them di-ie the death,
> And curse your name with their expiring breath. . . ."

The extravagance of his mood did not endure. But the underlying view persisted, buoying him when he needed buoying, giving him reason and purpose for going on, for working himself down to a nub as a scavenging bone pick when intelligence and ego told him he was cut out for better things.

The work schedule he kept was not conducive to a balanced life, but it produced results. By mid-August, he had gleaned the entire Rustler Plains of bones, with the single exception of the sector around Rifle Mountain. For reasons he still could not bear to examine, he did not intend to work the Rifle Mountain sector.

Altogether, when the collecting was done, he had what he computed to be a dozen full carloads of reeking calcium heaped up in ten huge dumps, ready for transport to Quadrille. Since it was time he was harvesting his hay crop, and since the homestead took precedence over all else, he swung a deal with a couple of idle farmers to do the long-distance hauling for a one-third share in the proceeds.

"Why should they divide with you?" a tobacco-chewing bystander challenged when the deal was made. "Hell, they's more skeletons around than pebble rocks. How come you got deed and title to 'em all?"

"You're welcome to what you find scattered around," Jeff answered shortly. "But the ones I've gethered up are mine. I'm the one that thought of doing something with them. And I've worked plenty hard."

244

"Christ, you sound like Wate Garrett."

"And you sound like a goddam fool!"

Before heading up to the homestead, Jeff drove off to Rustler Station, to purchase some more supplies. And the first thing he saw upon approaching the place was a corral full of young Hereford she-stuff, eating hay and resting. Inquiry brought the information that the whitefaces were being trailed to the Powder River country from Quadrille, where they had untrained a week or so before. They were owned by an Indiana breeder who was along, directing the drive. Jeff found him drinking watered whiskey in the station saloon, and introduced himself.

The breeder was full of drink and talk about the new breed of cattle he raised for brood purposes strictly. Jeff was an avid listener, and was able to impress the trail boss with his own book-learned knowledge of the type. But when Jeff mentioned the matter of purchasing a few head, the breeder was scarcely polite.

"Them sweetheart honeys are going to the English Haw-Haws, up on Powder River. Them boys know cattle, even if they are fugitives from Parliament and knee britches."

"Sure they know cows," Jeff agreed. "But from what I hear, they got plenty of Herefords up there now. The breed ain't known at all down here. Why not drop a few to kind of educate people to what they're missing?"

"I been trying to educate Wate Garrett for quite a while," the breeder confessed, implying that Garrett alone was worth dealing with. "But I ain't convinced him yet."

"Sure you haven't," Jeff agreed again. "Nobody convinces Garrett. He stopped thinking, back when Noah built the ark. But he can see what's put in front of him. Sell me a dozen head to show off with, and Wate'll beat a cow path from your door."

The breeder looked thoughtful, but when he'd sized Jeff up again, his expression was dubious. "That kind of stock costs money, boy. It does pay to advertise. But I got to have my money out of them. A dozen head would cost you a thousand dollars."

"It's a deal," Jeff said.

The breeder continued doubtful. But when Hackett vouched for Jeff and offered to endorse and guarantee Jeff's check, a deal was made.

245

"Remember they ain't as hardy as your longhorns. You nurse 'em through the winter, and next spring if you've still got the dozen I'll ship you out a bull on loan, for half the calves. I would like to whoop the breed out here."

"I'll buy the bull, and keep the calves," Jeff told him. "And if you'll pay me a commission, I'll guarantee that Garrett is stocking Herefords by spring."

"How would you influence Garrett on anything?" Hackett begged to know.

"I'll influence him to Herefords, just by stocking them," Jeff predicted. "I can't burn a brand, and that's one reason I'm going to a new color. If Garrett goes to the same breed, I got more troubles."

Hackett scratched his ear. "If you can't brand, and if Garrett goes to whitefaces, you're out of business, ain't you?"

"I wouldn't say so," Jeff differed. "Brand or no brand, I'll harvest a fair calf crop once a year."

"Why can't you brand?" the dealer asked. "You haven't been blacklisted, or something like that, have you?"

Jeff nodded, and the breeder looked distressed. "I'm sorry. In that case, I can't sell to you. Be cutting my own throat, if I did. The Association ever hears of it, I would be barred from ever selling another beevie in this territory. I hate it, sonny. But you can see my side of it."

Jeff looked down his nose. He could see the stone wall rise up in front of him again. He could hear a scratchy voice call "Whoa."

"You could sell to Jim Gentile, in Quadrille," he suggested, wondering as he said it whether the merchant would stand with him, against Garrett. "Jim's in the clear. He could resell to me —or let me run the herd on shares."

Regretfully, the breeder shook his head. "I'd like to accommodate you. But Quadrille is fifty miles the wrong direction, and I'm overdue, up on the Powder."

"Then sell to Hackett here," Jeff said in rising desperation. "How about it, Hack? You're not in the cow business. Garrett couldn't git at you."

The station man laughed tonelessly. "You don't need be in the cow business to be got at. The boys are all ahold of hands—

246

Garrett, the railroad maggots, the bankers, the pimping politicians in Cheyenne. They got things the way they like it, and they mean to keep it. A threat to one's a threat to all. They're holding each other by the tail—like a bunch of circus elephants."

Jeff's hopes shriveled. But it wasn't an outright and definite refusal. He didn't let Hackett off with just a half no.

"You wouldn't have to resell to me. We could run 'em on shares. You buy 'em, with my money. We'll go it, fifty-fifty."

Hackett shook his head.

"All right," Jeff pleaded, his voice cracking on a note of hopelessness. "You buy 'em. Hire me to run 'em, on my homestead. You can pay me off in livestock. By God, I'll buy 'em twice."

Hackett scowled unhappily. "I don't see where you stand to come out. You can't brand, and you can't ship. So what good's cows?"

"The farmers will all be stocking cows, in time. They can be persuaded to Herefords. They'll wipe their feet on Garrett's blacklist, too. Besides, there's going to be enough us renegades around in time to vote Wate off his throne. Then, by God, we'll pass laws entitling others of us to own property."

The station keeper frowned and chewed his tongue. Finally, he inhaled a long breath and spoke angrily. "The hell with it. I don't owe Garrett nothing. Not even respect. There won't be no buying them ballies and hiring you to run them. There won't be no running them on shares. I been waiting a long time to see somebody with insides enough to stand up to Garrett—and smart enough to make it stick. Damned if I don't believe that you're the one!"

"So—what?"

"So I'll buy the goddam ballies, with your money, and sign them over you. If Garrett gits my job, I'll take your offer of a pardnership, and move up there with you. Then we'll both git under the bastard's tail!"

So it was that Jeff set out for Hurricane again next morning, driving twelve head of coming two-year-old heifers, accompanied by a station roustabout who drove the wagon while Jeff rode herd on the cattle. No bullionaire in creation ever surveyed his bovine capital with more pride and self-congratulation. The stock was not registered purebred, according to the breeder. But it was good, line-back, grade stuff, uniformly colored and boxcar shaped. With one exception, Jeff thought it was the prettiest sight he'd ever seen. He babied the bunch along, letting it set its own pace, fearful even then of walking too much fat off the delicate, blocky bodies.

"You ain't took their temperature nor give them any physic since we left the station!" the roustabout jeered when Jeff permitted the herd to shade up for a couple of hours during the heat of early afternoon. "Strikes me you're gitting plumb reckless."

"Have your fun," Jeff invited good-naturedly. "I'm having mine."

He covered less than fifteen miles in an all-day's drive, and camped that afternoon on a small clear-water stream near Squatters Row. Before he had his team unharnessed, the farmers began stringing out in groups of twos and threes to look him over. Their manner wasn't friendly when they recognized him. But they were interested in the red bally cattle, and Jeff wasn't backward about bragging the heifers up. With Herefords for a common denominator, Jeff could talk to any man.

"So when you boys git around to stocking cows," he managed to put in, "you'll know where to come—Jimson Hereford Company, Hurricane."

The sun was sinking low, and Jeff was cooking supper when four riders hove into sight to southward, bearing rapidly down upon the camp.

"Comes ol' Scissorbill now," one of the visitors announced, almost in triumph. "And your heifers are feeding off his precious grass. He'll have a hemorrhage, sure."

"This is public ground, and public grass," Jeff answered calmly. "He'll just have to hemorrhage."

Now that trouble threatened, the farmers drew off a distance and sat to watch developments, making it plain beforehand that they were not involved in any unpleasantness that might develop. Jeff thought their attitude was short-sighted, but he could understand their feeling, and didn't waste his breath.

"Git on my horse, and ride herd on them heifers," he ordered

248

the roustabout. "Anything happens to one of them, the same thing will happen to you. And that's a by-God promise."

Then, rifle in hand, he took oil and rags from the jockey box, sat down on the doubletrees, and pretended to clean the gun—with the action closed.

Jeff recognized all four riders as they came nearer. With Garrett were Bowman and Powers and a gunman named Swift—personal enemies to a man. They veered from course and eased their pace to ride among the grazing Herefords, discussing them in undertones. Jeff pressed his back against the endgate and watched them narrowly, keeping up his oiling motions but holding the rifle ready.

"The Four Horsemen of the Apocalypse!" a farmer cracked.

"Famine, Conquest, Death and Slaughter!" And Jeff found a moment's amusement in allotting the identities among them.

The unofficial inspection over, Famine wheeled his mount and came toward the wagon, pressed closely by the others. He was riding the tall blue geld again. But the fact registered only distantly with Jeff. Jeff was watching Conquest and Death.

"So it's you!" Famine said, pulling up near Jeff. "Mind telling me whose cattle you're working down here?"

"Not a bit," Jeff said easily, finding he would always have strength to stand to Garrett. "It'll be a pleasure. These honeys are mine."

The thin eyebrows went up. "Where do you get cattle?"

"Stoled eggs and bought 'em," Jeff said, indulging a childish fancy. "How did you git yours?"

"Where are you taking them?"

"Up to my place on Hurricane."

"So you still intend to go on squatting up there?"

"Squatting is not the word, Mr. Garrett," Jeff explained, grimly patient. "You're the squatter here. The rest of us own our ground. We're here to stay. You stay only about as long as we decide to tolerate you."

Garrett almost smiled. "We don't seem to be quite in agreement on that point."

"No," Jeff said, "nor on some other points. But I guess we'll git around to settling them, in time."

"Would I be too personal if I asked whom you bought the ballies off?" Garrett asked.

Jeff nodded profoundly. "A heap too personal."

The old man colored a little. But he was too much master of others to be other than master of himself.

"You must know that this is Man Head range. Yet here you are, driving cattle across it without permission, feeding off my grass. You, who talk of blocking thoroughfare across that scrap of ground you claim, on Hurricane. Why shouldn't I reciprocate, and turn you back?"

"There's a fine point of difference, Mr. Garrett," Jeff said. "Like I just explained, I own my ground. This here is government land. I am a dues-paying stockholder in the government, the same as you. I got as much right to this ground and this grass as you have. You try to turn me back, you'll have something on your hands."

Garrett laughed shortly. "There must be something in the water up that way. You're starting to talk the way the Rae boys talked."

"That could be." Jeff nodded again. "I guess I'm starting to feel the way them two felt. But I learned a little from their case. I'm harder for your corpse-makers to come up on."

There was a drawn-out silence, during which Jeff's eyes warred once more with the acrid, faded blue eyes. There was a movement among the three riders, but Jeff kept his eyes on Old Starvation, knowing that trouble would not start unless authorized. After what seemed an eternity, Famine glanced at the rifle in Jeff's hands, and shrugged again.

"Well, you haven't caused us any real trouble, yet. Until you do, I don't suppose I've any real call to be hard on you."

"Make it easy on yourself," Jeff invited.

Garrett nodded. "Thanks, I will. . . . I won't wish you good luck with your heifers. But it strikes me you will need it."

20: One Man's Meat

Jeff had rather expected to find his homestead raided and laid waste when he returned, after an absence so long. But the place, strangely, did not seem much disturbed. The gate bars were down and scattered, to be sure, and a trail had been worn through his hay by traveling horses. But there were no signs of cattle, and the hay crop had not been knocked down to any great extent.

Jeff, while gratified, was puzzled. "Wate must be saving my grass for winter range," he told the roustabout. "Else feed is good on the mesa."

The meadow growth was ripe, browning at the top, and once he'd paid his helper off and put things to right around his yard, he tackled the task of making hay.

As when picking bones, he worked from sunup until sundown, with an hour's break at noon to eat and rustle wood and water for evening use. As when picking bones, he made a careful point of knocking off in time to have everything battened down by nightfall—the heifers confined to the corrals along with one horse in case of emergency. His evening meal was cooked and eaten behind locked door and shuttered window. Thereafter, he slept with his weapons and felt relatively secure, until daylight. But there was always a bad moment in the morning when it came time to open the door and step out into the revealing and friendless light of day.

Always, before showing himself, he searched the mud cliffs and the brush clumps around, for sign of a waiting killer. Always, he stepped through the door with rifle at the ready, every nerve and muscle keyed to the expected exigency. Not until thoroughly convinced that the coast was clear did he go to his chip pile and gather kindling to start his breakfast fire.

Once out on the meadow, out in the open with a clear view of the bluffs in all directions, he enjoyed the same sense of security that eased his sleep in the barricaded cabin at night. But he grew more and more reluctant to leave the cabin mornings, and after a week or so he knocked a hole in the earthen bedroom wall, back close to the supporting cliff, where a rock ledge and an overhang of brush concealed the tunnel's opening. Thereafter, he left the cabin for the first time in the morning crawling on all fours, like a rodent, feeling like a skulk and coward, but no longer dreading the dawn.

With the problem of the morning exit solved, he started feeling a similar reluctance to enter the cabin for meals. Always, it seemed that the interval he had to spend indoors cooking and eating and washing up the wrecks would give a killer ample time to quit some distant lookout point and move up within rifle range of the door. Convinced that too-frequent use of his secret passage would destroy its value, he stuffed old clothes with hay to form an effigy of himself, and made a custom showing the straw man in the doorway before stepping into sight himself.

But the days wore on, and no hunter came with peep-sights and wool socks pulled over his boots. No bullet came screaming down from the bluffs to rip the scarecrow or the man it represented. And though Jeff did not relax his vigil, he did become hardened to the notion of threatened death, and gradually slipped into a routine of caution, giving his conscious thought and planning to his hay and heifers. His senses were geared to report and interpret the smallest, most insignificant disruptions to natural sights and sounds. Any unexplained noise at night—a scolding of birds or a sudden curiosity on the part of his animals by day—struck a gong of warning in his mind, and brought his rifle to hand. But this was a matter of habit, and his work didn't suffer on its account.

The late summer weather continued hot and dry, spelling disaster for the dry-farm grain crops on the wind-scoured flats, but bringing ideal conditions for haying in Jeff's sheltered valley. His schedule of work was to cut for four days without interruption, giving the fifth day to raking the dried cuttings into windrows, the sixth day to hauling the sweet-smelling product to the innermost of his three corrals, now his hay yard. On the seventh day, un-Godlike, he began the cycle all over again.

The meadow's yield was surprisingly heavy. With the cattle confined at night and himself on hand to keep them hazed off the uncut stand by day, he lost little of his crop through trampling. Altogether, the harvest kept him occupied for most of a month. By the time it was finished, he had two fair-sized hay butts in the shelter of the corral—enough to feed him through any reasonable emergency in a land where snow did not lie in winter.

He was very low on supplies, by the time his hay was made. But he didn't relish the idea of leaving his heifers unguarded for the time required to drive to Rustler Station and back. What he needed, plainly, was a partner—or a wife. But he could think of no man he would welcome as co-sponsor of the Jimson enterprises. And the only wife he could fancy was as far out of reach as the pale polar star.

There still was plenty Man Head beef up on the mesa. But now that he had livestock of his own, Jeff found in himself a curious prejudice against eating other people's cattle. When his salted meat ran out, he lived on rabbits and sage grouse until he could bag a deer. He felt righteous as a bishop, eating venison and birds when the hills beyond offered better fare. And he was conscious of a sense of guilt, as well, particularly when passing Demps's grave.

"Goddamnit, Demps, I'm doing the best I know how!" he told the silently accusing mound on one occasion when the feeling of betrayal weighed especially heavy. "Things have changed some, since you was running the place."

But, say what he would to the grave, he couldn't shake the suspicion that his new-found respect for property was in some fashion a compromise of things that shouldn't be compromised— somehow another sell-out of things that ought to be held holy. Ultimately, when the venison had spoiled, he located a fat yearling steer in the upper canyon, and made a sacrificial killing in an effort to placate the nagging grave. But he didn't enjoy the meat as he'd enjoyed the venison.

Almost before he realized it, summer had thinned and faded into another fall, and still the looked-for assassin had not appeared. He didn't know quite what to make of the fact, but somewhere at the edge of his consciousness was the certain knowledge that Abby was the cause of her father's forbearance.

Since bidding her good-by in Quadrille, he had never permitted himself to think of Abby in any but the most oblique terms. Demps once had remarked whimsically that there was no benefit in itching unless a man could scratch. And from the moment he'd stood outside the dining-room door in the Drovers House, eavesdropping on the talk within, he'd known that his itching for Abby could never be scratched. But it had continued, painfully at times, even when his days and nights were so full of work and immediate worry that he had no time for profitless reveries.

Now that his hay was up and the pressure was eased, he found the girl more and more often in his thoughts. But thinking of her served no purpose except to bring back old ambitions which he had long ago renounced. Leave her to the Boston Bean Boys, Jimson, he advised himself many times. They will git her in the end.

But even as he thought it, another part of him went on knowing that she was the real reason he had stayed on in Wyoming, buying penny chips in a dollar-ante game in which he held no cards. The day when she did hook up with another man would be the day when he would follow Gentile's advice and get the blocks off his shoulders, and admit defeat. Or, barring that, would call deuces wild and buck the tiger as Demps had done—an act which would amount to the same thing, in the end. . . .

At the time of butchering his second calf, Jeff had observed that the Man Head roundup was in process, on the tablelands above him. Neither wagons nor riders had come up the creek road to cross his meadow, and he could only surmise that the roundup crew had traveled the southern trail. After two weeks had gone by without bringing sight or sound of the market drive, he began to hope and almost to believe that the cattle too had been routed to the dry trail. But one bright calm morning he heard a bawling up the canyon, pierced by the familiar high keening yells. And he knew then that he hadn't scared anybody, after all.

At one time he'd resolved that if Bowman tried to drive across the meadow in defiance of his ultimatum, he would meet the herd at the upper bars and hold it back with bullets. But now that he was faced with the actuality, he knew he had sold himself a lie. If he shot a Man Head cow in front of witnesses, to say nothing of a Man Head rider who might take the thing to heart, he would either have to flee the country or go to jail. And that was exactly the choice that Garrett wished to hand him.

He did saddle his dun, and hurriedly. But this was merely so he could ride around his Herefords and secure them in the corrals, so they wouldn't be swept down to the river with the Man Head stock. His heifers safely penned and all his horses up, he waited at the stable with his rifle, telling himself he would shoot, if the trespass extended to his yard.

It was shortly after noon when the bawling herd began spilling out of the canyon into the valley. It was all market stuff, tall and rangy compared to Herefords, and hungry as marching locusts. Big-hatted riders lazed insolently along the flanks, not hurrying the raiders any. Among the drovers Jeff spotted Strap Bowman, and sight of his ancient enemy set his teeth together.

Strap didn't offer to bother the corrals or house. But he managed to give outrageous provocation. Jeff's meadow provided the last grass the herd was likely to encounter the rest of the day, and Strap had the effrontery to call a noon halt there in the valley where he had no right to be at all. While five hundred three- and four-year-old steers and dry cows spread out through the bottoms to clean off the feed Jeff's heifers would need to winter through, the drovers watered their horses in Jeff's stream, then freed the animals to pick what grass the cattle missed. When the pack outfit came up, the jinglebob chopped Jeff's brush to build a cooking fire. And, when the meal was done, the men took their ease on Jeff's creek bank while cows and horses continued their work of destruction on the meadow.

The studied arrogance of the whole procedure filled Jeff with fury and a knowledge of the futility of fury. He considered firing a few shots into the ground near the reclining riders, just to relieve his feelings. But intelligence told him who would come off second best, if things came to shooting.

Tears of helpless rage stung his eyes, and while he skulked like a fugitive around his own corrals, fearing even to show himself lest that bring added insults, he plotted prodigious projects of reprisal. He would collect payment for his grass in Man Head beef that winter. He would eat all he could consume himself, and would make rural free deliveries of Man Head stock to all the

255

farmers on the Row. He would ride to Ekard tomorrow and offer his services to Drake, in any capacity that Drake could use him. He would organize a rustler ring, with Drake or on his own, and make Garrett pay through the nose.

But he knew throughout it all that he was only whistling past a graveyard. He knew that he now was committed to a course— that he couldn't voluntarily go to jail again, and the time was past when he could just climb his horse and ride away from things. He was trapped, by property and by his Herefords, and had to take the practical way. He couldn't bear to think of Demps down on the meadow, and it seemed that he would never be able to live with himself again, on any terms whatsoever. But he remained hidden until the trespassers were gone. Then, mute as the horse he rode, he set out to assess the damage.

Already depleted by the hay cutting, the meadow was now grazed clean. There was still some dry feed on the higher ground, but not enough to see him through. He cursed Man Head and Bowman until language failed him. But the cursing didn't alter anything, and, once he was calm enough to start thinking again, he began to plan anew.

There doubtless was grass up on the mesa. But he couldn't and wouldn't trust his Herefords up there alone and untended, prey to wolves and weather and Man Head line riders who were permitted to butcher fat strays but no company cattle. That meant he must stay with them at all times, like a sheepherder tending a flock. In order to do that, he must have a camp wagon such as sheepherders used.

He already had the wagon, with a double-bed box. He could make bows from green saplings, and there were tarps around out of which he could piece a hood. It wouldn't be pleasant, or easy, living like a gypsy sheepherder all winter, following the grass and hoping that deep snows didn't catch him fifty miles from hay. But he didn't see any other way of doing, without he just admitted defeat and cleared out. And the chips were still on his shoulders.

Next morning, he rose earlier than usual, and combed the riverbank thickets for willow that would do for wagon bows. By noon, he had the bows trimmed and fastened to the box, the tarps partly pieced together for a cover. He was knocking off to eat when three horsebackers emerged from the lower canyon, out onto the impoverished meadow. And even as his hands began readying the rifle he was never separated from, his eyes told him the weapon would not be needed. Two of the visitors obviously were farmers. The third was big Ben Hackett, from Rustler Station.

"Jeff," the station manager said when the three had pulled up at the cabin and preliminary greetings had been spoken, "I would like for you to meet a couple friends of mine—Dr. Woodrow and Preaching Lime Higgins, from the settlements. You may have heard me speak of them."

"Believe I have." Jeff nodded. Mystified and wary, he shook hands around.

"We've heard him speak of you!" Higgins boomed, plainly bent on flattery. "I'm glad to make your acquaintance!"

"Ben is quite an admirer of yours," Woodrow added. "This is a privilege."

More puzzled than ever, Jeff invited them to dismount and come inside. A check of the stove showed his breakfast fire was out, so he waved his guests to seats in the kitchen and made a trip out to his chip pile. The three were conversing in undertones when he returned, and the talk ceased with his entrance.

The uneasy silence persisted while he kindled a fire and moved the coffeepot to the front of the stove. Nor did anyone offer to speak during the time it took to add more water from the bucket and to grind the last of the berries to give it strength. But when he dumped the pleasantly pungent grindings into the pot with an air of casual prodigality, hoping that no one noticed he emptied the sack to do it, Ben Hackett spoke up jocularly.

"Bachelor coffee! Pound of grounds to the quart of water. Boil it an hour, and drop in a horseshoe. If the horseshoe sinks, boil it some more!"

Jeff bridled, sensing criticism in the observation. But his visitors laughed heartily, and laughter cleared the air. Jeff brought out his last sack of makings and offered it. Hackett and Higgins declined. The doctor started to follow suit, then changed his mind with startling vehemence.

"By God, I will!"

While rolling his own cigarette, Jeff managed to study the two homesteaders with more than cursory interest. Both were roughly dressed in ill-matching tag ends of old apparel, and both had what Gentile called "that hungry homesteader look." But here the similarity ended. Higgins was a huge, solid Percheron of a man, well fleshed but not fat, big enough to wrestle a bear. His hair and beard once had been deep red, but now were frosted with gray. Woodrow was small and intense, perhaps forty, dark complexioned and sharp featured as a ferret. His black eyes were bright and restless, seemed to snap when he blinked.

"How's everything on the Rustler?" Jeff asked finally, plunging in.

"Bad—and gitting worse," Hackett said instantly, as if he too had been impatient to get at the purpose of the visit. "County's on the verge of civil war."

Jeff's eyebrows lifted, but his laugh was cynical. "What's bad about that? Little civil war now and again is what this country needs."

"Needing is not affording," Preaching Lime Higgins interceded. "In the first place, civil wars have a way of destroying what they set out to fix. In the second place, a backhouse rebellion up here has about as much chance of succeeding as I have of converting people to the religion they swear by. If we start snapping caps around here right now, it's going to be a long, long night before morning."

From early youth, Jeff had built up a prejudice against preachers, as pimping apologists for the evil they fed on. He had come in his thinking to associate them with the toady hobo and Sundance and all who sold mankind out for a five-hundred-dollar reward. But here was a bunk-shooter who talked of things that mattered. Jeff was impressed with him.

"What's going on?" he asked. "Who's about to start cracking caps?"

"You remember a fella, a farmer, named Lin Mundy?" Hackett asked.

Jeff puzzled a minute, then nodded slightly. "Name sounds familiar."

"It should," Hackett said dryly. "Year or two back, he filed a

258

homestead down on Cat Crick. Says you rode up one day, shoved a rifle in his face, and told him to haul his freight. It was back when you was Garrett's—well, when you was deputy sheriff."

Jeff's face felt red and swollen. He remembered the incident, and its sequel, when the same man walked naïvely into the sheriff's office to enter a complaint against the company. He remembered the man's eyes when they finally realized who was sitting in the sheriff's chair.

"Yeah," he murmured, looking at the floor. "I remember."

"Well," Hackett said, "when Mundy moved off Cat, he filed a claim down on the river, not too far from me. About that time, the farmers' Grange started a irrigation project. Just so happened that farm of Mundy's is the only practical place to take a ditch out of the river, without going to the expense of a dam. They started work there about a year ago, and Garrett has been trying to buy Lin out or scare him off ever since, so as to shut that water off before it starts to run. The others all backed Mundy up, and he didn't scare. John Poe has contested the filing, in the name of one of Garrett's cowboys, putting him next in line in case the homestead shouldn't be proved up. Here the other week Lin was arrested for killing a Man Head cow to feed his family. If he's convicted, it means his filing is vacated, and Garrett's bullpuncher gits the land. In which case, there'll be no water on the flats, without a dam. And there can't be no dam for a good many years."

"Did Mundy kill the cow?" Jeff asked.

Hackett shrugged impatiently. "I suppose he did. But that's not what he's being arrested for—any more than Dempsey Rae was killed for stealing horses. That's what scalds a man."

"Unlawfully killing and possessing a Man Head beef!" Woodrow burst out, savage in his mimicry. "Defiling the sacred cows of Garrett. A high crime, deserving capitalistic punishment!"

"He killed the cow," Preaching Higgins put in more calmly. "But, in a sense, he had justification. His family was hungry, and there's no game around. It's possible to sin for righteous reasons, you know. And it's a rather common sin. His crime was getting caught."

"His crime was not being smart enough to guess the critter had

259

been planted on him, to be watched!" Woodrow exclaimed, his voice snapping like his eyes. "What the hell did he think it was? Manna from heaven?"

"Perhaps," the churchman intoned. And in the word was a rebuke that put the medical man to scowling blacker than before.

Jeff didn't know where the talk was leading, couldn't guess why the three were there, telling all this to him. But the talk thus far had been a revelation. The words were not the same, but the attitude of his three visitors toward Man Head and Man Head property was very like the attitude of the horse thieves he once had heard discuss the company, here in this very room. And these three were solid citizens.

"Well, it's a small world, after all!" he breathed, exulted by the discovery. "What's this about a civil war?"

"There'll be war, if Mundy is convicted," Hackett prophesied. "The farmers are not going to sit by and see their irrigation project knocked out. The whole community is up in arms, and Drake is making the most of a chance to even scores with Garrett. He's organized a vigilance committee of fifty toughs that say they're going to free Mundy by force. If that ever happens, it's good night ladies!"

"I don't see it," Jeff snapped, remembering the day before. "I'd say we'd all ought to join Drake, and run old Garrett back to where he come from."

"Then you ain't thought about it," Hackett told him. "Like I said once before, this thing is bigger than just Garrett. A threat to Wate is a threat to the whole damned fraternity. And them boys hang together. All Garrett's got to do is scream 'insurrection,' and the Governor will send up his bayonet boys, waving the country's flag, to give us what they gave the Indians."

"Step on Garrett's toe, and it's that son of a bitch in Cheyenne that yelps!" Doc Woodrow confirmed. "One groan from Garrett, and up comes the Governor's aide-de-cramp, to fix the situation. You know what that means. And you know who stands to get themselves fixed!"

"So what do you figure to do?" Jeff asked.

"Only one thing to do," Hackett said. "Let the case come to trial, in a legal and lawlike manner, and try to git Lin off. Doc and

Lime here can hold Drake back that long. But if Mundy's convicted and sent up, that's something else again."

Jeff grunted cynically. "Then why bother? You know how Garrett's court works."

"I know how it usually works," Hackett nodded. "But this will be a jury trial. And there's been a little change of feeling around here the last year or so. I've been talking to Gentile and some others about this case."

"I been talking to Gentile, too," Jeff broke in bitterly. "Don't look to him for help. He's got it good, way things are. Garrett boots him in the butt, he turns the other cheek. He don't want no change."

"Jim's old, and he's careful," Hackett conceded. "But he can see what we're headed for up here. He don't want that any more than the rest of us do. And he don't want any Drake taking over. We convince Jim there's enough of us to put the thing over, he'll kick over the traces and go with us—as long as we keep it peaceful, and don't start any ruckus the Governor can jump into. And there's plenty others in Quadrille we can count on, too. But we're going to need your help."

"My help?"

Hackett nodded so profoundly he practically bowed. "We want you to take the stand for Mundy. Tell what you know of Garrett's methods, and what you know of the way Mundy was treated, before he killed that calf."

Jeff shook his head. "Gentile and the others know more about Garrett's methods than I could tell in fifty years. It would be a waste of breath."

"It would show which side you stood on," Hackett persisted. "That's the big thing right now, in a lot of people's eyes."

Jeff laughed in sour derision. "What difference it make where I stand?"

"All the difference," Hackett said emphatically. "People have been watching you, since you broke with Garrett. You stood him on his head in that deal with Harley Rae, and made the court's ruling so damned transparent that even the blind men could see through it. You moved up on this homestead that two men got shot for squatting on. You're still here. You're still alive. You've even stocked cattle, and the hell with the Association blacklist. You've showed what can be done. People would pay attention, if you'd speak up."

Jeff was flattered, but confused and skeptical. Involuntarily, he glanced at Woodrow, and found the black eyes dancing. "You're the first man in this country that's kicked Garrett in the teeth and made it stick, and people like it. The jury knows you stand with us, they might do the same."

Jeff's wavering eyes went to Preaching Lime. The part-time reverend endorsed all that had been said with a nod of blessing. "We think you are one of us, boy. We'd like to have you with us."

Jeff walked to the open door, and stood awhile in silence, staring out at the cattle on his denuded meadow. His investment wasn't much, but it was all he had—as much to him as all Man Head was to Garrett. If he agreed to speak for the homesteader in court, it would mean leaving his heifers alone and unguarded for at least two days, and maybe three. There was grass enough to last them. But there were predators around, two-legged and four. There might be another Man Head drive, and ownership to unbranded cattle would be hard to prove. Last of all, if he opposed Garrett openly in court, the company would be bound to make more trouble.

Wryly, he remembered condemning Jim Gentile for being cautious and afraid to stand up for his convictions, because of hazards to investments. And there was Hackett here. By his own testimony, the station manager couldn't afford to invite the wrath of Garrett either. A man needed a guiding star.

"What about you, Ben?" he asked without turning. "You going to speak up for Mundy?"

"Hell, no," the answer came readily. "I can't talk for him. I'm on the jury."

The statement struck Jeff as being uproariously funny. "Hell," he said, "I'll join your club. I'll be mighty proud."

Later, when they'd all made a good meal of Man Head beef and no questions asked, Jeff stood in the doorway, watching the three depart, still warmed by the companionship he'd known,

262

wondering at his blindness in supposing that he stood alone, holding views unheld by others.

"Why, there's a lot of us around," he said in satisfaction. "The woods are full of us!"

21: Law of the Land

The opening of the district court found every able-bodied man in the county on hand in town again, to see the fire-works promised by the Mundy trial. The farmers had brought their guns and left their families home, in the expectation that the accused would be found guilty and trouble would result. Wate Garrett had heard of the farmers' state of mind, and had twenty armed cowboys on hand, all sworn in as special deputies. The jury had been chosen and the court was in noon recess. The farmers stood around the courthouse much as Jeff had seen them stand on one previous occasion. But this time Jeff stood among them, feeling himself one of them, secure in their company at last.

While he waited, Jeff alternately watched the Longhorn Bar where the Man Head deputies were fortifying themselves for whatever lay ahead, and the Drovers House Hotel, where Garrett and Coates and the whole Man Head clique were at lunch in the little private dining hall that Jeff remembered. A part of his mind was concerned with the Cheyenne attorney who had not yet shown up as scheduled, while another part of it listened to Duck-bill Drake's persistent plea for violence.

"That's adding insult to injury—them two butcher birds sitting over there deciding how the case will be decided, before the evidence is in! I got a barrel of roofing tar over on my rig. If somebody's got a featherbed, we'll have ourselves some fun."

The homesteaders had finished the cold, put-up lunches they'd fetched from home, and none had any money to spend in the stores or bars. The strain of waiting was beginning to tell, and they were in no mood to have Garrett's hook-up with the law thrown in their faces like a handful of runny mud. Those who

263

had tobacco were smoking, and Drake's proposal brought a sour rumble of endorsement.

"This is the damnedest way of doing—waiting till Garrett and all his pack are on hand, before we try to do anything. Time to have sprung Lin out was last night, like I wanted. Next best time is now—before he's been sentenced to twenty years at Laramie." The words were spoken to the group at large. But Jeff felt the acrid black eyes single him out for special message. Reluctantly, he turned to meet them.

"Take it easy, Duck," he said gruffly, feeling the other eyes on him, knowing the crowd was still willing to listen. "The place to whip a harlot judge like Coates is in his own cathouse court. And we've got a chance to do just that. We got a good jury lined up. Hackett and Gentile both got on the panel. They're for us. And I've talked with some the others . . ."

"You can talk, the good God knows!" the sage of Ekard sneered. "But that's about as far as this thing goes with you. You figure them boys in there are going to stick their necks out and vote a verdict Garrett don't want, just on your say-so, and Ben Hackett's, you better figure up again."

Jeff didn't like to preach to Duckbill Drake. Much less did he like to preach in front of people who knew Drake's history, and his own. But the crowd was still following their conversation, and Drake had to be answered.

"Duck," he said, "it's not Lin Mundy who's on trial in there. It's Man Head and Garrett that are up for judgment today, and the lawyer we got coming in won't let the jury forget it, for a minute."

"What loi-yer?" Drake challenged. "I don't see none around."

"Well, he's coming, on the one o'clock," Jeff predicted with a confidence he didn't completely feel. "Woodrow and Lime Higgins are down to the station, to hurry him on up. And this is our one big chance to right things around here. If we can bulldog Wate in his own court, that's two-thirds the fight. If we can't, well, there is still time enough to try things your way."

Drake made an obscene sound with his mouth and turned away. His purpose accomplished, Jeff let him go. The crowd still stood with Jeff. Drake would stand with him, too, if things worked out and Mundy was acquitted. If things went wrong and the jury convicted, Jeff's foot would be in his mouth, and he'd have no choice but to join Drake and his Warhawks—provided they would have him.

A wind came up, scattering dry dust over them. Hardened to wind and dust, patient as the horses at the tie rails, the farmers turned their backs and gave the elements no heed. They were starting to converse among themselves again. Their voices were bitter, their humor strained. But attention had shifted from Jeff and Drake and their quarrel, and that was good.

"Garrett planted that cow on Lin's place, and had it watched. There ain't no question about that."

"Sure he did. Lin ain't any greenhorn. Butchered at night, with no lights lit. Had everything out of sight by morning. But Bowman knowed right where to dig for the hide and head. Knowed where else to go, too. Lin fetched us some ribs in a gunnysack around midnight, and Desmond was around next morning, with a warrant to search. Didn't even git to cook 'em."

"Didn't lose no time gitting to my place, neither. Liked to tore the shack down, looking for the roast we'd et."

"Should of told 'em like Old Lady Cousins done, when Strap figured she was holding back on him. Walked over to the buckboard, put her finger down her throat, and puked right in the rig. Said, 'There's your cow meat, mister, and welcome to it.' Said, 'Come along, and I'll take you to what I et last night.' But the bastard wouldn't go!"

They laughed at that, bitterly but heartily, wringing the last drop of enjoyment from a probably exaggerated account of one humble person's triumph over the high and mighty lord of Man Head.

Jeff was looking toward the depot, wondering if the one o'clock was going to be four hours late again today, when an undercurrent of excitement broke against him, and he turned to see Judge Coates emerging from the Drovers House, immaculate in white linen and black broadcloth and planter's hat. Next behind came Garrett himself, with Abby holding to his arm.

"Old Man Head, and little Maiden Head!" someone quipped.

And, as Strap appeared, "The one and only Chuckle Head!"

265

The sallies brought a laughter so malign that Jeff was impressed again with the heritage of hatred that Garrett had built up, in the course of amassing a fortune for a sweet-faced girl who likely wouldn't want a fortune, and wouldn't know what to do with it, in any case. But the reflection was a brief one. Abby was talking now to Strap, and laughing, and the sound filled Jeff with an old pain that was almost too exquisite to bear.

He had told himself many times, out on the homestead, that he was well over his crush on Abby—that he'd merely confused her with his now-dead ambition to be a bullionaire. But seeing her again brought back all the old heartache, all the hunger he had known at Man Head. And he suddenly felt that, regardless of the principles at stake, he belonged at Abby's side, not here among the embittered men who were dedicated to the destruction of all that she represented. He suddenly felt conspicuous and ridiculous, somehow humiliated to be there among people he knew were despised as vermin by those with whom he'd tried to associate, but unsuccessfully. Yet, perversely, he felt a stronger pride in being there, and he put aside an impulse to turn and lose himself in the crowd while there yet was time.

Indifferent to those who blocked the way, the procession came leisurely up the walk, Poe and Gut Desmond bringing up the rear. The farmers to a man moved back to give it right-of-way, but Jeff himself did not yield the walk. Jeff stood immovable where he was, forcing Garrett and the judge to break step to get around him. His eyes received the judge's cool impersonal stare which looked at him and through him with no flicker of recognition. He saw the arrogant set of Garrett's head, the veiled eyes which did not deign to look at Jeff or anyone in the waiting crowd.

He saw the calm, speculative question in Strap Bowman's eyes. He saw the delicate white oval of Abby's face, proud but friendly, poignantly aware of Jeff, asking a different question from the one put by Strap. He saw the mouth his mouth had known prepare a smile of greeting. He felt the eyes of his new allies still gauging him half-distrustfully, and he rejected the girl's offer of renewed friendship with the same impassive mask that had rejected the judge's scorn. He saw the friendly eyes waver, the mouth tighten

266

in recognition of a chasm that never could be bridged by smiles, however bright and wistful.

He saw the girl sweep past him, cold and unbending as her father. He smelled the familiar exciting perfume she trailed, and stopped breathing until it had passed. He took one more pull at his cigarette and flipped it into the dust, seeing the smoke curl slowly upward, thinning in the wind like hope in the face of certainty.

Down the street, the doors of the Longhorn burst open, and Man Head's special deputies began spilling noisily out onto the street, their blood fired with whiskey and a monumental faith in their own righteousness, their own invincibility. They swaggered tantalizingly as they headed for the courthouse and another bloodless victory in a cause they mistakenly thought of as their own.

Jeff was preparing to go inside ahead of the deputies when he saw Higgins and Woodrow come out of the station, Higgins holding what looked like a telegram. Premonition weighed on him as he started down to join them. And as he drew near enough to read their faces, premonition congealed into bleak knowledge.

"Well, we got no lawyer," Higgins announced abruptly. "Cast your sunburned eyes on that."

Jeff accepted the proffered wire and read it at a glance. UNABLE TO KEEP COURT APPOINTMENT. VERY SORRY. BEST OF LUCK. JOHN HARMAN. When he looked up again, Higgins' hurt-child eyes were waiting.

"Don't that beat the Dutch? Why do you suppose he waited till now, to let us know?"

"Son of a bitch was bought off, that's why!" Woodrow's voice crackled. "If he'd let us know earlier, we'd have had time to round up another. When Garrett buys somebody, he gets his money's worth."

"Well, he has us where he wants us," Higgins intoned dolefully. "Outsmarted us at every turn."

"Well, we're not helping matters, crying in our beer," Jeff said impatiently. "Court'll be in session in another minute. We better git our haunches over there."

"Why bother?" Higgins gloomed. "Best we can hope for is a

postponement. You know well as I do that Drake and his pack won't stand for that."

"If I know Coates, there won't be any postponement," Woodrow differed. "It's judge's privilege, in absence of a lawyer for the defense, to appoint one out of the court. There being no other shyster in town, I don't doubt he'll give the honor to Hog Muldroon or maybe old Hitch, and get right on with his lynching. We are screed geese."

"Well, we can't let that happen," Jeff told Higgins. "You'll just have to speak for Lin yourself."

The preacher shook his head. "I'm just not up to it. I don't know from Adam about the procedure. I've never been in court in all my life."

Ever since the conference on the matter out on Hurricane, Jeff had felt himself committed to a plan of action—to a pattern of thinking and believing. His mind made a reckless suggestion, and he didn't hesitate to speak it.

"Well, I've been in more courts than I remember. And I'd as lief stand up as lawyer as witness."

The farmers looked interested but unconvinced, and Jeff's impatience rose. "You said your own selves it wasn't as much a question of law as of somebody standing up to Garrett. Sure, I ain't any William Jenny Bryan. But I can argue any goddam thing with old John Poe. Long as we got no choice, why not give me a crack at it? What you got to lose?"

"Nothing but our necks—if Mundy loses out in there," Woodrow growled. "But you're our best bet. Let's go."

They were almost too late. The judge was speaking across his lectern as they entered the stale-smelling room, and there was consternation among the farmers who filled one side of the small chamber—some standing in preference to crossing the aisle to occupy chairs with Garrett's crowd.

"I repeat: Is the attorney for the defense in the court? If not, I shall fulfill my statutory obligation and appoint counsel from the floor."

"That won't be necessary," Lime Higgins called out. "The Grange has retained Mr. Jimson to represent the accused."

All heads swiveled at the announcement. The Man Head peo-

268

ple looked taken back, but amusedly so. The farmers' basic re-action seemed one of suspicion and dismay. The most malign countenance in the room was that of Drake. The most coldly hostile was that of the accused, who sat manacled at one of the two tables up front, staring inimically at the man who'd once threatened him with a company rifle.

Jeff walked to the table with an outward show of confidence, and—refusing an encounter with the defendant's opaque eyes—appropriated a vacant chair. His glance went to Theo Coates, and found the judge's troubled eyes on Garrett. Jeff's eyes whipped to Garrett in time to see the ranchman's bemused nod of consent. They went to the farmer crowd in time to see that the friends of Mundy also had witnessed the transparent exchange.

Drake already was on his feet, thin lips writhing in a snarl. "It's a sell-out, just like I said! They never figured on gitting Lin no loi-yer. That was all eyewash. And look who's undertook the job! You ain't got to take my word he's Man Head spy. You all seen that Garrett heifer set her eyes on him when she come in . . ."

The words brought Jeff to his feet, cocked for violence. But the room was in uproar, and the surging crowd had him fenced off from the offender. Higgins and Woodrow were trying to wrestle the culprit down, but one maul of a fist sent Higgins sprawling against the wall, one flailing arm felled three men in one sweep, crashing chairs to kindling. Doc Woodrow came up with a chair leg, and swung it like a pick. Drake dropped from sight, and as he did so the hammering of Coates's gavel began to beat at Jeff's ears.

"Order. Order in the court. Throw the lout outside!"

In Jeff, the ill-selected words stirred an old grievance which all but brought him to the defense of the man he had sprung up to tear apart. But matters already had passed him by. The judge's brayed instruction brought Strap Bowman and a dozen Man Head deputies to their feet—to be confronted by a solid phalanx of grim-faced farmers, captained by Lime Higgins.

Disheveled and bleeding at the mouth, the huge man still managed to amass a formidable dignity as he faced the armed com-pany men, calm and immovable, somehow monumental.

"You may all resume your seats," he told the threatening cowboys. "We'll attend to him, ourselves."

He'd scarcely stopped speaking when the crowd parted, and Woodrow and three others emerged, carrying Drake's limp form toward the door. A tangible aura of relief filled the room as the odd procession disappeared without further disturbance. But when the four returned, empty-handed, roughly half the farmer delegation stalked silently through the door. A hollow feeling spread in Jeff, seeing them go. And, seated on his chair again, he had a brief impression of Abby's stricken, averted face. He closed his eyes against the sight and vowed that someday he would kill Duck Drake.

"The court will come to order," the bench thundered. "Another outburst like that, and I will clear the room!"

A minute passed while Coates glowered at the offending faction, now reduced by half. Then, his anger sated, he turned his gaze on Mundy.

"If counsel is acceptable to the accused, the court will offer no objection."

"This is your show, not mine," Mundy answered sullenly. "Appoint who you damn please."

Coates favored Jeff with a short nod, and spoke quietly to Poe. "The prosecution may proceed."

At a sign from Poe, Gut Desmond produced a wooden washtub containing a spotted cowhide with head and horns still attached. It had not been cured or properly dried, and the fetor that emanated from it caused visible distress to some, but was oddly reassuring to Jeff. It made him feel at home.

While Poe exhibited the hide, Jeff took opportunity to study his client. He'd heard from Higgins that Mundy once had punched cows for one of the English outfits to the north. But when you looked at him, it was hard to believe that he'd ever done anything but till the soil. The look of the soil was in his dirt-rimmed eyes and fingernails, in the stoop of his heavy shoulders. The smell of earth clung to him like musk, even after his sojourn in the jail, and granite was in his pale, unyielding eyes. Trouble had ridden him mercilessly, grinding the hard stuff of his interior down to a cutting edge that was dangerous to brush against.

Hunched and withdrawn and sodden, he might have been a bored spectator at another's trial, for all the interest he showed in the proceedings.

With the hide's brand and ownership established, Poe had Gut Desmond identify the decaying skin as the one he had dug from the earth on Mundy's property. Next he had the sheriff tell how he had driven to the defendant's farm on a tip from an unnamed source to find half a freshly butchered cow hanging from a tripod in some willows near the house.

"Your witness." Poe leered then at Jeff. And Jeff stood awkwardly. He was wearing his broadcloth suit for the first time since he'd left Man Head, and was doubly uncomfortable because of it. He carefully refrained from looking at the audience, or at Poe or Coates. He did glance at the jury box, and received a wink from Hackett. Encouraged, he turned to Desmond in the chair.

"You say you found *half* a carcass? Did you ever locate the other half?"

"I found parts of it," Desmond growled, plainly irked at being submitted to questioning by one he so thoroughly despisèd. "I had to drive over half of Squatters Row to do it."

"You mean Mundy shared the meat, and the whole community benefited?"

"I object!" Poe said, rising.

Coates nodded benevolently. "The objection is sustained. The witness will not answer. The question will be struck."

Jeff shrugged and tried again. "Who was it tipped you off that the cow had been butchered? Who was it drove the animal onto Mundy's ground—a fracture of the law all by itself—then hid in the brush to see what happened?"

"Your honor!" Poe exclaimed, leaping up again, "I protest the defense counsel's entire line of questioning!"

"Sustained." Coates nodded. "Counsel will confine itself to questions that pertain."

"You say it was night, when the cow was butchered. In that case, Mundy couldn't have seen the brand, could he? Couldn't it be that he just made a mistake?"

"His mistake—" Desmond smiled—"was in killing a cow when

he didn't own no cow. He didn't have to see the brand to know the critter wasn't his."

"I guess you're right, at that," Jeff conceded. "You come right down to it, he should have known the cow was Garrett's, because the law don't permit anybody but Garrett to own cows. That what you mean?"

"Your honor," Poe groaned, in actual pain, "this is insufferable. This has no bearing on the case. I must object again."

"You are sustained," the judge pronounced. "Recording clerk will strike from the record all questions and answers pertaining to defense up to this point."

Jeff shook his head, and resumed his seat. Desmond was dismissed, and Poe next summoned Lin Mundy to the chair. The sullen homesteader gave no indication that he'd heard the summons, and Jeff answered for him.

"The defendant won't take the stand. He can't be made to testify against himself."

"Then you admit he's guilty?" Poe pounced.

"I object."

"Sustained. It is not a proper question."

Poe next called Bowman, who repeated the salient points of testimony offered by the sheriff.

"Your witness," the prosecutor said when the twice-told tale was finished.

"Strap," Jeff said, meeting the scornful green eyes again, "what value would you put on that critter you say that Mundy killed?"

"Forty dollars, if a dime."

"You still pay forty a month and found, top-hand wages, at the ranch?"

Bowman nodded guardedly.

"Mundy needed that meat, and needed it bad. His kids was hungry, and any kind of man at all will see his kids git food. If he'd come to you and offered to work out the price of the critter, would you have put him on? If he'd offer to work it out now, would you drop this case and take value received, and call things square?"

"I object."

"Sustained. The question has no bearing."

272

"Your honor," Jeff said, "I beg to differ. To us people that have bet the government five years of our lives against a hundred and sixty acres of land that we can live in this country and make a go of things, it has a lot of bearing. If we all had free and equal use of the land we're all supposed to own, it would be different. But we don't. We can't own cattle. We can't work for the big ranches, unless we give up our ground. You can't hire us, here in town. What's a man with kids going to do? Let 'em starve, so's to keep out of jail? Is that the kind of people we want for neighbors?"

Poe was on his feet, shouting frantically. The judge rapped for order, instructed the clerk not to record the speech, then bent a stern gaze of censure upon Jeff.

"I will remind counsel that there is nothing in our laws which requires one person to give employment to another, no matter how great his need. I will remind you further that the Man Head company is not on trial here today, and warn that continued attempts on your part to put them on trial without filing of formal charges will result in your being found in contempt and punished accordingly."

With all the evidence in, John Poe made a quick and able summary. After reading from the statutes those provisions which defined and prescribed punishment for illegal butchery of animals, he touched briefly on the growing spirit of lawlessness which characterized the country, with emphasis on the threat which that lawlessness posed to property of every kind. He expressed a certainty that the jury would see its duty, and—secure in that certainty—he sat down.

The judge offered a few formal words of commendation, complimenting the prosecution on its able presentation of the territory's case, then turned a jaundiced eye on Jeff.

"The defense may make its summary."

"The defense rests," Jeff snapped.

The announcement created something of a stir. The farmers looked incredulous, let down, the Man Head crowd amused. Theo Coates's eyes communed for one savored instant with the eyes of old Wate Garrett. Then he placed his pince-nez in position and peered at Jeff as at some unknown species of insect.

273

"I should remark that your defense was most irregular. You realize, of course, that you spoke not one word in behalf of your client, and introduced no evidence in his favor? You realize that you leave me no choice but to instruct the jury to bring in a verdict of guilty?"

Jeff was silent for a moment, too angry to trust himself to speak. The spectacle of all the power and machinery of society conspiring at the ruin of a man who'd likely never harmed another human being out of malice, while the actual enemy of the people sat securely looking on, unaccused and unaccusable, filled him with a fury that knotted his stomach and put his head to pulsating. He thought of Demps and Harley Rae, and the price they'd paid for speaking out against this same evil, and suddenly he lost all fear of consequences.

"I realize that you would have instructed the jury just the same, no matter what I said or done!" he said. "I realize what Lin is up against, same as everybody else here must realize it, because I'm up against the same thing, and so are most the rest here. I realize Lin ain't being tried on the charges filed, any more than Demps and Harley was murdered for stealing cattle. He's on trial because he had the gut to exercise his right as a citizen and file a homestead on the public ground. There couldn't be no defense, because in this bought court, the defense don't apply! Well, there's thirty men outside with Duckbill Drake that will apply it, if you git your way and send Mundy up the river for doing what any man worth his salt would do in the circumstances!"

Poe was on his feet, trying to outshout Jeff. The farmers were applauding, and the judge was hammering his lectern, trying to make himself heard.

"Order! Counsel will come to order!"

"I'll come to order when I've had my say!" Jeff raged, shouting all others down. "This is a thing we've got to settle, in here with words, or out in the street with guns. In the eyes of the law, Lin Mundy's a criminal, for not letting his family starve. But who made the laws that read that way? I say there are other and bigger criminals in this room that we'd ought to consider ahead of Lin Mundy. There's other laws than them that safeguard cattle, even if we don't hear anything about them. There's law saying the

274

public land belongs equally to all of us. There's people in this room that have stole that ground, and hold it at gun's point. I say it's the big crime we'd ought to worry about—the one that's behind the little crimes like Lin's. I say we've got fair claim on Man Head beef, us that have been defrauded and deprived of our rights as citizens. I say the beef eats our grass, and that gives us legal share in them. I say the beef Mundy killed is damn small payment on what the company owes him. I say we've got moral right on our side, and the hell with company law. I say there's enough of us in the country now to run it for the benefit of the majority, and if we can't do it one way, we'll do it another. I and some others in this room have talked long and hard against knives and bullets as ways of gitting our rights around here. But I've got a rifle out on my rig, just like plenty others in this room have got. I say if we can't git satisfaction in here, I'll take my stand with Drake outside, and git it another way. And if this is rebellion, we'll make the most of it!"

Dead silence filled the room when Jeff had finished and sat trembling with emotion on his chair. There was no applause from the farmer faction now. The farmers seemed as shocked as the Man Head group by the intemperance of the outburst. And Jeff's anger was shot through with remorse that he had lost his temper. He felt he had made a colossal fool of himself, and damaged Mundy's chances as well. But he recanted none of what he'd said. He would stand with Drake, if the jury voted to convict.

Then the judge was speaking, ignoring Jeff completely. His voice was sirupy calm and well-controlled, shaming Jeff even more for losing control.

"It goes without saying that none of that scurrilous tirade will be entered in the record. It will be preserved, however, for use in contempt proceedings which will be instituted against defense counsel as soon as this trial is over."

Still without a glance at Jeff, Coates turned to face the jury. "You gentlemen will do well to remember that you are under oath to interpret the evidence as presented, in light of the charges and the statutes, not in accordance with your own prejudice or that of Mr. Jimson. I will point out to you that not one shred of evidence was offered in the accused's behalf. Whether such evidence exists, I cannot know, since the defense saw fit to give its efforts to belaboring in unfair fashion an eminent citizen of the community who can claim much credit for developing our city and county to their present state of high prosperity. I therefore charge you to do your duty and return a verdict which is in harmony with the evidence presented. I cannot recommend too forcefully that you view the case and its handling by counsel as a test of law and order in a county where the advocates of lawlessness are gaining in strength with each passing hour. I say to you that any verdict other than guilty would constitute a travesty on justice, the blot of which would never be cleansed from your names and conscience. And you may now retire, until you have reached a verdict. . . ."

Long after the jury had left the room, long after the judge had retired to his chambers in company with Wate Garrett and Strap and Abby, presumably to discuss the length of sentence to be meted out to a man not yet convicted, Jeff sat limply on his chair, exhausted in body and mind, still torn between remorse and high satisfaction in his performance.

Now that it was too late, his brain was presenting him with all manner of convincing arguments he should have made before the jury. He longed to walk to the door through which the twelve had disappeared and warn them again that if they ruled for the company they would rule against themselves and the entire country. Warn them again of Drake's plans for violence, of the blood they would loose upon the county if they did not act while there was time.

Then he perceived the futility of what he was doing, and turned his thoughts forcibly from the closed door to the room about him. To the people in the room, who were sitting tight, even though the court was in recess. To Lin Mundy who was slumped upon his chair as Jeff was slumped, eyes fixed on the floor. Hoping a little, maybe, but finding hope shrinking with each passing minute. He'd won the man's trust and friendship finally, with his reckless talk. But Mundy was more interested in freedom than in principles. If convicted, he would be less forgiving than before.

He thought of Abby in the judge's chamber with her father and Strap, and wondered what she might be thinking or saying. He hadn't been able to look at her while talking. But, afterward, he'd looked and found her cowed and puzzled, utterly confused by what she'd heard. Well, she'd always wondered at his bitterness. Now maybe she understood a little of it. She wasn't any great mentality, but she'd come to court that day, when the farmer women had stayed home because of threatened danger.

The thought touched off a process of comparison in his mind, of Abby with the farm women he had seen. But the contrast was too great to have anything like meaning. Abby Garrett could never become a farm woman. That would be like harnessing a thoroughbred to a plow.

Then his mind rebelled against a truth that was false and destructive to all he felt and wished to believe. Abby was no better than the squatter women. Well, she was, but being Garrett's daughter didn't make her better. She would be her bright, attractive self if she had no father at all. In such a case, she might have been available to Jeff Jimson.

The thought seemed a profound one, deepening his hatred of Wate Garrett to abysmal depths.

But such speculation was worse torture than watching the jury-room door, and he turned his thoughts elsewhere. He saw again how the room was divided cleanly between the hostile forces whose conflict was building to a climax. Between the owner-tillers of the soil and Garrett's rootless mercenaries with their Cossack pride and childish vanities, the twisted streak of the cavalier that delighted in serving the interests of an order that was dedicated to their own destruction.

They thought of themselves as rugged individualists. But they were the reverse of individuals. Even the archindividualist, Wate Garrett, was essentially a servant to other servants, working against the country and therefore against himself, enriching men whose only interest in the territory lay in the percentage return on their dollar investments.

What was Drake up to, outside? And what could the jurors be talking about, to take so long a time? Either it was one way or the other. Either they had the intelligence and the gut to stand up to Garrett or they did not. They had nothing to haggle over.

He should maybe have hammered harder at the angle of the

ditch and the farmers having to have the water. That might have helped . . . No, it wouldn't. The issue wasn't Mundy, and the farmers. The issue was Man Head—Garrett. In a way, the issue was Jeff Jimson. If he had convinced the jurors that he was man enough to stand up to Garrett, they would back him. If he hadn't —well, no one put money on a loser. Not in a fracas such as this one was shaping up to be. . . .

The door was opening. The jury was coming out. The realization left Jeff desolated, devoid of hope. The thing was settled now. Nothing he could do or say would affect the decision, now or ever. The things he could have said and still could say convincingly did not matter. It was over now.

The jurors were in the box, rattling the chairs. Word went to the judge and Garrett, and they reappeared to take their respective places. Throughout it all, Jeff had sat frozen, unable to look up or move a hand. Now, after an eternity of waiting, he brought himself to it. Like a man lifting a heavy weight, he raised his head and forced his gaze to Gentile—to Hackett—to Hitch. Their eyes did not elude or reject him, and his heartbeat pulsed into a powerful marching rhythm.

Jeff knew he had won.

"Gentlemen of the jury, have you reached a verdict?"

"We have, your honor."

"Will you announce it to the court?"

"We find the defendant not guilty—innocent of all charges."

Long after Gentile, the jury foreman, had finished speaking and sat down, his words seemed to hang in the silent air like pennants, for all to see. The first sounds of stirring came from the astounded farmers, and someone started a keening yell of triumph. But his neighbors quickly gripped him into silence. The victory was too devastating, too dangerous to be celebrated on the spot.

As it was, the interrupted outburst was enough to bring old Garrett to his feet, his thin face livid.

"Twelve good men, and true!"

With that single utterance, he took his daughter by the arm and stomped up the aisle without a glance to right or left. The door slammed behind them with a dull bang of finality, and silence closed over the sound like water over a hurled stone.

With Garrett gone from sight, all eyes swung back to Coates who, since the verdict was announced, had sat motionless as a statue, staring into space. But as the silence continued unbroken and all eyes continued to stare at him in anticipation, he seemed to realize that some kind of statement must be made.

"Well, gentlemen," he began uncertainly, "I must confess that I am somewhat taken aback. When a defendant is patently guilty of a crime and the jury returns a verdict of acquittal, it is evident that the jury system has broken down and that other means of dispensing justice must be found."

His voice faltered, as if unable to go on. Then it rallied, and the cherubic countenance assumed a severe mein. "It is not in my power to take action in the matter, or to punish you for your dereliction. But I will say that you have betrayed your trust, and at a time when your community stands on the brink of civil war. If blood is shed in this valley, that blood will be on your heads."

The rebuke received in silence, the jurist turned on Lin Mundy. "As for you, the accused, I can only say that you have escaped a punishment that is justly due you. The evidence and your own tacit confession will stand forever to condemn you. You are now discharged from this court a free man, because I cannot under the law detain you, even knowing your guilt. Your neighbors and those injured by your crime will have to judge you. I cannot."

But his most blistering denunciation was reserved for Jeff. "As for you, Mr. Jimson, I wish to congratulate you on as masterful an exhibition of demagoguery as it has ever been my lot to witness. In thirty years upon the bench, I never have beheld courtroom conduct so reprehensible. Even your obvious ignorance and inexperience at law do not excuse you. You will remain in court for consideration of the contempt citation that has been made against you.

"And now, the court is adjourned. . . ."

Instantly, the room erupted into a scene of noisy confusion, with the farmers pressing forward to shake Lin Mundy's hand and pound Jeff Jimson on the back, the Man Head aggregation meantime withdrawing from the room, crestfallen but still disdainful of the victors. Jeff, however, had unfinished business with the judge, and tore himself lose from the jubilant farmer crowd to approach the lectern.

"I take your speech to mean you're washing your hands of us secondhand citizens," he said in resurging anger. "Sounded like an invitation to Man Head to take the law in its own hands and punish Lin however they want."

The jurist stiffened and drew dignity around him like a cloak. "I refuse to dignify your insinuation by replying to it. I refuse to submit to mob interrogation in my own court."

"You just might submit to worse, before you're done!" Jeff warned him. "Another speech like that, and we might take a little law into our hands."

The judge bristled before him, threatening him with the awful weapon of his office. As he did so, he glanced in the direction of Bowman and the Man Head deputies—just in time to see the last of them depart.

"I will not be intimidated in my own court," he blustered. "Stand aside or I will find you in contempt without formality of a trial."

"You'll find me in contempt!" Jeff sneered, sensing an advantage. "Where in hell do you think we find you?"

Coates turned and looked around the room, his eyes spearing Gut Desmond. "Sheriff," he commanded, "arrest that man."

Desmond peered uneasily at Jeff, and quickly looked away. And for the first time in all the while he'd known him, Jeff felt halfway sorry for the first enemy he'd made on Rustler River. Gut Desmond never had made a move as sheriff without Wate Garrett at his back. Now Garrett was out of reach and hearing. Gut Desmond was alone, facing Jeff and a roomful of angry farmers. Desmond didn't move.

"Arrest that man!" the judge repeated, shouting in spite of himself.

"I wouldn't advise it, Gut," a flat, drawling voice intruded. "Us people have been pushed far enough. We're doing the pushing from here out."

Jeff turned to see Drake beside him. He had recovered from the head blow, and was wearing a pistol. Whatever his plan for violence had been, Jeff's victory inside the court seemingly had set him back. But, under pretense of aiding Jeff, he was bidding for the spotlight again. His thirty backers had come in with him, and all were armed. One carried a coil of rope.

"Simmer down, boys," Jeff counseled. "Gut wasn't going to arrest nobody. Gut knows the judge was joking. The judge is a great joker, ain't he, Gut?"

The sheriff shot Jeff a look of gratitude, and the shame Jeff felt for his ancient enemy seemed somehow to touch himself. Theo Coates was glaring around, seeking help from any quarter. But there wasn't any help. The judge was a prisoner in his own court, held by a rowdy crowd that was turning into a mob.

"Better hit the grit, Theo. In a minute, we'll git up a jackass judge and kangaroo court of our own, and sweat you some."

"I secont the motion. It's time we introduced the judge to justice. They been strangers too damn long."

"I got a coil o' Texas suddint justice, right here in my hand. What about it, boys?"

"I always heard he was a hanging judge. Let's see the bastard hang!"

"That's enough," Jeff said roughly, starting to feel alarmed. "You sound like a dog pack, when somebody else has downed the game. Stand back. The judge is leaving."

There were grumbles, some near-resistance. But the crowd was still a crowd. Under specific instruction from someone in position to instruct, it drew back, and the judge started toward the door, walking fast yet ploddingly. The succession of indignities and defeats administered in his own citadel had aged him singularly. His face was the color of unbaked dough, and his normally firm jowls hung down like dewlaps.

Jeff watched his dragging footsteps, and knew that his victory had been complete. But he felt little elation and didn't join in the noisy demonstration that ensued when Coates had gone. He sensed that he had just witnessed the final breakdown of the law in Ten Trees County, and the thought occurred that perhaps he had accomplished the very thing he'd set out to avoid. He suspected that the same suspicion was in the minds of the jurors who hadn't yet stirred from the box, because when he walked over to thank them for the verdict, only Hackett and Gentile received him with any warmth. The others seemed frightened, some resentful, and he suspected them of repenting their decision already. Minutes later, when the courtroom was deserted and he stood out on the steps with Hackett and Gentile, Gentile too seemed doubtful of their accomplishment.

"You was kind of rough on the old feather merchant, wasn't you, boy? Kind of tromped him when he was down?"

"Tromped him, hell!" Jeff differed. "I saved him from a lynching."

"You saved him—and you stirred the thing up to start with," Gentile pointed out. "He was still the honored judge in there, till you tore into him. I hope you never start after me, the way you waded into him."

"He had it coming," Jeff said defensively. "Calling on Garrett to take the law into his own hands and punish Mundy any way he seen fit. I remember two other guys that Garrett punished as he saw fit."

"You called on us twelve to take the law in our hands—and we done it," Gentile said. "And that may have been our mistake. When the laws are bad, you'd ought to change them, not ignore them. You take short cuts, it's revolution."

"Well, why be scared of the word?" Hackett scoffed. "It was revolution when a bunch of rowdies dressed up like Injuns and throwed a bunch of tea in Boston harbor. But things worked out all right in the end."

"Things worked out in the end," the merchant gloomed. "But there was a lot of bloody fighting in between."

They stood awhile in silence, watching the big dust plume the Man Head crowd stirred up, heading for the ranch—the bigger dust the farmers made, driving fast toward Ekard, where Drake had decreed a victory celebration for the night, a scalp dance with all the trimmings. Jeff had declined an invitation to the orgy, and was commencing to feel uneasy about his Herefords. When the irresistible force met the immovable object, sparks were bound to fly.

"Jim," Hackett said suddenly, "whatever came of the talk I

heard awhile back of the town incorporating, and setting up its own government?"

"Nothing come of it," the merchant informed him. "Garrett scotched it. Didn't want the competition, I guess."

"Well, if I lived here, I'd see what I could do about reviving the idea. Looks to me like the county government's on the rocks. There'd ought to be someone to take over and sort of keep the lid on things, until election."

"If there's trouble, it ain't likely to develop here in town," Gentile pointed out. "Town's authority don't extend beyond its limits."

"Town's authority is better than no authority," the station man argued. "Way it looks to me, Desmond and Coates are both washed up. And Garrett with them."

"Looks the same to me," Gentile confided. "But I don't see where a civic setup could accomplish anything. Anyhow, Garrett goes and does some damn-fool thing to touch things off, there's going to be a lot of people lose some hide. I don't hanker to be the man out in front when the Governor's occupation troops come up."

The talk added to Jeff's uneasiness, and he felt he had overstayed in town. But when he mentioned leaving, Hackett spoke discouragingly.

"I'd think you'd at least hang around here till you find out if Coates figures to press them contempt charges. Here in town, you got a friend or two. Out there, you're going to be alone."

"I don't expect Gut will be any more anxious to serve papers on me out there than he was here today." Jeff shrugged.

"I'm not thinking of Gut," Hackett answered. "I'm thinking of Strap Bowman and his twenty deputies."

"So am I," Jeff confessed. "That's why I figure I'd better light a shuck for Hurricane."

22: Crime and Punishment

Gentile had handed Jeff a check from the St. Louis commission house upon his arrival in town the night before. He had settled with the men who'd done his hauling, and now he spent the balance for stock salt and ammunition and canned food —purchased in that order. He loaded his wagon that afternoon, and after talking late with Hackett and Gentile, bedded down in Hitch's hay loft for an early start.

The sun was a burning bush on the eastern hills when he pulled out of Quadrille. He nooned on Cat Creek, and was preparing to hit the road again when a dozen or more horsebackers came into view, led by Duckbill Drake. The entire cavalcade was made up of farmers he'd seen at court the day before. They looked like the tail end of an all-night brawl. Faces were drawn and taut, and eyes were red and heavy. But they rode with an urgency that took no account of weariness.

"Howdy, men," Jeff called with wary cordiality. "You traveling, or just going some place?"

"We're traveling," Drake answered abruptly. "Lin Mundy was murdered last night. We aim to do something about it."

"Lin Mundy—murdered?"

The horsemen had pulled up around him, and he could smell sour whiskey fumes on every side.

"That's what happened. Drove into a ambush, up at the Wood Crick ford. Some son of a bitch was laying for him, in the brush. Waited till he was past, then blasted him where his suspenders cross. Took Seger's team that Lin was driving, led them up into the cottonwoods and shot both horses dead, still hooked to the wagon. How do you like them bananas?"

The speaker's face was queer with triumph. Jeff looked away to avoid the sight.

"What time was this?"

"Can't say, for sure. He left my ho-tel, some after dark, driving Seger's team. We was celebrating some, and he promised to come back. He didn't show, so some of us rode up to his place, and found he hadn't got there. We found him, quick as it was light."

The story was told with quiet vehemence, the speaker's emotions submerged for the moment in human preoccupation with imparting momentous news.

"Us boys had took up a purse for Lin. He bought some things to take to his wife and kids. When he was hit, he fell frontwards off the seat. Bled out all over them packages he was taking home."

As he listened, Jeff's gaze went beyond the speaker to the purple mountains to the west. Clouds were collecting about the jagged peaks—black thunderheads that predicted violent storm. Just now, the silence seemed oppressive.

"Horses both dead in their harness—and Lin bled out all over his kids' packages!" Drake repeated hollowly, as if the latter detail rendered an already outrageous crime somehow more heinous—as, indeed, it did.

Jeff felt the eyes of his informant and all the others upon him, waiting for his reaction to the news. But he could not react for them. He felt no anger, no real surprise. After all that had happened in Coates's court, this latest killing should have been expected. The question now was, Who is next?

"You mean you let Mundy start home alone—after Coates as good as called on Bowman's bunch to salt him down?"

"Now, hold your horses, Jeffrey," Drake advised, his face bloated and malign. "Don't go twisting this around to make it look like our fault. You're the one that brought this killing on. Don't try to make it look like something else."

"I'm the one that brought it on?"

"You, goddamnit! If you and Hig and Woodrow had kept out of this, we would've sprung Lin out, just like we aimed. That way, he would have knowed what he was up against and would have took care of himself."

It struck Jeff as a piece of the weakest reasoning he'd yet heard. But he didn't bother to argue the point. There were more important things to be considered.

"So, where you bound to, now?"

"We're bound for town, to swear murder complaints on Garrett and Strap Bowman. If Coates will draw the warrants and let us serve 'em, we'll bring that pair in for trial. If the bastard won't, we'll draw our own warrant, and our own conclusions. You can join us if you want. But understand beforehand that we're out for business. The time for talk has passed."

Jeff sat in indecision, his mind pulling in two directions at once. Jim Gentile had remarked in town that if Garrett did some damn-fool thing to touch things off, they all would be in the wringer. And Garrett certainly had touched things off. Or had he? Was it possible that Drake himself had killed his neighbor, in order to promote the violence he stood to profit from?

"Any real clue that it was Garrett or Bowman?"

"Only the big clue. Christ, don't you even believe yourself any more? Who killed Demps and Harley Rae—or had it done? Who'd have you and me both six feet under right today, if he could find somebody with gut enough to undertake it?"

"Well, I don't doubt you're right," Jeff admitted. "But I got to think things over, before I mix in any massacree. Where you going to be hanging out? Quadrille?"

"No, by God!" Drake snapped. "We have incorporated the City of Ekard, and we already have got a judge and a marshal. If Coates won't act in this matter, we'll handle it as a municipality. And we'll take our judge along to save us the trouble and expense of caring for the prisoners."

Jeff watched the Ekard delegation out of view, then clucked to his team and drove on. He knew an impulse to head straight for Man Head, to apprise Garrett of the farmers' plans, and learn what he could of the shooting—another to drive on to Squatters Row, and talk with Woodrow and Higgins to get their slant. But concern for his heifers won out in the end, and he continued on to Hurricane instead, reflecting as he went upon the ironies of his situation.

He had succeeded eminently in court the day before, and yet his final failure was about as grandiose as his victory had looked the day before. He and Higgins and the doctor had talked for peace, and promoted violence, after all. He and Drake had been working together all along, and just couldn't see it. But now that the thing had been decided, Drake was in the saddle and Jeff was on the outside, looking in—though he and Higgins and Hackett had set the thing up for Drake. Except for yesterday's trial and its outcome, Drake and his gang would be just another mob on horseback. As it was, with Mundy legally acquitted and illegally murdered, Drake had enough on his side to give him a big talking point when the troops came in to put things back to rights. Jeff, in bucking Drake, had merely set him up in business.

"Well—" he shrugged. "The reach exceeds the grasp—in a hell of a lot of ways."

But the feeling persisted that he lacked the courage of his convictions or he would have joined Drake on Drake's own terms, and would be riding with the mounted mob. Garrett was as big a threat to him as to any of the farmers. He would benefit as much as anyone in the county from the old man's hanging, and Dempsey Rae had used to say that a man should kill his own meat or turn vegetarian. But Demps had also told him once that you couldn't shoot a system, and Jeff found comfort in the memory. For if you couldn't shoot a system, it was likely that you couldn't hang one, either. And, come what would, he could not see himself officiating at the extermination of Abby's parent. He knew it was a mark of weakness. But he was content to admit the weakness and skip the lynching—if lynching was what it was going to be. . . .

Dusk had fallen by the time he reached the canyon on Hurricane. The evening star was out, glowing pale but steadily brighter in the still-light sky straight ahead of him, as if to guide him to his cabin. The powerful symbolism of it recalled the Christmas card he had received from Abby a million years before—of the wise men following their star, of his cynical reflections upon the matter of people who had stars to follow.

"I sure could use a star tonight," he said wistfully.

On childish impulse, he claimed the star, and made a wish upon it, but didn't speak the wish aloud. It was too personal, too much a part of his secret self, to put into words, as he once had done —braggingly—to Dempsey Rae. But it filled his whole being with a new sense of strength, and for the moment it seemed that no obstacle could withstand a force so consuming and sustained as his wish for Abby Garrett.

A full moon rose, filling the canyon breaks with fantastic patterns of shadow and light, intricately mysterious as life itself.

With star in front of him and moon behind, he was guided to his gate without incident, and was pleased to find the bars still up, as he had left them. But the moonlight now had reached the canyon floor, and when he climbed down to drop the bars, he saw horse tracks and boot prints on the ground in front of him, leading through the gate. Instantly the moon, so mellow and friendly a moment before, became an ally of his enemies, betraying him to unseen guns. The shadow patterns, once artistic abstractions beguiling the mind, became grottos of peril, each concealing a waiting assassin.

Stepping quickly into the shelter of the brush, he stood motionless for a time, every sense reaching out to detect any hostile presence. The only sounds were those made by his horses, but these very ordinary noises were terrifying—not in themselves but in the fact that they would guide prowlers to where he stood.

When his mind began to function again, he found himself damp with perspiration, though the night was chill and getting colder. He laughed softly in scorn, and called himself a name. But when he moved, it was to take his rifle off the wagon and go ahead on foot, holding to the brush, leaving his team and outfit behind.

When he came within sight of his meadow, he found it ominously deserted. It wasn't likely that his heifers would be brushed up at night, as in the heat of the day. But none of them were in sight. He didn't even see either of his horses. Weighted by dread, he started a search of the area.

The search at first was unrewarding. He was commencing to believe that the marauder had been content to drive off his stock when he rounded a big bush and almost fell over the body of his dun geld. That of the old bone-pile mare lay nearby, half in shadow, half in light. Glistening dark pools had formed around each, and closer examination showed that both had been shot cleanly in the forehead, almost exactly between the eyes.

When he had steeled himself to it, he left the dead horses and walked on through the brush. Other dark shapes soon were visible against the lighter background of willow. Shapes as unnaturally still as the first two encountered. Dull-eyed and dull-minded, he walked among the sprawled carcasses, counting his Herefords as

288

he had counted them religiously each day for weeks, finding eleven of the twelve at once.

After a time, he heard a muffled moaning from a pothole near the creek. He crossed over and there found the missing heifer, still living but not very much alive. Both front legs were broken at the knees, presumably by a bullet, and it had dragged itself to the water on protruding bone ends. Birds had been at its eyes.

Mechanically, like a man sleepwalking, he put down his rifle and opened the jugular vein with his jackknife, letting out what blood yet remained in the suffering body. Then, exercising the fanatic frugality the years had taught him, he dragged the carcass to high ground and let the warm entrails out to preserve the meat. This done, he wiped his bloody knife and hands off on the grass and squatted down to rest.

Throughout his choring, he had found it possible to avoid thinking. But now he could postpone it no longer, and had to look at things as they were. It wasn't any nightmare, as he had almost been convinced. It had happened. He was ruined. The sneak killers hadn't dared to strike at him directly. Instead, they had taken the coward's way of getting at him. He was right back where he'd started—on his haunches.

The thought came from somewhere that cabin burnings usually went with cowardly raids like this, and he looked in the direction of his house, fully expecting to see a smoking ruin. But the structure was still standing, along with the stable, both clearly revealed by the moonlight. He was thinking wistfully of bed when another thought occurred. The killers might be up at the house or stable, forted in, waiting for him to move within good shooting range.

Goaded to further action by the suspicion, he picked up his rifle and made a long circle through the brush, approaching his stable and corrals from the upper side. There was no animal, four-legged or otherwise, in the corrals. But the hay he'd half-expected to find burned still filled the innermost of the three mud pens. And this seemed to be the surest clue to the raiders' identity. Duckbill Drake or others bent on vandalism only surely would have burned everything ignitable, including the tinder-dry hay, whereas emissaries from Man Head would be inclined to spare anything that would be of value to the company, once the property had passed into company ownership.

The stable door was secured from the outside, so when he heard a stamping of horses inside, he felt relatively safe in entering. Once inside, with the door hooked shut behind him, he stood a moment, inhaling the rank horse smell, gun ready just in case. There was little chance of light showing through the thick earth wall or heavy slab door. So when his groping hands found the lantern hanging in its place, he scratched a match and lighted the wick to look around.

There were two horses in the place. Their eyes flashed light as they turned to oggle him, and the sight while eerie was reassuring. Demps had told him once that among all warm-blooded creatures, the human eye alone did not reflect light. And Jeff had yet to find a thing that Demps had been wrong in—outside of trusting Sundance.

He looked the animals over, and was both surprised and unsurprised to find he knew them both. Both were tall, rangy creatures, one a dark bay, the other a starred black, both branded in the Wineglass iron, and both the property of Strap Bowman—who, as foreman, enjoyed the privilege of riding his own horses. And other discoveries interested him even more. Both horses had been unsaddled, and the gear dumped carelessly in one corner. Along with the saddle was a crossbuck, a bedroll and warbag, and two bulging panniers. Since there were but two horses, and one was packed, the implication was that Strap was by himself, playing a lone hand.

A cursory examination of the panniers' contents indicated further that the Man Head foreman was embarking on a major outing. And as his hands worked swiftly at the packs, Jeff's mind was busy with the puzzle of it all. It was hard to believe that Garrett was so hard up for triggermen that the foreman had been forced to personally undertake the routine extermination chores. But Jeff was convinced that it was Mundy's murderer who had killed his animals on the meadow. Hurricane was a convenient ride from the farm settlements, and the same pattern of rabid, senseless ferocity was visible in both outrages: Killing Mundy's borrowed horses to compound the murder, when the added killings served no rational purpose; wantonly destroying all Jeff's stock, when to have let them live would have been to lessen the chance of alerting Jeff to his own danger.

"Must be a shortage of rugged individualists willing to muck for Wate!" he muttered bitterly.

There was still the mystery of Strap's full packs. But it was a minor puzzle, and didn't signify. Strap likely figured to drop from sight awhile, once his kills were made, not knowing of the farmers' threat to Garrett. What really mattered was that Strap was here on Hurricane to kill Jeff Jimson. The long-looked-for assassin had come at last.

Judging from the droppings on the floor, the horses had been in the barn all day. Belatedly, it registered with Jeff that Strap had carried liberal amounts of his hard-earned hay in from the stack and fed to them. He was reminded of a thing Demps had said concerning the killers' custom of eating a man's food and feeding his hay, then doing him in, and for an instant this seemed the most intolerable aspect of the entire outrage.

"Might not be a professional, but he sure as hell acts like one!" he growled.

He assumed that Strap was at the cabin, figuring to shoot him as he passed the window or opened the door. Strap might have heard his wagon down the canyon, might possibly have seen him walking around down on the meadow. But the chances were against both possibilities. Secure in the cabin where Jeff had to go eventually, he had only to wait for the kind of sure shot he wanted.

At one point, Jeff was inclined to play Strap's own game, to outwait him there in the shelter of the stable, and take the drop on him when he finally came out, as he would have to do. But after the lantern was blown out and he had stood for several minutes at the door, listening for sounds that weren't made, he knew that waiting wouldn't do. There had been too much waiting, where he and Bowman were concerned. And he had a secret entrance to the cabin, after all. There was an outside chance that Strap had found it, and would be waiting at the tunnel, not the window. But the hole outside was hidden by brush, on the inside by a heap of duffel. It was a chance. But Jeff preferred the chance to longer idleness.

Pulling off his boots, and freeing himself of his cumbersome pistol belt, he thrust the revolver in the waistband of his pants, and eased the door open. His searching eyes went first to the cliff where Sundance had lain in ambush to murder Demps. As down in the canyon earlier, the weird pattern of light and shadow lent an aura of dreamlike unreality to the whole situation. But Jeff was not dreaming, and his eyes probed the shadows for another minute before he moved, seeing nothing that looked like danger. It was like jumping off a cliff, and he knew that if he hesitated too long he wouldn't be able to bring it off.

"Here goes," he said under his breath.

He made it to the far side of the gate in two long leaps, shoulders drawn up against a phantom bullet. The bullet did not come, and he halted in the shadow of the butte, took one quick look behind him at the stable and the shadow-filled corrals, then turned and watched the house.

He couldn't see the cabin's front face from where he crouched, couldn't tell whether the door and window stood open or closed. But the whole west side was bathed in yellow light, and no Bowman was in sight. More than a hundred feet of open ground lay between him and the brush that concealed the tunnel he was aiming for. But there was no window through which he could be seen. Unless Strap were hunkered down in the fringe of brush that screened the hole in the wall, which wasn't really likely, he stood a chance of covering that ground without dying of sudden death.

Once again, he had the feeling the thing must be done at once, if at all. Gripping his rifle in both hands, he bent low and left the shadow in a kind of crouching hop, running silently as a shadow, zigzagging in case Strap was not inside the cabin.

He made it to the brush fringe, and Injuned through it, as he'd done many times before. Beside the hole he paused again, still crouched low, breathing shallowly to listen. No sound came from the cabin, and he didn't hesitate long. Leaning the rifle against the wall, he drew the pistol from his belt, placed it in his left armpit to muffle the ratchet's click, and eased the hammer back to cock. Then he lowered himself to all fours, and—pistol thrust out before him, finger off the trigger because he didn't trust his nerves—crawled into the chambered dark.

He had done the same thing so many times in different circumstances that he didn't have to think out every act. When he came to the duffel that blocked the other opening, he was able to push it aside soundlessly. Then, mind closed to the possibility that Bowman had outguessed him and was waiting in the dark, he slithered out into the room.

The expected blow did not fall. Apparently, he was alone in the bedroom he knew so well—knew by smell as well as sight and feel. He thought at first that a lantern was burning in the kitchen; the door was clearly outlined, and a patch of light fell through it to the bedroom floor, almost touching Jeff. But even as he thought in terms of a lamp, perception told him that the window shutter was up, that the light on the floor was moonlight, falling through the opening. Which meant that Strap was at the window, or had been, waiting for him to show up out in front. As if in confirmation, he heard a chair squeak in the other room, followed by a sound like someone drinking from a bottle.

Until that moment, Jeff had had to drive himself at every point to keep from turning back. Driven now instead of driving, he could not have turned back even if he'd known that Strap was onto him, waiting to blast him the second he showed himself in the doorway. He couldn't have postponed action longer, any more than he could postpone breathing. It was a thing which must be done. Silently, he inched toward the door.

Strap was not onto him. Strap was seated at the table, in clear silhouette against the open window just beyond. He was faced halfway from Jeff, watching the moonlit meadow, rifle and pistol on the table in front of him. There was a quart bottle on the table, too, and as Jeff watched, Strap hefted it to take a pull.

A strange unnatural calm had come over Jeff. It now seemed he had no nerves at all. He trusted his finger inside the trigger guard now—trusted himself to point the weapon, then to breathe deeply.

"That my likker, Strap?" he asked.

Bowman reacted exactly as if someone had set off a bomb beneath him. He choked, dropped the bottle, snatched up the pistol, and leaped to his feet—all in one wild burst of action. Jeff squeezed his trigger—felt the pistol shock back in his hand—heard Bowman's explosive grunt—saw Bowman staggered—hurled back against the wall as if struck by a club. Then bluish fire jumped at him from Bowman's hand, scorching his face as it went by. Jeff fired two more rounds, and Strap toppled, falling stiffly, like a timbered tree. He lay face down, muscles twitching like those of a beefed critter. His head and shoulders were in the patch of light upon the floor, and though he did not move except to jerk convulsively, Jeff did not stop shooting.

Like a man who keeps chopping at a snake he has already killed, Jeff kept firing into the hatless head until the pistol clicked empty. Then he jumped to the table, grabbed up the rifle, and stood ready to shoot again. But even the twitching had stopped by now, and it finally penetrated to Jeff's mind that no more shooting was required.

As soon as the realization dawned that it was really over, that Bowman was dead at last, and by his hand, Jeff's knees wanted to buckle, and he began to shake and twitch as Strap had done down on the floor. Collapsing upon the nearest chair, he picked up the overturned bottle, and drained it, using both hands to hold it to his mouth. Then he sat for a time, staring out upon the light-bathed meadow, teeth chattering as if he were in a chill.

When he was able to think again, he remembered his team down at the bars, and the butchered heifer that had to be cared for before daylight brought the flies to it. But, at the moment, he felt he could not bear to leave the cabin's shelter—until it was light again outside at any rate. It seemed a little strange that fear should take him, now that the peril was past. But, danger or no danger, the thought of venturing out in the moonlight again, target for other hidden guns, started him to shaking again.

"Old Ma Nature rations out fortitude in parcels to fit the occasion," Demps had remarked one time, when the matter of personal courage had come up. "Just enough to give a man guts to sneak through an Injun siege line, to fetch help, and just enough to sneak home after a spree, to face a cranky wife!"

Jeff smiled faintly at the recollection, seeing how completely it applied in his own case. And somehow it stiffened him to get on with the things that must be done.

23: Tally

He found his team and outfit where he'd left it. He'd carried an axe and rope down with him from the cabin, and on his way back up across the meadow he hoisted the dead heifer up to a limb and completed his butchering, then covered the cold carcass with a tarp to keep the flies off during the coming day. This done, he drove back to the cabin, unloaded his supplies, and contemplated the corpse on the floor.

Through all the violence of his last five years, through all the killings and near-killings he had witnessed, Jeff somehow had not personally slain a fellow human being until that night. But now that his first nervous seizure had passed, he was completely untroubled by conscience or remorse. It was as if he had killed an animal which had threatened him and had to be destroyed. And though he never would actually come to relish the role of undertaker, he was not without experience in the field.

He made a trip to the stable to fetch the dead man's bedroll tarp, then wrapped and roped the corpse much as he'd wrapped and roped another in that same house. Once it was fittingly prepared, he heaved the stiffening burden on the wagon and hauled it up to the corrals—not for burial in his manure pile as once would have been necessary, but for storage in the cool stable, where it would be out from under foot. He unharnessed his horses and turned them out on the meadow, and—after a moment's consideration—decided to keep Bowman's animals in the corral, in case he should have need of them.

"You might not know it, but you're Jimson horses now," he told them as he let them out into the corral.

Dawn was ghosting up gray and salmon-red to eastward when he returned to the cabin. The kitchen was in bad shape: splattered with blood and brains, littered with cigarette butts and dirty pots and pans—souvenirs of Strap's brief tenancy. It was fully light by the time he had things put to rights, and he was frying bacon and pan bread to eat before catching needed sleep, when he heard a blasting whinny from one of Bowman's horses, answered quickly from somewhere up country. The sound brought him to the open door, rifle in hand, there to stare like a man seeing his first mirage.

Two horses and two riders were coming down across the valley from the upper canyon, riding at a swinging trot. And to Jeff's numbed senses, the whole improbable sequence of events began to take on the irrationality of nightmare. Unless he'd lost his mind or power of vision, his latest callers were Wate and Abby Garrett—as unlikely a pair of visitants as could be imagined.

"Well, this breaks it," he murmured uneasily.

Abby pulled up down on the meadow, and Wate rode toward the cabin alone. He was dressed in broadcloth, and wore no hat. He carried a rifle in his hands, but as he came nearer, he signified a peaceful attitude by reversing it and holding it butt-end forward.

By now, Jeff was convinced he'd fallen asleep on his feet, and it was all a dream. The rider was Wate Garrett, but a very old Wate Garrett whose face was a lump of dough, whose eyes looked like two holes burned in an old blanket. He was riding the tall blue roan, and after he'd reined up in front of the cabin door, he greeted Jeff with a short nod. But his red-webbed eyes remained fixed on the corral where Bowman's horses, still neighing, stood with heads thrust out over the bars. Then he was speaking, his voice grating like a rusty hinge.

"It appears we arrived a little late."

Jeff nodded, angrily. "Too late to save your son of a bitch, if that's what you mean. He's up in the stable—with the rest of the muck."

Garrett turned to face him finally, and a shock went through Jeff as he looked fully into the shrunken eyes. Old Garrett was a sick man. A very sick man. A dying man, possibly.

"It isn't what I meant," the old man said. "To be frank, we came here to ask sanctuary, not having any other place to go. But I'd also hoped to get here in time to warn you that Strap had a bug in his hind end, and was waging a one-man war against you people. I surmise, from the looks of things, that you found out yourself, in time."

Never before had Jeff heard the gentleman rancher descend to vulgarity in his speech. He was impressed almost as much by this phenomenon as by the enigma of the preceding statement.

"Did you say 'sanctuary'?" Jeff inquired politely.

Garrett nodded. "Your farmer friends paid me a call last night, in force. Around a hundred of them, led by Duckbill Drake. We were warned in time, or they would have murdered us in our beds. Abby and I got out ahead of them, and I told the crew to skin out while they could, and not risk their lives. But you can't give some people advice. About a dozen hung on, and there was a lot of shooting. So I suppose they fought loyally, even knowing I was gone."

Jeff's eyes swung instinctively to the upper canyon trail.

"I don't think anyone followed us," Garrett said, anticipating his thought. "We tangled our trail. Anyhow, they were more interested in looting and burning than in us."

"Burning?" Jeff echoed.

Garrett nodded and looked quickly away. He was very close to breaking, yet he did not break. "They put the house to torch, and all the stables and outbuildings. After they'd cleaned my cellar, of course."

The voice was dry and bleak as winter wind, and as Jeff gazed at him he realized why it was that the old man's face appeared so disturbingly familiar. It was the same face, the same eyes, that he had seen on another old man two days before, creeping beaten and dishonored from the court that had been his strength and stronghold.

How are the mighty fallen. . . .

But the thought was a fleeting one, off one side of his mind, and occurring only as an offshoot of an infinitely more significant fact: Garrett's Castle had been destroyed! Vulgar Manor had been taken and now lay in ruins, together with the empire it had ruled.

In fancy, he saw the great white house as he last had seen it. Dominating the rich bottoms as its builder dominated an entire region. Symbol of the power-wealth of its lord-in-residence and his feudal hold upon the lands he exploited and held by force

297

but did not own. Monument to a philosophy inherited from the earlier trappers and miners who first plundered the country—taking everything out, putting nothing back, stripping the land of its wealth in order to enrich a handful of pale-cheeked investors who never had looked upon its canyons and rivers and plains. Edifice of a philosophy which held that nature's riches had been put on earth to benefit and enrich a favored few, to the exclusion of all others. A philosophy that had to be overthrown if Jeff Jimson and a million like him were to survive.

It was, of course, a thing which could not happen. Yet, miraculously, it had happened, or seemingly had. The Bastille had fallen, and here was its arrogant tenant, a mendicant at Jeff's door.

"We've been riding since long before midnight," the croaking voice went on. "If we're welcome to stop awhile, we'll both be thankful to part company with our saddles. Of course, if we are not welcome—"

The voice trailed off again, and the pallor on the drawn face bespoke an urgent need. A few hours earlier, when stalking Bowman in a deadly game of hide-and-seek, Jeff hadn't thought the day would ever come when a Garrett would be made welcome at his cabin. But now the world was turned upside-down, and everything was reversed. Jeff and his allies had wrought much better than they'd known. Toward Duckbill Drake, he felt a vast and warm affection. Everything as it was, he could be charitable toward a defeated foe.

"Why, sure, light down," he said almost heartily. "I wanted to talk with you about some dead horses and cattle, anyhow."

The old man toppled from the saddle, and would have fallen to the ground, if Jeff hadn't steadied him. Jeff assisted him inside the kitchen and onto one of the barrel chairs. Moved almost to compassion, he produced the cheap bottle of whiskey he had fetched from town, and filled a tin cup with water from the bucket on the stand.

"Here," he said, setting the two before the shrunken, staring figure. "I figured to use this for snake bite only. But you look snake-bitten. Help yourself."

The old man ignored the cup. With trembling hands, he up-tilted the bottle and drank thirstily. Jeff stood a moment, savor-

298

ing the spectacle of the lord of Man Head, accustomed to sipping fine wines and brandies from cut-glass cups, gulping Paddlefoot Renfro's rot-gut from a bottle—and liking it. Then he stepped outside to ask Abby up and in.

She still sat her mouse-brown pony down where her father had left her, and in her present state of exhaustion, her drawn face was bony and hard, remarkably like her father's. Jeff had a clue then as to what she would look like thirty years hence, and wondered vaguely if he would have gotten over her by then.

"Morning, Abby," he said evenly. "You look used up."

"I feel used up," she confessed. "May I get down, too, and come inside?"

Jeff gave her his hand and she leaped down. Like her father, she needed steadying, once she was on her feet. Unlike her father, she clung to Jeff a little, once she had her balance. Jeff turned away, offering his arm.

"I didn't get a chance to congratulate you, after the trial," she said tentatively, but with apparent sincerity. "I thought you were wonderful."

"It appears I was," Jeff said distantly. "Wonderfuller than I even imagined."

They moved along in silence then, one of Jeff's arms in Abby's hands, the other leading the Morgan pony. Jeff still wore his town clothes, and they were wrinkled and dusty and caked with dried blood and earth. He hadn't shaved in two days, and his eyes felt swollen and gritty. But Abby, too, was disheveled and sunburned and tawdry-looking for a girl that belonged in a catalogue. Her dress was made for hoops which were missing, and it had been snagged in many places. For the first time in all the while he'd known her, Jeff felt he was her equal. Felt even that he held the upper hand.

It was a novel sensation, and walking with Abby had always been like dancing, so closely did the cadence of her every movement harmonize with his. What with one thing and another, he found himself mellowing somewhat.

"I heard about the burning," he said awkwardly at length—pointedly refusing to tell the lie that he was sorry, but letting his tone imply the lie. "Did you save anything you wanted?"

"I saved my father," she answered in a tone so strange that he turned to look at her, and found her crying silently. "Up to now, at least."

"Well, you can stop worrying about that," he said huskily, feeling unaccountably strong and protective. "You both are safe enough here."

"It's what I told Dad," she informed him in the same strange voice. "He didn't want to come."

"That I can understand," Jeff said, bitterness taking him again.

Back in the kitchen, he found Garrett still seated at the table, the water cup untouched, the bottle's content reduced by half, the ailing man much revived. Assuming the role of host, he helped Abby into the other barrel chair and poured her a cup of coffee which she received as gratefully as her father had received the bottle. While they refreshed themselves, Jeff went on with his breakfast preparations, tripling the proportions, addressing his talk to Garrett.

"So Drake and his minute men took you apart last night! Well, I can't say I'm sorry, except for Abby's sake. That's what we was trying to head off in court. And we got it done. But you had to stir it up again."

"Head it off?" Garrett challenged, a ghost of the old impatient arrogance in his voice. "That's where you set it up. Do you suppose those dirt farmers would have had the spine to pull a raid like that, if there had been a functioning court and sheriff's office?"

"Depends on how the court and sheriff functioned," Jeff answered ironically. "I know those spineless farmers would have taken Mundy away from Gut by force, and mopped the ground with you and Coates, if the jury had voted the other way. That's why I got into the thing. . . . That's one reason, anyhow."

"Would you care to mention another reason?"

"Another reason," Jeff said, feeling his temperature rise, "is that I have as much God-given right to live in this country as you do. I've got as much right to own cattle, and to brand them, and graze them on the public land. I've got as much right to hold property as you have, and to protect it from trespass, by you or anyone else. I've got a right to git up of a morning, and walk out my front door like a man, instead of crawling out like a dog,

300

wondering from which direction I'm going to be shot in the back. I've got a right to be a man, and if I've got to sew you up in a suet sack to do it, why I'll git the job done, too."

All the old poisons poured back into Jeff's blood as he talked. By the time he'd finished, his face was flushed, and his voice was unnecessarily loud. After what seemed centuries of unequal and hopeless combat, he had brought the enemy to bay. The enemy would have to yield, or join the fight again.

"Well," Garrett said placatingly, "any man in this country has what rights he can enforce, through the legislatures and courts— or any way he can."

"You are right, for once!" Jeff glowered. "Alone, neither me nor Lin Mundy nor Duck Drake has got the rights of one your cattle. But once we git next to ourselves and stand together, we can tear your house down. As you say we did."

Garrett nodded. "That I'm willing to concede. The question is, in tearing my house down, does your own escape destruction?"

Jeff thought of his dead Herefords and horses, and found the question unanswerable. The old man's crust in sitting there at Jeff's table, drinking Jeff's whiskey and blandly reminding Jeff of his losses seemed insufferable. But Abby's presence and his own obligation as host imposed restrictions on his mind and tongue.

Later, when they'd finished the meal, Abby helped him wash the dishes, then asked permission to lie down and rest. Unabashed, Jeff turned his unclean bunk over to her and saw her flop on it without hesitation, falling almost instantly asleep. Then, back in the kitchen, he heard Garrett disclaim any responsibility for Bowman's actions, because he had fired his foreman ahead of the shootings.

"Fired Strap?" Jeff asked incredulously. "Why'd you fire him?"

"For getting me into an alley fight with you people over Mundy and his damned homestead," the old man said. "I knew things were going against us, and I told him to ease up. But you know Strap. He had the bit in his teeth, and wanted to show how efficient he was. Kept after that irrigation outfit, ignoring my advice. When it blew up in his face the way it did, I lost patience and fired him—right after the trial. I knew when he left the ranch that he had hell in his neck. But I didn't expect him to run amuck."

Things were coming too fast for Jeff's mind to assimilate and digest. He stared at his guest in dubious wonder.

"You mean to tell me that you had nothing to do with framing Mundy?" he asked skeptically at last. "You mean Strap just up and took all that on himself?"

"That's what I mean to tell you," the ranchman confirmed. "As you must remember, Strap was ambitious. Give him an inch and he'd take a mile. Wanted to please. Wanted to feel important to the company."

Jeff had reached the limits of credulity. "Next you'll be telling me he was acting on his own when he jumped Harley Rae!"

"I could tell you that, and be speaking the truth."

Jeff sneered. "Come off it, Wate. You're talking to Jimson now. Strap never even took a trip into the brush without he cleared with you first!"

"It's a funny thing," Garrett said wryly, "but people used to say the same thing about you. I guess you can judge for yourself how true it was."

"What do you mean?" Jeff countered, sensing an affront.

There was a shrug, a phantom smile. "You and Strap were a lot alike, in a lot of ways. You both were good men for the company. A little too good, maybe. A little too eager. A little too anxious to be the indispensable man. Send either of you after a cow, and you'd bring in a whole herd. As I say, you both meant well. But you put me against the blaze a lot of times."

"I put you against the blaze?"

"Oh, nothing as serious as this blunder of Strap's. Little things, mostly, adding up. Like turning the men in for butchering company cattle. Like informing on the ones that slipped off from the camps for a spree, and all that small-caliber meddling you went in for, in competition with Strap. You have to have rules, in an outfit as big as this one. But it usually pays to wink at the small infractions. In most of the cases you brought to my attention, I didn't blame the man. In their situation, I'd likely have done just as they did. . . . I mean, rules have to be applied with a little common sense. You and Strap both earned me more enemies than I could afford, over little things that weren't worth making enemies about. But once you'd raised an issue, I had to back you up or wreck the whole system. There were plenty of times when I seriously considered firing you both. But that would have set you both against me. And neither of you were exactly the kind of catamounts I relished for enemies. So, in self-defense, I put up with you. Though sometimes I wondered why the other hands didn't kill you."

Jeff was listening in a state of fascination. There were still times when he suffered agonies of embarrassment and regret for the role he'd played at Man Head, times when he wondered how he could have behaved so abominably. But never in all his misgivings had it occurred to him that he had served his master badly. The discovery added to his ignominy.

"It's a puzzling thing," Garrett was saying, plainly talking of a thing to which he'd given much thought. "I've been dealing with people, handling men—or trying to handle them—for a good many years. And that's a problem I haven't ever solved. I mean this business of abuse of authority and the eternal bickering and jockeying among ambitious employees, each wanting to be the one I can't get along without. Each trying so hard to improve on my ideas that everything I try to get done turns into something else. Yet I have to own it as my policy.

"Take you and Strap, as a case in point. You both were a damned sight harder to get along with than I ever was. Harder on each other, harder on the crew, harder on everyone. Raising hell over things I wouldn't have noticed, or would have overlooked. Worrying more over my interests than I did. And take that creature Hapgood that I first sent up here to deal with your friend Dempsey Rae. I knew that Rae was tied in with that horsethief ring. I didn't relish the idea of him being in so close to my range, knowing his record. I sent that detective up here to get evidence that he was stealing local stock, with the thought of having him locked up. Apparently Hapgood failed to collect proof that Rae was doing any more than breaking horses for the ring. So, thinking it would please me, he salted Rae away.

"Then I had you to deal with. Abby had been attracted to you, and nagged me about using you so harshly. You were young, and deserved another chance, so I sent John Poe to you to offer you your old job back, with no strings attached. But he was spoiling to distinguish himself as prosecutor by solving all the county's crimes, so he had to give you a big scare and a lot of wrong ideas.

"The same with you going out to knife everyone else on the place the minute I hired you. The same with Strap killing Harley Rae after the court had ruled he didn't own this homestead. The same with him rigging that case against Mundy. It was my stock the homesteaders were butchering. I knew they were up against it. I was willing to spare them a few cattle on the sly, to keep them from making bigger trouble. But Strap felt obligated to trap Mundy and make an example of him. The same with him killing Mundy and coming here to murder you, after I'd fired him for already crowding things too far—thinking, I guess, that I'd reinstate him. What's the answer?"

Whiskey had loosened the old man's tongue. He was staring moodily at the bottle, unbending to Jeff as Jeff had never heard of him unbending to any other man. He was giving a very biased account of things, deliberately forgetting or falsifying a lot. But the mere fact that he felt impelled to justify himself was a revelation, an indication that Jeff had never really known Garrett, the man.

"What's the answer?" the ranchman repeated.

Jeff shook his head, unable to supply it. Yet it seemed he had to say something in his own vindication.

"I don't know any answer. But I think you're being a little too hard on me and Strap, and a little too easy on yourself. We did everything you say. But we had the interests of the company at heart."

It was a weak and tepid attempt at justification of a thing that couldn't be justified. But Garrett wouldn't even allow this.

"I wonder. I wonder if you didn't all think first of your own interests, with the company. I wonder if there was a one of you wouldn't have sold me down the river, just as you sold everyone else you could, if you'd seen where it would benefit you, and if you'd found a way to do it."

The thrust found its mark. Quick, defensive anger was kindled in Jeff. "You don't need to pose as so damned holy and abused!"

304

he lashed out. "You can't push it all off on us. You set the pace for the rest of us. You've got your damned powerhouse association and your blacklist, and you make mighty free with both of them. You keep me and everybody else in the county but yourself from registering a brand. You shut us out of work anywhere around. You buy your judges, and sheriffs, and anybody you can use. You rigged that crooked deal to trigger Harley Rae out of this homestead! You wanted Demps killed, whether you arranged the details or not."

"I've done all those things—and some you didn't mention," the ranchman admitted with disarming candor. "But I've reason to do them—as long as I can. I've reason where you didn't have. After all, they are my interests I'm protecting. And after all, I didn't murder anybody, even if I did get the credit for a number of murders I had to condone because they were committed in the name of my interests. As far as I know, I never sold out a man I had owned as a friend. I always tried to stand with my own kind."

Stung beyond endurance, Jeff stood up to leave the cabin. "All right," he said, trying to speak coherently. "So it took me a long time to grow up. Well, I'm a big boy now. I look after my interests, too. Shielding you here ain't going to be in my interest. You're welcome to stay, till Abby wakes up. Then you better find some your own kind, and beg them for sanctuary!"

"That's what I thought I was doing, when I came here," Garrett sighed, staring out of the window. "But I guess I won't be going anywhere now. Here come Drake and all his angels."

Garrett erred in saying it was Drake and all his followers. By the old man's own report, upward of a hundred men had joined the raid on Man Head, and only twenty were in the group that came riding down the mesa trail. But as far as the percentages went, the differences were academic. The odds had as well have been fifty to one as ten to one.

Jeff stood in front of the cabin, rifle in the crook of his arm, watching them come up. The horses were hot and jaded from hard riding, mostly equipped with new saddles and bridles, which Jeff took to be prizes of war. The men were smoke-grimed and red-eyed, armed with almost every kind of firearm ever manufac-

305

tured. Duckbill Drake rode at their head, looking grim and capable.

Jeff's mind dredged up a dozen fantastic schemes for averting further bloodshed in the war he'd helped promote, discarding each before it was wholly born. "There is a tunnel through the bedroom wall," he said to Garrett without turning or moving his lips. "I'll hold them here in talk, while you skin out. Git into the breaks, you can give them trouble."

"I'll give them trouble here," Garrett answered. "I'm tired of running from them. But do me the favor of taking Abby out of it. They surely don't make war on women."

"You're a fool," Jeff told him. "There's been enough killing already."

"There'll be more killing, before I hand myself over to a mob like that," Wate promised.

The hard-looking company came up silently and spread out around the door. Jeff searched the ring of grimy faces but saw no friend, no friendliness. He looked at Drake, and received a cool half-nod.

"You didn't make it last night, Jeffrey. We missed you at the ball."

"I hear you had quite a party. How's the hangover, today?"

"No hangover yet, Jeffrey. Party is still on."

Jeff made no answer, and Drake grinned in patent glee.

"We noticed, coming across the meadow, that you lost some cows some time. How do you feel about things today? Still hell-bent for law and order? Still ready to turn the other cheek?"

"It depends," Jeff answered evenly, "on what happens to the first one."

"Still can't make up your mind, eh? Well, where is he?"

"Where's who?"

"Wate Garrett. We know he's here."

Words of denial came to Jeff's lips. But he didn't speak them. After all, they had followed the ranchman's trail right to his door. The Man Head horses were there to see.

"He's inside the house," Jeff said. "Where you think?"

"Well, we want him."

Jeff at the moment was remembering another mob on horseback that had ridden up to this same cabin this same way, a million years before. He remembered another victim who had waited with his heart in his mouth, hearing his fate debated in much this same fashion. He remembered the bird-faced old man who finally had spoken up for him, bidding the hangmen to put up their ropes and take him in to jail.

Jeff shook his head. "You can't have him."

Drake grinned again. "Then we'll take him."

Jeff hitched the rifle under his arm, but didn't point it. He wouldn't point it until he meant to use it.

"You might be able to," he admitted. "But you'll have to take me, too. It won't be easy, Duck."

Drake stared at him inimically, yet did not seem ill-pleased.

"You're proving everything I ever said about you, Jeffrey. Still sucking up to the boss of Man Head."

"You can give it any name you want," Jeff told him. "Garrett's here. He surrendered to me. He's my prisoner. I don't mean to hand him over to any mob."

"This is no mob," Drake said. "We are the board of aldermen from Ekard, the only lawful government in the county. We're entitled to take him into custody. It's what we figure to do."

"Then figure again," Jeff said. "I represent the county. Wate's a county prisoner. He'll git a trial in county court—as quick as we git one."

"How do you represent the county?" Drake challenged.

"Wate resigned as chairman of the board—in my favor," Jeff said, improvising boldly. "Told me to organize a new board and restore order around here. I'm appointing Jim Gentile and Ben Hackett and Abby Garrett. Lime Higgins will be judge, and—by God—I'm the sheriff. We're going to let bygones be bygones, and we don't figure to make anybody any trouble on account of what happened last night. I say Wate got what he asked for. But we're going to ring it down now, and start living like civilized people for a change. There'll be no more night riding and burnings. But in this county, beginning today, any man that wants can register a brand and run livestock on the public grass. Garrett will be investigated for land fraud, and every foot of land he got the crooked way will be reopened to filing. New committee will hold office until election time and they're voted in or out."

Jeff had been talking as much to Garrett in the cabin as to the farmers. He halfway expected to hear a roar of protest and repudiation as he blandly committed the hidebound tyrant to a program of liberal enlightenment and justice. But no such repudiation came. Even Wate Garrett knew when to talk and when to listen. Even Wate Garrett valued life over property—when the life concerned was his.

The listening farmers looked impressed. But Drake still wore a sneer.

"So, we're all going to forgive and forgit, eh? All kiss and make up, and call things square! And what happens to the son of a bitch that murdered Mundy?"

"The son of a bitch that murdered Mundy has been took care of," Jeff said, playing his trump ace. "I took care of Strap, while you was helling off to Man Head, burning buildings. He's up in my stable now, on ice. And just for your information, Garrett had fired Strap before he went on his rampage. Wate, of course, will stand trial, and be judged by a jury. But Strap don't need judging. Strap just needs a coffin."

"You mind if we look in the stable and verify that?" Drake asked nastily.

"Not a bit," Jeff said. "Then you can clear out. You stay around here, we could have trouble."

For a time after the farmer delegation had departed, Garrett sat slumped on his chair again, watching Jeff with eyes that were half-friendly, half-unforgiving. Jeff sensed the depth of the old man's grievance, but chose to ignore him, giving his whole attention to sharpening his skinning knife.

"Well, you're some promoter!" the stockman said ruefully at last. "I suppose I should be grateful to you, for saving my life. Question is, whether it was really any favor."

"That's one you'll have to answer for yourself." Jeff shrugged.

"Another question," Garrett went on querulously, "is how you're going to git me to resign—to make your bluff stand up."

"You'll resign," Jeff predicted with confidence. "You're in custody, and don't forgit it. You don't resign, or try any monkey-shines like gitting in touch with your Cheyenne friends, I'll take you to Ekard, and turn you over to them eldermen up there. They'd resign you—from the whole damn world."

Garrett shook his head in grudging admiration. "You get what you go after, don't you?"

"I go after what I git," Jeff answered.

His knife properly honed, Jeff walked down into the bottoms to skin out his dead heifers. Garrett accompanied him, and casually broached a new subject.

"There was one other reason why I rode this way, last night. I'm needing a foreman, now. Know anyone who might be interested?"

Somehow, Jeff had seen that coming. Six months before, six hours before, he might have been interested. Now he shook his head.

"Sorry. I got my own interests to look after."

Garrett was silent a time, then spoke almost plaintively. "I never did understand why you pulled out on me."

"If you have to ask, I can't explain," Jeff said shortly, unwilling to probe that sore again.

"I guess maybe I don't have to ask," Garrett conceded. "But Abby will be sorry to hear you won't come back. She's been hard to live with, since you left. And things won't be easy for her, now. The house is gone, and everything in it that she prized. I was thinking that maybe . . ."

"And I was thinking that maybe you'd have better sense than to dangle her to me as bait again!" Jeff cut him off. "It worked once, but it won't again. Ever I decide to make her another proposition, I'll talk to her—not you."

"Fair enough." The old man shrugged. "Fair enough."

Garrett lent a hand at the skinning, and proved himself no slouch at the work. They had all twelve head peeled by shortly after noon. On the way back to the cabin, Jeff carved a half-dozen thick red steaks off the carcass in the tree, to cook for dinner. When they reached the house, Abby was up, looking wonderfully restored. She'd washed and fixed herself up, and—to Jeff—looked good enough to eat. More impressive yet, she had been out to his chip pile and gathered kindling for a fire. The stove was hot, and she had the place so full of lovely smells that Jeff almost weakened on the spot. She had her hair in braids, and wore a flour sack for an apron. Her cheeks were red from the stove's heat, and in every way there was to look like Jeff's ideal of a wife and helpmate, Abby did. So much it made him blush to look at her.

When the steaks were fried, Abby served them with fresh biscuits and flour gravy. They all fell to and ate ravenously—Jeff thinking wryly of the other meals they'd shared—at Vulgar Manor.

"Best meat I ever tasted," Garrett pronounced. "But then the other fellow's beef always tastes better than your own."

Now that he'd heard Wateman Garrett repeat stale jokes about rustled beef, Jeff figured he'd heard everything. It truly was a day of miracles.

"Well, I'm glad you like it," Jeff told him. "Because you're going to pay for it. I'm billing you, right now, for all twelve head —whether Strap worked for you or not."

"How's this?" Wate said dryly. "The way you talked in court, I thought you approved the practice of killing other people's cattle. 'Feed the hungry stranger,' and all that! You mean it makes a difference when it's your beef involved?"

"A big difference." Jeff nodded. "You can pay me in cash, or I'll just help myself to what's up on the mesa—at four to one."

"Well, I refuse to recognize your claim," Garrett said. "And if you help yourself to any stock of mine, you'll have to hurry. I intend to liquidate my holdings, as fast as I can."

"Liquidate?" Jeff repeated, somehow displeased. "Sell out?"

"Certainly. Do you think I could go on living in this country —after what's happened, and what's going to happen? And me unable even to hire the foreman I want to look after my interests?"

"You haven't got to worry about what's going to happen," Jeff said gruffly, refusing to take the bait. "And what's happened, you had coming."

"That's your opinion," Garrett said. "But I don't have to go on living in a country I pioneered and made safe for those who ruined me."

"Hogwash!" Jeff snapped. "You haven't been ruined. And you never made this country safe for anybody but yourself. Made it unsafe, for everybody you could. You've had a good thing here. It had to end, sometime. You knew that."

"It'll be harder on Abby than on me," Wate went on, ignoring Jeff's statement. "I want to travel, some. And I've interests in the East to keep me puttering. She likes this country. She wants to stay."

Jeff saw Abby's blush, and looked quickly at his plate, still refusing to take the bait.

"I'm rather sentimental about it, myself," Garrett continued. "For that reason, I won't sell to just anyone. I'd like to sell to a man I know can cope with changing conditions, and salvage something out of the wreckage. If such a man would be interested, I'd even finance him. Let him pay the thing out as he went. From profits."

Jeff felt constrained to say something. "I don't know of anybody that would be interested. I thought once I wanted to make a million dollars. Then I got to watching how it was done, and it kind of cured me. I don't know if that's what I want."

"You have a time deciding what you do want," Garrett said sharply.

"I know some things I want," Jeff said slowly, eyes on Abby, pleased to see her kindle.

"But not how to get them, eh?" Garrett cracked.

"That remains to be seen," Jeff maintained.

The meal finished, Wate Garrett rose and filled the dishpan with water and placed it on the stove to heat. Then he borrowed Jeff's tobacco sack and tried awkwardly to fashion a cigarette. Jeff watched him fumble and spill tobacco all down his vest, and ended by doing the job for him.

"If I did undertake a proposition like yours, I'd do things a whole lot different," he surprised himself by saying, out of a clear sky. "I wouldn't try to ranch the whole damn territory. A man can have enough, without trying to have it all. A man can live and work with other people. That way, he won't have them at his throat."

"Well, you don't have to give me your answer now," Garrett said. "Take your time, and think it over. But I'll lay you a little

311

wager—say, your place against mine—that Abby will talk you into it."

Jeff glanced at Abby and, blushing again, shook his head.

Jeff wouldn't take a bet like that.